Demon of Lust

To my daughter, Patricia Rohr Krisch, who bears no resemblance to the demon in this story.

CHAPTER 1

The most beautiful woman in the world came into my life the night she was thrown down the stairs. She struck my bedroom door, awakened me from a troubled sleep. At the time, I was seventeen and lived with my father in a large brownstone house in Greenwich Village. No one else occupied the house, except an old artist named Togallini. He rented the attic apartment from my father.

Hearing a thump and a cry at my door, I sat up in bed thinking the tenant had fallen down the stairs. I was not allowed to offer him any help. Early in life my mother gave me this warning: Avoid the tenant Togallini! Never have anything to do with him. So that's what I'd do. I'd wait till my father came home. He could carry or drag Togallini back to his apartment.

"Oooooooooh!"

That cry didn't sound as if it came from Togallini.

Rolling out of bed, I hurried to the door, opened it, found someone on the floor. Shoulder-length hair hid the face. In Greenwich Village, shoulder-length hair doesn't necessarily belong to a woman.

I heard the sobbing words, "Help me, please."

The hand I grasped was the hand of a woman. Helping her stand, I saw her face.

Apart from a small bruise on her forehead, her face was breath taking. Never in all my life had I seen features so perfectly formed, eyes so gray and challenging, lips so luscious, skin so clear and white.

Demon of Lust

My heart pounded on my ribs, acted as if it wanted a release from its cage, get a closer look at the amazing woman. "You're one of Mr. Togallini's models, aren't you?" I managed to ask.

She was slow to answer. "I was a model."

Did that mean she was one of Togallini's models? I wasn't sure. Mesmerized, I stared at her hair. It glistened like highly polished gold.

"Can you help me?" she asked.

Her request gave me a sense of importance. "I'll be glad to help you."

The woman studied my face before speaking. "My ankle pains terribly. I'm afraid I've sprained it."

I could feel her pain. "Could I help you back to Mr. Togallini's apartment?"

"Heavens, no!" she exclaimed in a voice that contained music. "He threw me out of his apartment."

I couldn't understand why any man would throw a beautiful woman out of his apartment; especially a man like Togallini, who'd spent many years of his life painting lewd posters for porno films, jackets for hard-core paperbacks, dirty comics, and anything else that excited the male populace. He'd sold his work to his brother, Mario, who owned the largest and most diverse pornographic business in the world. I wanted to ask her why he threw her out of his apartment. I merely asked, "Could I telephone someone to come and get you?"

"There's no one to call."

"I could call a taxi. The taxi driver will take you home."

"I have no home. No money."

I'd no money, either. If I had, I'd have given it to the lady. Another thing I didn't have: authority in the house. If I'd anything to say about the house, I'd have gladly given her my bed. For the first time within recollection, I missed my father. As he so often reminded me, the house was his. He'd have to decide what to do with the woman. He wasn't one bit generous, but he couldn't throw her out of the house. The night was cold and bitter, the streets covered with ice.

"My ankle is throbbing," she said. "I'm putting too much weight on it. Would you mind if I leaned on you for support?"

"I wouldn't mind at all."

She put her arm around my neck. I put my arm around her waist, felt her body against mine. The contact generated a remarkable experience. My body grew warm, glowed, sparkled. The woman was six or seven years older than I, yet she had an astonishing effect on me. An effect I hadn't known before. I'd an overwhelming desire to do everything I could for her, regardless of the consequences. "My mother's bedroom is empty," I heard myself say. "Would you like to stay in her room for the night?"

Her words came in soft tones. "Your mother isn't home?"

"It's my father who isn't home. My mother died two months ago."

"I'm sorry."

I helped her into my mother's room; turned down the covers on the bed. I also helped her remove her shoes and stockings. When it came time to remove her dress, she turned away from me and slipped it off over her head. Through a mirror, I saw her breasts beneath her slip. She was truly a perfectly formed model. I felt my scalp prickle and a chill ran down my spine.

She smiled when I pulled the covers up around her neck. She was more beautiful every time I looked at her. I felt good about giving her the bed, something my mother would do if she were alive. My mother slept alone in that bed, said something about having an aversion to my father's snoring. I long ago concluded she had an aversion to my father.

"My name is Vivian," the woman said to me in her wonderful voice. "What is yours?"

"My name's Tommy. Tommy Davis."

She studied me with her fascinating eyes. "You're a generous young man. I hope I can repay you."

"You don't have to repay me," I said, thinking I received payment every time she spoke to me, every time she looked at me.

She suddenly asked, "Could you get me something to eat? I haven't eaten in two days."

Demon of Lust

My heart went out to her. "Sure I'll get you something. What would you like?"

"I'll settle for anything."

As I examined a large refrigerator containing a small quantity of food, I was glad the woman said she'd settle for anything. I practically emptied the refrigerator of edibles when I made two ham sandwiches with lettuce and tomato. I toasted the sandwiches, made a pot of tea.

While carrying the tea and sandwiches up the stairs, I still had the pleasant glow that started when she put her arm around my neck. The glow diminished somewhat when I looked at the thickness of the sandwiches. So taken by the fact that Vivian was hungry, I made the sandwiches especially thick with ham. My father wouldn't appreciate my generosity, nor would it go unnoticed. As an accountant, he took a mental inventory of everything purchased for the house...especially food. He called food a controllable expense. If a pound of ham didn't last a certain number of days, he wanted to know why. I was the only one he asked, the only one he blamed, the only one he punished.

Now I didn't care. A young man growing up has to make his own decisions. I was sure I made the right decision as I watched Vivian eat the sandwiches, drink the tea. Her face took on an angelic radiance. Though famished, she emptied her plate in a lady-like manner. I liked her for that. I liked the way she smiled at me, too. What perfect teeth she had. What heavenly eyes. What a perfect model!

When she finished the final crumb, I took the tray from her and put it on a table. I then returned to her bedside. Feeling somewhat paternalistic, I tucked her in and planted a kiss on her forehead. I'd have loved to kiss her luscious lips, but I wasn't feeling that paternalistic. She wasn't exactly a replacement for my mother, yet she did an awful lot to deaden the sense of loneliness I experienced since my mother's death.

"Good night," she whispered. Her voice launched little thrills in my body.

"Good night," I replied, resisting the temptation to kiss her again. Picking up the tray, I turned off the light and closed the door gently behind me. My legs refused to carry me away from the bedroom door. As if magnetized, I could neither walk down the stairs and return the tray with soiled dishes to the kitchen, nor return to my own bedroom. I closed my eyes, rested my head on the bedroom door, and thought of the wonderful woman who had come into my life.

Who was she, anyhow? Of course, I knew she was a model. But was she one of Togallini's models? Was she one of the hundreds of models who used the rear entrance and stairs to Togallini's apartment? All my life, I'd heard them coming and going.

They'd sometimes awaken me at night. When I was half asleep, I'd say to myself, "Women in the walls." In recent years, the number of women in the walls had decreased. Togallini had given up the work he did for his brother. He specialized in painting nude women. He'd also grown old. When last I saw him, he looked as if he'd shrunk. Why would a remarkable model like Vivian visit a shrunken old artist like Togallini?

Speculating on several possibilities, I focused on one plausible explanation. It made a great deal of sense to me. Togallini owed Vivian money. She was trying to collect it. He became angry, threw her down the stairs. That line of reasoning led me to a heartbreaking question: Did he owe her money because she posed nude for him?

No! No! Vivian was a model but she wouldn't pose nude for that old reprobate. Somebody else had posed for him. Vision's mother, maybe. Vision's mother had to be beautiful to produce such a beautiful daughter. If Vivian had no home, chances are her mother was dead. Her mother could have left behind a copy of an unpaid bill sent to Togallini. Dad would call such a bill an Account Receivable. Vivian tried to collect the Account Receivable from Togallini.

Without moving from the bedroom door, I asked myself some more deep and discerning questions about Vivian's visit to the house. Answering all questions to my own satisfaction, I came to the conclusion that Vivian's mother was dead. She was in heaven with my mother. Naturally, the mothers talked about their kids. Naturally, my mother told Vivian's mother I was lonely and unhappy because I'd no one to love, and no one loved me. Quite naturally, Vivian's mother suggested her daughter visit me. Vivian was the answer to my prayers. A Catholic kid must believe in such things. Otherwise, he has no faith.

A Catholic kid must also learn to suffer. My suffering began the moment I heard my father's voice.

"What the hell are you doing at that door with a tray in your hands?"

My heart jumped into my throat. "Nothing, Dad."

His voice was slurred, filled with indignation. "Did you eat an extra meal?"

I knew he'd attended an accountant's banquet, where the food and drinks were free and plentiful, and he was asking me if I'd eaten an extra meal. "No, Dad, I didn't."

"Then why the empty tray?"

I pushed the words out in fear. "There's someone sleeping in mother's room. Someone who was hungry."

A hard gleam came into his eyes. "You rented your mother's bedroom without my permission?"

"I didn't rent it. I gave it to someone who had no place to sleep, nothing to eat. I did what Mother would do…"

My father was quick with figures and quick with his hands. He had my face burning before I realized he'd slapped me on both cheeks. He spoke with bitterness: "Your mother is dead. When she was alive she didn't live with me. She lived in another world. She lived in a world of principles and prayers and priests and Papal nonsense. She passed her crazy ideas on to you. Now I've got to cope with them. I don't know what to do with you. You're not like a normal kid in Greenwich Village. You're in another world. A world that existed a hundred years ago."

I stammered out the words, "Dad, Mother always tried to do the right thing. I try, too."

His words were like stones, pelting me. "You gave away good food and a clean bed to some bum."

"A bum? No. I gave the food and bed to…"

"Did he come begging at the front door?" he asked like a district attorney, bent on getting a confession out of me.

My words quavered in my throat. "It's not a he, Dad. It's a she."

"You brought a *woman* into this house? You gave her food, a place to sleep?" He struck me again on both cheeks, shouted loud enough for Vivian to hear. "Get her out of here."

Regardless of what's taught in Catholic schools, there's no such thing as turning the other cheek when dealing with my father. "I wish you'd let me explain."

"No explanation is acceptable," he said with bitterness. "Get her out of here."

"I'm not going to do it," I said, bracing myself for more stinging slaps.

Through rimless glasses, he studied me in disbelief. His eyes were webbed with red and charged with disgust. "I'll show you how to throw a bum out of this house, then I'll deal with you."

Like myself, my father wasn't tall or strong. His size disturbed him greatly and I knew it. I wanted to hurt him as much as he hurt me. Tauntingly, I said, "You wouldn't be so brave if a man were in Mother's room."

The remark caused him to hesitate, but only for a few seconds. Before I could say anything else to stop him, he ripped open the door and charged into the bedroom. Switching on a light, he rushed across the room, pulled the covers off Vivian, shouted, "Get the hell out of here." He'd have said more, but when he focused on the beauty in the bed, he lost his voice.

With the gracefulness and poise of a reigning queen, Vivian sat erect. She fastened her lovely gray eyes on my father, and spoke with child-like innocence, "Is something wrong?"

My father's mouth opened wide. He seemed to realize, as I did, that he was not only confronted with an extraordinarily beautiful woman, but one who deserved gentle treatment and the utmost consideration. "I thought my son brought home a bum," he stammered. His voice was barely audible.

Vivian looked hurt. "Are you calling me a bum?"

"Oh, no, no," my father said quickly, apologetically. "My son led me to believe he picked up someone from the street, brought him home. Within the past year, he's brought home a turtle, a cat, and a snake. I never know what to expect. He failed to explain your situation to me. He hasn't learned to express himself well."

Vivian turned her breathtaking eyes on me, giving my father the opportunity to get a better look at her perfect profile and the fullness of her bosom. "I thought he expressed himself very well," she said, staring at him as if she couldn't understand how anyone could say such a ridiculous thing about me. "I wouldn't be here now if he hadn't convinced me I'd be welcome. I concluded he came from generous parents."

"Generous parents," my father repeated. The concept, new to him, brought a smile to his lips.

"Did your son tell you I had a business meeting with your tenant, Mr. Togallini? When I was leaving his apartment, I took the wrong door, tripped on the stairs and fell. I've injured my ankle."

My father stared at her ankles. Apart from a small bruise, they were about as shapely and perfect as ankles can get. "My son failed to tell me you fell." He looked at me as if I were a hopeless case. "I'm going to call a doctor for you."

"A doctor won't be necessary," Vivian said with a wave of her hand. "Besides, I'm low on funds. Just allow me to rest here tonight. I'll be on my way tomorrow morning."

My father spoke as if he were anxious to keep the greatest treasure he'd ever found. "You need not rush off. Your ankle needs attention. Tomorrow is Saturday. I've no commitments till Monday. I'll be happy to nurse you for the next two days."

"Isn't that kind of you?" Vivian said? Her smile was more radiant than the sun. And if my father's heart was anything like mine, it was beating madly.

CHAPTER 2

The morning after Vivian arrived at our house, my father burst into my bedroom at seven o'clock. He shook my bed, awakened me from a peaceful sleep. I thought the house was on fire.

"On your feet," he shouted. "Get your clothes on. I want you to run down to the grocer's. Buy a pound of good coffee, a pound of sugar, a half pint of cream, a loaf of bread, a dozen eggs, and a pound of bacon." He threw some bills on a chest of drawers.

"Are we going to have bacon and eggs for breakfast?" I asked, savoring the idea.

"*She's* going to have bacon and eggs for breakfast," he retorted with emphasis on the *she*. "What's her name?"

"Vivian," I answered solemnly, as if her name were sacred.

"Vivian's going to have bacon and eggs for breakfast and anything else she wants. Can you think of anything we don't have?"

"I like donuts."

"I don't give a damn what you like," my father said, looking a little nutty. "I'm concerned with what she likes. Whatever it is, I'll pay for it. She's without money, a place to live. If she's desperate enough, she'll agree to stay here with us. You may consider the idea preposterous, think I'm reaching for a star, but the star is worth reaching for. Vivian is so ghastly beautiful, she'd make a perfect mother for you."

"A mother for me!" I said, wondering if a psychiatrist could help my father.

"Why not?" he shot back. "Ever since your mother died, you've moped around this house as if you've suffered a permanent loss. You haven't. Your mother can be replaced."

My belly began to burn. It's important to set my father straight. "My mother can never be replaced. She did everything humanly possible for us. She was perfect." I wanted to say more, tell him how often she encouraged me to become a priest. She wanted me to save my soul; help others to save theirs. I couldn't explain this to my father. He wouldn't listen, wouldn't understand.

He shook his head. "You always were a mama's boy. Now you're without a mama. So what do you do? You make the best of the situation you're in. And so do I. I had the good fortune to marry your mother. Many people considered her beautiful. Now I have the opportunity to marry another beautiful woman. I intend to take advantage of the opportunity. If everything goes according to my plan, and out of respect for your dead mother, I'll wait a month before proposing marriage to Vivian."

I examined my father's sparse hair, the potbelly on his small frame. "Vivian is much too young for you, Dad."

"I agree with you," he said after contemplating my remark. "She's young for me, yes, however, I won't hold that against her. I'll be properly compensated. I'll get youth and beauty. She'll get a home and security."

"I don't know about that..."

"You don't know a damned thing," he said with a viciousness that caused me to wince.

∗ ∗ ∗

Six months passed without a wedding. I was relieved to know Vivian had refused to marry my father. However, she didn't refuse the room, board, and the money he gave her. Nor did she refuse the clothes he brought her. His gifts to her saddened me.

I asked myself why. Was it because he was generous with her and stingy with me? No. I was used to his stinginess and happy to know Vivian had a place to sleep, good food to eat, money to spend, nice clothes. Whenever she received a new dress, she'd model it for me, make me wish I had money to buy her a new car.

    Was I jealous of my father because he could give Vivian presents and I couldn't? That could be one reason. Was there anything else? The answer came one night when I was asleep and dreaming of my mother in heaven. She was frowning and waving a finger at Vivian's mother. She was saying something...

    "Have you taken a bath?"

    "Yes."

    "Then come in."

    I was no longer asleep. The question I heard didn't come from my mother. It came from Vivian, talking to my father. She invited him into her bedroom. I listened attentively for more talk. None was forthcoming. I wanted to believe she'd invited him into her bedroom for a little conversation, but I couldn't hear any talk, regardless of how hard I tried. Was Vivian sleeping with my father? No! No! She was much too perfect to sleep with him. Did Dad ever give anything away for nothing, especially food, clothes, money, a room? Again the answer was no. A sad and reluctant no.

    On two other occasions I'd reason to believe Vivian allowed my father into her bedroom. On each occasion, it took me a week or more to recover from the blow. My period of convalescence included a Saturday in my room without food or water, a Sunday walking the streets of New York with my head down and my hands jammed into my pants pockets, as well as five evenings at home living the life of a monk in a monastery. When not attending school, I spent my time reading the Bible and contemplating my good fortune in having had a virtuous mother, not interested in sex. What a wonderful example she'd set for me. What a jewel among women. She wouldn't do what Vivian had done.

Demon of Lust

As part of my contemplative life, I didn't talk. Whenever Vivian or my father asked me a question, I'd answer by shaking or nodding my head. I also learned I could do what my father told me to do without uttering a word.

"What's wrong with Tommy?" I heard Vivian ask my father one evening.

"I don't know what it is, but I like it," he replied. "Kids should be seen and not heard."

My father approved of my silence, Vivian didn't. As a matter of fact, I believe she finally realized what was bugging me. She stopped my father's visits to her bedroom, gave me more attention than ever. She fed me well, gave me a vitamin every day, and helped me with homework. She was a source of inspiration.

My general average during my senior year rose dramatically under her tutelage. Surprisingly, I won a gold medal for English Composition. It was to be presented to me the night of graduation. Since my father often called me stupid, I gave him a ticket to the graduation exercises. He'd see the medal awarded to me.

Vivian showed up with the ticket, applauded me. I proudly introduced her to some of the guys from my class, told them she was my Aunt Viv. They said she was the best looking aunt they'd ever seen. I was so happy I felt there were angels inside me, using my ribs for a harp. I forgave Vivian for the pain she caused me.

The day after I graduated from high school, I didn't know what to do. I was seventeen years of age, with no money or prospects for a job or college. I was also madly in love. I wanted to marry Vivian, get her away from my father. I thought of finding odd jobs in the neighborhood, making a few dollars, buying lottery tickets, winning big. I'd then buy my own home, get married and raise a family. It'd be fun having a son, being kind to him.

Would Vivian marry me? I suspected she would. She certainly didn't want to marry my father. If she did, she could've married him the first month she was in the house. Every now and then I'd see her staring at the ceiling. She seemed to be waiting for something or someone. I figured she was waiting for me to grow up, prove I could handle the responsibilities of a wife. What other reason did she have for remaining in our house for such a long time? I could think of no other reason, regardless of how often I tried. Was I was making the same mistake my father was making? Was I reaching for a star? A star that was evasive and mysterious.

I was successful finding a few odd jobs in the neighborhood, washing windows and sweeping floors. I made enough money to buy lottery tickets for two weeks. On no occasion did I come close to winning. I mentioned my bad luck to a John Donaldson, a redheaded boy who lived a block away from me. He'd graduated from high school the previous year, worked as a teller at Citibank. He spoke with great authority about money.

"Don't be a sucker," he said when I told him about the lottery. "When you play the lottery, you pass your hard earned money into the greedy hands of the politicians. They can't raise taxes any more, so they've moved into the gambling rackets. Next thing you know, they'll legalize pot and prostitution."

I felt frustrated. "But how can a guy make some big money in a hurry?"

"Sports," he answered spontaneously. "A champion fighter can make millions. If you're willing to fight, I'll be willing to be your manager. I can get you started in the Golden Gloves."

After a month of rigorous training, I found myself in a ring, facing a black kid. He looked skinny and weak. Shortly after the bell sounded, he landed a hard blow to my nose, made me see red. He knocked me out in twenty-two seconds. He also knocked all thoughts of becoming a fighter out of my head. I was feeling pretty low when I walked home, thinking of my failure.

Vivian met me at the door. "How did you make out?" she asked.

"I was knocked out in twenty-two seconds."

"Perhaps it's just as well. You're not meant to be a fighter. What prompted you to enter the ring?"

I felt my spirits lift. "I figured if I could win the Golden Gloves, I could get some professional fights, make some money, give it to you."

Demon of Lust

Her smile was beautiful. "You'd like to be able to support me?"

"I would if I could."

"How sweet."

She planted a kiss on my lips that lasted till the count of ten. I'd have fought the black kid every night in the week if I could come home and be kissed like that.

"Have you had supper?"

My heart was still fluttering when I answered, "No."

"You must be hungry." Taking my hand, she led me into the kitchen, sat me down in a booth in the corner. "Can you eat more than two sandwiches?"

"Two will be fine. And a glass of Ginger Ale."

She pulled out meat from the refrigerator, cut it for the sandwiches. Her body shimmied a bit when she cut the meat. The shimming caused my body to heat up. Why? I don't know. I do know she had me mesmerized.

She gave me the sandwiches. I wolfed them down. She returned to the refrigerator, withdrew a bottle, opened it, and filled two large glasses. Giving me one, she sat down close to me.

For several seconds I watched bubbles from her glass bounce into mine. The bubbles had unusual pep. I took a long drink. Sparks flew in my stomach.

"You aren't supposed to gulp champagne. You sip it."

"Champagne! You gave me champagne?"

"What did you think it was, Ginger Ale?"

"That's exactly what I thought it was."

She wrinkled her forehead. "Well, if you're not man enough to drink a little champagne, don't drink it."

"I'm man enough," I said, taking another long swig. The sparks in my stomach were pleasant, gave me a relaxed feeling. "Where did you get the champagne?"

"Your father gave me two bottles. His office is honoring him tonight, giving him a Distinguished Service Medal. He asked me to think of him while I drank it."

"Are you going to do it?"

"Do what?"

"Think of him."

She smiled. "I'm going to drink the champagne. Or we'll drink the champagne." She filled my glass, than her own.

She and I finished our second glass in a hurry. While she filled the glasses a third time, I studied her face. She was so unbelievably beautiful; I couldn't understand why she wasn't working as a professional model or movie queen. I figured it was a good time to ask her. "Vivian, would you tell me why you're living in this house? You could go anywhere, get a good job and make enough money to set up your own apartment. No employer would turn you down. You have talent, great beauty."

"It's good to know you think I have talent and beauty. As for why I'm here, I'd rather not say."

I probed deeply. "Is it because you love my father?"

Her frown was a thing of beauty. "I don't love him. How about you? Do you love him?"

My words came slowly, almost in pain. "He killed what little love I had for him when he was mean to my mother. My mother inherited this house, inherited the tenant Togallini. She let my father collect the rent for the apartment, deposit it in his own bank account. Despite her kindness to him, he was mean to her."

Vivian said softly. "He's not mean to me."

I hurried my words. "He's not mean to you because he wants to marry you. Once he has a ring on your finger, he'll turn sour. I've been told that's what he did to my mother."

Vivian shook her head. "I've difficulty understanding any woman like your mother."

I poured myself another drink. "For a long time I couldn't understand her either, why she stayed married to my father. She was his opposite…good, kind, gentle, considerate. As owner of this house, she could've made a life of her own. I think it was her religion that kept her bound to him. She also wanted to do what was best for me."

"Do you understand yourself?" Vivian asked.

"I know I've got a hereditary problem. I'm a product of a good mother, a bad father. My genes are forever playing tug-o-war. A constant battle goes on inside of me. I try to do what my mother taught...try to respect my father, even when I feel like kicking him in the...." I didn't finish the sentence.

Vivian shifted closer to me. "Environment is a factor. You spend time with me. Do you believe I'm a good influence on you?"

I looked into her lovely eyes, answered automatically. "You're great."

She smiled, poured another drink for me.

I finished the drink in a hurry. I'd another and another. All my sadness, worries, and frustrations were somehow transferred to the bubbles in my glass. I watched the bubbles break and disappear. I also watched the refrigerator move around the room, without making a sound. I didn't know how that could happen. There was so much I didn't know.

Vivian put her arms around my neck and nibbled on my ear. Her teeth sent painful pleasures through my body. When she stopped nibbling, she faced me. Her eyes were tinged with pink. "Do you love me, Tommy?"

I knew the truth of my words. "I love you, Vivian."

She pressed her large breasts against my chest and her mouth found mine. She gave me a wet, sweet kiss—long, hungry, passionate. She whispered in my ear, "Time for bed now, Tommy."

Staggering, I followed her up the stairs to my mother's bedroom. No doubt about it, I was drunk. But not so drunk I didn't know what I was doing. If Vivian had taken me to my bedroom, I'd have entered the room with her. She took me to *my mother's bedroom*. I couldn't enter the room. If I had, I'd have visions of my mother in heaven arguing with Vivian's mother, one blaming the other.

Vivian was holding my hand when she entered the room. I pulled my hand away, closed the door, and ran to my room. As I turned the key in the lock, I told myself that was the most difficult think I'd ever done in my whole life. My body cried for Vivian's body. My conscience shouted no, no, no!

Sleep was impossible that night. I must've traveled a couple of miles tossing from one side of the bed to the other. I kept thinking of my mother, wondering if she saw me kissing Vivian. She wouldn't appreciate my making love to a mature woman, or any other woman. Nor would she appreciate my getting drunk. What would she say? She'd say I ought to go to confession. In memory of her, I'd go. There was a church on Fourteenth Street. I'd go to confession there, be back home in time for breakfast.

I hadn't taken more than two steps beyond my bedroom door when I heard someone on the upper stairs. Turning, I saw Vivian descending the stairs from Togallini's apartment. She was wearing a bathrobe and carrying a tray of dishes.

"Good morning, Tommy," she said awkwardly.

I wanted to ask her what she was doing in Togallini's apartment. I said, "Good morning."

"You're up early," she remarked, giving me no explanation for visiting Togallini.

"So are you."

Did she blush at my remark? I don't know. I was down the stairs, out of the house before she could reply. On my way to church, I kicked a couple of cans and growled at a mutt. I tried to think of something to say to the priest in confessional. I could think of nothing. All I could think of was Vivian. I'd told her I loved her and what did she do? She visited Togallini, that's what. How could she visit a man who threw her down the stairs? How could she associate with a man who spent his time painting dirty pictures? How could she live in a house with my father?

I was approaching a theatre as these unanswered questions nagged at my mind. I saw a series of pictures leading to the box office. The first picture showed an innocent looking girl in an evening gown. The second picture showed her kicking off her shoes. The third picture showed her removing her gown. The fourth showed her discarding her slip. The fifth

Demon of Lust

had her removing her bra. The sixth had her poised to pull down her panties. In the seventh picture she was partly covered by a sign, *Continued Live In The Theatre.*

Finding myself at the box office, I stared into the face of an enormously obese black woman cleaning the glass. "Theatre ain't open," she said, glaring at me as if I were on the road to ruin.

"Show starts in six hours," someone behind me remarked. "Stand where you are. You can be the first one in."

Turning, I saw an old man who had no teeth. He was grinning at me with his gums. He carried two signs, fastened together with short straps resting on his shoulders. The signs advertised topless waitresses in a nearby tavern.

"I'm not interested in the theater," I said, feeling embarrassed.

"Ya was lookin' at the pictures," he said accusingly.

Hurrying away from him, I ran across the street; was almost struck by a truck. The side of the vehicle was covered with a picture of a scantily clad woman, advertising a sexy novel. The image remained with me till I reached the church. Why was I being confronted with so many sex symbols when I was trying to avoid sex?

I'd one foot on the first step of the church when I heard breaks screech. An old Cadillac, with its top down, stopped at the curb. The driver of the car was a powerfully built young man with bushy eyebrows, thick black hair, and the expression of a hurt hawk. He swung himself out of the car, moved towards me with his hands extended. "Tommy, my boy. You're just the guy I wanna see."

Several seconds elapsed before I could recall his name. Joe Scarpeo, a classmate of mine, who played football for the high school team; had the record for injuring competitors. He was a freshman for three years; was booted out of school for stealing computers. I hadn't heard from him since. He now had two shapely girls with him. One girl was in the front seat, the other in the back.

"What did you want to see me about, Joe?"

He slung a heavy arm around my waist; practically lifted me off my feet, carried me to his car. "First of all, I want you to meet my girl, Rosie, and her friend, Ingrid. He turned to the girls and said, "Girls, meet Tommy Davis. He's robbed more hearts than Robbie Redford."

Rosie, slouched in the front seat, had coal-black piercing eyes, a thin sallow face, and a tiny mustache. Without smiling, she said, "Absolutely delighted to know ya."

"Nice to know you too, Rosie."

Ingrid was a pretty Swedish girl with sunny blond hair, an oversized bosom, and large green hypnotizing eyes. She reminded me of my first love, a movie star I'd seen on TV when I was in my first year of high school. Before the movie was over, I was desperately in love with her. The following day, I thought fate had done me a favor. I learned she'd appear live in a New York City theatre. I sold my bike and bought a front row ticket to the show. I'd sit at her feet; somehow let her know I loved her. I could hardly wait to see her. The show finally opened in New York. She appeared on stage. What I saw was unbelievable. The woman I loved had gained thirty pounds and thirty years.

The years make a difference. Ingrid was still young, slender, and lovely. Maybe if I got to know her, she'd help me forget Vivian and the trip to Togallini's apartment.

Joe was watching me watching Ingrid. He knew I was interested in her. "Get in the car," he ordered.

"Where are you going?"

"We're goin' to Rosie's house, get in a little sack time. We've been out all night. We'll sleep a while; then raid the wine cellar. Rosie's old man and momma took an auto trip through Macy's window last night. They're in the hospital, all cut up. We're going to drink to their slow recovery." He laughed at his own joke.

I used what willpower I had to say, "I can't go with you, Joe."

"Why not?"

"I'm going to church."

Demon of Lust

"Ya a sexton or somethin'."

Before I could reply, Rosie spoke curtly. "Don't beg him, Joe."

Joe looked more like a hurt hawk than ever. "If you wanna go with us, say so."

"I can't."

"Okay then." He put out a hairy claw. "No hard feelin's, Tommy."

I gave him my hand. "No hard feelings, Joe."

He crunched my hand. An incredible pain shot up my arm, traveled through my body. Falling to my knees, I thought Catholics do suffer.

Joe and the two girls drove away.

CHAPTER 3

"Bless me, Father, for I've sinned. It's been six months since my last confession. I accuse myself of...." I'd a strong desire to run out of the dark confessional, out of the church, down Fourteenth Street.

"Yes," said the priest encouragingly.

"I keep forgetting to say my morning prayers, Father. I miss them two times a week. Maybe three."

"Anything else?"

I'd confessed an easy sin. A sin I confessed many times before. It wasn't as easy confessing a sin I've never confessed before. Bracing myself for a blast from the priest, I said, "Lust for a woman."

The priest allowed several seconds to pass before asking, "How many times?"

The question gave me confidence. The priest didn't sound surprised. He was used to listening to the weirdoes from Greenwich Village. Nothing I could tell him would startle him. "About five, six or seven times a day. Seven days a week."

The priest responded with a voice that betrayed an Irish ancestry and a sadness that made me think I was to be pitied. "You may think lust can be taken lightly. God thinks differently. He called lust a capital sin. A deadly sin, mind you. If not controlled, lust can become overmastering. It can lead to hell. How old are you?"

"Seventeen."

"At seventeen boys and girls are strongly tempted by sex," the priest said sympathetically. "When you handle the temptations properly, you gain merit from God. When you handle them improperly, you offend God. By offending God, you injure yourself, your partner, your family, your community, and your world. You don't want to offend God, do you?"

"No Father, I don't."

"Most of us are tempted by sins of the flesh, regardless of our age or station in life. The temptations are difficult to avoid, since our society is saturated with sex. We must pray often to avoid temptations. And we must avoid anyone who tempts us."

"I can't avoid the woman who tempts me. I live with her."

"You live with a woman?" the priest asked quickly.

"In the same house. She lives with my father and me…rent-free. My father would like to marry her. She isn't interested in him."

"Is she attracted to you?"

"She likes me more than she likes my father. Last night she got me drunk, gave me some hard kisses, invited me to go to bed with her. Worst of all, I wanted to go…"

"But you didn't go?"

"No. I was strongly tempted. She's a beautiful woman, Father. Friendly…intelligent."

"When she arouses your passions, she isn't showing signs of intelligence. You must do all you can to avoid her."

"I'll try."

The priest was silent for a while.

His silence made me wonder if he were thinking of his own passions, not yet conquered. If he could pity me because I've a problem with sex, I could pity him for the same reason. I overheard my mother once say, "Priests have their problems, too."

"Your mother, she isn't living?"

"She's dead."

"And your father, does he help you with your spiritual life?"

"No."

"You're pretty much on your own then?"

"Yes."

"It's you against the devil."

"The devil? I'm afraid I don't believe in the devil."

"That is precisely what the devil wishes you to believe. His deepest wile is to persuade you into believing he doesn't exist. But he does exist. The devil is constantly roaming the world, seeking the destruction of souls. He has an army of demons working for him. Each demon specializes in a particular type of sin. He may concentrate on a government, a city, a neighborhood, a house, or an individual. His objective is to win souls for the Master of Evil. He does this by getting us to offend God. He compensates us with pleasure, fame, fortune, or some other temporary attraction."

The priest then urged me to get a job; saying work will help me keep my mind free of impure thoughts, away from temptation. "If you can't find a job with pay, look for one without pay," he said. "Help a fellow human being. Sacrifice yourself for someone. Help him on his journey to eternity."

The priest gave me absolution and a penance, five Our Fathers and five Hail Marys. Not much of a penance to compensate God for my offense.

Leaving the confessional, I looked at the name on the door, Father O'Donnell. It was an easy name to remember.

Kneeling in the dimly lit church, I said the Our Fathers with my head bowed, my eyes closed. But when I said the Hail Marys, I raised my head and gazed at the pure white statue of the Blessed Virgin Mary on the altar. My mother used to say God gave us the Blessed Virgin Mary as a symbol of virtue. Maybe Mary would help me avoid the sin of lust.

Outside the church, New York City was aglow with a comforting sun. The world around me seemed bright and clean. Confession had lifted a cloak of gloom from my spirit, made me feel bright and clean again.

Traveling towards Eighth Avenue, I walked past a tavern where some of my friends from school would buy a drink and pick up a girl. The owner of the tavern drank more than any of his customers. Usually drunk, he didn't know if a customer were seventeen or seventy. And didn't care. He was behind the bar now, pouring himself a drink, smiling his silly smile, trying to keep his eyes open and attentive. An attractive girl with frizzy hair like Orphan Annie's was seated near the window. Her eyes met mine. She smiled, beckoned.

I wanted to talk to her. How could I? I'd just promised a priest I'd avoid temptation. I waved goodbye to her, started home. On the way, I wondered if the girl could use some help on her journey to eternity.

*   *   *

I looked at my father scooping cereal into his mouth. He splashed a couple of drops onto his rimless glasses. He wasn't concerned about the milk or helping anyone on a journey to eternity. He was concerned about Vivian. As a matter of practice, he took off his glasses when speaking to her. He thought he was better looking with the glasses off. But he couldn't see well without them, so after a while he'd put them back on, feast on her beauty.

I couldn't tell exactly what passed through Vivian's mind when she saw him feasting on her. I do know she'd snap at him if he pawed her while I was around. Her lower lip had a way of protruding when Dad gloated over her. For the millionth time, I asked myself why she lived in the same house with him. She certainly wasn't in love with his looks.

Dad was in his mid-forties, soft, slouched, and somewhat pot-bellied; the price an accountant pays when he takes advantage of his expense account. His hair was thin and two-toned, brown and gray. Whenever he returned home from his office, he carried a look of anxiety, or, to be more specific, the look of a man expecting to be fired any minute from his position.

When he was through eating, he wiped his mouth with a paper napkin and gave Vivian a detailed account of the Awards Ceremony, held for him and nine other accountants who'd performed well for the firm. "The applause I received was loud, spontaneous," he said with phony enthusiasm. "I was the first man called to the podium. The executive vice president made the presentation. He shook my hand, read my accomplishments. I hadn't realized I'd done so much for the organization. You should have heard the applause."

"I'd have heard it if I'd been there," Vivian said sarcastically.

"I've explained before, I can't introduce you to our top management until we're married. If they saw you with me at this time, they might conclude I'm misappropriating funds to support you."

Her reply was as sharp as a fork jammed into his ribs. "Ridiculous!"

"You don't know how accountants can pick up a couple of facts, like my salary and your beauty; then ask themselves if I'm taking money from clients, falsifying records, or doing something else not in strict conformity with generally accepted accounting principles and practices. My career could be jeopardized."

Vivian gave a short laugh. "All right, Willie," she said, holding up her hands as if to stop his flow of words. "Enough said about the Awards Ceremony. I didn't want to go, anyhow. I've no desire to meet accountants. I detest people who make a career out of counting and recording other people's money."

Dad's eyes flamed. For a moment, I figured he'd snap at Vivian like he used to snap at my mother for some small remark she'd make. However, he managed to remain quiet. He believed Vivian wouldn't stay in the house unless he treated her gently. He gave her a forced smile, made me feel ashamed of him.

She returned the smile and made a remark I couldn't believe she'd make: "Tommy and I were glad you weren't home last night. We had a ball together."

Dad frowned. "What is contained in a ball?"

Her answer was coy. "We can admit to a few jokes, laughs… champagne."

Dad gave me an angry look. "How much champagne did you drink?"

"I…I…drank…."

"Come now, Willie. Don't ask Tommy how much he drank. Ask me. I gave him the champagne."

Demon of Lust

"Just how much did you give him?"

Vivian smiled. "The right amount for what I planned.

"He shot out the words: "Must I ask what you planned?"

"If you do, I'll think you don't trust me, Willie."

Dad put on his glasses, studied Vivian like he'd study a complicated financial report.

I figured he knew he couldn't trust her, but he'd never admit it.

"I trust you, Vivian," he said meekly.

Dad's sudden capitulation drove the tension away.

Vivian immediately recalled it. "You have to trust me, Willie. Otherwise you'll worry about my making love with Tommy."

Vivian's words struck my father with the impact of a punch in the nose. "You wouldn't have anything to do with Tommy. He's just a boy," he managed to say.

Her laugh added to the turbulence in my head. "Don't be too presumptuous. A girl in my position may have reason to be interested in a young man." She swung a perfumed arm around my waist, drew me close to her.

I could've dived through the linoleum floor when she did that, for Dad's mouth took on a cruel twist. He glared at me in a strange way. If he'd been anybody but my father, I'd have sworn he hated me.

*   *   *

In bed that night, I tried to figure out why Vivian developed a line of conversation that could lead to trouble between my father and me. Why did she throw her arm around my waist when she knew she'd enrage my father? Or why would an intelligent woman do such a crazy thing? I once asked my mother that very same question: why intelligent people do crazy things?

"They follow the promptings of the devil," she answered. "The devil stirs up conflict in the world."

If she'd been anybody but my mother, I'd have laughed at her answer. Priests who want to scare sinners give such a response, or psychos in search of a reason for killing someone, or comedians looking for a laugh. Of course, I couldn't laugh at my mother. She was a saint, believed everything taught by the Church.

I was almost asleep when I heard a knock on Vivian's door.

"Go away," I heard her say.

My father's voice: "Let me in."

"No."

Vivian was no longer willing to allow my father into her bedroom. She probably figured she had him hooked, wanted to punish him for taking advantage of her when she was homeless. If that were the case, my father would blame me. I had to get out of the house. But first I had to find a job, become independent.

CHAPTER 4

Finding a job wasn't an easy thing to do. Especially for anyone like me, who wasn't big and strong. I spent about seven hours trying to convince the owners of butcher shops, restaurants, appliance stores, gas stations, pawnshops, undertaker parlors, and fabric shops that I was just the man they needed. They didn't believe me. Some were pleasant enough, suggesting I try again in a month or two. Others were not so pleasant, dismissing me with a shake of their heads or silence. I couldn't understand why they couldn't say no, instead of treating me as if I didn't exist.

Walking home, my spirits were on the same level as my sore feet. Getting a job was more important than anything else I could do. It meant money for food, a place to live, and freedom. I had to get away from Vivian and my father. Vivian would continue to pursue me; my father was sure to find out. Maybe I should approach him like a man, admit she was tempting me, causing me to lust for her. He'd blow off some steam, but eventually he'd cool off, realize Vivian was trouble. He'd tell her to leave the house. But would he? She was so pretty. Pretty enough to have him throw me out of the house.

Facts had to be faced. Admitting my problem to my father wasn't the sensible thing to do. Since Vivian had moved into the house, my father grew wackier every day. If I told him Vivian invited me into her bed, he'd say I was corrupting her morals, doing him a great injustice. He might even go berserk. I once read about a father in the Village throwing his baby against a brick wall. He said he did it because he lost his job. That was insane. Crazier than anything my father ever did. At least, up till now.

I thought about Father O'Donnell telling me to work for nothing. That was the most impractical advice I'd ever received. Even if I wanted to work for nothing, I didn't know anybody who could use my services. I was the only one I knew who needed help.

It was seven o'clock when I opened the door to my father's home. I heard him and Vivian talking in the dining room. Common sense told me to go to my bedroom. My stomach told me to go to the dining room, get something to eat. I hadn't eaten since breakfast.

When I entered the dining room, Dad was toying with some Vanilla ice cream. Seeing me, his mouth dropped at the left side. A little computer seemed to start in his memory, searching for the nastiest thing stored there. Rather than listen to it, I headed for the front door.

Vivian stopped me with a cry of welcome. "Oh, Tommy! Come in. We have roast beef. You must be famished."

"I'm hungry," I admitted, looked into her perfect face.

"You'll enjoy this dinner," she said.

My mouth watered watching her cut three generous pieces of roast beef for me. She heaped mashed potatoes and creamed spinach on the plate, poured hot gravy on the meat and potatoes.

"We were worried about you," she said pleasantly. "We thought you took a boat to Hong Kong."

Her voice lifted my spirit. I gave myself the pleasure of staring into her beautiful face. "I didn't get as far as Hong Kong in my search for a…" I stopped short, decided I wouldn't say anything about my search for a job. Taking the plate from her, I cut a piece of meat, jammed it into my mouth. The piece was too big for conversation. I chewed it slowly.

Vivian asked with interest, "Your search for a what?"

I continued to chew the roast beef till it was beef burger. Swallowing it, I could think of nothing to say but the truth. "I was looking for a job."

"Any luck?" she asked, her face tormenting my heart.

Instinctively, I shot another piece of meat into my mouth, chewed it slowly, hoping my father wouldn't find reason to start an argument with

Demon of Lust

me. I didn't want to be dismissed from the table till I finished the dinner. I knew he didn't intend to start an argument when he moved restlessly in his chair. He was interested in discussing the job market. As an expert on everything, he was anxious to demonstrate his knowledge to Vivian.

Without waiting for me to swallow the food, he demanded, "Did you locate work?"

"No, Dad, I didn't. I walked the streets, stopped every place that looked promising. I'd no luck."

Frowning, he said, "A day looking for work is a day without pay. You should've found something. You're not a bad handyman. You paint, do minor carpentry, some plumbing. You can wash dishes, sweep floors, clean toilets, carry out garbage. If you'd looked for work properly, you'd have found a job in an hour or two. I'm sure you could've talked your way into some sort of a job."

"I've no experience. What can I say to an employer?"

He gave me a long, dirty look. "I've already told you what you can do. If that's not enough for an employer, tell him you can do other things. You have a problem getting a job because you're stupid."

"Now just a minute, Willie," Vivian said quickly. "Please don't call Tommy nasty names. He has no experience outside this house. If an employer isn't interested in domestic chores, what experience can he say he has?"

"That depends upon the prospective employer," my father said derisively. "Tommy becomes a grocer's helper when talking to a grocer. A jeweler's aide when talking to a jeweler. A bank teller when talking to a banker. He uses his ingenuity, fabricates a story. Damn it, he lies…"

"Tommy doesn't lie!" Vivian said quickly.

"Don't make me laugh. He lies if he wants work. Without lies he can't cope with today's competition. Everyone lies…advertisers, scientists, statesmen, presidents, philosophers, priests.…"

My father continued to spout his views to Vivian, views based on his logic of lying. Once in a while he'd contradict himself. Vivian would pick up the contradiction, repeat it, and ask if that's what he meant. He'd tell her she was missing the point, the essence of the idea.

Dad's ideas were pure baloney to me. Whenever I could get away with it, I'd turn them off. This was one of those times. I concentrated on the spinach, the potatoes, and the roast beef. All were delicious.

I also concentrated on Vivian. She was delicious. I marveled at her memory, her poise, and her presentation of ideas. She was an enigma…brilliant one minute, foolish the next. I couldn't understand why she lived in a house my father occupied. Besides being a pain in the ass, he was much too old for her. Of course, I was much too young. Some day I'd be old enough to marry her. But what was I thinking? I was supposed to stay clear of her. She was temptation. And she had me all mixed up.

For the next two weeks I continued to search for work. I walked through the garment district, the shoe district, the jewelry district, and every other district that could be covered with two burning feet. I saw hundreds of people working; operating machines, making suits and dresses, packing boxes, decorating windows, sweeping floors, selling toasters, vacuum cleaners, television sets. Surely, I'd find a job. Out of the working masses a vacancy would occur. Someone would quit, get a promotion, leave town, marry a millionaire, drop dead.

I found no job. I had to admit I couldn't earn my own way. I had to depend upon my father. I was stuck with Vivian. Next time I see Father O'Donnell, I'll tell him I could avoid temptation if I didn't have to eat and sleep. He'll probably tell me the world is filled with problems. I have to cope with them.

My own father picked at me constantly because I couldn't find a job. "I don't understand why you can't find work in New York City," he'd state when I was all set to enjoy dinner. "New York is the Mecca of the world."

I kept my patience. "Maybe so, Dad, but today I walked as far as Central Park without finding a job."

Demon of Lust

"There's work in New York City," he said with annoying persistence. "In my office alone, there are two vacancies for clerical positions. The positions provide an excellent background for accounting."

I'd just put a piece of lean meat into my mouth. It soured at the thought of working in my father's office.

Vivian jumped into the conversation with enthusiasm. "You mean you can get Tommy a job? Why didn't you say so?"

Dad's words dug into my ribs. "I want him to get his own job. I want him to mature, become a man."

"There are plenty of good men looking for work today," Vivian argued. "Jobs are difficult to find. Tommy will report to your office tomorrow morning, file an application. Won't you, Tommy?"

I couldn't share Vivian's enthusiasm. I wanted work, but not in my father's office. If I worked in his office, he'd fire me if I left home with the money I earned. In a whisper, I said, "I'll report to your office."

"No, you won't!" he shouted. "Your stupidity could jeopardize my image."

Vivian and I winced at the remark. "Tommy isn't stupid," she said. He'll do well in your office. For a boy his age, he knows a great deal."

Again came words that hurt. "He knows what he's not supposed to know. What he's supposed to know, he doesn't know."

Vivian shook her head. "Let's not argue about what he knows, what he doesn't know. Are you going to get him a job or aren't you?"

"Yes, I am," my father said.

The news came as a surprise and a disappointment to me.

"You'll give him the address of your office, the room number, whom to see...the time?" Vivian asked.

"He's to report tomorrow morning, nine o'clock sharp, to my tenant, Togallini."

I immediately pictured myself in the nude, posing for a picture. "Is Togallini going to paint me?"

Dad's little eyes brightened as if he had the wittiest idea in the world. "Togallini's not going to paint you. You're going to paint his apartment.

His brother, Mario, is giving me a hard time about a rent increase. He questioned me about the attention I've given the apartment. The lease calls for a painting every five years."

"When did you have it painted last, Dad?"

"I've never had it painted. You'll do the first job, tomorrow morning."

I could find no words to explain why I didn't want to work for Togallini. I wasn't concerned about being exposed to pictures of naked women. I was concerned about being in the same house with Vivian during the day.

Vivian's face also showed concern about my working for Togallini. Her words confirmed the notion. "Don't ask Tommy to work in that apartment." Her request sounded like a plea.

"Why not?" my father asked with suspicion.

Her face flushed. She quickly gained her composure. "It's no place for a boy to work."

"Do you believe the paintings of nude women will corrupt him?"

"They won't do him any good."

"You aren't interested in his moral life," was the bitter response. "You're only interest is in your own objectives, whatever they happen to be. A painting of you is in Togallini's apartment, isn't it? You don't want Tommy to see it. You don't want me to hear about it. Have I analyzed your position correctly?"

For a split second, Vivian had the look of a tiger. She was crouched forward, ready to spring. She appeared capable of sinking her teeth into my father's throat. Then she relaxed and said, "To hell with you, Willie."

CHAPTER 5

Struggling with the paint supplies my father had given me, I stood at the door to Togallini's apartment, trying to gather enough courage to knock on his door. The door looked like any of the other heavy oak doors in the house, but there was a difference. The door was rarely ever used. Togallini and his models used the door at the rear of the house. My mother had forbid me to pass through either door. Never once had I entered the attic apartment.

I thought of my mother. She once said Togallini was a dirty, old man who corrupted the women he hired. My mother spent the early years of her marriage offering my father a variety of reasons for terminating the Togallini lease. My father had one reason for keeping it active: the check he received each month from Mario Togallini.

How much rent Mario paid for his brother's apartment was never revealed to me. I doubt that Togallini, the tenant, knew or cared. He cared only for his paintings and his women. Or his women and his paintings, whichever came first.

Togallini didn't care for kids. When I was little, I tried to walk a six-foot fence in our backyard. Losing my balance, I fell on a brick walkway, stunned myself. The door to the second floor opened. Togallini, tall, thin and aristocratic looking, stood before me. He was like a hero coming to my aid. He held an empty tube of red paint in his hand. He obviously wished to replace it in a nearby paint store. Despite my mother's warning, I was glad to see him. I needed help. His eyes shifted from me to the empty tube. Stepping over me, he hurried through the gate.

The incident left a scar in my memory. It helped me avoid the artist while I was growing up. Even now I wanted to avoid him; didn't want to knock on his door. Could I offer my father a reason for not knocking? Could I say the walls couldn't be painted because they were covered with paintings? He'd say I was looking for an excuse to avoid work. I knocked on Togallini's door.

No response.

I knocked again.

A frail voice answered. "The door is open. Please come in."

When I opened the door and stepped inside the room, it was like stepping inside a Greenwich Village antique and junk shop. The room was jammed with dust-laded furniture. I couldn't find the artist.

A frail "Hello" helped me. The greeting came from a large rocking chair, near a window with many cobwebs. I hardly recognized the deathlike creature sitting in the rocker. He was practically all bone, covered with loose flaps of skin, the color of mayonnaise. His eyes were small and black and sunken into their sockets. He spoke with a great effort.

"You're the Davis boy, aren't you?"

"Yes, Mr. Togallini. My name's Tommy."

He studied me thoughtfully with his sunken eyes. "You've enough paint there for a career as an artist. Why all the paint?"

"My father sent me to paint your apartment."

Togallini's face soured when I mentioned my father. "This apartment hasn't been painted since I moved here. Why now?"

"My father wants to increase your rent."

"My brother takes care of the rent. Has your father contacted him?"

"I think so."

"It's not so easy prying money out of my brother. When a rent increase was mentioned to him, I can picture him questioning your father about the condition of this apartment, reminding him the apartment hasn't been painted in years. My brother would tell your daddy the conditions of the lease have been violated."

I felt a sudden kinship with this man. "I'm sorry, Mr. Togallini."

The weak voice came again. "You're not to blame. It is I who spoke to your father, agreed to stay in this apartment when your mother inherited this house. I ignored a basic business principle the Togallinis have been following for generations."

After my unsuccessful search for a job, I was interested in learning a basic business principle that might help me. "What's the principle, Mr. Togallini?"

He raised a bony finger. "You get screwed when you deal with a prick."

He was talking about *my* father. What he said was lewd and crude but true. It'd shock my mother. Yet I had to smile, laugh. My laugh became uncontrollable, took on a funny sound that always caused other people to laugh. Togallini was no exception. Squeaking sounds broke from his thin lips. His bony shoulders bobbed up and down. His laugh didn't last long. He began to cough, wheeze, drool. His skin, mayonnaise colored, turned a pale green.

Apprehensively, I wiped his mouth with a clean paint rag. "I better go now. We'll talk about the paint job some other time."

"We'll talk about it now," he said with surprising vitality after a seizure that could have finished him. "And we'll make the talk brief. Forget the paint job. Tell your father to forget it. Tell him he'll have a law suit on his hands if one drop of paint is applied to the walls of this apartment while I live."

Nodding, I started for the door, thinking the life of the artist would end before any lawsuit could begin. "I'll tell him, Mr. Togallini."

"Just one minute. I have another job for you. A job more important than my life. But I'm not sure I can trust you to do it. If you're anything like your father, I know I can't trust you. If you're anything like your mother, I know I can."

I didn't like to hear him talk about my mother, as if he knew her well. "Get your brother to do the job. You can trust him."

The voice was weak but excited. "I can't trust my brother to do the work I want done. Besides, he's very busy. He owns the largest pornographic business in the world. The business is his only interest, apart from a few ladies he sees for recreational purposes."

I spoke impatiently. "Can't you tell him you're sick, ask him to visit you?"

The old artist tried to look through a window covered with dust and cobwebs. "He won't visit me till I'm dead."

I felt some sympathy for the human wreck. "There must be someone else."

"I've no one I can trust. I'm stuck with you. There's a fifty-fifty chance you're all right. I must take that chance."

"I'm not so sure I want to work for you, Mr. Togallini. My father owes you a paint job, that's all."

His voice grew stronger in his earnestness. "I'll pay you more than you can earn from others."

Now he's talking business, I thought. "How much?"

"I have very little money. I can give you a painting and some furniture."

My eyes roamed the walls of the room, looking for his paintings. I wanted to see if they had any value. The nails for holding the paintings were on the walls, long irregular rows of them, and the dirt marks which once surrounded the paintings were there, but no paintings.

His eyes grew sly. "You'll like the painting I have in mind for you."

"Could I see it?"

"Not till you finish the job I want done."

I studied the bony creature on the rocker, asked myself why he'd moved his paintings from the walls. Was he ashamed of them? Had he come to realize he'd no talent, moved the paintings so no one would see them? Maybe he didn't want his models to learn he wasn't a true artist. He was probably more interested in the models than the canvases he produced. He'd so many models. They used to awaken me at night, squealing on the stairs. Togallini was a lover, not an artist.

He seemed to be reading my mind. "My furniture will bring you some money," he said. "I bought it new, now it's antique."

I examined the furniture in the room. It wasn't worth much. The living room and bedroom furniture combined were placed without a plan. Togallini, or someone else, had pushed the bedroom furniture into the living room. I knew he'd a separate room for the bedroom furniture, as well as a third room, combination kitchen and studio. Why had he moved the bedroom furniture into the living room? Did he need the space for an ex-model who was now a corpse? Did he need me to cut her up, remove her body from the apartment, piece by piece?

Making believe I wasn't suspicious of him, I asked, "When can I have the furniture?"

He focused his sunken eyes on me. "When I'm dead."

I forced myself to reveal what was on my mind: "I can't wait for you to die. I need money now."

"We all need something now. But all of us must wait for certain events to take place before we get what we want. Sometimes we never get what we want. And sometimes we're better off when we don't get what we want. Do the job I want you to do and you'll be glad you did. Trust me, for I am near the end of the road. Have faith in me, Tommy. God will bless you."

When Togallini mentioned *faith* and *God,* I thought of Father O'Donnell advising me to work without compensation. I decided to follow his advice. "I'll do the job for you, Mr. Togallini."

"You will!" the old artist cried. The effort caused him to cough and hold his heart. When the coughing spell was over, he slumped in his rocker, looking drained. "This is the first time in months I've felt relaxed and happy," he whispered. "I'm indebted to you." And then he closed his eyes and died.

At least, I though he'd died until I examined him. I pressed an ear against his thin chest and listened for a heartbeat. Hearing nothing, I took a wide paint scraper from my pocket and placed its bright blade under his nose. Several moments passed before the blade turned dull. Togallini had breathed on it. He was alive! And my heart stopped its frantic pounding.

But he was asleep. A crazy thing for him to do. He hired me to do a job and then went off to sleep without telling me what he wanted done. I should have learned what he wished me to do before I agreed to help him. He might have a *corpse* in the next room. One way to find out, take a look.

I moved silently to the door of the next room, opened it gently. I was willing to bet anything I'd see a dead body. There was no dead body. There were two long rows of canvases, pressed neatly together. None was on display. None could be viewed without disturbing a row.

Moving quickly through the aisle formed by the paintings, I entered a large room. I saw a dusty oak table, mottled with paint, two chairs, a rusty gas stove, sink and refrigerator, which were manufactured before I was born. More than two-thirds of the room contained the tools of the artist: easel, palettes, bench, racks, paint, knives, brushes, and blank canvases. This was the studio and kitchen combination.

A bright sun streamed through a skylight, focusing on a brown leather couch, cracked and worn. What stories that couch could tell about Togallini and his trollops, I thought. What stories a boy could tell if he'd been able to peer through the skylight. But nobody with any sense would try to look through that window. Nobody but God.

What to do? What to do? I returned to Togallini, found him still sleeping. It'd be a shame to shake those bones, awaken him. Not that he slept so peacefully. Even asleep, he frowned as if he foresaw great trouble. Why was he so worried? Was it his health? A million germs must have feasted on his flesh, picked him clean. He said nothing about his health. He was worried about something else.

His women! Was he worried about them? They were his whole life. All he lived for. He didn't want them to learn he was a flop as an artist. Perhaps he wanted me to get rid of the paintings before he died. Peddle them for anything I could get.

I wouldn't object to selling his painting. They might be better than he thinks. I'd sell them on a commission basis. I might be lucky enough to find a dealer willing to pay as much as fifty dollars for one picture. At a commission of ten percent, I'd make five dollars. Not bad. At twenty percent, I'd make ten dollars. Better! If I could sell fifty paintings at that price, I'd make five hundred dollars. Great! If people can make money selling paintings by monkeys, I can make money selling paintings by Togallini.

Returning to the room in the center of the apartment, I pulled out the first painting my fingers touched. It was light to handle, yet long, roughly six feet. I brought it into the studio, stood it up against the couch. As I expected, the painting was that of a naked woman. As I didn't expect, I was looking at the most beautiful picture I'd ever seen.

The woman stood boldly before me, with her legs spread wide, her knees slightly bent; ready, it seemed, to seduce me. Her breasts were big, perfectly formed, inviting. They wrecked every resolution I made to avoid temptation. I was drawn to the woman by a force over which I had no control. I breathed heavily, burned below the belt.

Stepping back from the painting, and cupping my eyes with my hands, I told myself I was mad to allow paint on canvas to affect me so. The painting was influencing my mind, my imagination, and my will power. I wanted the burning in my pants to stop. I wanted my heavy breathing to stop. I looked at the picture again.

The woman was smiling.

I ran from the studio, through the room filled with paintings, into the room littered with furniture. Tripping over a rug, I sprawled before Togallini, awakening him.

"What's wrong? What's wrong?" he cried.

Without answering, I struggled to my feet, hurried towards the door.

"Please come back. Please! Tommy! Please!"

Again, I didn't answer. Not that I didn't want to help Togallini, I was driven to do something else. Reaching the second floor, I cried out with a voice shaking with emotion. "Vivian! Vivian!"

Her voice came from the bedroom. "I'm in here, Tommy."

Her door was ajar. She was in a flimsy negligee, seated on the edge of the bed. She looked as if she'd been waiting for me.

"Vivian," I said, moving close to her. "Could you...would you...do something...?"

When she stood, her thighs touched mine. "Anything you say."

My heart pounded against my chest. "Would you make love with me?"

Her arms moved around my waist, she gave me a passionate kiss. "Like that?"

My words sounded as if they came from some stranger. "Yes. In bed."

I clung to her for over an hour, experiencing wild pulsating painful pleasures that bathed every inch of my body. No one on earth could pull me from her. Not the strongest boy in school...not my father...not a team of horses...not the priest who heard my confession. I wanted Vivian with all my body, with all my soul. As a strange and new excitement gripped me, a fleeting question passed through my mind. Was it really Vivian I wanted, or was it the woman in the painting?

CHAPTER 6

We slept most of the day. I'd have slept longer, but the hands on the alarm clock shocked me out of bed. My father was due home from work in an hour. If he caught me in bed with Vivian, he'd castrate me. Putting my clothes on, I ran down the stairs, unlocked the front door.

Vivian came running down the stairs after me, grabbed my arm before I could leave the house. Her eyes were puffed a bit, her lips chapped. She didn't look as pretty as she normally looked. "Tommy, don't leave this house without something to eat."

For the first time in my life, the thought of food sickened me. The thought of what I'd done with Vivian sickened me more. "I'm not hungry."

"Where are you going at this hour?"

Trying to evade a direct answer, I said, "I don't want to be here when my father gets home."

"Don't blame you for that. But now that I think of it, I know where you're going."

"You tell me."

Her response was sarcastic. "To confession. That's were little Catholic boys go when they think they've committed a sin."

I could be just as sarcastic as she could. "How about Catholic girls?"

"They go, too."

"Shall we go together?"

"No thanks."

"Why not?" I asked, thinking I'd outwit her. "You said you're Catholic."

"A good one, too," she retorted triumphantly. "And a good Catholic girl doesn't go to confession and say she's sorry for a sin she intends to commit again."

I slammed the door in her face. Two minutes later I kicked an empty coffee can into a store window. The window didn't break, but the sound of the can brought a tall bearded man to the door.

He had a nasty manner, pointed a finger at me. "You hit my window."

If I'd weighed another thirty pounds, I'd have been nasty with him, not apologetic. At my present weight, he'd take me for sure. "A kid in a car threw a can at your window."

He glared at me. "I didn't hear no car."

"It was coasting," I said, hurrying off."

What a stupid lie! Worse than any my father ever told. Why did I lie? I could have told the truth. If that bearded character came after me, I could have put my thumb to my nose, pointed four finger at him, and taken off. He outweighed me. That didn't mean he could outrun me. I was disgusted with myself, getting more like my father every day. I ran my fingers through my hair to learn if my hair was getting thin like his.

And why did I make love with Vivian? I resisted her before, not this morning. I wanted her with all my heart...with my soul. The more I thought about it, the more I realized Togallini's painting had driven me into Vivian's arms. There was something about the painting that destroyed my willpower, suspended my ability to reason, and destroyed my desire to follow God's laws. I couldn't understand why I did something I didn't want to do. Many young people fornicate and forget it. I couldn't be like them...didn't want to be. My conscience wouldn't allow it.

To a great extent, my mother had formed my conscience. She once defined it as the intellect passing judgment on moral matters. She taught me what was right, what was wrong. She set a perfect example for me. I followed her example till this morning. I can't blame my father for that. Nor Vivian. Nor the devil. Besides, I don't believe in a devil.

Demon of Lust

I was walking without thinking where I was going. I stood in front of the church on Fourteenth Street, looking up at the stone structure. I couldn't go in. No sense in ringing for a priest, telling him I was sorry for a sin I'd commit again. Vivian was right. She wasn't much of a Catholic, but she knew what a Catholic should do.

A car door slammed, someone walked past me.

"Looking over the church property, young man?" The priest who asked was a big man with broad shoulders and an Irish brogue. His eyes were bright blue. He had brown hair with waves like a roller coaster. I hadn't seen him before, yet I recognized his voice. He was the priest who heard my last confession.

"No...yes...I guess so, Father."

Father O'Donnell didn't stop to talk. He took the church steps two at a time and disappeared through the door.

I was sorry I hadn't stopped him. I could've asked him what a kid could do who was doing things he didn't want to do.

I walked till I could walk no more. Tired and hungry, I returned home. Vivian met me at the door. She was excited about something.

"Come into the kitchen," she said, taking my arm. "I'll get you something to eat. I want to talk to you."

Her nearness brought a tingling sensation to my body. "Where's Dad?"

"I don't know," she said impatiently. "He's out somewhere. Who the hell cares?"

I was glad he was out. I wouldn't have to face him. I was sorry he was out because I'd be alone with Vivian, didn't trust myself with her, didn't trust her with me. "What do you have for supper?" I asked distractedly.

"Spaghetti. Eat it quickly. I've something important to discuss with you."

She gave me a generous portion of spaghetti, three slices of bread, a glass of milk. I ate quickly, watched her work. She disposed of a soiled pot, a half-loaf of bread, the butter and milk with surprising speed and efficiency.

She then sat down at the table opposite me, waited patiently for me to finish. I could tell she wasn't thinking about sex. She had something else on her mind. The moment I wiped my mouth clean with a paper napkin, she was all business.

"Tommy, you were in Togallini's apartment this morning. What did he say to you?"

"He said he didn't want his apartment painted."

A slight frown appeared on her face. "I could have given you that information last night. I didn't want to mention Togallini's name in front of your father. Togallini has cancer of the liver. I see him every day. I feed him, give him his medicine."

Vivian wasn't holding a grudge against the man who threw her down the stairs, I thought. "That's good of you."

"Not really. I don't look after him out of the kindness of my heart. Nor do I do it for the few dollars he gives me from the little money he receives from his brother. I do it for another reason. Something he promised me."

I pushed out the words quickly. "Did Mr. Togallini paint your picture?"

"He did."

I had to ask the next question. "Did he make love with you?"

Her frown deepened. "Now look here, Tommy. I want to know what Togallini had to say to you."

"He said he wants me to do a job for him."

Her eyes betrayed a deep curiosity. "What does he want you to do?"

"He didn't say."

"What do you mean he didn't say?" she asked heatedly. "If he asked you to do a job, he certainly told you what he wants done."

"He fell asleep."

She sat back in her chair, studied the ceiling a moment, then faced me. "And when he fell asleep, you looked at one of his paintings, didn't you?"

"Yes. I figured he wants me to sell his paintings on a commission basis. Naturally, I wondered if they're worth my time and effort."

Her smile was sardonic. "The painting you examined, is it worth your time and effort?"

I had to give her an answer. "The moment I saw the painting, I realized it was worth at least one hundred dollars."

"Why lie?" she asked with the sharpness of a razor blade.

I wanted to display some indignation. Her steady gaze changed my mind. "Well...."

"You didn't think of money when you saw the painting. You thought of me. You came running."

My cheeks grew hot. No question about it, I'd been caught in a lie. Vivian was uncanny. She knew I'd come running when I saw the picture. She was waiting for me. I couldn't argue with her. She was considerate enough to change the subject.

Her words came softly now. "Tommy, how would you like to leave this house, live without your father?"

"With you, Vivian?"

"With me, without me, any way you please."

"Is there a catch?"

"The catch is cooperation. We can earn money together."

I'd heard of couples cooperating, sharing expenses for rent and food. They managed because they were in love. I wasn't so sure I'd always love Vivian; she'd always love me. A future with her was filled with question marks. "I doubt if we'd have any luck..."

"Nonsense! You have doubts before you know what plans I have for the two of us. The plans are based on Togallini's paintings. We can sell them. Make a great deal of money."

"I've already thought of that."

Her eyes sparkled. "You have?"

"Yes. I think Togallini wants me to sell his paintings. That's the job he wants me to do. I thought of asking him for twenty percent of everything I collect. If I sold one hundred paintings at fifty dollars apiece, I'd make one thousand dollars, which is a lot of money but not enough for us to go off on our own."

Vivian broke into a warm and friendly laugh. I liked to hear her laugh, even when she laughed at me. When she was through laughing, her voice became low and serious.

"Tommy, I'm going to tell you something you must not repeat; especially to your father."

"I won't tell him. You can trust me."

"I do trust you. And that's why I don't want you to deceive me. I want you to trust me, do as I say. If we work together, we can become wealthy."

I began to suspect the truth. "A Togallini painting is worth more than fifty dollars, isn't it?"

Vivian was just about as serious as she could be. "A Togallini painting is worth ten thousand dollars, maybe twenty, and maybe more."

Impossible to believe, I thought. Togallini loved pleasure. If his paintings were worth so much, why hadn't he sold them, lived in his own home with all the comforts money can buy? Why did he depend on his brother for money?

Vivian arched her brow. "You don't believe me?"

"I'm afraid not, Vivian. If Mr. Togallini was smart enough to paint pictures worth a fortune, he'd be smart enough to know they're worth a fortune."

"He knows, but he won't sell. He's never sold a single painting. He's sold nothing but pornographic junk."

My words came fast, on the heels of hers. "I'll bet he can't find a buyer."

Vivian took my hand in hers. "Let me tell you a story. One night I was in the apartment. A buyer came in to see Togallini. His name is Botski. He owns one of the finest art galleries in New York City. As he examined each painting, his face revealed a strange delight. I asked him what he thought of the work. He said every painting is a thing of great beauty. Before he was through with his examination, he offered to buy every painting in the apartment at a price far above the market for an unknown artist. Togallini told him the paintings were not for sale. Botski said he'd pay ten thousand dollars for any painting Togallini wished to release. Togallini refused the offer. Botski then walked over to my painting, which was near completion. He offered to buy it for twenty thousand dollars. Togallini was so annoyed at the art dealer's insistence, he told him to leave the apartment."

I pulled my hand away from hers, finding it hard to believe her story. "He wouldn't sell one painting?"

"Not a single one. Several nights later, he finished my painting. He stood and admired it for a long time. It seemed to give him some sort of a weird charge. He led me to his couch, tried to make love with me. I refused. He opened his wallet, offered me every dollar he had. I refused him again."

I felt relieved. "I'm glad you did, Vivian."

"After I'd refused him a third time, he asked me to look at my painting. Up to that time, he wouldn't allow me to see it, which was all right with me. The other paintings I'd seen put my passions in such a turmoil I avoided them the best I could. I told him I preferred to leave. He said I could go as soon as I viewed my painting, his masterpiece."

My body grew warm at the thought of seeing her painting. My emotions were like Fourth of July sparklers.

"It was truly a great work of art," she said. "And it had an unbelievable affect on my passions. I not only wanted to have sex, I wanted to possess the painting more than anything else in the world. My instincts told me to get out of the apartment, or regret it the rest of my life. I started to go… Togallini grabbed my arm and said, 'If you give yourself to me tonight, I'll give you the painting.' I yielded to him."

The world seemed to crash around me.

"When the ordeal was over, Togallini gave me an excuse for not giving me the painting. In the months that followed, he continued to give me excuses. One day he asked me to help him move the bedroom furniture into the living room, take the paintings down from the walls, store them in the vacant bedroom. He had other paintings, too, in the studio…everywhere. I helped him, hoping to learn he'd sold some of his work. I expected money from him, as well as the painting he promised me. He told me he'd cleared the living room and the studio of his paintings to clear his mind of everything he'd done in the past. He was going to produce a painting that'd surpass everything he'd ever done."

"Everything?"

Vivian stared at me like a child just spanked. Tears formed in her lovely eyes. She sobbed as she spoke. "After we completed the work, he pointed to the door, told me to leave the apartment. He said he never wanted to see me again."

I found myself in a state of confusion. Should I feel sorry for her or jealous of Togallini? "I don't know how he could say he never wanted to see you again, Vivian."

"I'd have left in a minute," she stated defensively, "if he'd given me the painting he promised. He said he was sorry he had to break his word, but simply couldn't release any of his paintings."

"The painting was yours," I said, anxious to agree with her. "Why didn't you wait till he was out, or asleep, then take it?"

"His name is on everything he does. His work cannot be disguised. If I were to take a painting, he could have me arrested."

What could I say? "Couldn't you get him to change his mind, get him to give you the painting with a bill of sale?"

"God, how I tried. For a full year, I haunted the door leading to his apartment. I begged him to keep his promise. At times, he was firm in his refusal and drove me off. Other times, he was pleasant and sympathetic. He'd invite me into his apartment, not to make love, but to feed me and give me what little money he had. It was never enough to carry me for long. There were nights when I'd nothing to eat, no place to sleep."

"I'm beginning to understand how you got here," I said softly.

Her beautiful face showed her pain. "No one can ever understand how I got here. Even I can't understand it. I do recall the night. It was cold and damp. A penetrating wind swept the streets. I was hungry…had no place to sleep...no money." She paused. "I could have gone home to my father. Despite our differences, he'd have taken me in, fed me, given me my old room. Other avenues were open. But no! Some strange power compelled me to go to Togallini's apartment, force myself on him, even though I knew he no longer wanted me. Everything in my life became focused on my painting. I simply had to have it."

"Was the money you'd get for the painting so terribly important to you?"

"Strange you should ask. I never considered money terribly important. Not till my painting was promised to me. I like nice things, but I was never willing to compromise myself for them."

"You compromised yourself plenty when you posed naked for Togallini," I advised her.

"I did," she admitted. "I was sent to Togallini's studio by a modeling agency. Nothing was said to me about posing nude. When I entered his apartment, I saw the paintings on the walls, recognized some of the girls. I knew then the artist wanted me to pose nude. He also wanted me to take a sexually aggressive stance, as if I were ready and willing to seduce everyone who viewed me."

"You went ahead, allowed him to paint you in a compromising way. I can't understand why you let him do it."

She was slow to respond. "When I studied some of the pictures on the wall; pictures of models I knew, I saw that Togallini had captured on canvas a beauty these girls didn't possess. He'd caught something else, something difficult to explain. It's a power that activates the imagination and sexual desires of those who view the paintings. When I saw them for the first time, I wanted to discard my clothes and be painted in the nude."

"You hadn't posed naked before?"

Shaking her head fiercely, she said, "Never! Nor had I ever allowed any man to touch me. For me, keeping my virtue was keeping my wisdom."

Vivian was stupid and wise. A bundle of contradictions. She reminded me of a neighbor who taught at New York University, five days a week. On weekends, he'd get drunk, fight with his wife, his children, his friends, the police. He'd fight with everyone he faced till Monday morning, when it was time for him to return to the University, where he taught *Logic*.

"You haven't explained how you came to live with Dad and me."

She stared at me for a moment, hesitated, and then related the following:

"I went to Togallini's apartment that cold night to ask him to take me in. When he opened the door, I realized he'd aged considerably, appeared ill. Nevertheless he was pleased to see me, anxious to show me a painting he recently completed.

'This is the last painting I'll ever do,' he said. 'It's taken a great deal out of me physically. Mentally, it's helped me. I now realize there's more to life than paint on canvas.'

'Like money?' I asked the artist. 'Are you thinking about selling your paintings?'

'I'm thinking about selling one of them…or giving it away.'

I thought the battle was over. 'You're thinking about selling my painting or giving it to me?' I said to Togallini.

He shook his head. 'I'll never sell your painting, nor will I give it away.'

Before I knew what I was doing, I leaped at him, tried to scratch his eyes out. My fingernails cut the side of his nose. I wanted to hurt him for hurting me. I only infuriated him. He slapped my face, called me a tramp, and ordered me out of his apartment. I was hurt physically, mentally, spiritually. Yet I didn't want to leave that damned apartment. I was rooted to the floor.

'Get out!' he shouted.

'I've no place to go.'

'Spend the night with Davis. He collects the rent for this apartment. You two are alike. You're mercenary, conniving bastards. The whole world can go to hell as long as you get what you want.' Togallini grabbed the top of my dress, and with a strength he didn't appear to possess, he pulled me through the door leading to the interior of this house. He threw me down the stairs.'"

Demon of Lust

Vivian's face was contorted with pain, breathing hard, as she related these events to me. She couldn't understand why she was thrown down the stairs. Like a piece of garbage, a lover threw her away.

"That's when I found you, wasn't it?"

"Yes."

"Do you make love with my father?"

She evaded the question by saying, "I'm in love with you."

I was about to tell her she hadn't answered my question when she took my hand, kissed each finger.

"We don't have to waste our lives in this house, Tommy. We can get out soon. As soon as we have money." She looked hopeful.

That night I closed my eyes and tried to sleep. I thought about Vivian. She'd given me a great deal of information about herself, yet I still didn't understand why she remained in a house she desperately wanted to leave. Why should she find it necessary to cope with my father? Or Togallini? Why did a painting have such a strong hold on her? It meant more to her than the money it'd bring. I knew it; she knew it. There was no explanation. Tossing and tumbling in my bed, unanswered questions tormented me throughout the night.

CHAPTER 7

The following day I stood at Togallini's door. I'd decided to do my best to help Vivian obtain her painting. If she received the work of art, she could sell it, leave the house, and live a normal life. Whether I'd go with her was something to think about. It hurt me to recall she sold her body for the painting. If I married her, I'd know she was no virgin. Yet she had so many other wonderful qualities… I knocked on Togallini's door.

His frail voice answered. "Come in, Tommy."

Since I'd seen Togallini the previous morning, I should have been prepared to see him again; prepared to see a man days away from death. His conditioned had worsened. "Had your breakfast today, Mr. Togallini?"

"Vivian brought me a little gruel. But never mind that. I informed you yesterday I want you to do a job for me. In fact, two jobs. Both important." His eyelids drooped. I thought he'd fall asleep again.

I spoke in a loud voice. "Why not tell me what you want done. If I can do anything for you, I'll do it."

"I hope so, son. My first request: Get me a priest."

"A priest?" I repeated, surprised.

Togallini clasped his bony hands together as if he were praying. "I haven't been to confession in fifty years. I must see a priest as soon as possible, make my peace with God before I die."

It never struck me before that Togallini was Catholic. He wasn't one I'd brag about. He'd really drifted away from the Church. Must have some sort of a drift record.

"Do you go to confession?" he suddenly asked.

Demon of Lust

I tried to speak nonchalantly. "I've gone recently.
"Did you see the priest? I'd like to know what he's like."
"He's Irish, big, rugged. Seems to be on the ball."
Togallini's lips broke into a tiny smile. "He's the man for me. Think you can talk him into coming here?"
"I'll do my best. Vivian would do better. She's a convincing talker, has a lot of charm."
If I'd given Togallini a spoonful of gasoline instead of a suggestion, his face wouldn't have turned as sour. "I want you to do the job, Tommy. I can't trust Vivian. She might bargain with me, fight with me, finish me off."
My words were spontaneous. "All she wants is her picture."
That startled him. Disappointment showed on his death-like face. "We'll talk about the painting after you get me the priest."
My spirits rose. He'll give the picture to Vivian. She'll get her money. Everything is going to be perfect. "The painting is important to Vivian," I said. "Could I give her a hint?"
Shaking his head pathetically, he let out a cry, "The priest…the priest."
I made a quick decision. "Okay, Mr. Togallini. I'll try to get the priest. Do my best, anyhow."
He spoke with a great effort. "There's another thing you can do."
I figured he'd changed his mind, wanted me to deliver the picture to Vivian right away.
"What's that, Mr. Togallini?"
He stared at me with his sunken eyes. "Go to confession yourself."
Later, as I entered the church on Fourteenth Street, I could still feel the shock I experienced when Togallini advised me to go to confession again. Could he read my mind? My soul? Did he know I'd an affair with Vivian? Was he psychic or something?"
Entering the confessional, I thanked God the confessional was black, and the priest couldn't see me. After saying the preliminary prayer for confession, I got to the very heart of the confession: "…. fornication, Father. Once."

"For-ni-ca-tion!" The priest put an Irish accent on every syllable of the word.

"Yes, Father."

His voice was loud. "With a prostitute? An innocent girl? With whom?"

I thought he could be heard outside the confessional. I dropped my voice to a whisper, hoping he'd follow my example. "You know, Father. I explained before. I'm the boy who was tempted by a woman…I mean by Vivian…I mean by a woman who lives in our house."

"I remember you well. I told you to avoid temptation."

"Yes. And I tried…."

The priest snapped, "You didn't try hard enough. The devil has many snares for boys like you. If he doesn't get you with one snare, he'll try another. You must learn to avoid the snares. Otherwise, you'll lose your soul."

Father O'Donnell had to be more understanding, I thought. "It's not easy, Father."

"Of course, it's not easy," he said with a sigh. "Any great objective requires hard work, concentration, sacrifice. If you wish to save your immortal soul, you can't yield to every temptation that comes your way. You must be a soldier in God's army, willing to fight for your spiritual life. You're either in God's army or out of it. Neither you nor I make the rules. We follow the rules laid down by God. Do you have the strength of character to follow the rules?"

I felt a rise of courage. "I do. And I've got incentive now, more than ever. The woman who tempts me will leave our house if I help her get something she wants. You could help, too. You could come home with me and meet…"

His words cut into mine. "You want me to meet the woman?"

"Not the woman. A tenant named Togallini. He's dying. He wants to go to confession."

"Togallini," the priest murmured. "His name is familiar."

Demon of Lust

"You probably saw the name in the newspapers, Father. This man's brother is big in the manufacture and sale of pornographic materials. Dirty pictures, dirty films, and dirty comics, that sort of thing. You haven't seen our tenant's name in your list of parish members, though. The man's in our parish, but he's never been inside this church. He hasn't going to church for fifty years."

The priest mumbled something that had me wondering if there's a Christian way of cursing. Despite the brogue, the following words were unmistakably clear: "He hasn't gone to church for fifty years and now he wants a priest to go to him, hear his confession. Is that it?"

"Yes, Father. It'll help him an awful lot if you'll go. It'll help me, too."

"All right," said the priest after a pause, "I'll go with you. There's a blue Chevy in front of the church. The door is open. Wait in the car for me. I shouldn't be more than twenty minutes."

* * *

Priests are ordinarily punctual. This one kept me waiting an hour and ten minutes. When he finally arrived, opened the door and forced his bulk behind the wheel, he put out a huge hand. "Father O'Donnell," he said pleasantly.

I shook his big mitt. "Tommy Davis."

"Sorry I'm late."

"That's all right, Father. I don't mind waiting. I'm concerned about Togallini though. He's not going to last long."

"I broke away from confessions over an hour ago," the priest said, inserting a key in the ignition. "The moment I stepped into the rectory, the telephone rang. It was my pastor. He's in St. Vincent's hospital recovering from a minor operation. He's a pious man, welcomes the opportunity to suffer pain without complaining. Today he kept me on the phone a long time talking about his operation. I don't remember hearing him talk so much about himself."

"That's the way it goes sometimes."

The priest was pressing the ignition key forward. No sound came from the starter. He stepped out of the car, lifted the hood, and jiggled the battery cables. "They seem tight enough."

"Have you had any trouble with this car before?" I asked.

"It's been recently overhauled by an excellent mechanic. He put in new plugs and a battery. I can't understand why it won't start. I'll go in the rectory, call a taxi."

"We can walk."

Father O'Donnell closed the hood of the car. "An excellent suggestion. I should be the one recommending the walk. I'm trying to get my weight below two hundred."

I smiled. Wow! Wouldn't I like to weigh over two hundred pounds? With that weight, I'd train for the world's heavyweight title.

As we walked, the priest related another reason why he was delayed in the rectory. "About two minutes after I managed to say goodbye to the pastor, the phone rang again. It was the pastor calling a second time. In great detail, he apologized for making such an issue over the pain associated with his operation."

"I don't blame him for complaining about the pain. That's natural."

The priest tipped his hat to an old woman who smiled when she passed by him. "It's natural to complain about pain, but not for him. Most of us seek comfort; avoid pain as best we can. But the pastor has always accepted pain and other crosses graciously. He believes God places the heaviest crosses on those He loves the most."

"The pastor never cries for help?"

"Rarely ever. But I believe he should seek help more frequently than he does. Christ received help when He carried His cross. He also used the apostles to help Him spread His message. We all need help. We need one another."

He continued in this vain, discussed the importance of helping one another. As he did so, I realized I liked him very much. He was so sincere

Demon of Lust

in what he had to say, I felt sure he practiced what he preached. He did a little preaching when he told me to work for others without pay, sacrifice myself. He was sacrificing himself now as he walked towards Togallini's apartment. And so was I. By getting a priest for Togallini, I was doing something without pay. I felt good about it.

We were walking on Fourteenth Street, taking a right turn onto Sixth Avenue, when a shot was fired. A few seconds later, two Puerto Ricans, running at top seed, crashed into us. The older of the two runners struck Father O'Donnell; the younger one hit me. I flew back onto Fourteenth Street, stumbled at the curb, and landed in the street. Trucks, buses, cars, motor cycles raced towards me. I'd be dead in a second. The priest would give me the last rites.

A taxicab shot towards me like a rocket, brakes squealing. The cab stopped within three inches from my face. I could feel the heat from the motor.

Struggling to my feet, I made my way through a crowd that gathered. I saw two scared looking Puerto Ricans seated on the sidewalk with their backs resting against a building. An elderly Jewish man held a handkerchief to his bleeding scalp with one hand. The other hand held a big black revolver, pointed at the two Puerto Ricans. He'd have shot them if Father O'Donnell didn't stand between him and his line of fire.

"Give me the gun," the priest demanded.

The elderly man cried, "I'm killing these two punks."

"You can't kill them. You'll commit murder."

The man cocked his gun. "They hurt my wife."

"They'll be punished by the law. If you kill them, you'll be punished; separated from your wife."

The old man hesitated. He wouldn't hesitate long, I thought. A Jew is not going to listen to a Catholic priest. Even Catholics don't listen.

The old man handed the gun to the priest.

Holding the barrel of the gun with the butt down, Father O'Donnell turned to the two thugs. "On your feet! And give me the knife."

I hadn't noticed the knife before. The older of the two clutched a deadly looking knife in his right hand. The handle had the markings of a rattlesnake.

"All right, Padre," the bearer of the knife said, "I'll give ya the knife."

He gave it to him with a fast, brutal thrust.

The knife was aimed at the heart of Father O'Donnell. He was quick enough to avoid a fatal blow. Blood spurted from his shoulder. His left hand moved up to cover the flow. He looked surprised, disappointed, hurt.

The little thug, who'd knocked me down, scrambled to his feet, tore the gun from the limp hand of Father O'Donnell, swung it towards the crowd. "Back up! Back up!" he ordered, "Or I start shootin'."

The crowd backed up. The two young men dashed across Fourteenth Street, into a subway entrance. Father O'Donnell stood silently against a wall, holding his bloody shoulder.

For several moments, everyone was speechless. I worked my way through the crowd, towards the priest.

He smiled grimly when I reached him. "You all right, Tommy?"

My heart pounded my chest. "I'm okay, but you...you've been stabbed!"

The old Jewish man spoke. "It wouldn't have happened if he'd let me shoot those bums."

"I'm glad you didn't shoot them," said the priest.

The man shrugged, shook his head. "What can I do for you?"

"See if your wife needs you."

The eyebrows of the old man lifted as if he couldn't understand how he'd forgotten about his wife. He then hurried down the street, disappeared into a small store.

"Father, I'll get you a doctor," said someone in the crowd.

"My husband's calling an ambulance," said a woman with blond hair, black at the roots. "He has a cell phone."

A police car veered towards the curb at high speed, skidded to a stop. Two policemen rushed out of the vehicle, pushed the crowd roughly aside, headed towards us. One of the officers said to the bloody priest, "We'll take you to the hospital." Both officers helped Father O'Donnell into the car. Pushing me aside, they slammed the doors closed.

The priest leaned towards an open window. "It shouldn't take long to patch me up. I'll see Togallini as soon as I can get away from the hospital. What is his address?"

I gave it to him.

He seemed to be making a mental note of the address when the police car pulled away. Its siren screamed, added to the bedlam on Fourteenth Street.

My mind was also in a state of bedlam. A short time ago I was successful in getting a priest to agree to hear Togallini's confession. Now the priest was on his way to the hospital, blood pouring out of his shoulder. Would Togallini die before the priest was well enough to hear his confession? I didn't know. I'd have felt so much better if I knew the answer. Togallini's confession had suddenly become terribly important to me.

CHAPTER 8

Arriving home, I'd a strange feeling all was not well with Togallini. Taking the stairs two at a time, I was soon standing at his door. With only a moment's hesitation, I opened the door and moved quickly towards the rocking chair. Togallini was not in the chair. Nor was he in the living room. Was he in the bathroom? I opened the bathroom door. He wasn't there. Could he be with his paintings? He wasn't. He must be in the studio. He wasn't in the studio. I returned to the furniture-cluttered room with my head bent, my eyes focused on the floor. I told myself the artist had to be in the hospital or the morgue. Vivian had access to the apartment. Maybe she'd found him…

Raising my head, I saw him in the far corner of the room with his back pressed tightly against the ceiling. He was suspended in empty air, naked. His poor pecker, long and dark and thin, dangled down. A sausage with the meat removed.

The shock of seeing him naked, on the ceiling, was registered in every bone in my body. Each bone vibrated like a funny bone, struck at the same time. As soon as my legs would move me, I'd leave the apartment, never return.

A pathetic voice changed my mind. "Please help me, Tommy. Pull me down."

Mesmerized with fear, I could do nothing but stare at him, recall my mother's warning: Avoid the tenant Togallini!

His words, weak and trembling, came again: "Help me."

Demon of Lust

In a daze, I pushed a heavy oak table under him, stood on it. Grabbing his ankles, I pulled him down from the high ceiling. He was as light as a toy balloon and just as easy to move. I helped him into his rocking chair. His body shivered uncontrollably, and his teeth chattered like castanets.

I ran to a closet, ripped open the door, looked for a coat, a blanket, pants, shirt, anything to cover his naked body. I found an old bathrobe. Shaking out the dust, I asked myself what I'd do if he rose again. Turning towards him, I saw that he still sat naked in his rocking chair. He waited for me like a helpless child. I put the bathrobe on him. It was much too big. Togallini had shrunken plenty. Soon there'd be little left of him. Shuddering, I felt sweat run down my backbone; sweat as cold as a corpse.

"Where's the priest?" Togallini suddenly cried. "Couldn't you get him?"

His cry was so pitiful; I'd have done anything to comfort him. "I was able to get him, but on the way here…"

"He was killed," Togallini cried out, despair written all over his fleshless face.

I knelt beside him. "He wasn't killed. He was injured, stabbed in the shoulder by someone who robbed a store."

Two tears emerged from the sunken eyes, ran down the face of the artist. "Thank God he wasn't killed."

"No, he wasn't killed. As I've told you, he's rugged. He asked for your address. As soon as he's patched up, he's coming here. You'll meet him. You'll like him. He wasn't hard on me in confession, didn't lecture me on the way here. And even after he was stabbed, and he was bleeding plenty, he spoke to an old gent whose store had been robbed. He told him to see about his wife. She'd been hurt."

What little joy that can show on the face of a man who knows he's at the end of the road, showed on the face of Togallini. "Tommy, tell me everything that happened after you left the church. I know what happened inside the church. I know what you told the priest in confession."

How could he possibly know what I told the priest in confession? Was he too sick to think clearly? Or was he psychic? I wasn't going to question him. So I told him about the long wait I had in the automobile, the delays experienced by the priest, the problem with the car, the holdup, the collision with the two thieves, the stabbing of the priest.

"All those events can be attributed to Isacaron," Togallini said as if he were talking to himself. "Isacaron is a master of timing."

I felt the hair rise on the back of my neck. "Who? What…?"

With a bony hand, he waved away my questions. "Never mind. Continue."

I covered every detail I experienced during my return from the church. On two occasions I tried to divert the conversation to his trip to the ceiling. To my dismay, he wasn't interested in talking about his trip. He was interested in the thoughts I had about him before entering the apartment; that all was not well with him.

"Do you think you had a premonition?" he asked as if premonitions were a common topic with him.

"I don't know."

He leaned forward. "You could've had a premonition. Your mother had several before she died."

When he mentioned my mother, my belly grew hot. I felt like telling him that any information he had about my mother was meaningless. He hardly knew her. She wouldn't reveal anything personal to him…a sinner and womanizer. Nevertheless, all I said was: "She had premonitions?"

"She did, indeed," he replied with authority. "Too bad she didn't have one before she married your father. She must've been very young and exceedingly stupid in those days…" He then began to cough and drool.

I was so mad at him for calling my mother stupid; I didn't wipe away a yellow substance dribbling out of his nose. Before I realized what I was saying, I found myself bawling him out; bawling out a man close to death. "You think all women are stupid, don't you, Mr. Togallini? You think you can say anything you please about them, don't you, Mr. Togallini? You think you can do anything you wish with them, don't you, Mr. Togallini?

Demon of Lust

I don't like you when you call my mother stupid. Nor do I like you when you deceive and abuse Vivian."

That brought on another coughing spell. Togallini's eyes looked as if they'd fly out of their sockets if he continued to cough. He finally stopped coughing and fastened his watery eyes on me. "When I spoke about your mother, I'd no intention of criticizing her," he said, wiping his nose with his sleeve. "You mother was a splendid person...a lady...someone I respected. However, I could never understand why she married your father."

I felt my own heat. "Haven't you ever made a mistake?"

He stared at me with his watery eyes. "My whole life has been a mistake."

I experienced no sympathy for him. "Then why be so critical of others? You not only criticized my mother, you criticized Vivian. Out of all the women you've had, she's the only one left. She's the only woman who'll do something for you."

He gave me another long, watery stare. "Vivian is a mixed bag of tricks. She's consistent in doing the right thing one day, the wrong thing the next. A good time is her primary concern. Her god is pleasure. Don't put too much confidence in her, Tommy. She'll disappoint you."

As earnestly as I could, I said, "Vivian is a beautiful woman, Mr. Togallini. She's the most beautiful woman in the world. And I'll tell you something else. I'm in love with her. I...I can't help loving her."

His smile was weak. "You and I are basically the same, my young friend, except for a difference in age, health, and proximity to death. I, too, love Vivian, even though I know I can't trust her. I wouldn't harm her for all the treasures the devil can offer. More than that, I believe God loves her. She's His creation, a thing of beauty. If a human being can fall in love with something beautiful he creates, so can God..." Togallini stopped to mull over his own words, nodded his head as if he agreed with then, then closed his eyes and fell asleep.

I watched him for a while, wondering if all men standing on the brink of the grave think and speak of God and the devil. I wondered, too, what force, good or evil, carried Togallini to the ceiling. I tried to get him to talk about it, he wouldn't. That bothered me greatly. I was also bothered by something he did talk about: My mother! He certainly didn't know her well enough to talk about her with any degree of authority. What little information he had about her probably came from my father. That had to be the explanation. Togallini was a sinner. My mother was a saint. Sinners and saints don't mix.

Vivian was waiting for me when I came down the stairs. I paused a moment to bask in her beauty. She led me into the kitchen and asked, "What did Togallini say to you?"

"He said he wants to go to confession."

Vivian's lovely eyes were wide with wonder. "To confession? He's not Catholic, is he?"

"He was once. He'd like to be one again."

"He knows he's going to die. And I know we must work fast. If he dies before he signs my painting over to me, his brother will claim it with all the others." Vivian pressed a kitchen spoon against her chin. "Too bad Togallini hates me so much."

Her words came as a surprise. "He doesn't hate you. He loves you."

She threw the spoon into the sink. "Then why isn't he kind to me? I asked him for my painting a hundred times. Why doesn't he give it to me?"

"I don't know."

"Were you able to get him a priest? A little religion may help his spirit, make him more generous."

"I found a priest for him, all right. A Father O'Donnell. The priest was almost killed on his way here. He was stabbed by a thief who tried to rob a store."

"Stabbed?"

"Let me start from the beginning. Maybe you can help me figure out what's going on." I told her what happened to the priest, starting with the delays he experienced in the rectory and ending with the stabbing. I didn't tell her about the extraordinary event that took place in Togallini's apartment after the priest had agreed to hear his confession. If I'd told her I found Togallini on the ceiling, she might refuse to enter his apartment, care for him. Just thinking about the event left me feeling as if I'd my finger in an electric socket.

"But the priest wasn't killed," Vivian said, giving me the impression a stabbing wasn't terribly important to her.

"No, but nearly." I spoke with emphasis, hoping to convince her the stabbing was important. "The priest nearly lost his life. The knife struck within inches of his heart. He was cut badly. That damn thief stopped him from hearing Togallini's confession. But get this: Later, when I told Togallini what happened to Father O'Donnell, he acted as if he knew why the priest was delayed, why he was stabbed. Do you think Togallini is psychic or something?"

"Of course not," Vivian said irritably. "He's just a victim of his own colorful imagination. And he's scared of dying. You can tell he's frightened from his silence, the way he stares at you."

"He doesn't stare at me. Nor is he silent. He's talkative. Something is troubling him. It keeps him talking. Keeps him going."

Vivian nodded reflectively. "He does have drive, regardless of his health. I've seen him work for days without rest. I only hope he stays alive long enough to sign my painting over to me. He says little to me. He won't talk about my painting." Vivian put her hands to her head. "If he doesn't give me the painting, I'll go mad."

A sense of sympathy for her swept over me. "I'll try to get your painting tonight."

Rather than thank me, she said, "You better. If I don't get my painting, you can forget about sleeping with me again. That's a promise."

Her threat caused me to ask myself an important question: Should I give up the idea of marrying her? She's beautiful, no question about that. However, a beautiful woman can someday develop into a bitch. I'd have to be firm with her. "Vivian, do me a favor: Don't ever talk about sleeping with me while we're in this house. If my father ever heard you, he'd go berserk. He'd give me an awful beating."

My request had a strange reaction on her. Her face became hard, unfamiliar. "When are you going to grow up?" she said with cutting sarcasm. "Can't you defend yourself? You've been in the ring. You're younger than your father and just as big. Why not give him a beating?"

"Beat my father? That's something I'll never do. I've been taught to honor my father. Besides, if I tried to beat him, he'd throw me out of this house."

"Is that so bad?" she asked sneeringly. "You're not living in a happy house, you know."

"It's the only house I have. I can't support myself yet. I can't move till I find a job."

Vivian raised a manicured finger. "Get my painting for me and you won't need a job. The painting will keep us going for quiet a while. It'll also help me find work. Artists will be attracted to me."

"They'll be attracted to you if you don't get the painting. Why don't you give yourself a break? Forget the painting! Try to get a job on your own."

She shook her head vigorously. "I can't. You don't understand."

The words came unexpectedly into the room. "What doesn't he understand?"

My father's voice! He'd slipped into the house without making a sound. Standing in the doorway to the kitchen, he looked at me in a puzzled way. Was he suspicious of Vivian and me? He'd arrived home earlier than usual. If he'd arrived home moments before, he'd have heard Vivian refer to my sleeping with her. Some kids may think sleeping with a woman is great. I know it can cause an awful lot of trouble in a family…especially my family.

Vivian broke an uneasy silence. "Tommy doesn't understand how difficult it is to support oneself in New York these days. Rent and food are so expensive…"

"I'll countersign that opinion," my father said briskly.

Vivian frowned. She often frowned at some of the words he used, some of the ideas he expressed. At the moment, she seemed to be mulling over

Demon of Lust

two annoying facts: He snuck up on us. And he almost heard her say something about sleeping with me. If she lost her temper, she'd tell him he'd no right to invade our privacy…even if we were sleeping together.

I had to change the subject. "Dad, did you know Togallini is very sick? He doesn't want his apartment painted. He has some other chores he wants me to do for him."

My father wiped his glasses with a Kleenex. "Other chores aren't in the lease. Does he have money to pay us?"

"I don't think so. He let us off the hook for a paint job. We owe him something…"

My father glared at me. "What a dumb observation. The painting is one thing, the chores another. Let Togallini get the money from his brother Mario before you start work."

"Togallini is seriously ill, Dad. He's not going to last long. I'd rather not ask him for money."

My father's face grew grim. "If he's not going to last long, that's another reason why you should talk to him about money. Get the cash in your hands before you start work. When we look for a new tenant, I'll let you pay for the advertisement. The apartment can't remain vacant long."

"For heaven's sake, Willie. Give the boy a break," Vivian said with impatience. "Other factors should be considered when dealing with Togallini. For example, consider…"

My father suddenly opened his eyes wide, snapped his fingers, turned, and sailed out of the house. Before leaving, he said something about getting back to the office as quickly as he could. He'd left a report on his supervisor's desk without adding a crucial footnote.

After hearing the front door slam, Vivian remarked, "Don't let your father worry you." She stood close to me, stared innocently into my eyes. "You have a job to do for Togallini. Get the old rabbit a priest."

Her nearness caused my body to tremble. I tried to speak without revealing my inner feelings. "Father O'Donnell said he'd be here as soon as he's patched up."

Vivian shook her head. "Who knows how long that'll take? Togallini may die of worry. Get the priest on the phone, talk to him, find out if he's strong enough to leave the hospital."

Vivian's advice was sound. I hurried to the phone, found the number for St Vincent's hospital, the closest hospital to the scene of the stabbing. An operator responded. I told her I'd like to speak to Father O'Donnell.

She had a report on his condition. "Father O'Donnell is under sedation. He's unable to accept a call."

I relayed the information to Vivian.

She nodded with understanding. "You made an honest effort to get a priest. Togallini will appreciate the effort, as I do."

A desire to do something for the dying artist became important to me. "How about food for Mr. Togallini? Will he eat?"

"He doesn't eat much, sometimes nothing at all. Take him a cup of soup and offer it to him. Find out what he wants you to do. If you have the opportunity, ask him about transferring ownership of my painting to me."

"I'll do my best."

She drew me close, planted a kiss on my lips; made my spirits soar as if they were carried by a balloon to the moon. She continued to hold me while she said, "If you fail, as I've failed, we'll try something else."

Her remark punctured the balloon. Drawing away from her, suspecting she had something illegal in mind, I asked, "What more can we do?"

"We can wait till he dies, then take my painting and all the others. Togallini owes them to me for wrecking my life."

"You told me his work couldn't be disguised. His brother will have you arrested if you steal the paintings."

"He won't recognize them after they're removed from the apartment. They differ drastically from the junk painted for the porno business."

I was persistent. "How about the signatures?"

Vivian spoke with confidence. "I've talked to a man who can change them. He's a little nervous about doing the work, but I'm sure he'll do it for me." She looked at her watch. "He said he'd call me around this time."

Demon of Lust

The telephone rang, startled me. Before Vivian could get to the phone, I picked it up, held my hand over the mouthpiece. "Let me take this call, Vivian. I don't want you to get in trouble, land in jail." Removing my hand from the mouthpiece, I said, "Hello."

"Mr. William Davis, please." The voice was strangely familiar.

"He's not home," I said, trying to figure out who was on the other end of the line.

"Would you mind tellin' me who I'm talkin' to?" the caller asked.

Suddenly I realized the voice was Togallini's. But that couldn't be. He was too sick to call… had no phone… "This is Mr. Davis' son, Tommy."

"Tommy, this is Mario Togallini," he said as if we were friends for years. "Your father and I've been debatin' a rent increase for my brother's apartment. I've decided to give it to him. I want him to do somethin' in return for me."

"I'll give him the message."

"No! Wait!" Mario shouted into my ear. "You sound like a mature kid. You could do me the favor. Now that I think about it, I prefer dealin' with you. If you do me this favor, I'll give you a season pass to the best nudie show in town."

"I'm not interested in nudie shows," Mr. Togallini," I said with indignation.

Mario Togallini laughed. "You and two other kids in the world. If you don't want the pass, I'll give you cash. Ten bucks! You can spend it any way you like."

"What is it you want done?"

"I hear my brother's very sick. I want you to let me know when he dies."

The request sent a chill through my body. At that moment, I wished I had my father's ability to say something nasty. All I could think of was this: "You can read all about it in the newspapers." I slammed the phone down into its cradle.

CHAPTER 9

Togallini's face brightened when I arrived with the soup. He took four spoonfuls and waved it off. He was truly happy when I told him I called the hospital and inquired about Father O'Donnell. He was truly sorry when he learned the priest was under sedation and too ill to take my call.

The old artist rested his head against the back of his chair, studied my face. "In essence, you've told me the priest is unable to get out of bed to hear my confession. Now I'll tell you something: He'd be able to get out of bed to visit a prostitute."

A cloud of anger engulfed me. "What are you saying? Father O'Donnell is a good man. He's devoted his life to helping others. He wouldn't visit any..."

"Sure, he wouldn't!" Togallini cried out. "That's why Isacaron keeps him pinned to his bed, away from me."

For a split second, I thought I saw *an ape-like expression appear on the face of Togallini*. It happened when *Isacaron's* name was used.

To assure myself I actually saw such an expression, I studied the artist closely. There was no repeat performance of the ape-like expression. "This Isacaron you speak of, who's he?"

Several seconds elapsed before I received a response. "If I tell you who he is, you may not do the job for me."

I felt my annoyance. "Why not tell me, then I'll tell you whether I want the job."

He tapped four thin fingers against a thin knee. He paused, and then continued to tap without speaking.

Demon of Lust

As I watched him, I wondered if Isacaron had something to do with his trip to the ceiling. Whenever I recalled the scene, a cold fear took possession of me; caused me to tremble. "Have you known Isacaron long?" I asked.

"I've know him for five years. He's known me for fifty years."

I forced out the words. "You have me puzzled, Mr. Togallini. Is he a long lost grandfather?"

"A long lost demon."

"You must be joking."

A heart-breaking glumness appeared on the face of the artist. "My days for joking are over. Isacaron latched onto me when I first showed promise as a painter. He's influenced mostly all my work. He's influenced those who've viewed my work. He influenced you. That's why I knew what you told the priest in confession."

Surprised, I blurted, "You knew about…"

Togallini nodded his skull. "I knew about Vivian. Isacaron also knew. That damned demon joined you and Vivian in the bedroom, observed your performance. He mocked me about the affair."

A death-like silence filled the room. "Is Isacaron with us now? Can he hear what we're saying?"

Togallini shrugged his bony shoulders. "He keeps in touch. He hears what pleases him; what distresses him."

"What would distress him?"

Togallini whispered, "My asking you to get a priest."

The cold feet of fear ran up and down my spine. "You landed on the ceiling because you asked for a priest?"

"I did," Togallini stated without blinking a watery eye.

My thoughts began to collide. Was he crazy or was I? Did I see him on the ceiling or didn't I? Yes, I saw him on the ceiling. And he's explained how he got there. A demon put him there. But I don't believe in demons and devils. But just because I don't believe in them, does that mean they don't exist?

These thoughts gave me a cold and sickening feeling. "Mr. Togallini, I'm not feeling well. I'll have to go to my room, lie down."

Togallini raised a fleshless finger. "Going to your room and lying down won't help you. Isacaron can follow you to your room, enter your mind, and have you thinking about Vivian, or some other woman willing to seduce you. Leave your room and he'll accompany you, be with you in the streets, in the bars, anywhere you go. He'll have you meet attractive women and men who'll lead you astray. But you need not fear Isacaron if you're in the state of grace. You'll have a weapon to fight him."

All this talk was adding confusion to my already confused mind. "Now, just a minute…please. I'm not fighting a demon, whether I believe in demons or not. All I want to do is help you. I said I'd do a job for you, so I'll do it. That's all."

Togallini's eyes glistened. "And that's enough," he announced triumphantly. "By doing a job for me, you're fighting…" He was going to say more, decided against it. He moved back in the rocker, grasped the arms of the chair as if he wished to prevent himself from rising.

I asked nervously, "What do you want me to do?"

The artist leaned forward; spoke as intently as any man could speak. "I want you to destroy my paintings."

At that precise moment, I heard Togallini's stomach growl. Even as I listened to the sound, it was hard for me to believe a man's stomach could growl. In fact, it was more than a growl. It was like the sound of a vicious animal…an ape, maybe. Moreover, I'd trouble believing Togallini wanted me to destroy his paintings. "You want me to destroy *all* your paintings?"

He nodded his skull. "All but one." He pointed to a large cabinet against a wall. "The painting to survive me is in that cabinet. I've bequeathed it to you. The painting is yours if you help me."

"I'll help you." The words left my lips without conviction.

Togallini examined my face for several moments before saying, "You don't sound so sure of yourself, my boy. Don't be afraid to have strong convictions. And don't let anything or anyone influence you whenever you're doing the right thing. What I'm asking you to do is right for you and me, right for God and the world."

"I hope so."

Togallini's voice squealed, "No question about it. Do you like games, Tommy?"

"I like them very much," I said, thinking the conversation was about to take a lighter turn.

"The job you'll do for me is a game. It's a contest between good and evil. The game will be rougher than any game you've ever played. It'll be played for keeps. If you win, the prize is eternal bliss. If you lose…" Togallini's stomach growled so loudly his words were lost to me.

The sound caused my heart to beat hard against my chest. Togallini ignored the growling. Several torturous seconds passed before I could speak. "I don't have as much courage as you."

His words were dogmatic. "You can't measure courage till you're under fire. Isacaron has played many frightening and vicious tricks on me, especially during the past year. But he hasn't killed me yet, spiritually or physically."

I spoke up quickly. "He's weakened you."

The artist nodded his head in agreement. "He weakened me many years ago when I listened to his song of sex. The old pimp took advantage of my love for the female form, had me devote my talents to painting woman. With his inspiration, I've produced paintings that accelerate the imagination of viewers, stimulate their passions, distort their consciences, inflame their minds, and give them an overwhelming desire to commit sin. The temptations are hard to resist."

"I know, Mr. Togallini. I've been tempted. I've sinned."

"Sin can be a lot of fun," said the artist, stating a fact that caused him to appear extremely sad. "But the fun doesn't last long. It's replaced by a sense of guilt. The guilt is a signal from the soul. Your soul tells you that God created sex to people the earth; consummate the love between husband and wife. When sex is used as a play thing, God is offended."

"Can you be sure about the signal?" I asked the question because I figured I knew more about religion than Togallini, an old reprobate. He was telling me something I hadn't heard before.

"I received a clear signal from my soul the day I completed the first painting inspired by Isacaron," he said. "The painting had a tremendous influence on me, sexually. When I managed to rid myself of the sexual sensations, my soul burned with a desire to go to confession; tell God I'd not use my talents to offend Him. Instead of going to confession, I knelt in my studio, promised God I'd never sell any painting that'd cause viewers to sin."

Was he lying to me? "You sold plenty of sexy paintings to your brother, Mario. They wouldn't please God."

Annoyed, Togallini argued, "I sold my brother junk, sketches of nude women; nothing that couldn't be rejected by a healthy mind. The work sold to Mario is similar to marijuana. The work withheld is pure heroin."

The artist wasn't all bad, I thought. "You can be proud you didn't sell him the heroin paintings."

"I've no reason to be proud," he remarked, frowning and staring into space. "I continued to produce canvases inspired by Isacaron, one after the other. My mind became insensitive to God's signals. I wallowed in the sexual stimulation the paintings gave me, even though I knew they were evil."

"Still, you never sold any of them."

A spark of hope appeared on the emaciated face. "My only chance for salvation. With your help, we'll destroy the paintings before I die."

Togallini spoke with such honest conviction, I was almost willing to throw in Vivian's picture to make the destruction complete. The price offered for her picture put my imagination into high gear. So much could be done with twenty thousand dollars. "How do you want me to go about destroying the pictures, Mr. Togallini? I've lots of paint on hand. Could I smear them with it."

The old artist shook his head. "Paint can be removed, pictures restored. Any other ideas?"

"My father has a Benzene torch and several new cylinders of fuel in his workshop. Could we use them?"

Togallini's eyes shone with excitement. "Excellent! We'll use the devil's own device, fire. Do you know how to use a torch? You won't burn down the house, will you?"

I was glad Togallini liked my suggestion. He made me feel important. "I'm pretty good with any kind of tool. I do most of the work around this house."

He smiled a tired but happy smile, spoke with great sincerity. "I'll enjoy watching the canvases burn.

I felt an honest desire to let the artist know how I viewed the destruction. "If I were in your place, I wouldn't want to see my life's work destroyed. You don't seem to have any regrets. Your paintings will go up in smoke."

"Better them than me."

His remark was disturbing. "You don't believe in hell, do you? Even if there's a hell, you don't believe that God will let you burn?"

The artist ran his fingers through the few strands of hair left on his head. "God will let me burn in hell as he lets men, women and children burn on earth. He lets us suffer the pains of fire, wars, plagues, gonorrhea, leprosy, cancer, AIDS, poison, starvation, a bayonet in the belly. He wants us to know pain, what we can reasonably expect if we fail to conform to His laws. The pain we'll suffer in hell will be far worse than any pain we suffer on earth."

I thought I was making a major point when I said, "God is all Merciful."

"And He's all Just," Togallini said spontaneously. "He's a Judge who demands punishment commensurate with the crime. Since I became aware of Isacaron, I also became aware of God. He's more complex than all men put together. Who knows, for example, why He turned the world He created over to Satan? Why He admitted to Satan's predominance over the kingdoms of the earth? Why He called Satan the prince of the world?"

"These concessions are difficult to fathom."

"Why so difficult?" he asked, grasping the arms of his chair, pulling himself closer to me. "We know from the Bible that Satan tempted Christ in the wilderness when he showed him all the kingdoms of the world, and said, 'If you fall down before me and worship, I will give you command over all these things, for they have been given to me.' Christ answered by saying, 'Man does not live by bread alone, but by every word spoken by God.' Christ didn't dispute Satan's claim on the world; didn't say you can't offer me kingdoms you don't possess."

The artist seemed to gain strength as he scored his point. I found myself deeply interested in the subject. I wanted to learn more about Satan's predominance over the world. I wanted Togallini to continue.

"So much for the theology," he announced. "Let's get on with the burning of the canvases. Where's the torch?"

I answered with reluctance. "In my father's workshop. It's ready to use."

"Get the torch, the gas, whatever else you need. We'll blister the heart of the demon."

* * *

One thing I can say about my father, he kept his tools in order. Every tool had its place. I lost no time finding the Benzene torch and two canisters of gas. I returned to Togallini's apartment.

When I entered the furniture-cluttered room, he cried with glee. "We'll destroy the paintings in the studio, the place where they were born." He forced himself out of his chair, onto a pair of thin legs that appeared as if they might snap.

I swung an arm around his body, helped him into the studio. He was frail and light. A skeleton. I sat him down at the kitchen table, where he was as enthusiastic as a kid at a party. He studied the torch as he'd study a magical toy.

"A painting await us," he said happily. "Move it away from the sun."

The painting awaiting us was the one I'd selected from the storage room and placed against the couch. As soon as I lifted it, I realized the painting was much heavier than it was when I handled it before. It grew heavier with each step I took. It dropped from my fingers when I reached the wall.

Experience told me I shouldn't look at the picture. I did. I saw the same naked body, the same daring eyes, and the same inviting lips. But there was more defiance in the beautiful face. The defiance perplexed me, for there was no doubt in my mind that a change had taken place in the canvas. The depth of defiance was something new. I remembered every detail of the painting. It'd been photographed on my brain. I continued to study the woman, couldn't take my eyes off her. My body filled with a hot passion.

"Better get the torch lit before you get other ideas," Togallini cautioned.

Had I not gone to confession, I wouldn't have had the spiritual strength to pull away from the picture and return to the table. My hand shook as I applied a match to the torch. A bright blue flame popped out of the nozzle. It singed my hand.

"Keep your mind on the flame thrower," Togallini chided me happily. "You're supposed to burn the canvas, not your hand."

I adjusted the torch, had the flame shooting six inches out of the nozzle. The flame was steady, true. It hissed like a snake.

"Give it to her in the womb," the old artist advised.

Approaching the woman slowly, I aimed the flame at her privates. And as I drew closer to her, I became aware of an expression of absolute scorn on her face. At the same time, the length of the flame diminished. When I reached the painting, the flame went out. I turned quickly to Togallini for an explanation.

His mirth was replaced by anxiety. He looked at me pleadingly. "Please try again."

Again I lit the torch and approached the woman. This time I watched the flame, thought of Isacaron being a master of timing. With every step I took, the flame diminished an inch. When I'd taken my final step, the flame diminished to nothing. It was the precise moment before the torch touched the painting.

A horrifying laugh emanated from the bowels of Togallini. There followed a stench that no creature, living or dead, could equal. An odious, evil smell like burnt human flesh.

Togallini brushed a shaking bone of a wrist across his nose. His voice trembled. "Fire won't work. Use a knife. We can't stop now."

I'll never know how I crossed that room on legs limp with fear. Somehow, I reached a cabinet, opened a drawer, and grabbed a knife. It was long, sharp. Doing my best to ignore the stench and the laugh that was now fading away, I approached the painting; keeping my eyes fastened on the blade of the knife, wondering if it'd diminish in size. It didn't. I reached the picture, looked into the face of the woman. She showed no scorn, only fear. She was afraid of the knife, afraid of…"

"Slash her!"

Togallini's cry was startling. I couldn't help but hesitate. He didn't say slash the canvas, slash the painting, or slash the picture. He said, *slash her!* He was talking about a woman. Someone alive.

"Slash her!"

I thought he'd have a heart attack if he screamed again at me. So would I. I put the knife on the woman's breast. The breast was soft, human.

"Cut her!"

I closed my eyes, pressed the knife ever so gently against her breast. I didn't want to hurt her, yet I had to. I had to do it for Togallini, for Vivian, for myself, for God. I pressed the point of the knife into her flesh. Something warm and wet spouted onto my hand. I opened my eyes. *Blood!* Warm blood from the woman's breast was covering my hand.

Dropping the knife, I turned to Togallini for help. He couldn't help me, couldn't help himself. Though a human skeleton, he floated off the chair, moved upwards till he was twelve inches from the ceiling. He clutched hopelessly for me. He was so frightened, so sad, so much in need of help, I decided to pull him down from the ceiling, regardless of what happened to me.

Hardly had my fingers touch his skeletal hands, when they moved away from me. Togallini began to rotate, slowly at first, then faster and faster till he reached a high whistling speed. He was like the blade of a helicopter, broken loose from its shaft. His slippers and bathrobe flew from his body. He spun across the room, under the skylight. He bobbed from ceiling to floor; six, seven, eight times. Each time he shot from the floor to the ceiling, he came a little closer to the skylight. I expected him to crash through the glass, spin out into space, battered and torn.

Dropping to my knees, I cried, "Please God, make him stop spinning...make him stop spinning...make him stop. Please."

Togallini spun away from the skylight, shot towards me, over my head, through the narrow doorway leading to the next room. How he traveled through that narrow doorway in a horizontal position, without smashing against a wall, can only be attributed to Isacaron's power of timing. That must be the explanation. He spun through the second doorway and into the furniture-cluttered room without hitting the paintings, a wall, or any of the furniture.

Getting off my knees, I ran after him. He was in the exact center of the room. Spinning. Spinning. Spinning. A human propeller with the hum of a giant hornet.

"Please God..."

Suddenly Togallini spun towards the entrance to the apartment. He crashed against the heavy door. The crash was bone splintering, cruel, horrifying, the worst catastrophe I'd ever witnessed. The demon had no further use for Togallini on this earth. He discarded him.

Even before I dropped to my knees and held Togallini's broken body in my arms, I knew he was dead. A thin stream of blood ran out of his left ear. The blood blurred when tears filled my eyes. I pressed my face hard against his face. He was lifeless, clammy. I held him tight, rocked him like a father would rock a baby. Why did I do that? Although I didn't know him well enough to love him as a friend, I loved him as a fellow human being. I pitied him. Despite his great talent as an artist, and the many beautiful women he had when he was young, he was helpless and alone in his old age. He was desperate when he appealed to me for help. I was the only one he could ask for assistance…the only one he trusted.

I picked up his light corpse from the floor, carried it to his bed, and laid it out as neatly as I could. His eyes were still open. He seemed to be looking up at heaven, trying to see what was going on there. I closed his eyes gently. As I did so, I noticed his lips were pursed. He was trying to say something when he died. He was trying to say *priest* or *painting*.

He died without a priest. A Catholic can't wait fifty years to confess his sins and expect to find a priest in a hurry. Nevertheless, at the end, Togallini wanted to see a priest. He was concerned about his own immortal soul. He was also concerned about the souls of his fellow man. That's why he could have been saying *paintings* when he died. He didn't want his paintings to be a source of evil…a poison for men's souls.

I was unable to get him a priest. I am able to destroy his paintings. I can lighten his punishment in the world below if I do what he asked me to do. Hoping he'd hear me, I stared down at his skinny corpse. "I'll destroy your paintings, Mr. Togallini. The devil himself won't stop me."

I left the apartment, was halfway down the stairs when I heard a horrifying laugh. It was a laugh that could have come from the bowels of a dead man.

CHAPTER 10

At St. Vincent's hospital, an attractive receptionist with flaming red hair was exceptionally nice to me when I told her I wanted to see Father O'Donnell. She gave me the room number and a warm smile. "You're in luck," she said. "Father O'Donnell is without visitors. You're free to see him."

I thanked her, took an elevator.

The priest was awake, staring at the door. He smiled pleasantly when he saw me.

"Good to see you, Tommy." He extended his hand.

I moved awkwardly towards him, took his hand. "Good to see you, too, Father. Sorry to see you hurt, though."

He smiled a grim smile. "Getting hurt is part of living. We must be willing to take the pain with the pleasure. Tell me, how's your patient doing?"

I came directly to the point. "Togallini's dead."

Father O'Donnell's eyebrows shot up. "Dead?" he questioned. "Were you able to get him a priest before he died?"

"I didn't have time to even think about another priest. He was killed while he was watching me do a job for him."

The face of the priest registered concern. "Killed! How was he killed?"

My words rushed out. "A demon called Isacaron killed him."

For a few moments, the priest appeared perplexed. "Isacaron?" he questioned, making the demon's name sound Irish. "The demon of lust?"

I was surprised to learn the priest was familiar with the demon's name and specialty. "He's the one."

"What do you know about the demon?"

"I know he worked on Mr. Togallini for years, inspired him to paint pictures of women who excite viewers into performing sexual acts. Togallini was aware of this. When he knew he was going to die, he decided to destroy his paintings. He didn't want to corrupt the souls of those who viewed his work. He asked me to help."

The priest sat up in bed. "What kind of help could you give him?"

"I got a torch, tried to burn one of the women. I mean one of the paintings. The torch wouldn't stay lit. So I tried to cut the painting with a knife. Blood poured out of the canvas onto my hand. That's when the demon lifted Togallini off a chair, spun him around and around at tremendous speed, dashed him against a door. I couldn't believe my eyes."

The priest wrinkled his brow. "The story you're telling me is so fantastic, I can hardly believe my ears."

"I wouldn't tell you a lie, Father."

"I know you wouldn't, yet I can't understand why a demon would kill an old man about to die."

Who could explain what a demon would do? "When I went to confession, Father, I told you I didn't believe in demons or devils. Now I do. Do you doubt what I'm telling you now?"

Father O'Donnell gave me a friendly pat on the arm. "It's not that I doubt you. I'm just puzzled. After I decided to hear Togallini's confession, I became involved in a series of inexplicable events. I was delayed beyond reason in the rectory, my car wouldn't start, I was stabbed, and I was taken to this hospital. In effect, I was prevented from hearing your friend's confession."

"You can blame Isacaron for that. Togallini told me he's a master of timing. He arranged…"

The priest held up a hand. "Just a minute, Tommy. Evidently you have information Togallini has given you that hasn't been passed on to me. Start from the beginning, I'll try to make sense out of the information you have. First, tell me why Togallini decided to go to confession after being away from the Church for over fifty years."

"He was a sinner, knew he was going to die," I said with confidence.

Father O'Donnell's expression indicated he didn't like my explanation. "Deathbed confessions are possible. As a general rule, however, sinners don't change the course they've followed for fifty years. Those who live in sin, die in sin. Sin has a momentum, a powerful force engineered by the devil to carry a sinner through the gates of hell."

"I didn't know that," I remarked, picturing Togallini flying naked through the white-hot gates of hell.

The priest put a finger on his chin. He seemed to be reconsidering the information he'd given me. "Of course, something or someone could have changed Togallini's way of thinking at the end of his life."

"I can't think of anything or anyone changing Togallini's mind. His head was hard, not open to suggestions."

"Was he under the influence of someone close to God?" the priest asked.

I shook my head slowly. "As far as I know, Isacaron was the only one who ever influenced him. Togallini was set in his ways. No one could tell him anything."

"We all have guardian angels. It's possible his guardian angel warned him about the paintings."

The priest wasn't making much sense, I thought. "If you knew him, Father, you'd know his guardian angel has been sleeping at his post for decades."

The priest shot a countering point at me. "But in the very end, it appears to me Togallini was warned by someone or some event."

"Maybe so," I admitted. "Shortly before he died, he wanted two things. He wanted to go to confession and he wanted his paintings destroyed."

Father O'Donnell wiped his brow with a handkerchief. "Unfortunately, he lost out on both counts. He failed to have a priest hear his confession, and he failed to have his paintings destroyed."

"He failed to get to confession, Father; but he was successful in one respect. I promise him I'd destroy his paintings."

My remark silenced Father O'Donnell for ten seconds or more. "Before you make any rash decisions, tell me what you know about Togallini's relationship with the demon. If a demon actually killed him, he could kill you."

Now it was my turn to be silent. I didn't want to die as Togallini had died: spinning, spinning, and spinning. To rid my mind of the possibility, I explained what I knew about the artist and Isacaron to the priest. I tried to determine from his expression if he believed me.

His face revealed no information; his words did: "Anyone who fails to stay close to God may find himself close to the devil, doing the devil's work," he said. "He may find himself involved in fornication, adultery, sodomy, incest, murder, or some other sinful act. The devil is a liar, a seducer, a false god who demands attention and strict obedience from those who succumb to his influence...." The priest closed his eyes, kept them closed.

Had the priest fallen asleep as a result of his medications? Or had the talk of the devil proved too painful for him to continue?

I spoke to him in a loud voice, hoping to awaken him. "What else do you think?"

He opened his eyes, fixed them on me. "I think you need help."

Relieved and pleased to hear him say he was willing to help me, I said, "I don't know how to destroy the paintings. I don't even know what to do with Togallini's corpse. If I tell anybody but you he's dead, I'll be stopped from destroying the paintings."

Father O'Donnell threw his blankets aside and slid out of bed. Wavering a bit, he said, "I can't help you if I lie here. Get my clothes out of the closet. I'll go with you to Togallini's apartment. I want to see his body and the paintings."

He had some trouble getting a release from the hospital. None of the staff believed he was well enough to be discharged. By raising his voice, and assuming a dominating air, he received the discharge. He had one of the nurses call a taxi for us.

Demon of Lust

When we were in the taxi, and the vehicle was racing through the streets, I put this question to him: What do we really know about the devil?"

Father O'Donnell settled back in his seat, stared out the window at a vagrant who had his pants down, excreting in the gutter on Fourteenth Street. He turned towards me. "We have some facts about the devil and many theological speculations. For example, we know that Lucifer was once a good spirit with a brilliant mind. He enjoyed a high place in heaven. Like many people today who have power and wealth, he wanted more. He spread his dissatisfaction to other angels in heaven; turned them away from God with a promise of greater wealth and power. He enlisted them in an army. They tried to take over the City of God. St. Michael and other angels faithful to Our Lord defended the City. They drove Lucifer and his followers out of heaven, and cast them into hell. When Lucifer fell, he became known as Satan."

I couldn't understand how Lucifer, if he had any sense at all, could even think about taking over the kingdom of heaven. Nor could I understand how he convinced others to follow him. "How could Lucifer convince intelligent beings to follow him on a course that'd lead to their destruction?"

The priest stared at me as if he didn't have an answer, then he said, "Adolph Hitler did it in Germany. Jim Jones did in Guyana. Its been done by many other leaders who establish themselves as gods in the minds of followers. Almighty God warned us about such leaders. His First Commandment: 'I am thy Lord thy God, thou shalt not have strange gods before me.'"

I knew the words well; use to recite them in elementary school. Yet I never knew the true meaning of the First Commandment.

Arriving home, I searched my pockets for a key to the front door; didn't find it. By not having a key, I couldn't avoid ringing the doorbell. Vivian would open the door.

She looked bright, beautiful, and genuinely happy to see us. She gave the priest a good view of her perfect teeth, and turned to me for an introduction.

What could I do but introduce her? "Vivian, I'd like you to meet Father O'Donnell. He's here to see Mr. Togallini."

"Welcome to our home, Father," she said cheerfully. "Mr. Togallini will be happy to see you." She extended her hand gracefully to the priest.

"Thank you very much," he said, taking her hand and returning her smile. He gave no indication of knowing anything about her.

I ushered him quickly to the stairs, hoping Vivian wouldn't tag along.

She followed us to the bottom of the stairs. "Tommy, perhaps Father would enjoy tea and biscuits with Mr. Togallini."

"No, thank you," said the priest.

"Mr. Togallini may like a snack" she suggested.

"I doubt if he'll be up to it," I replied, thinking Togallini has had his last snack. Despite an uneasy feeling I had about returning to his apartment, I was comforted by the willingness of the priest to help me. Vivian's failure to see the corpse was also a relief. If she'd entered the apartment, saw Togallini stretched out dead on the bed, she wouldn't be talking about tea and biscuits.

Opening the door to the apartment, I expected to see Togallini's body floating beneath the ceiling. The body was just as I'd left it on the bed, beneath the sheet.

The priest turned down the sheet, exposed the waxen skull and bony chest of the artist. One eye had opened. He was winking. I wanted to ask if a dead man's eye could open all by itself, but the priest began to pray. His prayers were too rapid for me to follow. As I tried to follow them, I wondered if the rapid prayers could catch up with Togallini's soul on its flight to hell. As a Catholic, I wasn't supposed to judge a soul, conclude Togallini had lost his battle with the demon; even though I figured he had.

The priest finished the prayers, covered Togallini's body fully with the sheet. "I'd like to see one of his paintings," he said softly.

He could've used a better word than *like* when he asked to see a painting of a nude. I let it go at that. "This way," I said, leading him into the studio. We found the painting as I'd left it, standing against a wall.

"Don't look at the painting," I whispered to myself. Two seconds later I found myself gazing at the beautiful face of the woman I planned to destroy. Her defiance was gone. She had the faintest trace of a smile. She was amused because I'd brought a priest into her room when she was naked. Without any movement that I could see, her eyes shifted from mine to those of the priest.

Her eyes met his and he blushed. He couldn't have reddened more if he'd inadvertently walked into the girls' room of a Catholic school and found a nun sitting on a toilet. He was quick to react. "Tommy! The other paintings, are they like this one?"

I tried to be quick, too. "I haven't seen them, Father, but I think they are. Pornographic nudes were Togallini's specialty."

The voice of the priest quivered. "We'll check them later, after we deal with this one. He stared again at the woman. "This painting would bring a large sum of money on the open market, but...." He shook his head, seemed reluctant to continue.

"But what?"

He turned to me. "It should be destroyed."

"Togallini was right, then," I said, thinking that destroying the paintings wasn't as painful as plucking out your eyes if you couldn't avoid looking at sinful images.

"Togallini was absolutely right," the priest said, sounding more Irish than ever. "This painting is remarkably good...or I should say, remarkably evil. It'll cause controversy, dissention. Some individuals will call it pornographic; others will call it art. I call it a weapon in the devil's arsenal. If we don't destroy it, copies will be made, distributed around the world. Those who view them will be tempted to turn to sins of the flesh. Unwittingly, they will join Satan's army. Satan once fought for the souls of the angels in heaven, and lost. Now he's fighting for the souls of men, women, and children on earth, and winning."

My attention was drawn to the face of the woman in the painting. There was a definite change of expression on her face. She appeared to be listening intently to the words of the priest.

He sat down at the table, picked up the torch. "You attempted to destroy the painting with this torch?"

"Yes, I did. I lit that torch at this table, approached the painting. As I did so, the flame diminished in size, went out before the flame touched the picture."

"And Togallini, where was he when you attempted to burn the painting?"

"Sitting in the chair you're in."

The priest looked uncomfortable. "Light this torch again." He stood the torch on the table.

I applied a match. A bright blue flame shot from the nozzle. The moment I picked up the torch, took a step away from the table, the flame went out.

The voice of the priest was strained. "Try again."

The same thing happened.

"Is it possible the fuel is low?"

Without answering, I replaced the canister of fuel, lit the torch. This time I was halfway to the painting when the flame died.

The priest picked up the knife. "I'll use this knife."

I held out my hand. "Give it to me, Father. I promised Togallini I'd do the job."

Giving me an odd look, he released the knife, remained seated.

I was tempted to remind him he was seated in the last chair occupied by the artist. I figured he wouldn't let a demon frighten him out of a chair.

Without looking at the painting till I was close to it, I placed the point of the knife on the woman's nipple. My eyes were focused on her face. She looked apprehensive, frightened. I added pressure on the knife, felt flesh yield. No blood spurted from the breast, onto my hand.

"Ooooooh!"

Demon of Lust

The cry of pain came from Father O'Donnell. I turned to see him, realizing he might be floating off the chair. He remained seated. His face was white, distorted with pain. Blood spurted from the wound in his shoulder.

CHAPTER 11

Vivian lost no time finding the number for St. Vincent's hospital, dialing it. While she was calling for an ambulance, I helped Father O'Donnell into a large chair in the living room. I located a gauze compress, placed it over his wound, and secured it with several strips of adhesive tape. The blood continued to flow, soaking through the gauze, draining the color from his face. He clutched the sopping gauze, pressed it to the wound. He was silent, sad, and thoughtful.

He knew he'd confronted a demon that almost took his life. Would he be willing to confront the demon again? Or would he call it quits? Fighting a demon isn't always done with a homily from a pulpit.

Vivian looked out the window for the ambulance, said, "Too bad your father doesn't own an automobile. It'd be a blessing now."

Whenever an automobile was mentioned in our house, my father spoke of the practicality of using the subway. Every time he spoke of the subway, I thought of many places I'd like to go that had no subway. My father was too cheap to buy a car.... In the distance, I heard the whine of a siren.

The ambulance attendants who removed Father O'Donnell from the house were accustomed to carrying injured people on gurneys. They needed no help from me. I jumped into the ambulance, asked the priest if there was anything I could do.

Wincing with pain, he replied, "Come to the hospital tomorrow morning. We'll discuss the paintings, decide what can be done with them."

That was all the time he had to speak to me. I was told to get out of the ambulance. I returned to the house. Vivian took me in her arms, planted a big kiss on my lips. The time for kissing was inappropriate, I thought; nevertheless the kiss felt good. It had me so exhilarated, I was tempted to tell her Togallini had died. She was free to take "her" painting. But she'll want more than one painting, I reasoned. She'll attempt to stop me from destroying the others.

Standing close to me, she asked, "Do you think you can get Togallini to give me my picture tonight?" Her perfume was intoxicating.

I didn't want to be intoxicated by the perfume or the kiss. "I'm sure I won't be able to awaken him tonight. Let it go till tomorrow."

"You've spoken to him in my behalf, haven't you?"

"I have. And he promised to give me the picture after I do a job for him."

Her brows shot up in surprise. "He promised you?"

"He did. But I don't want it. I don't want to see you naked in a picture."

She smiled, gazed into my eyes. "What does he want you to do?"

I couldn't tell her, so I said, "That's between him and me. Don't ask me to break a confidence."

She was amused. "You can keep your confidence as long as I get my painting."

"You'll get what's coming to you, Vivian."

She gave me a little kiss on the cheek. "That's sweet of you…and generous. I can't understand though why the old rabbit decided to give you my picture. Perhaps he wants us to stay together. Who knows? He may give me one of the others. Maybe he'll give me more than one. He has so many."

My head began to throb. "He has paintings to burn."

"Indeed he has, and I'll take any of them as long as they can be converted to cash. I need money, Tommy. I'm so anxious to get away from this house, away from your father, I could scream."

"It won't be long now."

Her lovely eyes stared blankly out a window, and her soft mouth turned up into a smile. She was daydreaming. About what? I could only guess. She saw herself in a fashion shop, sitting before a parade of models, selecting gowns without asking the price. Somebody would comment on her beauty. She'd be sure to say she was once a model.

In one respect, it was a shame to deny her the pleasure of buying all the clothes she wanted. She was a gorgeous creature. Even God would enjoy seeing her look her best. But no! Not if other souls had to pay for her pleasure. God was fair.

"That reminds me, Tommy," Vivian was saying, "when you get up tomorrow, put on your better clothes. Your father has work for you to do in the morning."

A bucket of ice water thrown into my face wouldn't have startled me more. "Tomorrow morning! I can't work tomorrow morning. I'm going to the hospital, first thing. I've got to see…"

"You have work to do tomorrow morning," I heard my father say in his usual nasty manner. He'd stepped into the room without making a sound. He glared at me.

Vivian looked as startled as I felt. "Speak of the devil and he appears!" she exclaimed. "How dare you sneak up on us like that? You've done it before, too."

He stared at her accusingly. "Perhaps I've reason to sneak up on you, as you put it."

She gave him an angry look. "Well, I don't like it."

He gave her an angrier look. He had the face for it. "Isn't that just too bad. This is *my* house. If I wish to sneak around it, I have that prerogative."

She moved towards the door, her face flushed. "All right, Willie. It's your house and your prerogative. Sneak around the house all you like." She stamped out of the room.

Dad glared at her back, glared at the doorway after she passed through it, continued to glare after her footsteps on the stairs could no longer be heard.

Something had changed his attitude towards Vivian, motivated him to be snappy with her. I could think of only one reason. *He suspected her of seducing me.* If he could be sure, he'd go berserk. Even now, as he turned to glare at me, he looked a little wacky. I felt my heart pound.

Demon of Lust

Like a five-star general talking to a private, he gave me this order: "Tomorrow morning at nine, report to a Mr. Leonard Smith in the Woolworth Building. You'll find him on the fiftieth floor, doing an audit for the Galbreath Drug Company. I told him you'd help him with some postings. He's having trouble reconciling an account. Mr. Smith is my assistant. Tell him your name is Tommy. Don't tell him your last name. Tomorrow, you're not my son. He expects you to be there on time."

I felt a sickness roil in me. "But Dad, I can't work tomorrow morning. I've got to see a friend in the hospital."

Pointing a thumb at himself, he said, "I'm the only friend you have. Understand? I've given you an order. If you don't do the postings tomorrow, you'll be in serious trouble."

He left the room. He also left me with the desire to leave home. I once met a boy from Long Island who ran away from home. He came to the Village. What would it be like to leave the Village and run to Long Island? I'd be like the boy from Long Island; have no place to sleep, nothing to eat. I couldn't go! Besides, I had to see Father O'Donnell, decide what to do about Togallini's paintings. I'll postpone a run away decision, and everything else, till after I do the work my father wants me to do.

The following morning I left a note in the kitchen for Vivian. It read: Don't worry about Togallini's breakfast. He can't eat anything.

I walked to the Woolworth Building, took an elevator. As it shot up to the fiftieth floor, it turned an egg over in my stomach.

Mr. Smith was waiting for me at the door to the Galbreath Drug Company. He was very much like my father: small, bent, pot-bellied, and crabby. Spotting me, he looked at his watch and told me the time: "It's one minute after nine."

Bowing my head, as if I'd committed a murder, I muttered, "Sorry I'm late."

"Don't let it happen again."

He escorted me to a desk, showed me ten bundles of paper. He removed a rubber band from the first bundle and said, "You're to post the date, invoice number, name of the company, and the dollar amount on these worksheets. The invoices are in numerical order. Make sure there are no missing invoice numbers. When you have posted the ten batches, run an adding machine tape on the dollar amounts. If the total is $1,427,621.82, your job is finished."

"And if I come up with some other figure, what do I do?"

Frowning, he looked at me as if I'd asked a stupid question. "You run another tape, boy. Make sure the two tapes agree."

"How long will the job take?"

"I could do it in a day and a half. It'll probably take you two days. Maybe three."

A wave of desperation washed over me. "Two or three days! I can't spend that much time here."

Smith showed no sympathy. "You'll have to talk to Mr. Davis about that. He hired you, told me you'll complete the job, regardless of the time involved. You have his permission to work till midnight."

"I better get started."

"Yes. You're late starting."

I realized Mr. Smith was an expert at needling an employee, but that's all he said to me. He sat down at a desk close to mine and became lost in his work. Every now and then he'd look up, study me. I don't know why. He'd no reason to complain. I was working as fast as I could. My work was neat, accurate, and I was able to concentrate on what I was doing. At noon, Mr. Smith went to lunch. He neither advised me of the time nor invited me to eat with him. It was just as well. I wanted to finish the job, get to the hospital as soon as I could.

At three o'clock in the afternoon, I completed the postings, began to run an adding machine tape. I'd some experience with an adding machine. I used to help one of the sisters in school with office work. I'd picked up about half the money amounts on the worksheets when Mr. Smith spoke to me.

"You haven't completed all the posting, have you?"

"Yes, sir, I have."

Demon of Lust

He shook his head in disbelief, scowled, and said nothing.

I continued to pound the adding machine. The adding machine tape grew longer and longer. The noise from the machine seemed to annoy Mr. Smith. I put in the last amount I'd entered on the worksheets and struck the total bar. "Mr. Smith," I said cautiously, "What's the total I'm supposed to reach?"

"It's about twice the amount you have in your machine."

Puzzled, I asked, "Why do you say that?"

He examined me critically over his glasses. "Because you couldn't possibly complete the job in the time you've spent on it. I know I couldn't do it. And the man who hired you, Mr. Davis, I doubt if he could do it. And here you are, with no accounting experience, implying you've done it."

"What's the figure, Mr. Smith?"

"You tell me what you have on your tape."

"I've got $1,427,621.82."

"That happens to be the correct number," Mr. Smith said, leaving his desk and approaching me. "You can't have it." He took the tape, studied it. He then examined my work papers, nodded his head begrudgingly. "Exceptionally fine work," he whispered, as if the words hurt him.

"Am I finished?"

"You are, indeed. I'll tell Mr. Davis you're a highly proficient worker. Incredibly fast. You have the potential to make an outstanding accountant and..."

"Would you do something for me, Mr. Smith?"

"Why yes, I'll be pleased to recommend..."

"Just tell Mr. Davis I did the job he asked me to do. Don't say anything else."

As I walked to the hospital, I thought about Mr. Smith's observation. So I have the potential to become an accountant, have I? Does that mean I'll follow in my father's footsteps? I don't want to be like him. I want to be like my mother. She was thoughtful, considerate, kind. My father is the opposite. It's impossible to know what a kid's genes will do to him. Too bad genes aren't like jellybeans. Jellybeans can be sorted out by color. A kid can keep the ones he likes, ignore the others.

I was still thinking about genes when I reached the hospital. I asked a wrinkled nurse with dyed black hair if I could see Father O'Donnell.

"No more visitors," she said. "He has two priests with him now, several nuns are waiting..."

I left the hospital, stood outside the large structure, wondering how I could be dismissed from the hospital in a couple of seconds after spending the day trying to get there. Where could I go now? I didn't want to go home. My home was occupied by a demon, a corpse, a woman who tempted me, and a father who disliked me. I couldn't decide who caused me the greatest grief. If I could destroy the paintings, the demon and Vivian would leave. Perhaps I could then learn to cope with my father. Would he always be a problem? If he gave me the opportunity, I'd do my best to get along with him. I decided to go home.

On my way, I found an empty whiskey bottle, small enough to fit into my pocket. The bottle gave me the idea of going to church. Stopping in the church on Fourteenth Street, I filled the bottle with holy water, said a prayer to the Blessed Virgin Mary, the Queen of Virtue. I asked her to keep my mind clean while I was trying to destroy Togallini's dirty pictures. I also prayed to St. Michael, who evicted Lucifer from heaven. I asked him to drive Isacaron out of Togallini's apartment if he happened to be there when I arrived.

Arriving home, I ran up the stairs and into Togallini's apartment, without being seen by Vivian or my father. The apartment was as quiet as an empty tent in the middle of the Sahara desert, and just as hot. The outline of the body beneath the sheet made me realize poor Togallini's corpse needed embalming, a decent funeral, and burial. Was it my responsibility to look at the body, see how it was taking the heat? If it were, I decided to shirk the responsibility.

Going into the studio, I'd the feeling of being watched. Was the Blessed Virgin Mary watching over me? St. Michael? Isacaron? I was glad I'd prayed to St. Michael. He'd drive Isacaron out of the apartment. I hadn't prayed so fervently to any saint since I'd prayed to all the saints in heaven the night before a football game between Notre Dame and Ohio State. I'd three dollars on the game. Notre Dame suffered a humiliating defeat. The loss of money should have taught me I couldn't always rely on the saints.

Yet I had to keep my faith in them, as well as religious objects. So when I approached the painting in the studio, I threw some holy water on the lady's face. She drew back an inch or two and growled. Frightened, I backed towards a cabinet, listened for another growl. I heard nothing but the beat of my heart. Opening the cabinet drawers, I rummaged through Togallini's supplies in search of a can of paint remover. I once used the chemical to burn varnish off an old chest of drawers. Devastating stuff.

There was no chemical remover in the cabinet. I ran down the stairs, found several cans in my father's workshop. Returning to the apartment, I opened a can and poured its contents into a pail. Taking a firm grip on the pail, I moved halfway across the studio, threw the paint remover at the woman.

A long blob of the chemical hung suspended in midair. A horrifying sound, like the cry of an ape, broke from the woman's lips. A flame shot out of her mouth, struck the chemical. The paint remover was transformed into a brilliant ball of fire. Within seconds a black, acrid smoke replaced it. A smoke that burned my eyes; stung my nostrils. A smoke that could be found in hell.

Through the smoke, I saw the woman in the painting. She was glaring at me. Her beautiful face was filled with defiance.

Struck with a bolt of fear, I backed away from her. My hand hit the bottle of holy water. It turned my thoughts to St. Michael. He didn't win his battle in heaven by running away. I couldn't run either. With hands that shook, I took another can of paint remover, poured its contents into the pail. I poured some holy water on top of it, tried to mix the two together. They didn't mix well. What did it matter? This was the potion that'd destroy the painting. I was sure of it.

Louis V. Rohr

I suddenly felt my father's presence behind me. He'd snuck up on me again. I could feel him…smell him. He wasn't going to stop me! I took a firm grip on the pail, turned around to tell him he could go to hell for all I cared. I didn't see my father. I saw someone else. *The dead body of Togallini, dangled before me.* One eye was open. Winking! The sight was too much for my fevered brain. My legs turned to spaghetti. I lapsed into oblivion.

CHAPTER 12

Awakening, I was wet with perspiration. Togallini's body was gone from the studio. Fearing the demon had transported it to my father's bedroom, or moved it to another place where it could easily be found, I rushed to the furniture-cluttered room. Was it there? The body was in the bed, beneath the sheet, as I'd left it. Approaching the corpse slowly, I felt the toe. It was as hard as a rock. Had the body been moved to the studio? Or had I seen an illusion? It made no difference. Isacaron had stopped me from destroying the painting.

I was sure of one thing. The demon didn't like holy things. When I attempted to throw holy water on the painting, he took action, scared me senseless.

Although I was never one to pray at great length, I decided to say a long prayer to the Blessed Virgin Mary, ask her to help me combat Isacaron. I'd forget St. Michael. What happened when I asked him for help? I landed senseless on my back.

Blessing myself, I began aloud, "Hail Mary, full of grace, the Lord is with thee...."

I heard someone open the door gently. I smelled perfume...felt the presence of a woman.

"Tommy."

Was the Blessed Virgin Mary here to visit me? No! The woman who spoke my name had hysteria in her voice. She also had dropped something on the hardwood floor...something that broke like glass.

I was afraid to turn around. The demon is a woman, I thought. I didn't want to pass out again.

"Tommy!" she cried. Her voice filled every crevice of the room. "Togallini is dead?"

Vivian's voice. Yet, I couldn't be sure. I'd been tricked before.

"Tommy! What's wrong with you? Why don't you answer?"

I turned around and saw Vivian standing in the doorway. She'd dropped a small jar of applesauce. Baby food. Baby food for Togallini. He didn't need it now…didn't need his paintings….

"Tommy! What's wrong with you?"

That was a good question. There was something wrong with me. I was cold, clammy, shaking. She'd frightened me almost as much as the demon had frightened me with his trick. I stared at her in wonder. She was a link between the devil and me. It's females who land males in hell, I thought. It's the males who need liberating.

"Are you ill, Tommy?" She spoke in a normal tone. She'd gathered her wits. I'd gather mine.

"I'm all right," I said with a voice that didn't sound like mine. I wiped sweat from my brow.

"When did Togallini die?"

"He died yesterday."

"Yesterday!" she exclaimed, moving towards me. "Why didn't you tell me?"

I felt too weary to answer. "I promised Togallini I'd do something for him. I wanted to do it before anyone knew he was dead."

She gave me a sharp look. "What did he want you to do?"

"I'm not telling."

Vivian's tongue snapped like a whip. "Look here, Tommy Davis. You and I have a deal. The deal is based on cooperation. You help me. I help you. How dare you refuse to tell me what Togallini wanted you to do?"

Demon of Lust

I studied her for a moment. She reminded me of a tigress, beautiful but deadly. "You wouldn't want me to break my word to him, would you, Vivian?"

"Break your word? Oh, no! I wouldn't want you to break your word to a cadaver. You do realize he's dead, don't you?" Her words were loaded with sarcasm.

"I know he's dead. I also know he needs embalming, a funeral, and burial. He…"

She interrupted me. "Nothing will be done with his body till I decide what can be done with his paintings."

"His paintings!" I repeated, forgetting momentarily they existed. "You intend to take yours?"

Looking as smug as a well-fed cat, she said, "I intend to take mine and all the others. Mario Togallini isn't going to get them. He doesn't deserve them. No one deserves them more than I do."

Her words surprised me. I decided to use my best logic on her. "If Togallini wanted you to have his paintings, he'd have given them to you, Vivian. He didn't want you to have them; not even the one you call your own. I was with him when he died. I know what he wanted." I spoke calmly, convincingly. I'd her best interest at heart.

She wrinkled her nose in a funny way. "Just what did he want done with the paintings?"

I wasn't prepared for the question. I remained silent.

She fixed her wonderful eyes on me. "You said yourself Togallini was in love with me. If he loved me, he'd want me to have the fruits of his labors. Millions of men work for the women they love. When they die, they leave what they have to them. Togallini left his paintings to me."

She spoke with such conviction I felt some sympathy for her. "You're right about one thing, Vivian. He did love you. And that's why…"

"He wants me to have his paintings."

Shaking my head, I spoke emphatically. "He didn't want you to have them. He wanted them *destroyed*."

The word *destroyed had* difficulty penetrating her mind. I could see she was going to reject it. "Destroyed! Togallini wanted his paintings destroyed?" she gasped.

"That's the job he wanted me to do. He wanted me to destroy them."

She looked at the floor as if she were searching for an explanation. "The old goat was out of his mind. He was as crazy as another artist I've read about. The loony artist set his paintings on fire before he died. He was mad at the world."

I took her hands in mine, tried a different approach. "Togallini loved the world. That's why he wanted his paintings destroyed. His work was inspired by a demon called Isacaron. His paintings are evil."

She pulled away from me, gave a short laugh. "You aren't serious, are you? You can't be serious. Not unless you're as crazy as Togallini or your father."

I now understood why Togallini threw her out of his apartment. I couldn't throw her out of the apartment, I could appeal to her common sense. "Maybe we're all crazy, Vivian. Look at you. You're spending the best part of your life trying to get something that'll do you more harm than good."

She raised a finger, pointed it at my nose, her eyes blazed with anger. She rejected my logic. "You little hypocrite," she said accusingly. "Don't tell me what's good for me. You've spent an hour with a priest, now you're talking like a living saint. How about the hours you've spent with me in bed? Talk about them! Or why not let me talk to your father about them?"

"You wouldn't."

Her voice had the shrillness of fingernails scratching a blackboard. "Wouldn't I?"

She would! She'd do anything to get those damned paintings. I'd do anything to keep them from her.

Before I could give her any more of my logic, she walked gracefully across the room, stopped at Togallini's body. She acted as if no animosity existed between us. "We'll have to work fast, Tommy. A corpse can't

Demon of Lust

remain unattended indefinitely. A dead body deteriorates rapidly. In what condition is it?"

I shrugged my shoulders. "Don't know."

The look she gave me indicated I was stupid for not checking the remains. She raised the sheet, viewed Togallini's body. She then looked a little stupid herself. "I'll get in touch with Botski," she said. "He'll move the paintings from this apartment, change the signatures, store them in a safe place; eventually put them up for sale."

"He can't do that," I said heatedly. "They're not his to sell. Not yours, either."

Vivian shouted, "They are mine."

I shouted back, "No, they're not. They were Togallini's. He didn't want you to have them. He wanted me to...."

Her face took on the same look of contempt I'd seen on the face of the woman in the painting. "Say it and you'll be sorry." She turned, left the room.

I wondered how far she'd go to get what she wanted. A sense of worry curled around inside me.

Later, I took a bath, flopped on my bed, tried to think of some way of destroying the paintings before Vivian could turn them over to Botski. Calling the police would stop her; but the police would notify Mario Togallini of the death of his brother. My job would then be impossible. Actually, I could think of no solution. Maybe I could think of something if I weren't so hungry. Darkness had blackened the windows. It was well past my usual dinnertime. I hoped Vivian had prepared something for me. Dressing, I hurried to the dining room.

Arriving, I found no dinner. Nor did I find Vivian. I did find my father, pacing the floor. He reacted to my presence like he'd react to a muddy crocodile getting into bed with him.

He asked, "Where is your future step-mother?"

I didn't like him calling Vivian my future stepmother. Nor did I like to argue with him. "I don't know."

He speculated, "Someone could have picked her up while you were working. You did work today, didn't you?"

I tried to stay calm. "Yes. I finished the job."

He couldn't hide his surprise. "You balanced that account in one day?"

"Yes."

Nodding begrudgingly, he said, "Not bad. Not bad at all. But getting back to your future stepmother, I was a bit sharp with her. I had reason to be. However, I don't want to lose her. She's a beautiful woman."

"No question about that, Dad. She's very beautiful. More beautiful than any woman you'll ever see in the movies."

He gave me an angry look for agreeing with him. He was going to say something nasty, decided not to waste words on me. Obviously, he was more concerned about losing Vivian than anything else. "I'm going out to dinner," he said abruptly. "You eat at home. You might find something in the refrigerator."

"And then again I might not," I said aloud after searching the refrigerator and finding it practically empty. Vivian hadn't stocked the fridge. She wasn't thinking about food lately. I ate half a head of lettuce and a carrot, enough to satisfy my hunger.

* * *

Something wonderful about America is the mobility of its workers. They come and go. When I arrived at the hospital that evening, the attractive receptionist with the flaming red hair was back on duty. She gave me an okay to see Father O'Donnell and a pleasant smile. It boosted my spirit enormously. "Some people like me, some people don't," I repeated to myself as I rode the elevator.

Entering Father O'Donnell's room, I noticed he was pale and limp. He was also having trouble keeping his eyes open. "How are you making out?" he whispered.

"Not so well, Father. How about you?"

"Not too well tonight. I felt better this afternoon. I was able to discuss our problem with two visitors from the Bishop's office. They said they'd get back to me with some recommendations. I don't expect a quick response. The Church is slow to act, you know."

"All good people are slow to act," I heard myself say to him. "That's why they always take it on the chin. The martyrs were good people, taught everyone to love one another. Government leaders tortured and killed them. They should've fought back. St. Michael fought…"

Father O'Donnell smiled faintly. "We avoid violence, follow procedures, and try to act rationally."

I felt a sense of annoyance. "The character who stabbed you didn't act rationally. He got away with it, too."

"We can't use his method. An evil method."

We could lose all the time, I thought. But I wasn't in the hospital to argue with the priest. I was there to get his advice, bring him up to date on what had happened. "Father, I tried to throw paint remover on the painting you saw in Togallini's studio. In midair, the paint remover burst into flame."

A look of apprehension appeared on the face of the priest. He seemed lost for words. "It…it frightened you?"

"Scared the daylights out of me," I said, thinking his question wasn't well thought out. I then related my other experiences. He was interested in the news I related, but he had trouble keeping his eyes open. When I'd finished, he was still awake. "Take this," he said.

I first thought he was giving me a gold coin. He dropped a tiny gold locket into my hand. "You're mother's picture?" I asked.

"A relic of Damien's."

I had no chance to thank the priest for the relic. A heavy hand fell on my shoulder. An authoritative voice spoke: "Father is allowed no visitors tonight. He's been heavily sedated." The voice belonged to a black man dressed in white. He was big enough to escort me out of the room before I could get the advice I needed.

But I had the relic. Relics come from the body, the clothes, or anything else intimately connected with a saint. This relic came from a Belgian Roman Catholic priest and missionary, who lived in the nineteenth century. He devoted his life caring for lepers on the island of Molokai. Apart from God, he wasn't afraid of anything or anybody. The relic was something I could use against Isacaron...something that'd scare the demon as much as he scared me.

Returning to Togallini's studio, I asked myself how I could use the religious object to drive Isacaron out of the apartment. Several ideas came to mind. None seemed to be any good. I took a quick look at the painting to see if the lady knew what thoughts were passing through my mind. She appeared extremely sorry for me. I began to feel sorry for myself. The sorrier I felt for myself, the more I regretted my promise to Togallini. Why should I risk my life for him? When I fell from the fence, he didn't even stop to help me.

I walked into the furniture-cluttered room, sat in the rocking chair, thought about people helping other people. In the Catholic schools I attended, the sisters taught students to help others. Most of us weren't sold on the idea. We wouldn't carry a sister's books, or help her erase a blackboard, or give her the respect she deserved. One nun lectured a classmate of mine about it. When she turned her back on him, he gave her the finger. I thought of other incidents proving the hopelessness of trying to help others. The cases were depressing, fatiguing. So much so, I fell asleep.

I can't say how much time I spent sleeping in the rocker. Awakening at the sound of a key scraping a lock, I heard someone trying to open the outside ground-floor door leading to the apartment. It could be only one person. Or two. Vivian and Botski. Vivian said Botski planned to get in touch with her. She'd brought him to the apartment to see the paintings. He'd take them away.

Should I help them or Togallini? My hand touched the relic in my pocket. I felt compelled to help Togallini. I had to stop Vivian and Botski. What could I do? Touching the relic again, I prayed for inspiration. A

Demon of Lust

grotesque idea popped into my head. It made sense. Damian had many weird and fantastic experiences living among the lepers on the Island of Molokai. I'd act on his idea, gruesome as it was. It was the only idea I had.

Vivian and Botski were laughing when they entered the apartment. They were happily anticipating the great works of art they'd soon be selling. They stopped laughing when they saw the corpse on the bed, which I'd illuminated with a lamp. Togallini's head, chest and arms were exposed. He appeared to have died attempting to pull a knife out of his bloody chest.

"My God!" shouted Botski. "You murdered him."

"Murder?" Vivian choked. "I didn't murder him."

"I'll have nothing to do with this."

Before Vivian could respond, Botski turned on his heel, left the apartment. She followed, pleading innocence, begging him to return.

I came out of the shadows, looked into Togallini's face. It seemed to be coated with a purple wax. Removing the knife stuck in the mattress between his chest and left arm, I scraped off the red paint I'd squeezed onto his chest. I then returned Togallini's wink.

CHAPTER 13

I slept peacefully till ten o'clock the following morning. After dressing, I went directly to Togallini's apartment, bringing a clean sheet with me. Removing the paint-stained sheet, I paused to examine the body of the artist. A sickening sight! My stomach bolted. I closed my eyes to block out the image.

Shuddering, I realized I could block out the image. I couldn't block out my thoughts. Regardless of how a man is fed, pampered, honored and loved, he eventually dies. He disintegrates, becomes food for worms. If there's any long-term hope for anybody, it must be in the spirit. That's why the demon deals with the spirit. He dealt with mine last night, filled me with doubts, depression, and negative ideas. He wanted me to give up the battle I was making for God. He wanted me to quit.

I'm not quitting. I'm going to destroy Togallini's paintings if it's the last thing I do on earth.

Armed with this resolution and the relic, I went into the studio, placed the relic on the sink. How far its power would extend, I'd no way of knowing. I'd be safe if I stood between the relic and the painting. The relic would back me up. Rummaging through Togallini's paint supplies, I found a large medieval hatchet. The hatchet was just the thing I needed to destroy the painting.

Focusing my attention on the face of the woman, I let the hatchet swing back and forth at arm's length, gradually increasing its speed. The woman in the picture watched me with horrified anticipation. Suddenly I felt sympathetic towards her. But I couldn't allow my feelings to determine my actions. Sometimes a boy has to do what he doesn't want to do. I had to strike the lady in the face with the hatchet...even though I didn't want to do it.

When the hatchet had picked up considerable momentum, I whipped it around twice more and let it go. It was thrown perfectly. The sharp edge of the hatchet was headed for the face of the lady. As if struck by a powerful blast of air from the floor, the hatchet veered up and over the canvas, crashed into the wall.

The woman growled, gave me an angry look. A thin film of her image emerged from the canvas, and moved towards me with arms opened wide. Her breath was foul. She embraced me...disappeared within me.

A cold terror swept through my body. My head reeled. I felt faint. I didn't pass out. Standing in the center of the room for a minute or more, I was too shocked to move, afraid to ask myself if an evil spirit had entered my body...taken possession of me.

The woman in the picture gave me no information. She appeared innocent, lifeless, and incapable of luring me into sin. Or could she? Sexual sensations tantalized my body. They were extremely pleasant. I knew Isacaron was responsible for them. I figured so what? Why couldn't I take advantage of the pleasures the demon had to offer, dump him later on? Plenty of people enjoy lives of hedonism and go to confession before they die. Togallini had waited too long to make his peace with God. A mistake I'd not make.

As I moved out of the apartment, down the stairs, the sexual sensations increased. I'd an overpowering desire to make love with Vivian.

With a package under her arm, she came through the door at the precise moment I reached the bottom of the stairs. Anger was written all over her lovely face. "Played a trick on Botski and me last night, didn't you?" she said, putting the packages on a chair.

She never looked more attractive. I was drawn to her. "A trick?" I asked, making believe I didn't know what she was talking about.

She took a step backwards and spoke heatedly. "Don't be cute. And don't get too close to me. I'm so disgusted with you I could scream."

I inched closer to her. "But why?"

She stared at me hard. "Because I'd one hell of a time getting Botski to agree to visit the apartment last night. He wanted nothing to do with the paintings until Togallini's body is removed, the estate settled. After much hassling, he finally agreed to visit the apartment, take my painting with him. He changed his mind fast when he saw Togallini's bloody corpse with a knife sticking out of it. He was terrified, ran out of the apartment as fast as he could. Who in hell ever prompted you to pull a stunt like that?"

I thought of Damien's relic. "It wasn't anyone from hell. It was a saint from Molokai."

Vivian dismissed my remark with a look of scorn. "Your damned nonsense can cost us a fortune."

"Cost us! We still partners?"

She paused. "We're still partners as long as you do what I say. Frankly, I wouldn't want you as partner if I weren't desperate for help. Botski will do little to help me. Not till the paintings are out of the house. He gave me an address where they can be stored. When he's certain Mario Togallini has no knowledge of them, he'll have someone remove Togallini's name from each canvas. Then we'll ship them out of the country; sell them one at a time."

I bought out my words fast. "We? That means you and me?"

"That means Botski and me. He knows people in the art world. He can get the best prices."

I felt a thrust of jealousy. "Does he like you a lot?"

Vivian didn't answer right away. "He likes me well enough to leave his wife and daughter. He wants to marry me. I'm not so sure I can avoid it."

I couldn't picture Vivian married to Botski or anyone else but me. "If you marry him, we'll never make love together again."

She put her arms around me, drew me close. "Marriage to him would be a temporary affair," she said with affection. "It wouldn't change anything between us. You and I will get together when our future is assured."

My body filled with lust. I picked her up, carried her to the stairs. I was surprised at my own strength.

She too was surprised at the ease with which I held her in my arms. "We better postpone the romance, Hercules, till we move the paintings to storage. I plan to rent a van and…"

I held her in a grip of steel, ran up the stairs to my room, dropped her on the bed. She offered no resistance. One thing certain about Vivian, she was always ready for romance. At that moment, so was I. The good resolutions I'd made were gone…gone…gone….

Ten minutes later I heard the most brain piercing words I've ever heard in my life: "*Caught you!*"

The words sounded as if they came from a lunatic.

"You damned, dirty, stupid punk!"

I was right. They did come from a lunatic. My father!

He grabbed me by the neck, yanked me out of bed, punched, slapped, and clawed my face. His glasses flew to the floor. Making no effort to retrieve them, he continued to strike me, adding a couple of kicks to my shins. Blood splashed from my face. I tried to hold his arms, couldn't. The tremendous strength I had a little while ago was gone. I was just as weak as ever. Isacaron had betrayed me. The demon had given my father the strength, the hate, the motivation to punish me.

I deserved the punishment for playing the demon's game, so I stood as erect as possible. With my hands pressed tightly against my side, I allowed my father to strike me. He not only struck me with his hands, he lashed me with his tongue. Vile words flowed from his mouth. They were endless. I took them all, believing I'd no right to defend myself.

"You filthy dog," he cried sanctimoniously. "I knew you weren't any good. You're the product of a bitch. A bitch who posed nude for Togallini, slept with him."

A knife through the gut wouldn't have caused more pain. "That's not true," I shouted. "My mother wouldn't sleep with Togallini. She was a good woman…clean…virtuous."

His voice was as hard as steel. "She was a bum."

Vivian was now on her feet with a sheet wrapped around her body. She stood between my father and me, shaking her head. "Come now, Willie. There's no reason to drag your wife into this situation. Tommy has pleasant memories of her. He's told me she was kind to everyone she knew."

My father's sweaty face took on the look of a man greatly wronged. "She was kind to everyone she knew, all right. I caught her coming out of Togallini's apartment one day. I forced her to admit she posed for one of his damned paintings."

"That was rotten of you," Vivian responded.

He retrieved his glasses from the floor, pointed them at her. "Rotten. She was the rotten one. She and her son." He then pointed his glasses at me. "He's worse then his mother. He seduced you."

Vivian weighed the ridiculous charge. A tiny smile formed on her sensuous lips. For a moment, I thought she'd admit seducing me first; accept the blame. She remained silent, studied me with amusement. She knew my father intended to forgive her, place all blame on me.

She was right, for my father spoke gravely to me. "Pack your things, get out of this house."

Vivian's tone was submissive. "Aren't you being too harsh on him?"

"He's lucky to get out alive. I felt like killing him."

Vivian left the room, followed by my father. What they had to say to each other made no difference to me. They'd find words to twist the truth, satisfy their need for each other. What mattered was what my father said about my mother. I wouldn't have believe it if I hadn't recalled Togallini's talk about my mother's premonitions. He spoke as though he knew her well. Very well! My mother was a saint and she sinned. A saint is more responsible for her sins than anyone else. I'm sure the angels in heaven wept when she posed nude for Togallini, slept with him. I never want to think about her again. I regret being part of her.

Opening one drawer after another, I tried to decide what to take with me. My supply of socks, underwear, shirts, was small. The traveling bag

Demon of Lust

my mother gave me on my fifteenth birthday was small. Somehow I couldn't move the clothes into the bag. So why bother? I'd leave them behind. I'd no place to take them, anyhow.

Vivian had a way of flying out of the kitchen whenever I came down the stairs. She did that again. I was going to ignore her as I headed for the front door, but her look of sympathy changed my mind.

"Don't you have a bag?" she asked.

"I have a bag but no place to take it."

"You need not worry…"

What a dumb thing to say. "Goodbye, Vivian."

"Take this, Tommy. And don't say goodbye."

She gave me a twenty-dollar bill, wrapped around a key. "This is a key to Togallini's apartment, rear door. You can stay in the apartment."

I heard my father scuffling around in the kitchen. I lowered my voice. "I can't stay in his apartment. Especially now that I know what he did to my mother. I hate his dead guts."

Vivian's voice was little more than a whisper. "Don't think too harshly of him or your mother, Tommy. There's good and bad in all of us. When you're older, you'll understand."

Jamming the key and money into my pocket, I moved away from her, out the door, down the stairs and onto the sidewalk. I didn't want to hear another word from her.

For a long while I walked the streets of Greenwich Village, thinking about my mother. How could she yield to Togallini, that dirty old man? How could she talk to me about religion when she wasn't religious herself? She was a hypocrite. A Catholic hypocrite.

The thought of my mother being a hypocrite had me feeling so low I'd difficulty holding back the tears. Maybe Vivian was right. Maybe I was being too harsh on my mother. How do I know Isacaron didn't possess her when she gave herself to Togallini? It happened to me. It could've happened to her. Isacaron might have urged her to be friendly with Togallini.

He appreciated her beauty. Or perhaps Isacaron offered her some peace away from my father. Could I blame her for yielding to temptation?

Could I blame myself for going to bed with Vivian when I knew I was possessed? I saw the image of the lady in the painting fly at me. After the initial shock, I went along with the game Isacaron was playing. I accepted the exotic sexual sensations. Enjoyed them…enjoyed picking Vivian up, carrying her to my bedroom. She was as light as a feather. I knew Isacaron had given me the strength to do that. Then he took it away, gave it to my father. My father used it to beat me up. Isacaron couldn't be trusted. People get hurt trusting a demon.

Had my mother trusted the demon? Was she in hell? Regardless of what she'd done, I'd help her if I could. She'd help me, regardless of what I've done.

I found myself walking on Eighth Avenue, at Forty-Second Street. Prostitutes were soliciting trade near the Port Authority Bus Terminal.

A girl my age approached me. Though pretty, she was gaunt and dirty. Forcing a smile, she asked, "Care for a good time, Honey?"

"No," I said, wondering how a girl so young could fall so low. But I'd fallen, too. I'd…

"I'll sell myself cheap."

"I'm sorry."

She leveled tired, gray eyes on me; spoke bitterly. "Why should you be sorry? You don't have to cheapen yourself. A pimp is not watching you. You're not trying to get home." She started to move away.

I grabbed her arm. "Just a minute. Where's your home?"

"If it's any concern of yours, Philadelphia."

"What's the fare?"

A spark of hope appeared on her tired face. "Around eighteen dollars."

I slipped the twenty-dollar bill into her hand. "Take the next bus to Philadelphia. That's all I ask."

She shot a glance across Eighth Avenue to a red Lincoln limousine, parked near the corner. "That black man in the Lincoln takes every dollar

Demon of Lust

I get," she said nervously. "I think he saw you give me the money. If I go into the Bus Terminal, he'll come running after me."

"Don't worry about him," I said with a confidence I didn't feel. "If he comes after you, I'll stop him. I've done a little boxing."

Before hurrying into the Bus Terminal, the girl looked at me dubiously. She pointed a thumb at the man in the Lincoln. "He's done a lot of boxing."

The pimp must've done a lot of running, too. He was out of the Lincoln and across Eighth Avenue in less than four seconds. He was a well-built man of medium size, which meant he was bigger than I was. I waited for him with my fists clenched. The moment he reached the curb, I blocked his path and said, "Stop right there."

He examined me critically. "Outta my way, man."

I raised my fists. "I'll let you have one on the nose."

He crouched forward; spoke mockingly. "Go right ahead."

Bent on knocking him down with one blow, I threw a hard right at his chin. He quickly dropped his head. My hand struck a skull as hard as a bowling ball. Pain shot through my arm, made it useless.

The pimp threw a left jab at my face, stunning a spot already sore from the blows my father had given me. He'd have flattened me with the next punch if two detectives hadn't grabbed him. They hustled him off to an unmarked car, not far away. A third detective, behind the wheel of the car, winked at me as he drove away. He knew I'd helped the young girl. Evidently the detectives were waiting for the pimp to do something illegal so they could arrest him. I'd given them reason for an arrest. I was glad of that. I'd helped a girl who'd gone astray.

Crossing Eighth Avenue with the intention of walking east on Forty-Second Street, I felt good about helping the girl escape from the clutches of the pimp. Maybe that's what life is all about, helping others; not hurting them.

So engrossed in these thoughts, I failed to see a motorcycle bearing down on me. The cycle came within three inches of sending me flying through the air to my death. I'd a fleeting look at the riders. They were the two Puerto Ricans who ran into Father O'Donnell and me the day we were on our way to Togallini's apartment. The larger of the two stabbed the priest, prevented him from hearing Togallini's confession.

Could I be mistaken about the identity of the two Puerto Ricans? Anyone who knows anything about coincidences would say I was mistaken. But anyone who knows anything about demons would say I was right. Isacaron didn't like my helping the young prostitute. He sent two of his disciples out to punish me.

When I was on Forty-Second Street, a young girl with a low cut blouse, short skirt, and high boots approached me. Her eyes were terribly tired. For a despairing moment, I thought it was the girl I helped escape from the pimp.

"Would you like to..."

"No."

She hurried off, looking for another prospect. I was sorry I'd no money to give her.

Another girl eyed me inquiringly.

I shook my head. She moved away.

There were so many girls on the street, so much sex for sale, I felt disheartened, frustrated. I could help only one girl on Forty-Second Street. I couldn't help them all. Quickening my pace, I turned right on Seventh Avenue, headed for Greenwich Village. On the way I felt dreadfully exhausted. I searched for a quiet place to sit...rest. I reached Fourteenth Street before finding such a place. A place filled with empty seats, more seats than any porno show in town. I sat in church.

There were neat little rows of candles on both sides of the altar. Some were long, some short. The long ones burned brightly; the short ones flickered out. Candles live and die like human beings, I thought. What's the use of living or dying? My mother used to say we live to serve God. We die to be with Him. I wish I knew how to serve Him.

My mind offered no suggestions. If I'd a quarter, I'd light a candle, pray for inspiration. I'd no quarter in my pocket, nothing but a key. Could the

Demon of Lust

key to Togallini's apartment be the key to serving God? I'd serve God if I could destroy the paintings. I'd reduce the number of prostitutes doing business on Forty-Second Street. I'd reduce the number on other streets throughout the world.

*   *   *

I'd lived in the same house all my life. Never once had I entered the house through the rear door; that is, the door leading to Togallini's apartment. The entrance was dark and dismal. Mouse-like dust balls slept on every stair. The stairs creaked like mice caught in a trap.

At the door to the apartment, the stench of death prompted me to turn back. I couldn't turn back. I was there to perform a service for God. By serving God, I'd also serve Togallini. That I didn't like. I couldn't forgive him for ruining my mother. I hated him for diminishing my love for her.

As I moved past his corpse, through the room where the paintings were stored, and into the studio, I kept asking myself how I could destroy the paintings. Sitting down on the kitchen chair, I tried to think of a way to do it. Studying the canvas might give me an idea.

To my surprise, the entire canvas had drastically changed. The bright colors Togallini had so skillfully applied had faded, as if the painting had been left on the roof for the summer, exposed to the sun. The expression on the woman's face was lifeless. Had Vivian or someone else substituted one canvas for another? No. It was the same canvas I'd seen before. Apart from the fading and the lifeless expression, there was one significant difference. The picture didn't excite me sexually.

The demon that possessed the picture was away, I thought. He could be counseling local terrorists; roaming the United Nations to promote discord among nations; visiting hotels to applaud those engaged in fornication, adultery and sodomy; riding the subways to provoke stabbings among different racial groups; observing ghetto families to delight in their poverty; or spending time in havens for criminals, where men and women gather together to abuse the rights of others. While the demon's away, I'll play. I grabbed a knife. I'll slash the canvas.

"Don't!"

The command sounded like the crack of a whip. It came from the painting, caused me to hesitate. I took a firm grip on the knife; spoke to the woman. "I'm going to destroy you."

"I read your soul, know your intentions." The voice coming from the canvas was rough, guttural, male and female, contained many accents. The demon was not only a disciple of the devil, he was a linguist; spoke all languages.

I wasn't sure if my own voice could speak a few words of English. "You won't be able to stop me," I said, with faltering tones.

The response was quick. "I have stopped nations. Do not think you stand in my way. You are nothing more than a poodle's excrement in my path." A foul smell filled the air.

Brushing my nose with the back of my hand, I said, "If I'm so insignificant, why are you concerned about me? Why have you revealed your voice to me?"

"Penetrating questions for a shit your age. Ordinarily, I would remain quiet, wait for you to screw your way to hell. However, I have decided to speak to you as a counselor."

I couldn't control my curiosity. "Are you really a demon…the demon called Isacaron?"

"My friends call me Lord Isacaron."

"You have friends?"

"Innumerable friends… from all over the world…from all centuries. I can be your friend; take you out of this stinking apartment, put you in a penthouse, make you wealthy. Accept my counsel and you will have more gold than King Tut, more pleasure than any Hollywood star, and greater strength than Samson. I showed you how strong I can make you. Show me what you can do for me."

Demon of Lust

The voice had taken on a New York City accent. It was persuasive, soothing, musical, friendly. I knew I shouldn't have been listening to it, but I found myself anxious to catch every word. "What can I do for you?"

"Take one of two courses of action. Assist Vivian in getting the paintings to Botski, or notify Mario Togallini of the death of his brother."

Isacaron didn't care if Botski or Mario received the paintings. Both men would use them commercially; distribute them around the world. Neither man would concern himself about the millions of people who'd view them and sin. "I'm sorry," I said firmly. "I can't do business with you. I'm going to destroy all the paintings. I promised Togallini..."

"Togallini!" Isacaron cried out in a wild and harsh voice. "How perverted can you get? You owe no allegiance to Togallini. Not unless you want to thank him for making a whore out of your mother."

The room seemed to collapse on me. "My mother was a wh..."

"She was, indeed," Isacaron declared with conviction, glee. "After Togallini was through with your mother, he discarded her as if she were a piece of used toilet paper. She then worked the taverns, uptown on Lexington. Your father gave her little money. She earned her own way by meeting men..."

I thought my head would explode. "You're a liar!" I shouted. "A damned, dirty liar! I don't believe you. I won't believe you. I'm going to destroy you for saying depraved things about my mother." With the knife raised, I ran towards the painting..."

Something cold struck my entire body, filled my head with horrifying sensations. Sensations that buzzed, shocked, pained. Dropping to my knees, I covered my face with my hands. I felt the bones in the upper part of my face shift. My chin widened. The back of my hands became prickly. Needle-sharp hairs, black and ugly, grew out of them.

I stared at the woman in the painting. Her eyes glistened with excitement. Moving away from her, I stood before a mirror. The face I saw chilled my soul. It was foreign...wicked...angry...the face of an ape. From somewhere within me, I heard a hideous laugh. The laugh shattered the stillness of the studio.

CHAPTER 14

The laughter that filled the studio didn't come from me. It came from Isacaron. He laughed alone, for I saw nothing funny about the face glaring at me from the mirror. I looked more like an ape than a boy. I'd the strength of an ape, but I was no longer interested in strength. I wanted my body back, weak as it was. I wanted to be the same as I was before Isacaron possessed me. He'd entered my body, not my mind. I was still thinking my own thoughts, controlling my own ideas.

Since that was the case, I'd get away from the painting. Backing out of the studio, I ran through the room filled with canvases, the room containing Togallini's corpse, down the back stairs, and halfway up the street before slowing down to a walk. A woman, who was leaving an apartment building, took one look at me and hurried back into the building. A black cat stared at me suspiciously, slunk away. I came to an abrupt halt. Where could I go? Who'd help me? Should I go back to the house, ask Vivian for help. Maybe she'd call Father O'Donnell, ask him to recommend a good exorcist. But would she call him? When she saw me, she'd be too frightened to call.

Frightening her wasn't a bad idea. It was time she learned that demons have a great influence in the world; time she forgot her painting. No! I wouldn't ask her for help. She was the link between Togallini and me. She was linked with the demon. The demon was linked with the devil. I must break the link!

I made my way through the dark, narrow streets of Greenwich Village, hoping I'd not be noticed. The few people who saw my face veered away from me; except for a thin, young, bearded man, whose bare tattooed chest was exposed beneath an open shirt and vest. Staring at me, he smiled and whispered to an emaciated girl hanging on his arm. "New York City has the strangest characters in the world."

My God! What has happened to me? I've more problems now than ever before. Looking like an ape is worse than being unemployed, tempted by Vivian, dependent on a stingy father, or dealing with the lady in the painting. Most of my problems are traceable to Isacaron. That damned demon wants me to cooperate with him. He wants my soul.

Maybe he'll get it. After all, I'm the product of a weak father and a weak mother. There's not much spiritual strength in me. Not much strength in most people I know. A little more pressure from Isacaron and I'll fold.

No, I won't. I'll remember what Father O'Donnell said. What was it? We're here on earth to be tested. I've passed other tests. I'll pass this one, too. If I'm knocked down, I'll get up. I'll try again. I know where to go for help.

Walking past a cheese shop, I caught my reflection in the window. Stopping short, I put my hand on my chin. My face was weird, ugly…the price I had to pay for trying to help a fellow human being, Togallini. When he was near death, I promised him…

"Your promise means nothing."

The harsh word of Isacaron flowed from my mouth, made my lips move. Fear chilled my bones. I hurried away from the window, walked a block or more, hoping I'd never again hear from the demon.

Once again, his words flowed from my mouth. This time they hurt my throat. "You're being punished for trying to help Togallini. Yet you persist in thinking of him. Are you seeking more punishment? Do you wish to remain a monkey all your life?"

My words came out in a pleading manner. "No…please…."

"Blame no one but yourself. I dislike having you resemble a monkey. I much prefer you to be handsome, attractive to women. I'll give you money to spend on them. You have no idea how you suppressed my pain when I saw you in bed with Vivian."

"That was a mistake," I confessed. "Why can't you leave me alone, associate with other demons? Why can't you just go where you belong...to hell?"

"Watch your tongue!" Isacaron shouted.

The shout was so explosive; it gave me a sore throat. I'd have to be careful what I said to him. He could stop me from reaching my destination...the church.

Isacaron seemed to be considering what I was thinking, for his tone became pleasing. "Tell me something, my good friend. Where are you going?"

"You don't know?"

"For some inexplicable reason, I am not getting information on your present destination."

God wouldn't object to my lying to a demon, so I said, "I'm looking for a place to live. You know I lost my home."

"I can give you a home," he said rapidly. "You may have everything you wish to enhance it. Furniture from the Roman Empire, a swimming pool, a new Rolls Royce, Vivian..."

I had to refuse the best offer I've ever had. "What do I get if I say I don't want anything from you?"

The scent of flowers, and an imaginary picture of my being lowered into a grave, accompanied his answer: "Death."

"You going to kill me the same way you killed Togallini?"

"There is a multiplicity of ways to kill a human being. We aren't restricted to using the same method twice. We demonstrated only one way when we destroyed Togallini."

"We? You used the plural." Had I caught Isacaron in an error he can't explain?

"There were seven of us with Togallini when he died," he said matter-of-factly. "I propelled him through space, six other demons went along with him for the ride."

Demon of Lust

The viciousness with which Togallini was bashed against the door was still vivid in my memory. I had to know why he was killed. "Togallini was old, sick, near death. Why did you have to kill him?"

"He attempted to confess his sins, repent, reject me after I had spent years giving him pleasure. Throughout the ages, a multitude of fools have attempted to pull this traitorous trick on me. The penalty is death, even though I dislike killing human beings. I much prefer seeing them kill one another."

I had to get away from the demon, I thought. I can't go on this way.

"You are thinking bad thoughts," he warned.

"I've got to think of something."

"Think about spending an evening with me. A night with me will transform you from a wimp to a man's man." His voice was pleasant.

Could I bargain with him? "If I go out with you, will you exorcise yourself from me? I don't enjoy being possessed...don't enjoy looking like a monkey."

The laugh was eerie. "I'll exorcise myself. You have my word for it."

What would an evening out with a demon be like? I tried to sound interested. Where will we go? What will we do?"

"We will find Joe Scarpeo, the punk who brought you to your knees in the presence of two sexy girls, Rosie and Ingrid."

I'd forgotten about the incident. "I can forgive Joe for that..."

Isacaron responded quickly and heatedly, "I speak all languages. *Forgive* is not a word known to me. Use the word again and you will resemble a monkey for the rest of your life. I will withdraw my invitation. I will not go out with you tonight."

I had to beg. "No, please don't withdraw your invitation. I'll go out with you. I'll do anything to be myself again. But I don't know much about Joe Scarpeo. I've seen little of him since he was thrown out of high school. I don't even know where he lives, or where he works."

"Joe is a small time racketeer, a punk who is compensated for crippling gamblers who fail to pay their debts. I want you to give him a taste of his own brew. I want you to give him a beating."

"Give Joe a beating!" I gasped. "I can't beat him. He can beat everybody I know."

The demon shouted at me. "He can't beat you if I am in your corner."

I wasn't going to argue with him. He'd tongue-lash me with my own tongue. "If you're in my corner, I can beat Scarpeo," I said, trying my utmost to pacify him, be agreeable, and stay calm. "Could you tell me where he lives?"

"Find his address without my help. I'll help you when you confront him."

So I started my search for Joe. I knew he lived near New York University. I stopped in a tavern, opened a Manhattan phone directory. There were only two listings for Scarpeo. One showed a downtown address; the other, uptown. Ripping the page from the book, I closed the directory, lifted my eyes.

Two women and five men were standing at the bar. All were watching me. A fat bartender in a white shirt was wiping a section of the bar that didn't need wiping. He focused a pair of faded blue eyes on me.

"Something wrong?" I asked him threateningly. I wasn't sure if the question came from me or Isacaron.

The bartender shook his head, dropped his eyes to the rotating rag. The men at the bar turned away from me. Some nervously sipped their drinks; others stared at themselves in a long murky mirror on the wall. None talked. I was pleased to see they were uneasy in my presence. Before leaving the tavern, I decided to do something to appeal to the cultural instincts of the demon. I goosed the two women.

The experience in the tavern gave me a wonderful feeling of power. Never before had I created fear in anyone. Never before had I goosed a woman. A night out with the demon could be fun. No question about it, I'd enjoy beating Joe Scarpeo. Nobody would believe a little guy like me could do it. Another fun thing I'd like to do was see Ingrid again. What an attractive girl! Maybe she wasn't quite as beautiful as Vivian, but she was more my age and less trouble than Vivian. I'd look her up first chance I got.

Demon of Lust

I'd no trouble finding Joe Scarpeo's house, a four story gray stucco building, decorated with graffiti. I recognized two Italian obscenities written in red paint. I was trying to translate a third one when I heard a low chuckle in my bowels.

Joe's mother answered the door. She wore an old pink dress, stained with tomato sauce. She had the same bushy eyebrows, black hair, and the look of the hurt-hawk that characterized her son, Joe. A pair of giant breasts hung halfway down her body.

"Joe home?" I asked in my own natural voice.

She examined me suspiciously with her keen bird-like eyes. "Whadda ya wanna see Joe for?" she asked in a husky voice.

"I've something to give him."

"He ain't home," she scowled.

A small boy appeared at the door. He wrapped an arm around his mother's legs, looked up at her piously. He was an exact miniature of Joe.

"Know where Joe is?" I asked the mother.

"Chicago."

The boy frowned, shook his bushy head. "Joe ain't in Chicago, Maw. He's with Rosie." He pointed to a soiled brick house on the next corner.

Grabbing the boy by the hair, Mrs. Scarpeo jerked him away from the door, drove a bunioned foot into his behind, lifting him a couple of feet off the floor.

The boy yelled an Italian word that could be found in graffiti on the front wall of his house.

I felt the evil grin of Isacaron on my lips.

Knocking on the door of the soiled brick house, I had my fist clenched, ready to let Joe have it in the event he opened the door.

Rosie answered the door. Her coal-black eyes glistened with tears. She examined me with skepticism and fear.

I took a few moments to examine her body. She had a terrific figure but a terrible face. "Know me?" I asked.

"I don't know you," she responded, eyeing me as if I were a talking monkey.

"I'm a friend of Joe's."

She wiped the tears from her face with the back of her hand. "I know Joe's friends. You ain't one of 'em."

"I'm one from Frisco, here on a special assignment."

She took a backward step. "If you're a hit man, don't tell me. I don't wanna know nothin' about mob business."

I spoke threateningly. "If you don't tell me where Joe is, you're involved in mob business."

She shrugged her shoulders. I don't know where he is."

"Is he hiding in this house?"

"He was here earlier. He ain't here now."

Without knowing whether Isacaron or I initiated the action, I pushed her aside; entered the house. "I'll see for myself." The voice I used was a little harsher than my own.

I searched nine rooms. Every room was furnished with heavy oak pieces. The walls and ceilings were done in red. I searched the cellar. It contained enough red wine to keep a family of ten drunk for a decade. Joe was not in the house.

Returning to the living room, I found Rosie near the telephone. Tears were in her eyes. "Did you call the police?"

She stared at me as if my education had been neglected. "People 'round here don't call the fuzz. We take care of ourselves."

"If not the police, whom?"

Her expression indicated I should have used *who* instead of *whom*. "I didn't call nobody."

"But you were thinking of calling someone."

I wasn't sure if those words came from me or Isacaron. Nor was I sure if I were acting on my own when I grabbed Rosie by the arm, pulled her close to me. "If you refuse to tell me where I can find Joe, I am going to screw you."

Demon of Lust

Rosie was surprised at the threat. And so was I. Never before had I threatened a girl in such a manner. But it wasn't my threat. I could blame Isacaron. Yet I couldn't do anything about him. I agreed to play his game. Now I had to play it.

Rosie struggled to break the grip I had on her. I ripped off her dress gave her a big kiss on the mouth. The sharp hairs on my face reddened her mouth; made her look as if she were about to puke. I drew her close.

She put nail-bitten fingers on her chapped lips. "Don't kiss me again," she begged. "I'll tell you where Joe is."

"So where is he?" The question came from my mouth.

Tears ran down Rosie's face. She was unable to speak.

An impatient voice within me spoke. "Tell us where Joe is."

"Tell us?" Rosie asked spontaneously. "You think you're more'n one person?"

Isacaron had made a mistake! He'd used my vocal cords to give a command, but used the plural pronoun instead of the singular. I was fascinated by the discovery. The demon wasn't infallible. How could he be infallible when he'd linked himself with Lucifer, rebelled against God, lost his home in heaven?

Isacaron must have read my mind, for he nearly ruined my vocal cords when shouting at Rosie. "Where is Joe, you dumb Dago dog?"

Rosie's black eyes shot around the room searching for a weapon. Not finding one in the room, she used the one in her mouth. Her tongue lashed me with cutting curses. Between curses, she said Joe had dropped her that night for Ingrid. He was in Ingrid's apartment now. Rosie gave me the address to the apartment, located over a candy store named *Vinney's*. "Go there," she shouted hysterically. "Stop his romance. Kill him! Or maybe he'll kill you. Joe is a first-rate killer now, as well as a first-rate lover."

Ingrid's apartment was ten blocks from Rosie's house. As I walked towards the apartment, the fight I had in the ring became vivid in my memory. The black kid knocked me out in twenty-two seconds. He wasn't big, less than half the size of Joe Scarpeo. Now I was thinking of fighting

Scarpeo. Was I a fool? Not if I could rely on the super power within me. The demon gave me his word. Could I believe him? Could I believe Rosie?

Rosie had time to telephone Joe before I reached the apartment. Did she warn him or didn't she? It's impossible to know what a woman scorned will do. Joe might be waiting for me. I was in danger of losing my life.

I appealed to the demon within me. "Isacaron, I'm walking towards a place where I believe I'm going to take a beating. I don't know why I'm not turning around, walking in the opposite direction."

"You are doing what I want you to do."

"I...I think I'll go home."

"You have no home!" Isacaron cried in a loud, triumphant voice. "You have nothing but this assignment. If you deal with Joe in the manner in which I dictate, you will have a home; money, Vivian, everything for which you lust."

My response was shaky. "And if I refuse?"

The scent of flowers struck my nostrils. "You will be a dead monkey. You die unless you kill Joe."

I stifled the words, *"Kill Joe?"* I agreed to fight Joe, not kill him. The thought of killing anyone horrified me. I didn't want to work for Isacaron. I wanted to work for God...do something worthwhile in life before I died.

The streets on which I walked became darker and darker. They eventually became pitch-black. Chances are the demon had something to do with knocking out the lights on the streets. Demons don't like light. They like to keep people in the dark. I bumped into a trashcan, knocked it down. Something scurried out of the can, ran away.

The voice within me spoke. "We have a short distance to go before reaching Ingrid's apartment. As soon as Joe opens the door, use your left hand to cripple him with a blow below the belt. Then hit him in the nose with your right. When..."

I'd lost all interest in fighting Joe. "I can't fight Joe," I blurted. "I certainly can't kill him. Even if I could, I wouldn't want to."

"You *are* going to fight Joe, kill him."

Demon of Lust

I pleaded, "I can't go through with this."

"Follow my directions or receive a bullet from Joe's gun. The bullet will travel through your stupid brain. BANG!"

The *BANG* was like a bomb exploding in my throat. A sample of what Isacaron can do if I fail to cooperate. I decided to follow his directions. The moment I made that decision, a strange confidence possessed me. I'd do my best against Joe Scarpeo; hoping one of us would go down for the count of ten. Maybe both of us would be able to walk out of Ingrid's apartment, alive.

CHAPTER 15

Isacaron and I knew we'd reached our destination when we came upon a small candy store with an awning reading *Vinny's Candy Shoppe*. An unlocked door to the right of the store led us up a flight of worn wooden stairs. A dimly lit bulb illuminated the landing. There was only one door at the top of the landing. I knocked on it.

"Expectin' anyone?" I heard Joe ask.

The reply was a whisper, "Could be Rosie."

Before Joe opened the door, I worried if I'd get out of the apartment alive. My heart was tapping a code against my chest, saying it wanted to leave immediately. What chance did I have against Joe Scarpeo? I felt my arm. The muscle was large, hard.

Joe opened the door. His hawk-like features registered surprise. Then he appeared relieved. Relieved, I thought, because he didn't have to face Rosie. She hadn't phoned him.

I was unable to see beyond Joe's bulky body, but heard Ingrid say, "Who is it, Joe?"

"A little ape," replied Joe, smiling. He stepped aside so Ingrid could see me.

I entered a fairly large room, containing living room, bedroom, and kitchen facilities combined. Ingrid was sitting up in bed with a sheet covering her bare body. She was just as pretty as ever. However, I thought there must be something wrong with her brain when she'd go to bed with a punk like Joe.

Joe kept staring at me in amusement. "Ain't he the ugliest thing you've ever seen, Ing?" he said, taking delight in my misfortune.

She eyed me from head to toe. Disgust clouded her lovely face. "Is he from the mob?"

That possibility brought a look of concern to Joe's hawkish face, and then he shook his head. "The mob don't know we got somethin' goin', Ing. Even if Rosie told 'em, nobody'd care. All the guy in the mob, married or livin' wit' somebody, got a lady friend on the side."

Annoyed, Ingrid asked, "What does he want?"

"A damned good question," Joe said. Turning to me, he snapped, "Whadda ya want?"

I was stuck for an answer.

Isacaron answered for me. "I want her. And I want to destroy you."

Joe's thick eyebrows moved up as far as they'd go. "You carryin' one of those?" he asked skeptically, pointing to a holstered gun and a long thin-sheathed knife, hanging on a clothes rack near the entrance to the apartment.

"My only weapons," Isacaron replied innocently. Somehow he raised my small fists to show them to Joe.

Joe raised his own fists; three times the size of mine. He approached me like a bull on the run. The punch I threw at his privates traveled so fast it was almost invisible. Joe's knees buckled. I threw another punch at his nose. It landed with the impact of a mallet. It straightened him up, drove him back...back...back. He managed to retain his footing till he struck a closed window. He disappeared through the window. His disappearance was accompanied by sounds of splintered wood and broken glass.

There were other sounds: Isacaron laughing and Ingrid screaming. Ingrid dropped the sheet, clenched her fists, took a deep breath, and increased the intensity of her scream.

I stifled her screams by getting into bed with her, planting a kiss on her open mouth. I wasn't sure if I'd acted on my own initiative or Isacaron's.

The kiss seemed to shock Ingrid more than the shock of seeing Joe go through the window. She tossed her head rapidly from side to side, scratching her lovely face on the hard hairs on my face. Repulsed, she stopped to spit; then continued to shake her head from side to side.

I grabbed her hair, held her head firmly.

Tears streamed down her face. "Why are you doing this to me?"

"I love you."

Her eyes narrowed. "Love me? You don't even know me."

"I know you, Ingrid. You once flirted with me, got me excited."

She examined my face as if I were mad. And then her eyes shifted to the door leading into the apartment. Somebody was coming up the stairs. Somebody was *running* up the stairs.

Almost as fast as Joe disappeared through the window, he reappeared at the door. His clothes were torn and soiled. He had a red and purple bruise over his right eye, a bloody nose, and a split lip. But for all practical purposes, he was uninjured. He moved rapidly towards his gun and knife.

From somewhere within me, I heard Isacaron curse. He cursed because Joe wasn't dead. The *awning* had broken his fall.

When Joe's hands grasped the gun, I shouted to the demon, "Joe lives and I die?"

"Right, you are," Isacaron responded after a pause. "Satan has corrected my error. It is better that Joe Scarpeo lives and you die. Scarpeo has a greater capacity for crime than you will ever have."

I should have known a night out with Isacaron would have an unhappy ending. But I thought a friendship had developed between us. "Do you actually want me to die tonight?" I asked with a spark of hope.

"Your death doesn't mean I won't see you again," he explained with a humorless laugh.

Ingrid looked at me with a great deal of curiosity. She couldn't understand why I was talking to myself with two different voices. Though fear still showed on her pretty face, she was beginning to show signs of courage.

Joe gave her the courage. He was now strapping the holstered gun to his chest, fastening the long silver knife to his arm, putting on his coat. He was in no hurry to kill me. He moved as if he'd been instructed to move without haste when preparing to kill.

Perhaps I could talk to him. "Are you playing a cat and mouse game with me, Joe?" I asked, thinking he'd find some friendly humor in my words.

"Cat and monkey," he replied, without cracking a smile. He looked more like an animal than I did.

I still had my arm around Ingrid. Her body was wet with sweat. Taking a firm grip on her waist, I pulled her out of bed, dragged her towards the window, using her as a shield against the bullets that Joe might fire.

Joe pulled the gun out of its holster, cocked it. Since I hid behind Ingrid's bare body, Joe was without a target. Or was he? The expression on his face was wild, making me wonder if Isacaron's friends from hell had taken possessed of him. They'd urge him to start firing. Would he shoot Ingrid to get me? He seemed to be weighing the possibility. He hesitated long enough for me to get through the window, drop to the awning, and fall to the sidewalk.

Running like an escaped lunatic, I was halfway down the block, when Isacaron screamed at me: "Don't run! Don't allow that goon to scare you. Stand firm! Fight!"

"Fight?" I gasped. "I don't have a chance."

"I will help you. You can beat Joe. Believe me."

"Believe you? Why should I believe you? I can't trust you. You're on Joe's side."

"No, I'm not."

Defying Isacaron gave me added strength, more speed. I ran through the dark streets with a feeling of freedom, exhilaration. Never again would the demon trick me into injuring others or myself. Never again would he lead me into a trap. Never again would he rot my soul.

BANG! BANG!

Both shots slammed through a mailbox, three feet to my left. The shots didn't frighten me. If I could escape from Joe in Ingrid's apartment, I could escape from him on the street. Nothing could stop me now. I felt a burst of courage.

Suddenly my left foot struck something. Something that sailed through the air, screeching, hissing, clawing. A black cat with bright amber eyes. Bad luck? I thought so. The cat caused me to stumble and fall. My head narrowly missed a fire hydrant.

Stunned, I scrambled to my feet, began to run again. I ran with less speed, less confidence. If my head had struck the hydrant, Joe would have caught me, killed me. Would he have beaten my head against the pavement or strangled me? What did it matter? I'd be dead. There are so many ways for one human being to kill another human being; the end result is the same. I shuddered at the thought of dying.

My left knee ached. Must have injured it when I fell. The knee became more painful as I ran. Taking a quick look over my shoulder, I saw his dark image in pursuit, a block away. The speed with which he traveled was incredibly fast for a smoker, a drinker, and a man of vice. I hadn't reduced my speed so very much, despite my aching knee. Yet he was gaining on me. What motivated him? Who motivated him?

Foolish to ask. It was Isacaron. The demon was giving Joe the strength, the hate, the fury, the drive to catch me. Isacaron could move from me to Joe, back to me, back again to Joe. At Ingrid's apartment, he had laughed when he thought I'd killed Joe.

The pain in my knee was getting worse, traveling through my body every time my left foot struck the pavement. If only I could stop for a while, hide. Where could I hide? Was there a place in the world where a killer, inspired by an evil spirit, couldn't find me?

I was running towards Fourteenth Street, hoping to find a policeman there who'd help me. Could a New York City policeman help me? Probably not! Joe would kill him while he was in the process of deciding whether it was legal to draw his gun. The police can't compete against killers. Police are handcuffed with laws, while killers killed without explanation or reference to a thousand legal decisions.

Demon of Lust

BANG!

The shot came dangerously close to my left leg. It slammed into a Buick, beautifully polished. Gasoline spouted from the tank.

I reached Fourteenth Street, made a sharp turn. In doing so, I took a quick look at Joe. He was closing the gap between us. My leg had slowed me down more than I realized. No matter how hard I tried, I couldn't ignore the pain; couldn't increase my speed. I ran another three or four blocks. My knee was on fire. I'd have to find a place to hide...now!

I limped towards an apartment house, tried to yank open the door. In my frenzy, I almost pulled my arm out of its socket. The door didn't budge. I tried a door to a store. Locked. Taking a quick look down the street, I expected to see Joe with his gun pointed at me. He was somewhere in the shadows. I didn't know where.

I was at the rectory in which Father O'Donnell lived, tempted to try the door. Odds were a hundred to one the door was locked. I wouldn't take that one chance. Knowing it was customary to keep the church open at night despite the thieves in the parish, I made my way up the stairs to the church. I avoided running, thinking Joe might take me for someone else if he saw me on the stairs. Reaching the top of the stairs, I'd a tremendous desire to turn around, see if he had me in his sights.

I didn't turn around. Limping inside the dimly lit church, I saw it was empty. I took several steps towards a confessional box. I'd hide there. No! The confessional would trap me. I walked up the center aisle, knelt in the first pew.

Knowing that death was near, I bowed my head; tried to think of a prayer for my own departing soul. No prayer came to mind. Vivian's face came to mind. Her beauty was unimportant now. She'd rotted my soul. I did the same to her soul. We called it *love*. Would the Master of Love call it *love* or *lust*? He'd select the latter. I feared Him more than I feared Joe with his knife and gun.

Maybe I wouldn't die now. Maybe Joe would look around the church and leave. Common sense told me he wasn't going to leave. He was going to shoot me in the head...or stab me in the back. I was certain I'd be murdered when I heard his footsteps in the church...heard him coming up the aisle...breathing hard. He was working himself up into some sort of an emotional frenzy. He was like a cat creeping up on a sparrow. Why didn't he fire his gun? So much time is wasted in the preparation and slaughter of human beings.

I looked up at the cross of Christ. For the first time, I noticed the head was turned to one side. Christ wasn't looking down at me, wasn't looking down at the world. Was He disgusted with me, disgusted with the world? He could be. He suffered and died for everybody. Everybody wasn't willing to suffer, die, or even be inconvenienced for Him.

"My God," I whispered. "Could we make a bargain? If you let me live, I'll do everything possible to destroy Togallini's paintings..."

A powerful hand grabbed my hair, jerked my head back. Another hand held a long silver knife against my throat, against my Adam's apple. Wet with perspiration and crazed with anger, Joe stood before me. He was ready to plunge the knife through my Adam's apple. His eyes suddenly narrowed, making him look more like a hurt hawk than ever. The pressure of the knife against my throat lessened.

"You ain't the ape," he said as if he'd never seen me before.

In my panic, I stuttered. "I'm...I'm...."

Joe released my hair. As quick as a magician, he made the knife disappear up his sleeve. And then he was gone. Somehow I couldn't believe he was gone. I couldn't understand why he hadn't killed me.

My neck bled from the knife. Compared to losing my life, the loss of a little blood meant nothing. I put a finger into the wound to learn how badly I was cut. In so doing, I was struck by an amazing fact. Bringing both hands to my face, I verified it. The hard hairs were gone. The apelike features were gone. The demon himself was gone.

I looked up at the figure on the cross, said a prayer of thanks. After the prayer, I sat in the church for a half-hour or more, thinking I'd come to the right place to avoid being murdered by someone inspired by a demon. Isacaron's power over Joe was eliminated when he tried to use it in church.

CHAPTER 16

The walk to my former home was short. The walk up the rear stairs to Togallini's apartment was endless. Unable to find the switch to light the stairs, I walked in darkness. Halfway up the stairs, I smelled death. Though carpeted, the stairs creaked. The creak seemed to speak: death...darkness...death...darkness...death... darkness...death...darkness...death...darkness. I wasn't afraid of death and darkness, I told myself. Then I told myself there was no sense lying to myself.

I switched on a light in the apartment, thinking there was only one think worse than darkness. Light! The light revealed a bed sheet on the floor. The sheet had fallen from Togallini's body. In a room without a wisp of air, how could a bed sheet fall to the floor? If Isacaron had ripped it from the corpse to frighten me, he was successful. I was horrified at the ghastly figure on the bed. Every pint of blood I possessed seemed to drain out of my body.

Togallini's skin had purpled; his eyes, mouth, chest and knees had sunken into his bony frame. A pungent odor filled the room. Butterflies winged around my stomach. I felt compelled to leave the apartment. But hadn't I promised God I'd destroy the paintings? Funny thing about doing a job for God. The only way is to help His creatures...the good and the bad, the strong and the weak, the living and the dead.

Turning from Togallini's corpse, I headed for the studio, thinking God made life terribly complicated. If ever I see Him, I'll ask him why.

Switching on the light in the studio, I saw the woman in the painting. Her head was turned towards the door. She was waiting for me. Her naked beauty caused pangs of passion to pass through my body. I was able to control the passion; for that, I was grateful. I was there to destroy the paintings, not to be destroyed by them.

But how can I destroy this particular painting? I'd tried before, failed. This time I couldn't fail. Time was short. My father would soon detect the odor in the apartment, find the corpse, and notify Togallini's brother. He'd also throw me out of the house. What would I do then? Probably pound the pavements, thinking of what I'd do if I'd another chance to destroy the paintings.

I'll seize this very moment; destroy them now. Catching sight of the relic on the sink, I decided to enclose the relic in my hand, use my fist to smash the canvas. It'll hurt a bit. I wouldn't mind.

The woman in the painting seemed to know my plan. She appeared threatened. This change of expression gave me a sense of satisfaction. The moment I felt the sense of satisfaction, a smirk appeared on her face.

I was familiar with the smirk. The type appeared on the face of a boy who challenged me to a fistfight. He was smaller than I, so I figured he must have some sort of a secret weapon. I talked him out of the fight, and later learned he had a pair of brass knuckles he wished to try out on me.

The woman in the painting wasn't wearing brass knuckle, or anything else. She did have a secret weapon. I was sure of it when I reached for the relic on the sink. The sink dropped from my grasp. Actually, the sink didn't drop. I was lifted about two feet off the floor by a strange force. Levitation, I think it's called.

I thought of Togallini suspended in space. He'd spun through the rooms, was bashed to death against a door. Would that be my fate? Would I die as he'd died? I kicked my feet, waved my arms, tried to lower myself to the floor. My body rotated halfway around till I faced the woman in the painting.

She was now confident, in control of the situation. Her expression suggested a surprise for me. She was in no hurry to show me what it was. While waiting, my body became rigid and angled towards the skylight, open an inch or two at one end. She was going to bash me through the

Demon of Lust

glass, kill me. Was death my surprise? Or would it be the monsters I'd meet after death?

As if this question triggered an invisible cannon, I shot towards the skylight. Instinctively, I braced myself for striking the glass. My face was inches away from the skylight when the cover flew up, allowing me to pass unharmed through the narrow opening. I shot up, up, up, and into the hot night sky, angling towards the Hudson River. At breath-taking speed, I passed over box-like buildings, amber-lit streets, and lines of honking automobiles.

Suddenly all the lights went out. I became lost in a dirty mist that blew across the sky from New Jersey. Unable to see, I didn't know if I were still moving towards the Hudson River or towards one of the high buildings in downtown New York. I'd lose my life in a hurry if I struck one of the buildings.

The power propelling me from Togallini's studio and into the black sky suddenly lost its thrust. I fell towards the earth, plummeting faster and faster as I fell. I dropped fast enough to break every bone in my body. Isacaron would enjoy seeing me suffer, get the peak amount of pleasure from my death.

When I struck the water, I felt no great pain…only a stinging sensation in my back. The sensation traveled rapidly to other parts of my body. I found it impossible to breath. The world turned red, white and black.

* * *

How long was I unconscious? I can't say. When my mind functioned, I thought of Isacaron. He'd have the job of punishing me in hell for the good things I did on earth, the bad things I didn't do. He'd treat me worse than my father treated me…worse than a lake full of snakes and crocodiles would treat me.

Someone with a smooth voice spoke: "Where did the boy come from?"

A demon, I thought, in charge of new arrivals.

A voice sounding like a foghorn answered, "That's the big puzzle, Doctor. We don't know where he came from. I was at the wheel of my tug. I saw him drop outta the sky. He nearly hit the foredeck of my boat before he plunged into the water. That's all I know. I don't even know how I avoided runnin' over him, chewin' him up with the propeller. A minute after we fished him outta the river, a dirty fog shrouded the whole damned Hudson River, shrouded my boat."

"Did you hear any aircraft?"

The moment I saw the kid come plummetin' down outta the sky, I shut off the engine; listened for an airplane. I didn't hear any."

Another voice said, "The police checked for planes, Doctor. At the time, none was flying in the area. There were no boats in the river, either. We're as mystified as the captain."

The doctor replied, "It's a pity I can't rely on a tugboat captain, and a New York City detective, to give me some idea of the height this boy fell. My only recourse is to ask the boy."

That was an appropriate time for me to open my eyes. I saw three men scrutinizing me with the intensity of competing hypnotists. The man standing in the center was dressed in white, carried a stethoscope around his neck. He was tall and thin and had a fine head of brown hair, grained with gray. The second man was short, broad and bald, with a belly big enough to keep him afloat for days. He wore a black windbreaker over a tee shirt. The third man was dressed in blue slacks and a gold sport jacket. He was long and stringy, gave me the impression of a marathon runner.

The doctor smiled at me. "Feel all right now, son?"

I didn't answer him. Instead, I closed my eyes and thanked God I didn't die and go to hell. To assure myself I wasn't in hell, I opened my eyes and gazed around the room. It contained a television set, a table with a pitcher of water, a large cushioned chair, and a clean white bed. The room was designed for comfort, not torture. Everything was beautiful. Most of all, the men waiting for me to speak were beautiful.

Demon of Lust

They continued to look beautiful even when tears formed in my eyes. They were good men, I thought, doing something worthwhile with their lives. I was happy to be with them. So happy, I suddenly laughed and cried at the same time.

"Cry a little if it makes you feel better," said the doctor, touching my arm with a long thin finger.

"Laugh if you like," advised the tugboat captain.

The detective said nothing.

Wiping away tears, I was able to control my emotions and say, "I'm feeling all right now, Doctor." My voice was little more than a whisper.

"Feel strong enough to talk a bit?" he asked.

I nodded.

"What is your name?"

Doing my best to increase the volume in my voice, I said, "I can't tell you my name. And I can't tell you why I can't."

The three men registered surprise.

The doctor asked, "Aren't you interested in having us notify your family you're in the hospital?"

Again, my voice was weak. "I have no family. My mother's dead. My father threw me out of his house."

The doctor studied me sympathetically. "Were you aboard an airplane when you fell in the river?"

"No."

"Were you carried aloft by some sort of kite?" the detective asked.

"No."

The tugboat captain scratched his head. "You weren't shot from a cannon, were you?"

"No. I…"

"Enough of this!" the doctor snapped. Focusing a pair of penetrating eyes on me, he demanded, "How in hell were you propelled halfway across the Hudson?"

I remained silent. I couldn't explain what was done in hell to propel me through space. Nor could I explain my dealings with the demon. The doctor would believe in a generous God, anxious to give life. He wouldn't believe in a damned demon, anxious to take life away.

The tugboat captain pressed a stub of a finger on my knee. "Answer the question, boy. How'd you get up in the sky?"

The captain was the man who fished me out of the water, saved my life. He deserved an answer. I gave him one. "I was in a studio in the Village when I was projected through a skylight, carried across town, and dropped into the river."

"But how were you projected through a skylight, carried across town, and dropped into the river?" demanded the doctor, frowning.

"By a demon."

The doctor knitted his brow. "By a what?"

"A demon."

The detective spoke as if he were trying to humor me along. "This demon you mention, did he have a mechanical device for propelling you through space?"

I shook my head. "I don't know how he propelled me through space, I do know he did it. I'm not even sure if the demon is a man. He could be a woman. He lives in a picture of a naked woman in a studio where I used to live. The picture was painted by an artist inspired by..."

"An inspired artist!" the detective exclaimed. "Tell us his name."

"I can't tell you his name. Even if I did, you wouldn't recognize it. Only a few people know he's produced masterpieces inspired by a demon. The masterpieces can have a tremendous influence on the world."

The detective spoke sharply. "Give me the name and address of the artist. I intend to talk to him."

"Talk to him?" I blurted. "You can't talk to him. He's dead."

My remarks brought on a heavy silence. The doctor left the room, returned with a tray of medical supplies. He opened a box of cotton and a bottle of alcohol. While he was soaking a piece of cotton with the alcohol,

Demon of Lust

I became concerned with revealing too much information to the detective. I'd made the mistake of admitting the artist was dead. If he found Togallini's body, he'd jail me.

The doctor struck me as being extremely intelligent. When we're alone, perhaps I can confide in him. I'll say the demon attempted to kill me because I tried to help an old artist concerned with saving souls. Would that be wise? I guess not. Many doctors have no interest in souls, not even their own. They're more interest in a pimple on a wealthy lady's buttock and the fee for removing it.

The doctor gave me no time to think of anything else. He lifted my arm, swabbed it with alcohol and asked: "Do you still maintain you were projected into the sky, propelled across Manhattan by a demon?"

"I do."

My answer might have been different if I'd seen the needle first. The doctor jabbed my arm with the needle. He jabbed my mind with a remark that hurt more than the needle. "In this hospital, anyone who seriously speaks of demons is considered delirious."

The drug administered by the doctor made me feel sleepy. I didn't want to go to sleep. I had to combat Isacaron. If I slept, the demon might defeat me. Stop me from....

* * *

When I awakened, Father O'Donnell was slouched in a chair, wearing an old bathrobe, reading a book. It didn't occur to me before that he and I could be in the same hospital. He was very much unlike the robust man I'd met a short time ago. His encounters with Isacaron had left him looking like he'd received a transfusion of milk. He smiled when he caught me staring at him.

"Good afternoon, Tommy."

"Afternoon?" Had I slept for half a day or more? I couldn't afford sleep. "Father, hello! And what time is it?

Without referring to his watch, he said, "Three o'clock."

"Three o'clock!" I shouted, sitting up in bed. "I must get out of here. I've things to do."

"The two of us have things to do. Together. But first we should consider our next move. We need a plan."

"A plan, yes," I said with enthusiasm. And then I lost my enthusiasm, realizing Father O'Donnell hadn't fared so well in his dealings with the demon. "I'm surprised you're still willing to help me, Father. You may get hurt again. Killed, maybe."

A tight smile formed on his milky lips. "I could be drowned in the Hudson."

"You know about my flight into the Hudson?"

"Your experience was the topic of conversation in the hospital last night and this morning. Speculation was rampant. Doctors and nurses were betting on the various ways you could have traveled halfway across the Hudson without any visible means of transportation. While you slept, one of the nurses checked you over for wings."

I simply had to confide in the priest. "I told the doctor who treated me about the demon. I also told a detective and a tugboat captain. I didn't omit anything. I explained exactly how I was transported across the sky, dropped into the Hudson. And they…"

"They didn't believe you," Father O'Donnell said, finishing my sentence. "Getting anyone to believe in a demon is a difficult proposition in today's world. I tried to convince one little girl in this hospital that your story is true. She just smiled, shook her head. And this particular girl likes you. She's the girl who works at the desk. She saw you brought into the emergency room. She let me know you were here."

I was concerned about the information revealed to me. "Did you tell the girl my name? Does the hospital staff know who I am."

"No one here knows your name except me. You're listed in the hospital records as John Doe."

"That's a nice name, Father."

The priest gave me a funny smile, and then became serious. "The name will do till we accomplish our mission. We must destroy the paintings without delay. Today."

"You realize the paintings don't belong to us. When we destroy them, we break the law."

"Not God's law," he shot back. "Whenever there's a conflict between God's law and man's law, it's always wise to follow God's law. It pays off in the long run."

The priest would make an excellent partner, I thought.

"Now for the plan. Our clothes are in the closets. We'll dress, and go to your home. Can we enter Togallini's apartment without going through the front door."

"We can. I've got a key in my pants…"

"Good," he said, without waiting for me to finish. "Once inside, we go to work."

"Don't ask me how to destroy the paintings, Father. Last time I decided how to do it, I landed in the Hudson River." My memory took me on an imaginary flight over Manhattan, caused me to shudder.

"Your experience with the demon is not to be discounted, Tommy. You know what he likes, what he dislikes. What you know about him is important."

"I know he hates holy things," I said, feeling a sense of importance revealing this information to the priest. "The relic you gave me annoyed him. When I reached for it, he lifted me off the floor, aimed me towards the skylight, shot me into the sky."

"You didn't have the relic in your hand when he lifted you off the floor, did you?"

"No."

"Then we have the first stage of a plan," he said with a firmness that gave me confidence in any plan he'd suggest. "When we enter Togallini's apartment to destroy the paintings, we'll have the Blessed Sacrament with us. I can assure you the demon won't toss the Blessed Sacrament around."

"How is it carried?"

"In gold containers. They're used to carry Holy Communion to people who are ill. When they contain the sacred hosts, and we have them with us, no power from hell can harm us."

The priest said more about the power the Blessed Sacrament has over evil forces, but I was no longer listening to him. His voice had become monotonous, loud, irritating. Something strange was taking place in my body, in my mind. My body was churning with uncontrollable sexual sensations. My mind was focused on Vivian. I had to see her… possess her. My body swelled, became strong. Hard hairs grew rapidly on my hands, on my face, prickled my neck.

Father O'Donnell's eyes opened wide, his chin dropped in amazement. "Good God, Tommy! What is happening to you?"

I knew what was happening. Isacaron had visited me in the hospital, listened to my conversation with the priest, didn't like it. I wanted to relay this information to Father O'Donnell. Instead, I cursed him vehemently, using all the vile words I knew…and many I didn't know.

CHAPTER 17

Whether all the words I spoke to Father O'Donnell came from me or the demon, I can't say for sure. After they were spoken, I experienced no remorse. Sex sensations perverted every idea that came to mind. If only Vivian were here in bed with me....

The priest was at it again. "Tommy, can you...will you talk with me?"

The priest wanted to talk. I wanted to act. He wanted to discuss a problem. I wanted to become involved with one. He was a typical modern priest, a loser in today's battle against evil. He used words and logic. Isacaron used pleasure and death.

The priest stood and moved closer to me. "Tommy," he said softly, pleadingly, "I want you to listen carefully to what I have to say. You..."

I struck him with both fists, drove him across the room. He hit the wall; fell to the floor. The white bandage beneath his hospital gown and bathrobe turned red. He struggled to his feet, staggered to the door, pulled it open.

He was a poor adversary, ready to run at the first blow. He didn't go beyond the door. He sent his voice booming through the corridor. "Nurse! I need help. Get some strong men. Orderlies, doctors, police, anyone. Quick!"

I slid out of bed, watched him with amusement.

He turned to face me. "Tommy, get back in bed. You're not yourself. You need assistance. You can get hurt."

"I can get hurt?" I mimicked him mockingly in a harsh voice. "You're the one who can get hurt. Stand aside; let me pass. I'm going home."

"You can't go home," he said, blocking the door. "You don't understand what has happened to you. Please do as I say. Get back in bed. I don't want to use force on you, see anyone else use force on you. I don't want to see anyone strap you to the bed."

Almost unaware of what I was doing, I struck him a hard blow on his injured shoulder, another blow on his cheek. Stunned, he reeled back into the corridor, held the wall for support.

Two heavy-set black orderlies rushed to his assistance. He pushed the men away, ordered them to get me...hold me. They came running.

Like twin bolts of lightning, my two fists struck the groins of the two men simultaneously. They looked surprised; fell to their knees, knelt as if in prayer. I heard them groan.

I was out the door, into the corridor. A guard flung open a door, came after me. Two men, possibly doctors, followed him. I wanted to fight the three men. Thoughts of Vivian changed my mind. I had to hold her.

Running through the corridor in my bare feet, I struck a gurney, bearing an unconscious woman. A team of doctors and nurses wearing surgical masks accompanied her. The gurney shot unattended down the corridor, tilting one way, then the other. It struck a wall. The patient fell to the floor. I turned a corner, thinking I had my own problems. The sex sensations in my body demanded satisfaction.

The three men chasing me picked up two more volunteers. They shouted, "Stop him! Stop him."

Why wouldn't they let me go? They didn't understand a man's passions. Some men kill for love. I'd kill for Vivian. I'd not stop running till I found her.

Reaching the end of a corridor, I entered a long narrow room with beds on both sides. The center aisle, the only aisle, was filled with visitors preparing to leave the ward. The patients were a sad collection of humanity, so old they could hardly say goodbye to their visitors. Some had legs and arms in casts; others were in tractions; still others had saline solution bottles above their heads, tubes running out of their noses...out of other places.

Demon of Lust

This I saw as I stopped momentarily to look for an escape route. The visitors in the aisle blocked my passage. I'd be caught if I tried to barge through them. My breath was hot, had a sickening stench.

An emaciated man occupied the first bed with a thermometer in his mouth. He cried when I jumped onto his bed. Other patients cried and "oohed" as I ran from bed to bed. Visitors watched in awe. They saw their friends and loved ones bounce into the air, land in agony on their beds. They were too startled to act, too humane to believe anyone would do what I was doing.

Two orderlies waiting for me with open arms suddenly blocked the passage at the end of the room. I jumped across the aisle, onto the last bed. Retreating, I ran from bed to bed, creating more pain, cries, and bedlam. I exulted in the confusion.

I'd three more beds to travel to make a complete circuit of the room. The men who first pursued me blocked my exit out of the room. Again, I leaped across the aisle, reversed my course. The cries of pain were now louder, more heart breaking, more desperate. The passage out of the room opened. My pursuers were caught in a crowd of visitors. I dashed through the passage.

At the end of a short corridor, I found a service elevator, took it down to the ground floor. Finding no outside exit, I ran through a corridor, made a sharp turn, and almost slammed into a man and woman walking towards me. Though no taller than I, both were heavy enough to block the corridor. The woman examined me as if she were examining the contents of a disposal receptacle in an operating room.

"Grab him, Henry," she shouted. "He shouldn't be running through this hospital."

Henry shook his head, stepped aside.

I was soon outside the hospital, running faster than I dreamed possible. I was free to visit Vivian, my only desire.

Reaching the house, I'd an impulse to rip the door off its hinges, enter the house with the door under my arm. I'd impress Vivian with my strength. I'd also attract neighbors and police. I didn't want to be disturbed when making love. I pounded on the door.

The pounding had to be continued for thirty seconds or more before Vivian opened the door. "Whatever you're selling, we don't want any," she said with annoyance in her sweet voice.

"Is that any way to talk to someone who came here to see you?" I asked. My voice didn't sound like my own.

She spent no more than two seconds studying my grotesque features before she tried to slam the door.

My foot shot forward. Despite the strength I possessed, the door sent a hot pain through my foot. I struck the door with both hands, sending Vivian sprawling to the floor. Her dress flew up as high as her panties.

Making no effort to pull down her dress, she cursed me with a vehemence I hadn't heard from her before. "You stinking baboon. You belong in a cage."

I had my back to the door, which was slightly open. I closed the door with my rear end. "I belong here with you…to make love."

Alarmed, she scrambled to her feet; backed away from me. "If you don't leave this house at once, I'll call my husband."

I relished the idea of throwing my father out of the house. "Go ahead, call him."

"Honey! Honey! I need you. Come into the living room."

Honey turned out to be Botski. He came out of the dining room obviously ill at ease. He viewed me as if I violated every concept of beauty he held in his artistic head.

"This *thing* forced its way into our home. Throw *it* out."

Looking pained and speaking with a sickening meekness, Botski said to me, "Leave or I call the police."

"Call the police," I said with all the arrogance I could muster. "I'm here to make love with Vivian."

Botski retreated to the kitchen, made sounds with the telephone. "A trespasser is in our home," he said. "He appears dangerous. Send a police car to…"

I was no longer interested in Botski. I was interested in Vivian. Even as she listened to the art dealer give the address of the house, she was enticing. "Shall we go to the second floor now?" I asked politely.

"To the second floor?" she repeated scornfully. "I may be able to arrange a second floor cell for you."

Botski returned triumphantly. "The police are on their way."

Vivian appeared relieved. "Good."

Botski peered down his nose at me. "If you wish to manifest some intelligence, you will leave now. The police will be here any minute. Why not slip away before they arrive?"

I shot out the words. "Follow your own advice, Botski."

He turned pale. "You know my name?"

I grabbed him by the throat, held him against a wall. "I know your name. I know where you work. I know you're planning to steal the Togallini paintings. I know you intend to leave your wife and daughter. I know you're looking forward to a trip to Europe with Vivian. I know you tried to deceive me with a phony telephone call to the police. And I know you'll be ruined if I call the *Daily News* and tell them what I know about you."

A hard blow from the heavyweight champion of the world couldn't have stunned Botski more. He stared helplessly at me. "What do you want?" he whispered.

Releasing my grip on his throat, I said, "I want you to get the hell out of here."

Dazed, he moved towards the front door.

Vivian took some quick steps towards him. "Just a minute, Nicholas. This gentleman has information that may prove embarrassing to you, but that's no reason why we can't come to some amicable agreement."

Without responding, Botski continued to walk towards the front door. He opened it and slipped out of the house.

Vivian's lovely face was livid with rage as she watched Botski pass from sight. She sprang towards me as if she intended to scratch my eyes out. "You filthy baboon," she cried. "You don't know what you've done. You've made me lose a fortune."

"You haven't lost the paintings yet," I replied in a harsh voice. "They're still in Togallini's apartment." The words came from Isacaron, not me. The sex sensations were mine. The demon was adding heat to them.

"You know so much, don't you?" Vivian said with a voice indicating emotional distress. "Only one person could have given you the information you have. Tommy Davis. I made the mistake of trusting that kid…liking him. Today's kids are weak, unreliable, selfish."

"To hell with Tommy Davis!" Isacaron shouted in his harsh voice. "I will help you get the paintings if you will sell your soul to me."

Vivian couldn't have looked more shocked if she'd put her tongue into an electric socket. "Sell my soul?" she gasped.

"Don't force me to rape you. Go to bed with me willingly, and I'll help you get the paintings."

I figured Vivian would tell Isacaron and me to go to hell. Instead she said with a sob, "If you help me get the paintings, I'll go to bed with you."

CHAPTER 18

As I followed Vivian up the stairs and into her bedroom, I'd difficulty keeping my hands off her. My passions were on fire, almost impossible to control. I had to control them, for I wanted my time with her to last as long as possible. Somehow I knew I'd never make love with her again.

She went directly to each window, closed the mini-blind. Shafts of sunlight pierced the room. Annoyed, she opened a bureau, found a scarf. Dubiously, she asked, "Mind if I blindfold myself?"

"You're not going to be shot. You're going to be…"

She tried to reason with me. "You're so ugly…disgusting…you smell and…"

My words cut into hers. "And you're so beautiful. We'll make a fine pair. The beauty and the beast."

"The scarf, may I wear it?"

"When I make love with you, I want to look into your eyes." I drew her close. "And you must look into mine."

Frowning, she turned her head away from mine, brought a hand to her face. "Your beard is razor sharp."

I laughed a harsh laugh. "I'm the sharpest man you'll ever meet."

She closed her eyes and let me kiss her. She pressed her body against mine; then drew it away. I knew she wanted to cooperate with me, yet she didn't. Something within her nature seemed to say, *let him make love with you.* Something else said, *don't.* The *let him* won the conflict. She gave me a long, sexy kiss.

I was about to throw her on the bed, when I heard a wild cry at the door. "Caught you! Caught you! Caught you!"

The devil, I thought. Turning to see the figure in the doorway, I saw I wasn't far wrong. It was my father.

"Caught you! Caught you!" he repeated with the glee of a madman in charge of an asylum. *He held a hammer in his hand. I felt the impact of his anger.*

Vivian stared at him, stared at the hammer.

His full attention was on her. "I should have known you were a tramp," he said with biting bitterness.

Her tone matched his for bitterness. "You should have known that the moment I agreed to live in this house."

He pointed the hammer at her, then at me. "You're consorting with a monkey."

She smiled with the grimness of a woman who'd lost all sense of shame. "I consorted with you. What's the difference?"

His face twisted with rage. He seemed to become another person. A person possessed by a demon. Snarling, he rushed at Vivian with the hammer held high above his head.

For a split-second, I experience a strange thrill. A desire to see Vivian killed. A thing of beauty smashed. The thrill ended the moment I saw the hammer speed towards her skull. My left hand shot up, grabbed the head of the hammer. It was only inches away from her head.

"Oh, my God," she cried, her eyes bulging.

My father grabbed the hammer with both hands. With surprising strength, he pulled it away from me. Stepping back, he raised the hammer above his head...hesitated. He wouldn't hit me with it, I thought. He swung the hammer at my head.

I turned and twisted my body to avoid being hit. The hammer grazed my shoulder. Painful pins and needles raced through my arm. The injury wasn't severe. It was infuriating. Feeling a surge of power, I grabbed the hammer, ripped it from my father's hands, tossed it on the bed, and threw him against a wall.

Like a rubber ball, he came bouncing back. He ran towards me with his skinny fingers outstretched, attempting to gouge out my eyes.

I stopped him with a stinging slap on the cheek. It knocked the crazed look off his face. As far as he was concerned, the fight was over.

Momentarily, the fight was over for me, as well. *I'd struck my own father.* Vaguely, I realized I was doing what the demon wanted me to do. He possessed me. He was the instigator of family fights…the instigator of wars, all other conflicts. But my father was inclined to cooperate with the demon.

I recalled him insulting my mother, slapping me for no apparent reason, calling me stupid, denying me pleasures other kids took for granted. I became blinded with anger; felt compelled to strike back. I found myself striking him again and again.

His face was red with finger marks, and his eyes were wet with tears, when he staggered towards the door. I decided to let him go. I'd given him a worse beating than he'd ever given me. Besides, I wanted to get back to Vivian.

She cried frantically. "He's trying to get away. He'll go to the police. I'll lose my home…lose the paintings. You must stop him! Kill him! Her voice had become as hoarse as Isacaron's.

My father stopped at the door. Turning around, he acted as if he had no recollection of trying to kill Vivian or me. "Vivian! What are you saying? I'm in love with you. I've been kind to you. You want me dead?"

She answered by offering me the hammer. "Kill him. I'll do anything you ask." Her voice was cold, harsh.

I moved towards her. The sex sensations in my body were at a feverish pitch, driving me out of my mind. "You'll do anything? You'll love me?"

"I'll give you love, money, friendship, everything you desire."

Taking her in my arms, I gave her a long hard kiss. Every molecule in my body glowed with pleasure.

She struggled free. "Take the hammer. Kill him."

I didn't want to kill him. I knew Isacaron was giving Vivian ideas. I wanted to please her.

"Take the hammer," she begged."

"I don't need the hammer. I'll kill him with my bare hands." I was impatient to get the job done, get back in bed with her.

My father had vanished from the room.

He couldn't go far. I ran down the stairs, searched the living room, dining room, and kitchen. He must be hiding in his workshop. I'll kill him there; hide his body beneath the workbench. He wasn't in his workshop. Could he have reached the front door, ran down the street? Hurrying to the front door, I found it bolted.

Vivian appeared on the stairs, sobbing like a child denied something due her. "Come quickly," she said. "He can get away. He's in the attic."

Togallini's apartment! Running up the stairs, I went directly to the apartment. My father was trapped. He was hiding behind the furniture, under the bed, in a closet, somewhere. I'll find him. Moving through the furniture-cluttered room, I examined each piece of furniture that could provide a hiding place. I looked in a closet. I didn't find him. Where could he be?

I stared at the corpse of Togallini, stretched naked on the bed. An odor from the body stung my nostrils. He was still winking. The joke is on him.

Looking under the bed, I saw nothing but heavy layers of dust. Moving towards a cabinet large enough to hide two men standing side by side, I realized I hadn't searched it. Togallini had once pointed to the cabinet when talking to me. I couldn't remember why. Nor did I try to remember. It wasn't important now. The important thing was to find my father, strangle him. He might be in the cabinet. I tried to open the cabinet door. It was unlocked but stuck. My fingers kept slipping as I pulled the small handle. The door finally opened.

The cabinet contained a canvas facing the rear. Togallini had reversed the canvas to paint the following:

> This painting I bequeath to my
> friend forever, Tommy Davis.

Demon of Lust

He'd dated the canvas and signed his name, T. Togallini. I wondered what the *T* stood for. Maybe his name was Tommy, same as mine. I also wondered what he meant by *forever*. Did he wish to keep my friendship while he was in hell?

There was no question in my mind about *the other side of the canvas*. I didn't have to turn it around to know whose picture I'd find. It'd be Vivian's. This was the painting that drove her from lover to killer...from a sweet human being to an animal.

I could now take the picture and legally give it to her. The thought had a calming influence on me. The fury that had driven me up the stairs to kill my father had subsided. Let the old crank live. Life as an accountant could be more of a hell than an eternity with Isacaron. Besides, I've been taught to honor my father...not to kill him.

But it was hard to honor someone who'd tormented me since I was a little boy. Isacaron converted my dislike for my father to hate. Now he was urging me to kill him. I should fight the urge. But what's the use? Fighting the urge was tantamount to fighting the genes within me. There was hope for me when I thought I'd come from a good mother. Now I knew there was no hope, since there was no good mother. I'll go along with Isacaron. I'll have Vivian, satisfy my passions.

Completing my search of the furniture-cluttered room without finding my father, I walked into the room filled with canvases. No place to hide there. He had to be in the studio. Appropriate, I thought. The lady in the canvas will watch me kill my father. She'll be expecting me, smile when I come through the door.

When I came through the door, her attention was focused on the skylight. It was open, the cover thrown back. Below was the table, a chair on it. My father had used the table and chair to get through the opening in the skylight. Had he escaped? Not unless he found another open skylight on another roof.

The woman in the painting suddenly gave me her full attention. She looked very much like Vivian...wild, beautiful, disappointed. She was disappointed because I'd allowed my father to get away. I was disappointed, too. I was taking too much time trying to rid the world of my father. I felt compelled to kill him, get back to Vivian. My desire for her dominated every thought in my mind, every nerve in my body. I wiped sweat from my eyes.

Using the table and chair, I climbed to the roof, saw my father. He was four or five house away, desperately attempting to open a skylight. He spotted me as soon as I climbed onto the roof. He ran to the last roof in a row of ten. He cringed in a corner. The anticipation of killing him gave me a thrill.

"Please don't hurt me," he begged.

"Hurt you?" I questioned in a harsh voice. "I am going to end all your pains and petty worries." Grabbing him by the neck with one hand, I jerked him to his feet.

"You can have the woman," he gasped. "Have her with my compliments. She's no good."

The kettle calling the pot black, I thought. "How good are you?" I asked sarcastically. Squeezing his throat, I dragged him to the edge of the roof, held him over the side, feeling an unprecedented power in my hands.

Someone from the street shouted, "There's the ape. He's on the roof!"

The street was filled with radio cars, emergency vans, station wagons, people carrying TV cameras, sound equipment, and wires. There were policemen, orderlies from the hospital, men and women in civilian clothes. One man wore a bathrobe, stained at the shoulder with blood. He rushed towards a policeman who was aiming a rifle at me. He ripped the rifle from the officer's hands.

Well, all right, I thought. If the policeman wants to shoot me, let him. I lifted my father high above my head, stood on the edge of the roof. "Go ahead and shoot," I cried in a rough voice.

A bald policeman, with a mustache resembling half the tail of a shaggy black cat, aimed a revolver at me. He pulled the trigger.

The shot sung harmlessly over my father's head. He cried, "Oh! Oh!"

Demon of Lust

The bullet would've hit one of us if the arm of the policeman hadn't been struck by the figure in the bathrobe. He shouted in a loud voice, "You'll kill them both!"

The policeman lowered his gun.

The near-death experience gave me a strange thrill, a feeling of wild and stimulating excitement. "Try one more shot," I called to the policeman.

The crowd murmured, became still. Many faces looked up at me. There was hope in those faces...hope that I'd throw my father off the roof. The crowd was also hungry for a thrill, I reasoned.

I moved down the roof with my hostage held high above my head. I came desperately close to falling. The crowd gasped. They'd gasp more if I threw him at them.

He begged, "Please let me down. I'm a family man. I've a wife and son. If I can't provide for them, they'll be in great need."

"Liar!" I shouted angrily. "Liar! Liar! Liar!" I was so mad at my father I wanted to throw him as far as I could into the crowd. My anger lessened when a question popped into my head. "Your wife, where is she?"

"My wife? My wife...she is..."

My hate pounded at me. "Don't say she's in your home."

"No. No. I won't lie to you. The woman in my home isn't my wife. My wife is dead. She died..."

From somewhere deep within my mind came another question: "Do you have a son?"

The question seemed to give my father some hope. He spoke rapidly, pleadingly. "I have a son. Believe me, I have a son. He's a bright boy who loved his mother. He's young...too young to support himself. He relies on me."

"He's in bad shape if he relies on you."

Isacaron whispered in my head: "Throw the miserable bum into the crowd. Break as many necks as you can."

I'd ask my father one more question. If he lied, he'd lie for the last time. "Your son, where is he now?"

"He's..." My father had difficulty continuing.

He was afraid to admit he'd thrown me out of the house. As soon as he lied about it, I'd throw him into the crowd.

"Don't wait for him to lie," Isacaron whispered in my head. "Throw him into the crowd. Aim for the big slob wearing the bathrobe."

Sobbing, my father cried out: "I don't know where he is. May God forgive me? I gave my son a beating, told him to get out of the house."

It's been said the truth will set you free. That was true in my father's case. The strength in my arms waned, and I lowered him to the roof. He was free but exhausted from his experience; he was unable to stand. He panted like a terrier after a race against a greyhound. He was no hero, but for once he'd told the truth.

A gun went off below. Heat from a bullet singed my hair.

"Hold your fire!" commanded the man in the bathrobe. The man could silence a crowd, silence a gun. He was looking up at me now, shouting, "Get back into the house. Get the relic."

The relic? The relic? I remembered it only vaguely. A priest had given it to me. Relics are holy things, I recalled with a mind veiled with mist. Holy things attract trouble. Last time I reached for a relic, I was blasted across Manhattan, dropped into the Hudson River.

The man in the bathrobe was now arguing with a policeman bent on pointing a revolver at me. Several other policemen ran to the entrance to our house, rang the bell, pounded on the door. I could have told them Vivian wouldn't answer the door. She wouldn't want them barging through the house discovering Togallini's body...his paintings. I wanted to do something about those paintings. I couldn't remember what. My brain ached; my body was tired...so tired I thought I'd drop.

Leaning over the side of the roof, I saw the police at the front door. I leaned too far, toppled forward. The crowd gasped. The gasp ended with a sigh of disappointment when I grasped the edge of the roof, climbed back to safety. I'd denied the crowd the pleasure of seeing me fall. That saddened me.

Demon of Lust

The crowd would get a thrill seeing me fall from the roof, strike the sidewalk. I'd get a thrill, too. After hitting the sidewalk, I wouldn't have to think anymore…wouldn't have to talk. I'd have nothing to do but die. Everybody dies. Life was a weary experience, dragged me down.

Isacaron whispered, "Go ahead and jump…end your troubles."

I moved to the edge of the roof. "There's one thing I'd like to know before I die. I'd like to know why my mother posed nude for Togallini. How can a saint become a sinner?"

"Your mother was an attractive woman with little money to spend. She was a magnet for men. They paid for her services. Your father was a tight wad, drove her to prostitution. You will see your mother when you jump. She is waiting for you."

The man with the bathrobe shouted, "Get away from the edge of the roof." With both hands, he motioned me to step back, away from the edge of the roof. His voice had a booming quality.

For the first time since I was on the roof, I recognized the booming voice. It belonged to Father O'Donnell. The priest looked ridiculous in his bathrobe, stained with blood. We all look ridiculous at times; do ridiculous things, I thought. My mind was working a little better now. The priest is a friend…

"Get the relic!"

The voice of the friend penetrated my mind, swept it clean. The priest didn't ask me to get the relic, he ordered me to get it. He was talking like a father interested in his son. A son needs a father interested in him.

Again came the words, "Get the relic!"

I stepped back from the edge of the roof. The idea of getting the relic was suddenly important. I ran towards the skylight, jumped through the opening. The chair and table broke my fall. Stumbling towards the sink, I grabbed the relic, threw it into my mouth.

The woman in the painting registered surprise. I didn't wait to see if the spirit within her would fly out of the canvas, tackle me or embrace me. With all the speed I could gather, I ran out of the studio, through the room containing the canvases, past Togallini's body, down the stairs to my bedroom. I heard wood splintering, Vivian screaming. The police were smashing in the front door. Vivian was letting them know she didn't like it.

I didn't like it, either. Soon I'd be dragged from my home, put behind bars. People would say I looked like a monkey in a cage. They'd laugh at the gown I received in the hospital. No, they wouldn't. I ripped off the gown, stuffed it into a hamper. When I'm in jail, I'll be dressed as well as any of the other convicts.

I found underwear, dungarees, shirt, socks and shoes. All were clean. I could thank Vivian for that. She always kept things clean. Everything but her soul and mine.

After putting on the clean clothes, I fell face down on the bed, closed my eyes, gripped the pillow with both hands. *I almost killed my father.* The thought was terrifying…torturing. Isacaron had nearly succeeded in making a killer out of me. He'd go to jail with me, corrupt other prisoners. He'd be with me till the day I died, for an eternity thereafter. If only I could think of a way to free myself from him.

I couldn't even think of a way to free myself from the police. They were cutting through the door. Vivian was shouting at them. The police would soon come up the stairs; arrest me.

I heard the door below splinter open. Men swarmed into the house, rushed up the stairs. It was too late for me to escape.

In a futile effort to stop them, Vivian followed the men up the stairs. "We have a right to privacy. You have no search warrant. You're violating our rights. You…you…you overpaid monsters."

I realized Vivian was crazed with anger because the police were on the verge of discovering the paintings. They'd take them away from her…away from me. I'd be unable to keep the promise made to God and Togallini. I'd be unable to destroy them. Isacaron had defeated me!

My door burst open. An Italian policeman, big enough to play tackle for the New York Giants, came into the room. He stopped dead in his tracks when he saw me. He was looking for me, yet didn't expect to find me. He did nothing but stare.

Vivian was in the hallway, trying to prevent other policemen from opening doors, searching rooms. She was also trying to keep them away from the stairs leading to Togallini's apartment. Her efforts produced no results. Policemen rushed past her, ran up the stairs to Togallini's apartment. Spotting me, she darted into my bedroom, stared at the policeman staring at me.

I expected her to curse the officer for not grabbing me, handcuffing me. It was she who grabbed me. With her face charged with emotion, she rushed to my bed, threw her arms around my neck, pulled my face into her bosom. She held me so close I'd trouble breathing.

Sobbing, she said, "You won't believe what's happening. The police are searching this house; looking for an ape. Your father is on the roof, trying to escape from the ape. The police will find...they will see... Everything we've worked for has gone up in smoke. Tommy! Tommy, my love, how can this happen to us?"

CHAPTER 19

I was slow to realize Vivian had called me *Tommy;* slow to realize the policeman standing at the foot of my bed hadn't made a move to handcuff me. I knew why when I placed a hand on my chin. The hard hairs were gone, my resemblance to an ape was gone, and Isacaron was gone. He couldn't reside in me while the relic was in my mouth. *The police weren't looking for me.*

I took the relic from my mouth, placed it in my shirt pocket, next to my heart.

Vivian asked nervously, "What's that?" Without waiting for a reply, she said, "The police are in the house, searching for someone who resembles an ape."

"An ape?" I repeated, not knowing how to respond.

"A brute that tried to force himself on me. I'd an awful time fighting him off. When your father tried to help me, the ape turned on him. He ran to the roof to avoid being murdered."

I'd only a bleary picture of my father lying on the roof. He could have fallen over the side. "Dad all right now?"

"I really don't know," Vivian said, making an ostentatious effort to appear interested in my dad's welfare. She turned to the policeman. "Would you know?"

He was staring at her as if she were Miss America. Awakening from his reverie, he said, "I'll find out." He took a phone from a hip case; spoke into it.

Static and a garbled reply followed: "...sprawled on the roof...appears to be in shock...."

Vivian rewarded the policeman with a forced smile. "Shock won't kill him," she said philosophically. "We all receive the occasional shock. Somehow we recover, continued with our lives, make the best of the situation we're in, regardless of how difficult it is." Her last remark seemed to be directed more to herself than the policeman.

For some unexplainable reason, I felt a pang of sympathy for my father. "I'm glad Dad's all right."

Vivian seemed reluctant to spend much time talking about him. "We need not be overly concerned about your father," she said.

"Why not?"

"He's a survivor. We ought to be more concerned about Mr. Togallini. The poor dear was ill and terribly depressed about his health. Imagine his state of mind when your father ran through his apartment with an ape chasing him. And now the police are in his apartment, disturbing him."

The finest actress on stage or screen couldn't have spoken her lines better. Vivian knew Togallini was dead, yet she created the impression she was totally unaware of his death. I'd have believed her myself if I didn't know better. Moreover, she did a remarkable job in gaining control over her emotions. She was no longer the hysterical woman on the stairs. No longer the shouting, cursing, arguing woman. She was now composed and thoughtful, a master at planning strategy. She'd lost one battle. She didn't intend to lose the next one.

Her next battle was to convince the police she didn't know Togallini was dead. She was now building up notions of her innocence by casting shy glances at the policeman, who was trying to take notes without taking his eyes off her. She informed him the ape had followed her home from church, forced his way into the house. She didn't give any details of the attempted rape, as she called it, but she did speak at length of the peace she experienced when she made her daily visit to the Blessed Virgin Mary.

The visits helped her stay in the state of grace. She recommended them for all women, especially those concerned with worldly goods.

The policeman made a note of the latter remark and nodded. When Vivian spoke to him, looked into his eyes, he'd have believed she was a living saint, a replacement for Mother Theresa.

As I listened to her remarks, I felt sorry for her. She'd played a game and lost. Her many months of sacrificing, scheming, and screwing were lost without compensation. Should I give her the painting Togallini bequeathed to me? Obtaining it was her first goal. She could sell it, live in comfort for a while. No! I couldn't give it to her. I'd keep my promise to God and Togallini. One painting, perhaps the most damaging of all to the souls of men, would be destroyed. Vivian would never appear naked on canvas. I'd see to that.

Father O'Donnell filled the doorway. He looked concerned, beaten, and sick. His health seemed to improve when he saw me. He was relieved I no longer looked like an ape. "You all right, Tommy?"

"I'm fine, Father."

"We're calling him Rip from now on, Father," Vivian said with a pleasing smile. "Someone resembling an ape tried to rape me. Then he chased Tommy's father through the house, onto the roof. The police smashed open the front door, charged up the stairs. Would you believe it? Tommy slept through the racket, didn't hear a thing...."

While Vivian was talking, distorting the truth, I became aware of people shuffling about in Togallini's apartment. Two policemen came running down the stairs, their radios squawking. The hall rapidly filled with more police, photographers, newspapermen, and others. The confusion they caused in the house matched the confusion in my brain. Togallini had said my fight against the demon would be a game, the most important one in my life. Now I was being pulled out of the game. I could no longer fight Isacaron. I was a loser in my battle against evil. I felt numb, empty, terribly disappointed.

Demon of Lust

Father O'Donnell examined me closely. He appeared satisfied that all signs of my possession were gone. "If you're questioned by the police," he said in a low voice, "simply tell the truth. No reservations."

The detective and the doctor who'd questioned me in the hospital nudged Father O'Donnell into the room. "Father, I'm Detective Costello, and this is Doctor Hanson. We wish to question the boy."

The priest stepped away from my bed. "Go right ahead."

Detective Costello took a small, black notebook from his pocket. Without any other preliminaries, he asked, "Your name, please?"

Suddenly I felt nervous, couldn't understand why. Why should a human being make me feel nervous after I willingly confronted a demon? My response showed the nervousness. " My name is Tommy. Tommy Davis."

He recorded the name in his book. "I'm happy to know you're well enough to give us your name. When we spoke to you in the hospital, you refused to identify yourself. You told us you were transported across Manhattan and halfway across the Hudson River by a demon. Remember? I hope you're now willing to admit you were delirious."

"I wasn't delirious," I said, losing my nervousness. "I was transported into the Hudson by a demon."

The detective shook his head. The doctor moved closer to me, peered into my eyes.

"No one saw you move from the hospital to here," Doctor Hanson remarked, as he continued to examine me. "Please don't tell us you traveled by air."

"I ran all the way."

"What time was that?" the detective asked.

"Between three and four."

He made an entry in his notebook. "When you arrived home did you ring the bell, have someone open the door for you? Or did you have a key?"

"I'd no key. I pounded on the front door…" I stopped talking… didn't want to get Vivian involved with the police. I looked at the priest for help.

Vivian involved herself by breaking into the conversation, tried to answer the question for me. "Tommy has a key to a rear door. He could have let himself in…"

The detective turned to her. "You weren't here to let him in?"

"I? No!"

The Italian policeman was anxious to say something. He blurted, "She was in church."

The detective's voice softened. "You were in church?"

Vivian bowed her head, clasped her hands as if in prayer. "Yes."

Detective Costello then fixed his dark brown eyes on me. "How did you get into this house?"

I could foresee trouble, looked appealingly at Father O'Donnell."

"Tell the truth, Tommy."

"I came through the front door. Vivian let me in."

If I'd jammed a sparking high voltage wire beneath her brassier, she couldn't have sounded more shocked. "What? What? What are you saying?"

"I'm saying you let me in the house, Vivian. You let me in, but you didn't know…"

"I didn't let you in," she said, raising her voice in anger. "I wasn't here to let you in. Father O'Donnell told you to tell the truth. So why the hell don't you tell the truth?" She stared at me hard.

"I'm sorry I have to contradict you. You didn't know me when I showed up at the door."

The detective asked sharply, "Why wouldn't she know you?"

Father O'Donnell broke in. "She didn't know him because he looked like an ape. He was possessed by a demon. She didn't recognize him."

The detective trained his dark probing eyes on the priest, studied the pale face, the bathrobe, the slippers. He concentrated more on the bathrobe and slippers than on the pale face. The bathrobe was faded, so small it was funny. The slippers were worn, ripped, turned over on one side. Not the clothes worn by an expert on anything. The detective shook his head hopelessly. "Father, if you wish to contribute something to this investigation, please don't talk about possession. I don't believe in it. And I don't know anyone who does. How about you, Doctor Hanson? Do you believe in possession?"

"There's no scientific basis for it. However, I do have Catholic friends…clever medical people…who believe in it."

Vivian spoke, sounding authoritative, "I'm Catholic and I don't believe in possession."

She didn't believe in anything taught by the Church that interfered with her pleasure, I thought. "You saw me possessed, Vivian. I pounded on the door of this house. You let me in."

"Like hell I did," she snapped. "I'd have known you if you came through that door. And you know why. I don't know what your game is, Tommy. Whatever it is, I don't like it. Another thing I don't like: Before that ape grabbed me, he gave me information known only to you. You know him, don't you? You told him about me, didn't you? You told him about the private affairs of this house, didn't you? Don't bother to answer, I know you did."

Detective Costello was attentive to every word spoken by Vivian. When she was through, he turned to me in anger. "Did that ape take your place in the hospital?"

"He was me."

The detective scowled. "I've a damned good reason to believe you were the ape. Then I could hold you responsible for injuring a number of elderly patients in the ward. Are you willing to assume responsibility for their injuries? Are you willing to pay for their additional medical expenses? Possible litigation? Court costs?"

I'd only a shadowy image of running through the hospital, jumping from bed to bed. "I didn't have control over what I was doing," I said to the detective. "I was possessed."

Before the detective could respond, the voice of the priest boomed at him, boomed around the room. "He's telling the truth. He struck me. I wouldn't dream of holding him responsible for striking me when he was possessed by a demon. The patients won't hold him responsible, either."

The face of the detective soured. "Nobody is going to believe this kid is the beast who ran through the hospital, showed up on the roof of this house."

"I believe it," said the priest. "Moreover, I witnessed the transformation, saw Tommy change from boy to beast. And why did the beast, as you call him, show up at this house? Why not any one of a thousand other houses? He came here because this is where he lives. Take my word for it..." Sweat broke out on the face of the priest. He took a handkerchief from a pocket, wiped his brow.

Doctor Hanson was quick to notice the sweat. He was sympathetic. "Your fever is breaking. Too bad our staff didn't do a better job combating your infection."

The priest shook his head. "Your staff couldn't combat my infection. It was given to me by a demon called Isacaron."

The detective howled, and kicked an old sneaker of mine that was on the floor. "Now I understand why this kid has been talking about a demon transporting him through space...possessing him. He's been listening to you. He's gullible enough to believe anything you tell him. The drugs you've taken in the hospital have affected your process of reasoning, Father." The detective put a sarcastic twist on the word *Father*.

I felt like punching him in the nose.

The priest ignored the sarcasm. "Tommy and I had a discussion before and after he was possessed. I can assure you, I witnessed the transformation."

The detective gave a shrug of hopeless annoyance, spoke firmly: "The possession of a human being by an evil spirit is absurd. Possession is no explanation. This boy had an accomplice. An accomplice who'll be jailed as soon as I find him."

Father O'Donnell raised his voice. "You won't find an accomplice. If you look for one, you'll waste time and taxpayers' money."

Flinching, the detective raised a warning finger. "Let me conduct this investigation in my own way. And let me get back to something, which requires an explanation from you. When the ape was at the edge of the roof, you called to him, told him to get a relic. Why?"

"I'd given Tommy a relic to protect himself from the demon Isacaron. When he was on the roof, I thought he was being urged by the demon to jump...destroy himself. I told him to get the relic, hoping he'd move away from the roof... hoping the relic would drive the demon out of him."

Unconvinced, the detective turned to me. "Where is the relic now?"

I took it out of my pocket, offered it to him.

"Don't release the relic," the priest ordered. "It may be your only protection."

Recoiling, the detective snapped, "Keep it! It's just an old souvenir, sold by the church at an exorbitant price for money making purposes."

Father O'Donnell clenched his fists. I figured he'd forget he was a priest long enough to throw a punch.

The detective moved towards the door, spoke to Father O'Donnell, Vivian and me. "I'll ask you not to leave the house without my permission."

The priest retorted, "And I'll ask you not to release any information to the press without checking it with me."

Detective Costello raised his eyebrows. "Information? I have no information. Certainly nothing to release to the press concerning a boy possessed."

What did he mean by that? Did he mean he'd not say a word about possession because it conflicted with his beliefs? Some detective!

He turned to Doctor Hanson. "I'm going upstairs. Care to join me?"

The doctor nodded, moved towards the door. "If you'll excuse me, Father, Tommy, Miss...." He smiled, gaped at Vivian, paused to give her an opportunity to supply her last name. She didn't. He left the room, followed by the policeman.

Vivian slammed the door, snapped. "Tommy! You made me sound like a liar in the presence of those men."

I was almost too weary to answer her. "If you didn't lie, you wouldn't sound like a liar."

The priest spoke to Vivian. "You lied. Why not admit it?"

Irritation showed in her words, loaded with sarcasm. "With all due respect, Father, you're the one who lied. You and Tommy. You tried to convince a New York City detective and a medical doctor, two intelligent men, that Tommy and the ape were the same person. They didn't buy the lie. Neither did I. And remember, I was on the scene. An eyewitness. That ape followed me home from church, forced his way into this house. When I opened the front door, he grabbed me. Talked to me. I talked to him…smelled him. I'm the girl he tried to rape. I'll swear, on a Bible, the ape who tried to rape me wasn't Tommy."

I could hardly believe it was Vivian who was talking. She was a human puzzle, a beautiful creature spouting ugly words.

A rap sounded on the door. The Italian policemen who first spotted me stuck his head inside the room. "Detective Costello wants to see all of you upstairs."

Vivian was through the door without delay. She ran up the stairs, entered the furniture-cluttered room, stopped short as if shot in the heart with an arrow. She immediately caught the attention of Doctor Hanson and Detective Costello, who were standing near Togallini's body, listening to a man with a stethoscope and a Schnauzer's beard. She also caught the attention of many other people milling about the room, including a police sergeant and a photographer. As she stared at the dead body, she gasped a couple of times and put on an act that'd convince anybody she viewed Togallini's corpse for the first time. The photographer snapped her picture.

The detective asked her, "You didn't know this man was dead?"

She appeared hurt. "No! No! Of course not."

Without turning his head, the detective turned his eyes on me. "And you?"

"I knew."

His face showed disgust. "Why you morbid little delinquent, why didn't you notify someone?"

"I had a job to do first."

Demon of Lust

"That I believe," he stated curtly. "You and your accomplice had a job to do. You were going to pick this place clean."

Father O'Donnell showed his indignation. "You're making an irresponsible accusation…a great mistake."

"This kid and his accomplice intended to rob this apartment. More important, they murdered the old man. He has a broken skull, ribs, an arm, a…"

"Murder?" questioned the priest.

"I'll stake my reputation on it. The left side of this man's body is a series of broken bones. Only one explanation is reasonable. The man was thrown from the roof of this house."

"Not true," I said.

"It is true," the detective stated as if he'd solved a difficult case, and no one could deny him the honor. "You and your accomplice lifted Mr. Togallini through the skylight, onto the roof. You then threw him into the back yard, retrieved his body, carried it up the back stairs, put it on the bed…"

The detective's words rang in my ears. I could only shake my head and say, "Not true! Not true!"

"Give me the ape's name and address," the detective demanded. "Or stand alone, guilty of murdering a defenseless old man."

CHAPTER 20

The detective's charges struck me dumb. My mind became a jumble of disoriented ideas. I wasn't able to say anything in defense of myself.

After making a quick survey of the contents of the apartment, Father O'Donnell returned to stand by my side, take up my defense. "This boy is incapable of murder. He's honest and as kind as any boy I've ever met. Not long ago he asked me to hear Mr. Togallini's confession. Not many boys today would be interested in the confession of an old man, near death."

"Some boys would. Others, wouldn't," Detective Costello stated, as if he knew more about confessions than the priest. "There are boys in New York City who'll do anything for money. I see them every day in the streets, in the police station, in court. I know them as well as I know myself. If this kid did Togallini a favor, he had a selfish motive for doing it. Obviously, he wished to steal something from this apartment, sell it in the Village. People in the Village buy anything."

Father O'Donnell tapped the detective on the chest, looked into his eyes. "This boy wanted to help Togallini. The artist recognized him as a friend. If you've any doubts about it; that is, if you want some hard evidence, read what Togallini wrote on the only canvas in this room." The priest pointed to the canvas in the cabinet.

Detective Costello drew close to the canvas and read:
This painting I bequeath to my
friend forever, Tommy Davis.

Demon of Lust

The detective kept reading it and reading it. He finally spoke to Doctor Hanson. "Doctor, if you'll help me remove the painting from the cabinet, we'll take a look…"

"Don't touch that painting," I shouted spontaneously. "It belongs to me. And I'm going to destroy it, first chance I get."

Vivian's voice was louder than mine. "Destroy it? You're talking about *my painting*, the one promised to me."

Detective Costello completely ignored my plea and Vivian's outburst. He and the doctor removed the canvas from the cabinet, rested it on two tables of equal height. The painting blocked the center of the room. Father O'Donnell was on one side of the canvas; everyone else in the room was on the other side. The priest was the only one in a position to view the painting.

He took several backward steps to examine it. His eyes widened with wonder. I could forgive him for taking a quick look at Vivian's naked body, blushing a bit, muttering some stupid apology, and then letting it go at that. I couldn't forgive him for the way he stared…and stared…and stared. He was transfixed. A pink color rushed to his face. He was drawn closer to the canvas. "The most beautiful painting…the most beautiful woman I have ever seen!" he exclaimed.

Vivian smiled happily and bowed. "Thank you, Father."

"In my judgment, this painting equals anything done by Michelangelo Buonarroti."

Vivian was now beaming. She grasped the arm of Doctor Hanson. With a gesture, she brought his attention to the affect her picture was having on the priest.

Detective Costello was impatient. "We'll turn the painting around, so all of us can see it."

As the painting was being turned around, I dropped my head. I didn't want to see it. I was afraid of again becoming subjected to Isacaron's power. A power that killed Togallini, lured me into sin with Vivian, sent me flying high in the sky, dropped me into the Hudson River, converted me from a rational boy to an irrational monkey, transformed a dedicated priest to one who gloated over a demonic painting.

Vivian changed my mind when she shouted, "That's not my painting!"

I raised my head. The woman in the painting was *my mother*. She wore a long blue dress, which fitted her lovely form with a gracious dignity and modesty. She knelt in Togallini's drab studio, staring into space. She seemed to be staring beyond the studio, beyond the house; beyond the golden rays of sunlight breaking through the skylight, shining on her like a spotlight from heaven. She appeared to be contemplating another world, confidently anticipating a happiness she never enjoyed on earth. Tiny words, almost imperceptible, were spun into the golden rays: *A Good Mother.* I couldn't see anything more in the painting. Tears of joy welled in my eyes. A monstrous demon had been evicted from my mind. A demon that convinced me my mother had posed nude for the artist.

The detective's face registered pain. It hurt him to know my mother resembled me. It hurt him to know a woman with the face of an angel had a son he suspected of murder. It hurt him to know I was a friend of Togallini's. It hurt him to know he'd lost his prime suspect.

He moved away from me, looked around the room, spoke sharply to Doctor Hanson. "A few minutes ago, the medical examiner was here, several policemen, newspaper reporters. I don't see them; hear them. Where are they?"

The response was haughty. "Why ask me? You're the detective."

Stung, the detective addressed the priest. "Father, do you know where they are?"

"In the studio."

"They're in the studio," I said, "but I wouldn't advise you to go in there."

Scowling, the detective led the way into the studio. He pushed his way through a group of people standing before the painting of the nude woman. When his eyes focused on her, he was struck immobile. His face flushed with lust.

Demon of Lust

"No place for us," Father O'Donnell said to Doctor Hanson, Vivian and me. "We better leave now."

The doctor stuck out a hand to the priest. "If you're leaving, I'll say goodbye to you now, Father. Before returning to the hospital, I'd like to speak to this young lady."

Baloney, I thought. The doctor wanted to view the painting, get himself all charged up, and then ask Vivian out. I knew it. So did Vivian. She was sizing him up, smiling to herself.

Someone was smiling at me, too. I could feel the smile on the back of my head. Crazy? To know for sure, I turned around and looked at the woman in the painting. Because of the people in front of me, I could see only her face. It was enough. She was smiling at me. A smile of victory.

She'd beaten me, all right. I'd not have another chance to destroy her painting or any of the other paintings in the apartment. I'd failed Togallini. And he'd failed himself. His one great work of art, the painting of my mother, wouldn't generate enough good around the world to counteract his many works of evil. God claimed those who did good. The devil got the rest. Togallini's soul was one for the devil. I could hope and pray I was wrong. Perhaps his desire at the end of his life to go to confession, make peace with God, was enough to save his soul.

*   *   *

I sat in the rear of the church during Togallini's funeral Mass, celebrated by Father O'Donnell. The church was filled with New Yorkers attracted by vivid newspaper accounts of the life of the artist. Overnight, he'd become famous. Vivian's painting and several others appeared in the newspapers. One columnist said the paintings had the male population of New York City panting.

Friends and business associates of Mario Togallini attended the funeral Mass. They'd arrived in Jaguars, Cadillacs, Lincolns, Mercedes Benzes, and other expensive cars. None of their cars could compare favorably with either of the two cars used to transport Mario Togallini's family. The first car pulling up before the church was a new Rolls Royce, Chianti colored and chauffeur driven. Mario's five kids occupied it. They blew bubble gum, laughed, shouted dirty remarks at passersby, and made rude gestures at mourners.

The second car pulling up before the church was also a new Rolls Royce, the color of pink champagne. The rear seat was occupied by a woman whose obesity made it difficult for her to squeeze through the door of the limousine. When she finally stood alone and embarrassed on the sidewalk, with her silk dress in disarray, she searched the crowd of people assembled outside the church. Her eyes were the saddest I'd ever seen on anybody.

A tall handsome man, flawlessly dressed, emerged from the crowd and approached her. He greeted her with overdone respect. He told her that Mario had an all-night business meeting with a very important person, but promised to arrive at the church in time to attend his brother's funeral Mass.

Mrs. Togallini, probably accustomed to listening to lies, wasn't convinced. She continued to search the crowd for her husband.

About ten minutes after the Mass had started, a man entered the church with a gorgeously dressed woman on his arm. The woman was so strikingly beautiful, I hardly noticed the man. She sparkled with diamonds, had a bearing that was absolutely perfect. It was Vivian.

The shock of seeing her glide down the center aisle of the church like a reigning queen, made me feel weak and helpless. Somehow I knew Isacaron had something to do with her lavish clothes, jewels, and renewed confidence. I didn't know what to think.

Seeking more information about Vivian, I turned my attention to the man who accompanied her. Another shock! I thought the deceased Togallini had come back to life, left his casket, erased ten years from his age, garbed himself in fine clothes, and accompanied Vivian into the church to attend his own funeral. Was he playing a demonic joke on those of us who knew him?

Demon of Lust

Common sense finally struck me. I was looking at Togallini's younger brother, Mario. The sad-eyed woman, who sat in a front pew, straining her neck to see her dapper husband walking up the aisle with a beautiful woman, confirmed this conclusion.

As I watched Mario take a seat in the church, I thought about my father. He used to curse Mario whenever a rent check was late. My father wouldn't receive any more rent checks from Mario. At present, he was too disturbed to focus on the loss. Released from a hospital the previous day, he returned home shaking, crying, telling me how lonely he was, and begging me to forgive him.

I let him know I'd no intention of forgiving him for his miserable conduct. He argued I was forced to forgive him because I'm Catholic. Like it or not, he pointed out, the Church requires me to pardon him. I told him he'd slapped me in the face and kicked me in the can so often, I'd satisfied all Church requirements. Sobbing, he said he'd do anything if I forgave him. Would he promise not to strike me again? He made the promise. Would he treat me like a father ought to treat a son? He agreed to do that. Would he love me? Yes, he would.

I forgave him. And I felt so much better. So did he. But he had a hard time understanding why I'd soon leave home; enter a seminary and study to become a priest. Weak and imperfect as I was, I felt compelled to continue my battle against Isacaron and all the other demons roaming the world, seeking the destruction of souls. Father O'Donnell was going to help me find a suitable seminary.

Like the blast from a cannon, the voice of the priest boomed around the church, hit every ear. It startled me.

"The name of the man who lies before you today is now known throughout our city," he said. "His name and fame will spread to other parts of the country, to other parts of the world. Art dealers will clamor for his work, offer large sums of money for it. The artist will be recognized as a genius. Why? Because his paintings have a powerful influence on the thoughts and actions of those who view them."

I knew where Father O'Donnell was going with his talk.

He asked this question: "If the artist could speak to us this morning, would he say he's accomplished everything he wished to accomplish in this world?"

Many of the people in the church nodded.

Father O'Donnell slowly shook his head. "At the close of his life, the artist Togallini was not concerned with accomplishments. Nor was he concerned with fame and fortune. He was concerned with his immortal soul. Like the rest of us, he had sinned. But, unlike some of us, he wanted to make his peace with God before he died. He expressed this wish to a young man who asked me to hear his confession. On the way to his apartment, I was struck down by a thief, sent to a hospital. I was prevented from hearing the artist's confession."

There was dead silence in the church.

Father O'Donnell allowed several seconds to elapse before continuing: The man who prevented me from hearing Mr. Togallini's confession was possessed by a demon."

No longer was there silence in the church. Many people commented on the startling statement. The comments were hostile, heated, and irreligious. People shook their heads, snickered, and stared at the man on the altar as if he'd broken every law ever discussed in the coffee shops of Greenwich Village. A bearded hippie, wearing a cap and horn rimmed glasses, uttered a curse. His friend, another hippie and just as dirty, gave the priest the raspberry.

The priest listened to some of the comments before continuing: "The concept of demons is difficult to accept, isn't it? Many of us are inclined to disbelieve their existence, even though our most reliable source of information, the Bible, is filled with passages relating to them. I can assure you, demons do exist. They are powerful forces, spiritual by nature, trained by Satan to lure us away from God. They are secretive, crafty, persuasive, with an uncanny and unholy objective to lead us to hell."

Some old guy in the rear of the church said, "I don't know about that."

Demon of Lust

The priest took out a handkerchief, wiped his brow. "Demons can break down the willpower of some of the most talented people on earth. With regret, I tell you that includes men and women who profess to serve God...priests, ministers, rabbis. It includes members of the Supreme Court, political representatives, businessmen and women, doctors, lawyers, mothers. The journey through life isn't easy. We must forever be on guard, be willing to forego the pleasures the demons have to offer. Our greatest defense against evil is sacrifice. By sacrificing something we wish to have, we not only help our own spiritual lives, we help others save their souls. We help them, regardless of whether they are living or dead."

For ten minutes or more, Father O'Donnell continued in this vein. On no occasion did he look at Mario Togallini. However, there was no question in my mind the priest was making a final pitch to Mario for the paintings. His arguments were beautifully presented, difficult to dispute, impossible to ignore. Surely Mario would accept the plea from the priest, relinquish the paintings. By doing so, he'd carry out his brother's wishes; the wishes of a dying man. Most important, he'd help his brother save his soul.

*   *   *

The following day, I was alone in the house when the front door bell rang. Opening the door, I was greeted by Vivian, Mario Togallini, and two men dressed in work clothes. Vivian took my hand, kissed me on the side of the mouth, and introduced Mario, a truck driver, and the driver's helper, to me.

I was hardly aware of the presence of the men. Vivian received my full attention. She was dressed in expensive clothes and was more vivacious and happier than I'd ever seen her. Her beauty was so fresh and startling, I felt myself being hypnotized. "I'm...I'm glad to see you again, Vivian," I said truthfully. My heart began to pound.

"We're here for the paintings," she said, stepping inside the house. She directed the men up the stairs to Togallini's old apartment. As we climbed the stairs, she took my hand and held it tightly. Before reaching the second floor, she stopped, drew me close, and whispered, "We'll keep in touch."

As I contemplated her words, a glorious thrill passed through my body. Keeping in touch with her would bring me more pleasure than anything else in life. Nevertheless, I said, "I won't be able to keep in touch with you, Vivian. I'm…I'm going away. I'm going to study to become a priest."

As if it were contaminated, Vivian immediately released my hand, gave me a puzzled look. She ran up the stairs and into the apartment; ordered the men into the studio.

I tagged along, resolving to never again look at a Togallini painting.

"What a lady!" Mario exclaimed when he stood before the woman I tried to destroy.

"Wow! Wow! Wow!" barked the truck driver.

His helper could only stare.

I stared, too.

The woman in the painting looked deeply into my eyes, my heart, and my soul. She set my passions on fire. While my body burned, she looked at Vivian. Without saying a word, she encouraged Vivian to make love with me. Suddenly I wanted to make love with Vivian. We could meet in some secluded motel…

The woman in the painting smiled.

Her smile made me grit my teeth, decide I'd never again make love with Vivian, regardless of the poundings my passions gave me. Isacaron would never again seduce me.

The driver's helper picked up the painting to remove it from the studio. As he did so, the smile disappeared from the beautiful face.

I'd miss that face, I thought. I'd also miss Vivian's face…not to mention her body. Could I forget her when I was alone in the seminary? Not unless I dropped dead the moment I arrived there. I'd remember her as long as I lived. She'd be with me when I studied, when I prayed, when I became a priest, when I'm on my deathbed. Would I ever attempt to see her again? No, I wouldn't. I've learned my lesson. The struggle through life isn't easy. No sense inviting trouble.

Nine Years Later

CHAPTER 21

The doorbell rang.

I couldn't pull myself away from the article I was reading. It appeared in every newspaper in the country. It dealt with a priest who'd fallen by the wayside, yielded to temptation, committed a horrible sin, and disgraced himself and his Church.

Such a catastrophe could happen to any priest, I thought. A priest is a target for the devil. A prize! I know that because I've battled the devil and one of his demons. I know that because I'm a priest. My name is Father Tom Davis. I was twenty-six years old when I was stationed at Saint Matthew's Rectory, located in a poverty-stricken section of a borough of New York City, known as the Bronx.

The doorbell rang a second time.

Ignoring it, I realized I'd the same weaknesses as other men...the same weaknesses as other priests. I was supposed to be a fisher of men, bring them closer to God. From my experience, I had to admit Satan was a better fisherman than I. He reeled in men, women, boys and girls, as if they were poor fish starving for the bait he offered. The bait was usually some form of sex.

I took the bait when I was a boy of seventeen. The bait was an ex-model named Vivian. She came into my life the night she was thrown down the stairs by an artist named Togallini, who rented the attic apartment from my father. She landed at my bedroom door, awakened me from a troubled sleep. The sleep was troubled because I'd recently lost my mother.

Demon of Lust

Vivian was the most beautiful creature God ever created. I fell in love with her. So did my father. Having no funds, she agreed to live with us for her room and board. She cooked and cleaned and rendered my father special favors, too painful for me to relate.

Not long after she moved into our house, I found myself in bed with her. At the same time, I fell under the influence of a demon called Isacaron. I soon learned that every demon has a specialty. Isacaron's specialty is sex.

The doorbell rang a third time. The ring was long and persistent. It disturbed my train of thought.

"What a nuisance," I muttered.

My pastor, Monsignor Blazer, saintly and sickly, had assigned the task of answering the doorbell to me. The housekeeper was in Ireland taking care of a mother unable to care for herself.

While walking on the worn carpet leading to the front door, I examined my wallet to see if I'd a few dollars to give to any one of a hundred beggars who frequently rang the doorbell. I'd two five-dollar bills and several meal tickets. I recalled the pastor's admonition: "If a drinker rings the bell, give him a meal ticket for Joe's Diner. Joe will bill us at the end of the month."

Drunk or sober, I'll give the bell-ringer a meal ticket, I thought before opening the door.

I've always been a lover of fine automobiles. Perhaps that's why I saw the new Rolls Royce parked at the curb before I focused on the woman who had a shapely finger on the bell, poised to ring a fourth time.

"Tommy Davis!" she exclaimed the moment I opened the door.

"I'm Father Tom," I replied, almost apologetically.

Her smile lit up the Bronx. "You're Tommy Davis to me," she said, taking me in her arms.

My mind exploded into a million remembrances of my past. I knew the feel of her large breasts pressing against my chest. I knew her perfume, the soft texture of her skin, her power to weaken every fiber in my body. I knew her name. "Vivian," I whispered.

"Tommy," she said passionately.

I wanted to hold her. I couldn't! Not if I wanted to hold onto my priesthood. Stepping back, I gave myself the pleasure of staring into her lovely face.

In nine years since I'd last seen her, she hadn't changed much. The soul-piercing eyes were the same, except for a sign of sadness. The perfect features, the heart-warming smile, the winning personality, all were the same. And her body, the body that turned men's head, was the same. She was dressed to perfection in a dark business suit. Several large diamonds sparkled on her fingers.

I said precisely what was on my mind. "Vivian, I never expected to see you again."

Her response set my heart hammering. "I expected to see you. Thought you'd drop out of the seminary. Not many young people today have vocations. Those who think they'd like to become a priest, drop out when they're told to do a little work, make a few sacrifices."

"It never occurred to me to drop out."

Vivian's smile showed understanding. "I should have realized you're no quitter. From the past, I know you've more determination than any kid I've ever met. I just hoped, for my sake, you'd quit."

I was going to tell her I was no longer a kid, but I suddenly realized the Rolls Royce was attracting a crowd of young blacks and Puerto Ricans. Several were staring at us, as we stood in the doorway. "Vivian, you and your car are attracting a crowd. I've a friend who's a policeman. He's off-duty now. With your permission, I'll call him, ask him to guard your car."

"The car's insured. I'm not worried about it."

"If you're not worried about it, I won't be worried about it, as long as you realize the Bronx isn't the ideal place to park a Rolls Royce."

She smiled. "I'm not worried about it."

I was going to give her more reasons for not parking the car outside the rectory, but decided not to do so. "Come into my office, we'll have some privacy there."

Demon of Lust

The moment she stepped inside the door, she asked, "How'd you like to have lunch with me at the Trump Towers? I'm living there now."

I thought of the ten dollars I had in my pocket, hardly enough for a gratuity for a waiter in the Trump Towers. "I'd prefer talking to you in my office."

"Don't be an old fogy. We'll have a good time."

"I'm afraid I can't accept your invitation."

Without a change of expression, she said, "Afraid of my inviting you to my apartment after lunch, seducing you?"

The question rolled off her lips as easily as a "Good morning, Father," from another woman. "Of course not!" I snapped, thinking I have a lie to report the next time I go to confession.

Vivian had a slight smile on her face as she walked into my office. I believe the worn carpet and the faded wallpaper amused her.

Her chair creaked when she sat down. "Well," she remarked, "I never expected to find you living in a rectory."

"And I never expected to find you living in the Trump Towers. I hope you're happy now."

She gazed out a window, had her eyes fixed on an old oak tree, devoid of leaves. "I expected happiness when I had everything money can buy. I learned the hard way, money doesn't buy happiness."

I disliked seeing the sad look. "Money is often a help," I volunteered. "There are many poor people in the world; people without food, clothing, shelter. I'd like to have enough money to help them."

She shook her head. "I know you would. You worry about the world. That's your problem, Tommy. You can't worry about the world, not unless your world consists of you and me and maybe a kid or two."

I was lost for words.

She shrugged her shoulders. "If the kids bother you, I'll hire a nanny. A half dozen of them if necessary."

"Are you proposing to me, Vivian?"

"What if I am? I love you and you love me. So why shouldn't two people in love get married?"

I tried to ignore the wonderful feeling that came over me at the thought of being married to her. "You don't seem to realize I'm a priest," I said without conviction. "Priests don't marry."

"Some do and some don't," she shot back. "The world won't come to an end if you say goodbye to your Church."

"Break my vows?"

"Smash them into tiny pieces for the woman you've loved ever since you were seventeen."

"I can't break my vows, Vivian. I'm a priest now. I'll be a priest till the day I die. Maybe longer."

She shifted uneasily in her chair, and spoke in slow, low tones. "Okay, Tommy, I won't press the issue. We haven't seen each other for nine years. I should've known you wouldn't jump at my proposal in ten seconds. Actually, I didn't come here today to propose marriage. I came because you're the only person I can trust. I need your help."

Her words puzzled me. I felt sure she wasn't requesting spiritual help; nor was she looking for money. What help I could give her was a mystery to me. "How can I help you?"

Before she could answer, a blue jay pecked at the window. Her beautiful face registered fear as she turned towards the window. "I thought there was someone at the window. That damned bird frightened me."

"How can I help you, Vivian?"

She was slow to answer. "You remember Togallini?"

The name brought back a thousand memories. I actually knew two men named Togallini. They were brothers. The first one I met was the artist who rented our attic apartment in Greenwich Village. He painted some of the most erotic images ever set to canvas. The power of his paintings was simply remarkable. They set off a complex tale of lust, power and madness that ultimately led back to a struggle between God and Satan. Satan had appointed the demon Isacaron to inspire the artist into painting nude women. The nudes had the power to turn men's thoughts to sins of the flesh. Togallini wanted me to destroy his paintings before he died. I was unsuccessful in doing so. Isacaron saw to that.

The second Togallini, named Mario, inherited the paintings after the death of his brother. He intended to use them in his business...the largest pornographic business in the world. And although he was a married man with a large family, he asked Vivian to join him. He supported her. She was his mistress. The idea of her being his mistress broke my heart. I was truly in love with her, even though I was only seventeen.

What justification did she have running off with Mario? She posed for a Togallini painting. The artist promised her the painting when it was finished. He later changed his mind, thinking it'd do her more harm than good. She was obsessed with the idea of getting it, regardless of what she had to do. She went off with Mario because he inherited *"her"* painting.

Vivian awakened me from my thoughts of the past. "Do you remember Mario Togallini?" she asked in a subdued voice.

"I remember him."

"The son-of-a-bitch is trying to kidnap me. He'll torture me; murder me, if he finds me. That's why I need your help."

CHAPTER 22

It took me several seconds to recover from the shock of learning that Mario Togallini wanted to kill Vivian. I asked myself why. Was he tired of her? That couldn't be. She was just as beautiful as ever. Was she trying to break away from him? That could be! A man who made a fortune in the pornographic business didn't care whom he injured. However, his pride would be injured if *his woman* tried to break away from him. The money he spent on her would be a factor. Why was I speculating? Why not ask her?

Her head was lowered and she looked uncomfortable in the creaky chair when I put the question to her. "Vivian, why would Mario want to kill you?"

Her answer was child-like. "Do you really want to know, Father?"

Now she was calling me *Father*. If I refused to be her husband, I could be her father. "Of course I want to know." I raised my voice. "How can I help you without knowing what has provoked Mario into threatening you? Has he gone mad?"

"He's mad at me, I can tell you that. Mad enough to kill me. And he's a member of the Mafia, has friends who make their living killing people. Can you imagine such an occupation?"

"I know all forms of evil exists in our society. I don't know what provoked Mario into threatening you."

When responding, Vivian sounded like a little girl admitting a prank. "I took the pictures."

A sense of annoyance brought blood to my face. "What pictures?"

Demon of Lust

"You know, the pictures his brother painted. The pictures you tried to destroy when you were a boy."

I shouted, "You took those pictures?"

"I took them and hid them. You know as well as I do that Mario's brother painted my picture and told me I could have it if I made love with him. I made love with him and the picture became mine. You also know he loved me more than any other woman on earth. He wanted me to have all his paintings when he died."

Vivian was an intelligent woman. At the moment, she was stupid. "Vivian!" I said emphatically, "I told you this nine years ago. I'll tell you again. Togallini loved you deeply. He promised you the painting he made of you. But he reneged on the promise when he knew the painting would do you more harm than good. It was inspired by a demon from hell. He didn't want you to have it. Nor any of the others."

Even before I finished my remarks, Vivian began to shake her head. She spoke as if I were the stupid one. "Nine years ago you told me that same crazy story. I told you then and I tell you now, I don't believe it. I don't believe in devils or demons. I simply can't. I do believe in guardian angels that protect us. Demons? No!"

"If you believe in angels, you should believe in demons. Demons were once angels who enjoyed all the pleasures of heaven. They became restless, power-hungry, and jealous of a being superior to themselves. They attempted to take over the City of God. They were banished from heaven, cast into hell. They roam the world seeking souls. God allows them to do this. If we fail to resist the pleasures and temptations offered by the demons, we're unworthy of a place in heaven."

"So if we have a little fun, enjoy ourselves, we go to hell. Is that what you're saying?"

"Draw your own conclusions."

Vivian looked at me quizzically. "I hope you realize you're preaching to me, Tommy. To be perfectly frank with you, I came here for your help, not your sermons."

"Well, all right, Vivian, I'll keep my sermons to myself. But all I'm trying to do is warn you those paintings are trouble. You can be in danger…"

"I'm already in danger. If Mario finds me, he'll kill me if I don't give him the paintings. But I'm willing to risk my life for them… even though I admit one thing about the paintings…." She hesitated.

"What?"

"They're jinxed. Mario sold one to a Russian official. Shortly after, the Russian murdered his wife and married a belly dancer. Mario sold another painting to the Royal Family in England. The pride of the castle, a prince, gave his wife the boot and became involved with a married woman. Mario sold another painting to a Hollywood playwright, famous for family themes. The playwright switched to sex themes. There were other instances that had me wondering. Of course, I could be wrong."

"And you could be right. Those paintings were inspired by a demon. I'm not surprised at anything you tell me."

Vivian's words were discouraging. "Surprised or not, jinxed or not, they're worth a fortune." I'm going to cash them in, keep the one of me."

"You'll go to jail for stealing."

"Mario hasn't paid a dime in taxes on the sales he's made so far. He won't complain to the police about what morally belongs to me. Get the point?"

The soft life Vivian has led since I saw her last has softened her brain, I thought. I tried to be as blunt as I could: "No, I don't get the point. You're putting yourself in great danger. I advise you to call Mario and tell him you'll return the paintings without delay."

Vivian's tone was sarcastic. "You want me to return the paintings to Mario? Didn't you once tell me he'll distribute them around the world, corrupt the souls of everyone who views them?"

Her question awakened memories of promises not kept. How could I forget promises made to the artist Togallini, my confessor, my God? I promised to destroy the paintings if I had to die doing it. Now I was telling Vivian to return the paintings to Mario Togallini. What a fool I am! I've another opportunity to destroy them. "Vivian, where are the paintings now?"

"They're stored in an apartment I rent in Brooklyn."
"You think they're safe there?"
"I'm sure they are."
"The paintings may be safe in Brooklyn, but you won't be safe if you continue living in the Trump Towers. You'll have to move."

Vivian looked puzzled. "Where can I go?"

"Why not go to Brooklyn, live in the apartment you rent."

Vivian's response was immediate. "If I lived in the apartment, I could be followed home by one of Togallini's men. That'd be the end of the paintings, the end of me."

I stared at her. She was right. One hundred percent right! She was brilliant one moment, stupid the next. A saint and a sinner. "Is there any other place you could live?"

"Not that I can think of."

"Do you know anyone in California? The climate's great there and you'd be far removed from Mario."

"I don't know anyone in California. If I did, I wouldn't go there. I want to stay close to the paintings. I also want to stay..." Her voice dropped to an unintelligible whisper.

"What do you want to do?"

"I want to... Forget it."

"You mentioned something else you wanted to do. What was it?"

She stared deeply, unashamedly into my eyes. "I want to stay close to you."

Her words set my emotions on fire. I loved the woman. The love was something over which I had no control. That didn't mean I'd break my vows or let her know I loved her. She was a thing of beauty, a temptation put in my path. I intended to avoid the temptation. I thought it best to change the subject. "Vivian, will you tell me where you're hiding the paintings, the address of the apartment?"

She was quick to answer. "No, I won't."

"You told me you loved me."

"I said I loved you. I didn't say I trusted you. You think Togallini's paintings are evil. How can I be assured you won't try to destroy them? You tried before."

"Well, all right. We'll talk about them later. First things first. I think you should call the Trump Towers, tell them you're checking out. Ask them to store your things."

"Store my things?"

"Yes. It's much too dangerous for you to return to the Trump Towers. From what you've told me, you'll be under surveillance the moment you step into the hotel."

"I hate to give up my things. I've some beautiful clothes, shoes, jewels."

Your life is more precious. You'll also have to store your Rolls Royce in some remote garage. That Rolls can be spotted a block away."

"I love my car."

"And you love your life. I won't ask you which is more important."

"All right, Father," she said, emphasizing the *Father*. "I'll do as you say."

"And now we must decide where you'll live. Do you have any money with you?"

"Not much. A couple thousand."

"That'll be enough for a while. Have you any idea where you'd like to live? I'd suggest somewhere economical, inconspicuous, as far away from Mario as possible."

"I'd like to live as close to you as possible."

Before I could think of a response, a knock on my door sounded.

Monsignor Blazer entered. He was a man with many degrees behind his name and many accomplishments in the fields of Philosophy and Education. He could no longer discuss them, simply because he could no longer remember them. Someone said senility was the reason. Because the Monsignor had refused to retire, he was given a small parish in the Bronx and a young priest to carry the load. I was the young priest.

The old pastor leveled a pair of tired blue eyes at me. Eyes, incidentally, that required a surgeon's attention for the removal of cataracts, which

Demon of Lust

greatly impaired his sight. The surgeon's attention was delayed, since the pastor believed the poor of the parish needed medical care more urgently than he.

"Father Tom," he said to me, "excuse me for disturbing your interview, but I can't wait any longer. Will you satisfy my curiosity?"

"In what way, Monsignor?"

"I'd like to know if this lady is to be our new housekeeper."

A week ago, the pastor had me place an advertisement in the church bulletin for a temporary housekeeper. He thought Vivian was applying for the job. I had to muffle a laugh at the idea. The old pastor's eyes were worse than I thought.

Standing, I said, "Vivian, I want you to meet Monsignor Blazer."

"Nice to know you," she said.

"And Monsignor, it is my pleasure to introduce you to Vivian."

"My pleasure," said the pastor, approaching her.

While they shook hands, I decided to straighten the pastor out. "Vivian is a friend of mine, here to discuss a problem. We haven't seen each other for nine years. She used to cook for my father and me. She took care of our house in Greenwich Village." The moment I made this statement, I knew I made a mistake.

The pastor's eyes widened despite his poor vision. He repeated my words: "She cooked for you and your father, took care of your house. Maybe she'd be interested in cooking for you and me, taking care of our house." He turned to Vivian. "We can't afford to pay you much, but we'll give you room and board. You'll have your own room on the fourth floor."

"I'm sure she wouldn't be interested, Monsignor."

Vivian stood and shook the hand of the Monsignor for the second time. "I'll take the job," she said. "And I'll feed you well."

CHAPTER 23

When Monsignor left my office, I turned to Vivian and said, "Were you joking when you told my pastor you'd take the housekeeping job in this rectory?"

Vivian's eyebrows arched. "Did I sound as if I were joking?"

"No, you didn't. That's what worries me."

Vivian threw one shapely leg over the other. "All I did was follow your advice."

"My advice? How can you make such a statement?"

"Didn't you advise me to move out of the Trump Towers, find another place to live?"

"Yes, but I didn't advise you to move here."

"You didn't think of it but I did. Two heads are better than one. This rectory is a perfect place to hide. Mario and his thug friends won't find me here."

"Don't be to sure of yourself. Thugs have city-wide and world-wide connections."

Vivian spoke quickly. "They don't go near a rectory or a church. Not unless their babies are being baptized, or a daughter is getting married, or one of them has been murdered. Chances are they'll go to another church. This church of yours is small for big time racketeers."

"We have our share of racketeers in the Bronx," I declared.

"I admit they're everywhere. But, as I've mentioned, they don't hang around a rectory or a small church."

She made other arguments and counter arguments to every idea I presented. When I failed to agree with her, she surprised me by saying,

"Monsignor will be interested in learning his young assistant was once in bed with me."

"You wouldn't tell him…"

"Wouldn't I?"

She would. Alarmed, I gave in to her decision to live in the rectory. Rationalizing my position, I'd more to gain than lose. Not only did I want to protect her from the thugs who were looking for her, I wanted to learn where Togallini's paintings were hidden. I intended to destroy them. If I couldn't destroy them, I'd bury them in a hole so deep no one would ever find them or view them again. "Okay, Vivian," I said after thinking about it. "You're our new housekeeper. That means you must learn to take orders from me. I'm second in command around here. Your first order is this: Give me your keys."

Her mouth dropped open in wonder. "You want the keys to my apartment?"

"I want the keys to your car."

"Why the keys to my car? You going out for a joy ride?"

"I'm going to store your car in a garage. I know a garage owner about ten blocks away. He'll take care of the car for you."

Vivian dangled the keys before my nose. "Tell him to bill me at the rectory. I'll pay him on a monthly basis."

Since I was accustomed to driving an old Ford Fairlane, I wasn't sure if I could handle the Rolls Royce, so I asked Vivian, "Is there anything I should know about the Rolls?"

"It cost a lot of money."

"I know that. I'm asking if there are any gadgets I wouldn't find on an old Ford Fairlane?"

"About three hundred."

I grabbed her arm, led her to the door. "You'll have to explain them to me if I'm to drive your car."

Opening the rectory door, I saw an open space where the Rolls Royce was parked. Stupefied, I gasped, "The Rolls Royce, your car is gone. Stolen!"

Vivian took the loss by pulling herself loose from my grasp. She headed back into the rectory without saying a word.

I closed the door and followed her. "Don't you realize someone has stolen your magnificent automobile?"

"To hell with it," she said.

I couldn't believe my ears. The Rolls Royce was worth more than the rectory, yet she wasn't concerned about it. Maybe she was right. If the police and her insurance company were notified, the news media and Mario Togallini would also be notified and Vivian's hideout would become common knowledge. Her decision was correct, better than mine.

She was opening and closing doors, finally found the one she was looking for. She entered the kitchen and immediately went to the refrigerator, inspected its contents. "Not bad," she muttered. "This fridge is pretty well stocked."

"It is," I said. "We've a generous butcher and grocer in the parish. They anticipate our needs; send us the best they have to offer each week. They save us the shopping chore, as well as a considerable amount of money. We buy at cost."

She nodded approvingly and spoke as if she were the head of the house. "We must have them in for dinner some night."

I was amazed at how quickly she'd forgotten the theft of her Rolls Royce, thinking how I mumbled and grumbled when someone stole a hubcap from my Ford Fairlane.

She pointed to an old rocking chair, one imported into the rectory by the housekeeper now in Ireland. "Tommy, if you'll sit in that rocker and tell me where I can find the pots and pans and anything else I might need, I'll prepare dinner."

"You'll prepare dinner?"

"Of course I'll prepare dinner. Dinner is part of my new job. Remember?"

"We don't expect you to prepare dinner the first evening you're here. I'll phone for pizza…"

Demon of Lust

"No, you won't," she stated firmly. "I'm going to prepare dinner for the Monsignor, you and me. We're going to celebrate my new job. I'm happy to be here!"

She looked happy as she went about preparing three steaks that I'd been nursing along for a special occasion. I recalled her proficiency, how quickly she worked...no lost motion.

She was truly a thing of beauty. A masterpiece created by God. As I watched her work, I wondered if I were committing a sin being in love with her. I'd asked myself that same question many times when I was in the seminary. The answer I usually came up with was no! Not as long as I failed to yield to the temptation of making love with her...not as long as I kept my hands off her. Besides, God wanted us to love all human beings.

The dinner that evening proved to be an event worth remembering. The Monsignor sat at the head of the table; simply delighted at the attention Vivian gave him. He enjoyed every dish she prepared. His compliments were numerous. "You prepare lavish dishes," he said on one occasion. I can well imagine you've toiled in some of the best restaurants in New York City, observed the chefs at work. You've learned your trade well."

Vivian smiled at the compliment. "I've never worked in a restaurant, Monsignor, but I have eaten in some excellent ones. I've also collected recipes that struck my fancy. I'll be trying them out on you from time to time."

He smiled. "I'll look forward to them."

Vivian served the Monsignor and me a large steak. She then sat down beside him and served herself a larger steak, dropping gravy on the tablecloth in the process. The pastor appeared surprised.

In the history of the Church, as far as I knew, no housekeeper ever sat down at a dinner table with a pastor. I figured her days in the rectory were numbered. No, her hours were numbered.

"Pass the potatoes," she said to the Monsignor.

Unable to think of anything to say to help her, I studied the face of the pastor, expecting him to explode any minute. I knew he was a traditionalist and the former head of a major seminary, where strict discipline was observed. He was accustomed to having those under his supervision toe the line.

Unaware of her faux pas, Vivian stared into the face of the pastor and repeated, "Pass the potatoes."

The normally reserved countenance of the pastor suddenly relaxed, he smiled and passed the potatoes. Then he laughed, softly at first, then uncontrollably loud. He exposed gold-capped molar teeth I didn't know he had. The laugh continued for three, four, maybe five minutes, while tears ran down his face. Finally, he was able to control his laughter. Wiping away tears with a napkin, he said, "Please forgive me for laughing."

Vivian responded quickly. "We'll forgive you if you'll tell us what's so funny."

"Oh, I can't..."

"Oh, yes you can," she insisted.

"No, I'm sorry."

Vivian raised a finger. "You needn't tell us, Monsignor. I know why you laughed. You thought of something funny and you just laughed. That's the reason! And that's a sign of a healthy, uninhibited mind. I've had the experience. I once broke out laughing in church. The priest was talking to a congregation of senior citizens, whose sex lives were nothing more than a dim memory. He stopped talking and looked at me. I'm sure he thought I was laughing about the subject he'd selected for the seniors, but I wasn't. I was thinking of something else that struck me funny."

I saw him smile and close his eyes. He enjoyed having Vivian at the table. I was glad. Whenever possible, authorities in the Church relax rules that make no sense in today's world. Would the rules ever be relaxed to the extent a priest could marry? I doubted it. Priests were soldiers of God, called upon to make sacrifices. Their motto: No pain, no gain. Christ had thorns on His head. In a sense, so did I. Christ survived, rose to glory. Would I survive?

Demon of Lust

The dessert was ice cream, topped with chocolate syrup, a combination that put the finishing touches on an excellent meal. The pastor ate the last morsel of food on his plate and stated, "The best dinner I've had in months."

"Thank you, Monsignor," Vivian said, blushing like a schoolgirl.

The Monsignor announced he'd retire to his quarters, say his office, watch the news on his television set, spend an hour in contemplative prayer, and then go to bed. "I should sleep well after having such a wonderful dinner."

Vivian gave him a warm smile, thanked him again.

He turned to me. "Have you any plans for the evening?"

I glanced at my watch. "Seven o'clock. A little early for me to go to my room. I'll help Vivian with the dishes, show her where she'll sleep, and then I'll follow your program: say my office, watch the news, pray...."

The pastor remarked to Vivian. "I consider myself fortunate having Father Tom with me. He and I think alike. We both recognize the power of prayer."

Vivian stammered, "I pray too, Monsignor. I say a Hail Mary every night before going to sleep. I try to be a good Catholic, but I'm not as good as I'd like to be."

"None of us are," the pastor responded, turning and leaving the room.

I could hear him on the stairs, climbing them slowly, painfully. Each stair was an effort for him.

"I like that man," Vivian said when the pastor could no longer hear her.

I spoke earnestly. "He's a very good person, has accomplished a great deal; but he's slowed down considerably because of a weak heart. We must do all we can to help him, never do anything that'd cause him concern."

Vivian sounded impertinent. "What could we possibly do to cause him concern?"

I didn't answer. I merely enumerated a number of things in my head that'd cause him concern.

"Well," Vivian said, after several moments of silence, "are you going to help me with the dishes?"

"I'll help you."

There was no dishwasher in the rectory. Every dish had to be done by hand. I didn't mind. I enjoyed working with Vivian despite the fact she worked so fast it was all I could do to keep up with her. She washed and I dried. We both put the dishes, the pots and pans away. A sense of disappointment ran through me when the job was finished.

Vivian expressed my sentiments precisely by saying, "I enjoyed working with you."

I knew the truth of my words: "And I with you. Now I must show you to your room."

Her room was on the fourth floor. It was small with a high ceiling, flowered wallpaper in vogue about forty years ago, a chest of drawers, a single wooden chair without a cushion, a black and white TV, an iron bed that squeaked whenever it was used, and green linoleum that matched nothing in the room.

She was puffing less than I when we reached it. After climbing the stairs, I expected her to say what other stair climbers have said: "You need an elevator in this rectory."

She took in the room with a glance. Her only question: "Where do you sleep?"

"I'm on the third floor, directly under this room."

"Do you have a big bed?"

"It's big enough for me."

"But not for me. Is that the idea?"

"Vivian, you wouldn't be here if your life weren't in danger. And even though it is, I'm not sure if this arrangement is going to work out. Just remember, I'm a priest, and I intend to be one for the rest of my life. Say your Hail Mary and go to bed."

"It's too early to go to bed."

"Not for anyone who lives in a rectory. Our first Mass is six o'clock. The coffee should be perking at four-thirty."

"Four-thirty! I very often get home at that time."

Demon of Lust

"Four-thirty? Curfew time in this rectory is midnight."

Opening the door to my bedroom, I had to smile. I'd the last word with Vivian, a remarkable achievement. I picked up my breviary, read it for a half hour or more, and put it down. I couldn't recall a single passage I'd read. My mind would concentrate on nothing but Vivian, the paintings she'd stolen, and her love for me.

I turned on my television set, tried concentrating on the news. Violence and sex dominated the airwaves. The Haitians were killing one another; the Chinese were shooting their own people; an occupied federal building in the United States was car-bombed; an actress, married and divorced eight times, slit the throat of her lover because he was unfaithful; an elderly Congressman raped a teenager; a married couple had sex changes; the budget for condoms in the local schools was being increased.

The news was so depressing; I turned off the television set. Vivian was right about one thing. I worried about the world. I couldn't help it. There was too much sex and violence in our society. I wanted to do something about it. But what could I do? What can any one man do?

I'd asked myself that question before. There was only one answer. Each of us, regardless of our position in life, must realize there are forces of good and evil in the world. Forces led by God and forces led by the devil. From the beginning of time, a battle has taken place between God and the devil. We must be on God's side...set a good example for others; do everything possible to minimize evil.

I prayed for an hour before going to bed, felt relaxed when I dozed off. I'd slept less than forty minutes when I saw myself, as a seventeen-year-old boy, naked in bed with Vivian.

I knew I was having a nightmare created by Isacaron, the Demon of Sex. He punished me for attempting to destroy Togallini's paintings. Punished me for becoming a priest. For the past nine years, he made my life miserable.

The demon had access to my memory, used it as a movie screen to reflect vivid images of a naked Vivian in my arms. How I prayed he'd stop reminding me of sins I wanted to forget.

I opened my eyes, sat up in bed, and stared into the blackness of the room. As a priest, I felt it was my duty to face the demon without fear. Nevertheless, I trembled. A cold sweat ran down my back.

Why should I be afraid? The demon could defeat me, that's why. There were nights when I'd get down on my knees, beg God to erase all sins from my memory. There were other nights when I wanted to repeat my sins. God, forgive me for thinking that. Fornication is like a drug. It gives a user a happy high; eventually it drags him down into the deepest pit in hell.

There was a period in my life when I didn't believe in a hell, run by Satan and legions of demons that roam the world seeking the destruction of souls. I was a pick-and-choose Catholic, believing some things taught by the Church, disbelieving others. Belief in hell was ridiculous, I thought.

But that was before I met the artist Togallini, his model Vivian, and the demon Isacaron. That was before I attempted to interfere with Isacaron's work. I tried to destroy the paintings he inspired....

"Don't ever try it again." The voice came out of the darkness, startling me. It was a voice I'd heard before...a voice representing all nationalities, all cultures.

I did my best to keep my own voice under control. "Is that you, Isacaron?"

"You know who it is?"

"I know you're the one who disturbs my sleep at night."

"More than your sleep will be disturbed if you attempt to destroy the Togallini's paintings."

"I don't know where they are."

"Find them and you find trouble. Enjoy yourself with Vivian. She won't be here indefinitely."

"Did you bring her here?"

There was no answer. I waited several minutes for Isacaron to respond. I heard nothing but a bird chirping outside my window. Switching on a lamp, I saw the room empty. My heart hammered on my ribs.

CHAPTER 24

Vivian was nowhere to be found when I arrived in the kitchen at 4:30 a.m. I'd plenty of time to prepare for the six o'clock Mass. Coffee at 4:15 wasn't important. It was just a bad habit, nothing more. Vivian's rest was more important. At least, she thought so.

I offered my Mass for her, assuring God I'd no plans to share my life with her. Nevertheless I wanted her to be safe and happy, successful in making her own way in life without financial help from Mario. Perhaps she could find some decent fellow who'd marry her, give her a home.

As I gave out Holy Communion at the end of the Mass, I've realized there were few people in church. The numbers were dwindling with each passing year. Vocations for priests and nuns were also down. I was convinced the demons roaming the world had something to do with it.

Returning to my room, I spent an hour in meditation, or silent prayer, opening up my mind so God would talk to me. God knows every idea ever conceived, yet he whispered only two words to me: "Be careful!"

Be careful of what? Was I being warned about Mario Togallini? Was Mario a threat to those of us who lived in the rectory? God knows I love Vivian. Was He concerned about my soul, think I'd choose her over Him?

No, I wouldn't. If a priest doesn't have enough character to avoid the temptations dangled before him, he doesn't deserve to be a priest. And he certainly doesn't deserve an eternal reward. Such is the theory. Theory and practice sometimes collide. God tells us what to do. Demons tell us to do the opposite.

Vivian was frying bacon and eggs when I entered the kitchen. Grease suddenly spattered from the pan and struck her arm and skirt. Her voice could be heard on the fourth floor of the rectory. "Damn!"

"Did you burn yourself," I asked sympathetically.

"I did," she said, blowing on a red spot on her wrist. "I don't care so much about the burn. It'll heal. But look at my one and only skirt. It's ruined."

I examined an ugly grease stain on her skirt. "I'll buy you a new skirt, Vivian. I've ten dollars."

"Ten dollars won't do it. But don't worry. I've money. I'll buy the clothes I need. Of course, I could return to the Trump Towers…"

I felt my own panic. "Oh, no! Don't go back there."

"I won't if you think it's dangerous. If I go shopping, however, I'll need a car. Where can I rent one?"

"It's best you don't rent or leave your name and address anywhere. Use my Ford Fairlane. It's a station wagon."

"Shift or automatic?"

"Automatic?"

"I can drive it then."

She served breakfast to the pastor, herself, and me. Despite the accident at the stove, breakfast was a success. The pastor enjoyed her company and said he liked the way she prepared the bacon.

She beamed. "I won't be serving you bacon every morning, Monsignor. It's bad for the cholesterol. However, on special occasions, bacon is okay. Makes a nice treat."

He nodded his head in agreement and smiled.

I knew he had unwavering philosophical beliefs, but beliefs regarding cholesterol? It appeared he'd let Vivian decide for him.

After eating breakfast and washing the dishes, I showed Vivian how to operate the Ford Fairlane, which had long ago passed the age of a normal retirement. Vivian took my instructions graciously, did me the favor of not comparing my Ford Fairlane with her Rolls Royce.

Demon of Lust

She asked only one question about the Fairlane. "Did you pay much money for this car?"

"It was a gift from one of the parishioners. He had trouble selling it, decided to give it to me. It was a tax deduction for him."

"That parishioner deserves to be audited by the IRS." Smiling, she put the car in drive, waved goodbye and drove away.

As the car disappeared from sight, I realized I should have asked her to drop me off at the high school, where I taught Religion once a week. The school was ten blocks away. The walk would afford me the opportunity to think of something to say in class.

I enjoyed the students in my class. They were Hispanics, Blacks, Chinese, Polish, Japanese, Russians, Whites, and a mixture of nationalities that no genealogist in New York could figure out.

When Christ said, "Go forth and teach all nations," He made the task easy for priests stationed in the Bronx, because the people from all nations came to the Bronx to be taught. Teaching them wasn't always easy but always worth the effort. They were God's children, the least of the little ones. I did all I could to drive a few ideas into their heads.

Upon entering the class, the students greeted me with a "Good mornin', Padre."

I responded with a "Good morning, Scholars." This prompted a few chuckles.

While I was trying to think of a good opening for my talk, a small, dark-skinned Puerto Rican raised his hand.

"Yes, Jose."

"How come we don't get free condoms in dis school?"

"Because we want to protect you…"

"Dat's what the condoms are for, Padre. Dey protects ya. Ya should know dat."

"They don't protect your soul. If you want to live a life based on intelligence, you'll protect your soul as well as your body. You do this by avoiding fornication, with or without a condom. Your soul is more important than your body."

An emaciated black boy in the front row asked, "Why's it mo' impo'-tant?"

"Because your body is a temporary thing that'll someday turn to dust. Your soul will live forever."

"We don't have to worry about our bodies then?" a white boy asked.

"You certainly do! Your bodies are a gift from God. The instant God creates a body; he creates a soul to give it life. The fact that you can wiggle a finger indicates the presence of life. When your soul leaves your body, you die."

"I've seen a dead man," one boy said solemnly. "He was shot through the neck, died with his eyes open."

A Cuban with dark circles under his cold black eyes stood, said, "He's talkin' about Senor Roberto. He raped Marie Angelina, got her pregnant. She jumped in front of a subway train. Cut to pieces. Her father killed Roberto. Tell us, Padre, is Senor Roberto burnin' in hell this mornin'?"

I pushed out the words, "I wouldn't know…"

The Cuban spoke in anger. "Why wouldn't ya know? He raped Marie. She killed herself…her baby died. Maybe her padre's gonna die for murderin' the bastard."

I disliked the Cuban's choice of words, but decided not to call him down for it. Another time, perhaps. I spoke gently, "I wouldn't know because I'm not allowed to judge another soul. God decides who goes to hell, who goes to heaven. He sees all angles, knows all the facts in every case. His judgment is infallible. Mine isn't and neither is yours."

The Cuban was persistent. "Ya think that makes sense?"

"Yes, I do. God gives us every opportunity to save our souls. Regardless of the crime we commit, we can be saved if we are truly sorry for our sins and ask God to forgive us. That man Roberto committed a heinous crime. We don't know if he was truly sorry for his crime, asked God to forgive him. We don't know his mental state when he raped the girl. Our knowledge is limited. That's why we can't judge...."

This statement brought on a heated discussion among the students. The discussion lasted till the bell rang, ending class.

Returning to the rectory, I went to my room. A convert had given me a copy of the new Catechism of the Catholic Church. I felt duty-bound to read it. The text was far more complex than the Catechism I studied as a boy. Nevertheless, I read about two hundred pages before my mind wandered. I began to think of Vivian.

When I knew her nine years ago, she'd little money for clothes. On special occasions, my father gave her money to buy a dress. I was always the first one to see it on her. She'd model it for me. She could model a dress better than any woman who ever lived. I wanted her to look her best. I thought God wanted her to look her best, too. After all, God created her. He must have been proud of the remarkable job He had done on her.

I heard her on the stairs, breathing hard. She was carrying clothes, I thought. She probably bought quite a few. She was struggling with the load...tripping, bumping into the wall, and cursing.

Leaving my room, I approached the stairs and saw her carrying an object wrapped in bed sheets. The object was approximately six feet long, four feet wide, and four inches thick.

She was halfway up the last flight of stairs when I called to her. "Vivian, do you need help?"

She paused momentarily on the stairs. "No, thank you."

I ran up the stairs, grabbed the lower section of the object she was carrying. "I don't mind helping...." My words were cut short by a strange vibrating sensation in my hands. The sensation emanated from the object we were carrying. It traveled to an area near my crotch. "What have you brought into this rectory?"

We were at the top of the stairs, the fourth landing, when Vivian answered: "Nothing."

Irritated, I snapped, "How can you say nothing?"

She pulled the object from my hands, carried it to her room. "I mean nothing important."

Nothing important? No! I knew what she had. She had a Togallini's painting. A painting inspired by a demon. "How could you bring that thing into this rectory?"

"I couldn't leave it in the apartment, take a chance on losing it. If Mario Togallini finds the other paintings, he won't find this one. Not if it's close to me. I love this painting. You'll love it, too. Look!"

Before I could stop her, she removed the sheets covering the painting. It was a masterpiece. A beautiful picture of Vivian. She was stark naked and glared defiantly at me. A picture painted by Togallini, the artist who'd rented the attic apartment from my father when I was a boy. A picture inspired by the demon Isacaron. It was a painting with the power to turn virtuous men's thoughts to sins of the flesh.

"Isn't it beautiful" Vivian whispered.

"It is," I heard myself say, knowing I should not be looking at a painting inspired by a demon from hell; especially now when I felt passion stronger than ever before. My body began to burn. I'd a great desire to throw Vivian down on the bed, have sex with her.

Vivian's voice was gentle, soothing. "You remember the first time you viewed one of Togallini's paintings? You came running to me. We made love."

"I remember."

"What a wonderful, noble, unforgettable experience that was."

I wanted to agree with her, say I'd never forget it. Instead, I stared at the intoxicating face in the painting, realizing the expression had changed. The woman in the painting seemed to be waiting for me to respond to Vivian's remarks…her invitation. She wanted me to undress, crush Vivian's body against mine, and satisfy the passion that had been ignited in my body. Wasn't this the natural thing to do?

Closing my eyes, I tried to eradicate from my mind the beautiful face, the beautiful body, before me. I couldn't. Every detail in the painting was stamped on my memory. The heat in my body intensified.

Vivian's voice came as a whisper, "Tommy, would you like to…"

"No. No! Yes! Yes, I'd love to. But I can't."

Although my legs were weak, I somehow summoned enough strength to run through the door, take the stairs three at a time, enter my bedroom, fall on my knees, and focus my attention on the crucifix above my bed. "An Act of Contrition. 0h, my God, I'm heartily sorry for having offended you. I detest all my sins because I dread the loss of heaven, the pains of hell; but, most of all, because they offend you…"

CHAPTER 25

Prayer is man's best defense against sin. But as I prayed, I wasn't sure my prayers were being heard. I'd difficulty asking God to help me control my passions, while I kept asking myself what I could do about the painting Vivian brought into the rectory.

Vivian also distracted me on the stairs. She made several trips. I concluded she was carrying the clothes she'd purchased from the Fairlane to her room. I couldn't object to her bringing clothes into the rectory.

My objection was her painting, the devastating effect it had on me. Bringing the painting into the rectory was tantamount to bringing the demon Isacaron into a home for priests. But wasn't he here before the painting arrived? He often spoke to me while I slept. His ideas carried over into my waking hours. His ideas never caused me to sin as a priest.

Was it possible he brought Vivian and the painting into the rectory to assist him in destroying my soul? The idea brought sweat to my brow. I loved Vivian and she loved me. Why would she join forces with the devil's disciple? She wasn't aware of what she was doing. Not unless she wanted me to go to hell.

Vivian sought happiness on a road devoid of the God who created her. She moved from one wrong road to another, failing to think of her ultimate destination. It was up to me to put her back on the right road. But she wouldn't listen to me. She thinks I'm preaching. Nevertheless, I must try.

I descended the stairs, heard her in the kitchen. Opening the door, I saw she was preparing dinner. My mind became a jumble of ideas. Could I extract one idea from the jumble to open a delicate subject? "Vivian, I…"

Demon of Lust

"Care for some raisins?" she asked. "They're delicious."

"No, thanks..."

"They won't spoil your dinner."

"Vivian, the painting in your room, all the other paintings you've taken from Mario Togallini, we have to decide what to do with them."

"I've already decided. I'm going to sell the ones I have in the apartment, keep the one I have in my room. I'm going to make a lot of money."

"I've told you before, the paintings are evil."

Tossing several raisings into her mouth, she said, "If money is the root of all evil, then I'll agree with you. The paintings are evil."

Her remark frustrated me. "It's not the money. It's your immortal soul...and mine."

"Oh, come now, Father," she said impatiently. "You promised not to preach to me."

"I know. All I'm trying to do now is convince you the painting you have in your room, and the other paintings you're hiding, were inspired by a demon called Isacaron. He'll destroy you if you aren't careful."

Vivian wiped her hands on a towel. Her face suddenly hardened. She threw the towel into the sink with force. Her voice became loud, irritating: "What the hell's the matter with you? You become a priest and you see devils and demons everywhere you look."

"I don't see them, but I know they exist. I know they can influence your thinking, your passions, your actions, and your dealings with me. All the experiences we had nine years ago in Togallini's apartment should have convinced you that demons do exist."

Vivian pointed a finger at me. "Demons are figments of your imagination. Figments of Togallini's imagination before he died. On his deathbed, he was afraid of going to hell because he painted sexy, nude women. He was out of his mind."

"He wasn't out of his mind. He wanted his paintings destroyed. That was an act of intelligence. I promised him I'd destroy them."

"Tommy, please! How can you talk about destroying paintings worth a fortune? You know I love you dearly. Do you want me to believe the man I love is a fool?"

For more than an instant, she looked a little foolish herself. What could I say to convince her? I tried this: "We need not go back nine years to know what a demon can do. A while ago, this very afternoon, when you pulled the sheets away from your painting, I'd an almost uncontrollable desire to throw you on the bed, make love with you."

"Why didn't you do it? I wouldn't have screamed rape."

"I didn't do it because Isacaron used the painting to fill my body with lust. If I'd sex with you, I'd have succumbed to the demon's temptation."

"You admitting my painting had you all charged up?" she asked, as if she were a student interested in solving a difficult problem.

"Precisely that. You're a beautiful woman, Vivian. I've the same instincts as any man attracted to beauty. But I'm a priest, which means my intellect must always take precedence over my instincts."

Laughing, she tapped my chest. "That's really funny, Father. Why would God give you instincts that tell you to take me in your arms, and an intellect that tells you not to do it?"

Vivian asked a legitimate question. "Well, as I see it, God wants our journey through life to have a few obstacles. We not only have to deal with outside forces, such as demons, peers, and environment, we have to deal with ourselves. You knew my father before he died…"

Without a moments reflection, she said, "I knew him well. He was a first class bastard."

"May God have mercy on his soul," I said, hoping Vivian would have no more derogatory remarks to say about my father. "I'll admit my father had his faults…sinned. You never met my mother. She was a saint. Now here I am, the offspring of a sinner and a saint. Is it any wonder I experience a constant tug-of-war?"

"A tug-of-war between good and evil?"

Demon of Lust

"Yes, and that's the way God wants me to live my life. He wants me to combat evil, embrace that which is good."

"Of course, I know you're a priest. I didn't know you're so damned religious, Tommy Boy."

"Not as religious as I'd like to be. Life is rough on the religious. All priests, nuns, ministers, rabbis…regardless of whether they're Catholic, Protestant, or Jew…are targets for Satan. He'd rather snare a religious leader than anyone else. I'm aware of this, Vivian. I need your help."

She seemed surprised. "How the hell can I help you?"

"By behaving yourself."

A smile crossed her luscious lips. "I'm the most behaved girl in this rectory."

She had a way of making me feel helpless. While I was trying to pull her up and out of a quagmire of sin, she was pulling me down. I've studied every branch of Philosophy; I should be able to think of some argument….

Suddenly she asked, "Do you still like apple pie?"

"I do."

"Well, I'm going to make you one. An apple pie with raisins. You'll love it. The pastor will love it, too."

And we did. The dinner that night ended with coffee and apple pie. The pastor put a question to me after finishing his second piece of pie. "How can young women like Vivian know more about baking pies than an old lady like Marie, our Irish housekeeper?"

I searched my mind for a proper response. "She knows much more than you can imagine, Monsignor."

He was pleased with my answer and didn't press me for details.

I heard the doorbell ring.

Vivian had her hands full of soiled dishes, so I called to her. "Don't worry about the door. I'll answer it."

She called back to me, "Don't attempt to do any counseling at this hour. You have dishes to dry."

Opening the door, I was fully unprepared to meet the three men standing there before me. I thought they were from a local funeral parlor, for all were dressed in black. The two men flanking the man in the middle were enormous, big enough to play football with the New York Giants.

They stared at me with cold black eyes and expressions as motionless as a tombstone. I felt vulnerable...frightened. The men had a sense of death about them.

"Hello, Tommy," said the man in the middle. He was much shorter than his companions. His greeting was cold, threatening.

"It's you! You, Mr. Togallini," I said, gasping out the words, wondering what I could say to a member of the Mafia.

"It's me, all right. Mario Togallini. I'm surprised you remembered my name."

"You look so much like your dead brother."

Annoyance showed on the swarthy face of the king of pornographic sales. "You mean to say I look like a skeleton? My brother's been dead for nine years. You gotta know he's a skeleton now."

"Oh, no! Of course not. I just couldn't help but associate you with your brother. I liked him. I knew him well."

"I know you knew him. That's why I'm here. I wanna talk to you." He turned to the two thugs who accompanied him. "You guys wait for me on the doorstep. Don't let anyone in this joint till my meetin' is over."

He then pushed me aside and opened the first door he came to... the pastor's office. With his index finger, he beckoned me into the office. "I wanna talk business with you."

"What kind of business?"

"The business of making money. You help me. I'll help you."

"I don't need any help."

He shook his head in disgust. "Maybe you don't, but this old house needs help. Look at the threadbare carpet, the crappy wallpaper, and the old furniture. This joint could collapse any time a taxicab rumbles by. You could be killed."

Demon of Lust

The rectory needs renovating, I thought. That doesn't mean I'll accept funds from anyone who makes his money in the pornographic business. I tried to show my annoyance with a question: "Did you come here this evening to tell me the rectory is in need of renovating?"

He shook his head and prefaced his remarks with a foul word. "I don't give a damn about this rectory. I mentioned money to get you to answer a few questions."

"What sort of questions?"

"I'd like to know if Vivian ever got in touch with you when you was in the cemetery, studyin' to become a Holy Joe."

"No, she didn't."

"That's strange. She used to talk about you once in a while. Told me you weren't interested in women. All you wanted to do was become a Holy Joe. She later told me you made the grade."

"Nothing strange about her talking about me. We were good friends."

"I know you was. I also know there's a damn good possibility she'd get in touch with you when she's in trouble."

"Is she in trouble?"

At this moment, Vivian was in the kitchen at the rear of the house. Mario and I were in the front of the house. Nevertheless, we could hear her voice: "Oh, Holy Night, the stars are brightly shining..."

I didn't know what to do. I couldn't rush to the kitchen; tell her that Mario Togallini was in the pastor's office. Moreover, he had two thugs at the front door, anxious to take her to some remote spot in the Bronx and apply a blowtorch to her face.

"It is the night of the dear Savior's birth..."

Mario's face took on an inquisitive look as he listened to the song. He finally asked, "Who's that singin'?"

I wanted to lie but I couldn't. "Our housekeeper."

"What a lousy voice," he said, opening his mouth and making a vomiting sound.

"At times, that voice drives me nuts."

"I can't listen to somebody singin' who can't sing," Mario said as if he were imparting important information to me. "I like good voices, like Sinatra's, Madonna's, the leadin' rap singers. If my wife, or any of the kids, starts to sing when I'm home, I teach them a lesson."

"What do you do?" I inquired.

"I give 'em a kick in the ass."

Evidently Vivian, fearful of being kicked in the rear, never attempted to sing when she was with Mario. He didn't recognize her singing voice. For that I was grateful.

I closed the door. Barely audible was, "Long lay the world in sin and sorrow..."

Thanks for shutting out that racket, Mario said. "Your housekeeper's lucky she don't work for me. Now we can get down to business."

"What sort of business?"

"The business of what you're gonna do if Vivian calls you, asks for help."

"And what is that?"

Mario's eyes were like the eyes of a serpent peering at me. "If she calls you, I expect you to call me, let me know where she's stayin'."

"I can't do that."

"You'll do it if you don't want this rectory wrecked. I can have it reduced to a pile of bricks, dirt, dust and prayer books."

Mario's threat was given so casually, I could hardly believe he was serious. "You wouldn't bomb this rectory, kill the priests who occupy it?"

His grin was humorless. "Priests are passé today. Nobody will miss 'em."

"Priests are out and pornography is in. Is that what you want me to believe?"

His face flushed with anger. "I want you to believe I'm not foolin' around. If you cooperate with Vivian and don't cooperate with me, you're in trouble."

"I'll remember the warning."

"You better. And now I've gotta go. I've wasted enough time 'round here." He opened the office door.

As he did so, Vivian's voice could be heard coming from the kitchen: "The weary world rejoices...."

The singing seemed to give Mario Togallini added impetus to rush for the front door. He opened it and was gone.

CHAPTER 26

I didn't realize sweat was running down my back until Mario Togallini slammed the door behind him. Nor did I understand why he failed to recognize Vivian's voice. True, he admitted disliking the singing voices of amateurs, but there must have been something in Vivian's voice to raise his curiosity; bring him back into the kitchen.

It's a miracle, I thought. If Vivian had selected a popular song instead of *Oh, Holy Night*, she'd have been dragged out of the rectory, tortured, and killed. But God, in his infinite mercy, had protected her, because she selected a song honoring the birth of Christ.

Could I be sure of this? Well, pretty sure. Not absolutely sure. God generally allows men and women to kill one another if they are disposed to do so. God's gift of free will to mankind can be a curse as well as a blessing.

I told Vivian about Mario Togallini's visit to the rectory with two thugs and his threat to bomb the place if I helped her.

She turned white, began to cry. "I'll have to leave," she said. "I can't put your life and the pastor's life in danger." She looked desperate.

She reminded me of my first encounter with her. I was a boy. She was hungry and homeless. My heart went out to her then. My heart went out to her again. She needed help. "Vivian, let's not make any hasty decisions now. Stay here until we can locate a safe place for you."

"Thank you, Father."

She was calling me *Father* again. I wish she'd look upon me as a father, trust my judgment. "Vivian, your troubles now…your troubles in the past...stem from Togallini's paintings. They're evil. They should be destroyed."

She furrowed her brow. "Please don't get on that track again. My painting is a wonderful work of art. All the other paintings are great works of art. When you say they should be destroyed, you pour hot coals on my head; add to my worries. You don't seem to remember I've Mario Togallini to worry about."

"You wouldn't have to worry about him if it weren't for the paintings."

Tears welled up in her eyes. She threw a dishcloth into my face, ran from the kitchen. I heard her on the stairs...heard her bedroom door slam.

I picked up the dishcloth, finished drying the dishes. After putting them away, I considered counseling her. She couldn't expect to solve her problems by running away. No use. She wouldn't agree with me. Why was it so difficult for men and women to agree on issues, regardless of whether they're simple or complex?

Why were reasonable people constantly at odds with one another? Why were educated people declaring war against one another? Shooting wars were ridiculous. An elderly leader disagrees with another elderly leader. They settle the dispute by having young people fight and die.

Feeling frustrated, I went to my room and picked up a copy of the Bible. Flipping through it, I read passages relating to Eve tempting Adam in the garden of Eden; Mary Magdalene, in her role as a prostitute; and Mary, the mother of Christ, exemplified as the queen of virtue. Women are the world's rudders, I thought. They steer men into doing that which is right, or that which is wrong.

Hearing Vivian on the stairs, I felt compelled to talk with her. I met her as she reached the bottom step of the third floor. She was wearing one of her new dresses...a red one. Her beauty was breath taking.

"You look as if you're going out," I said awkwardly.

"I look that way because that's what I'm going to do."

"Where do you intend to go?"

"Some bar. I'd like to have a few drinks, do a little dancing."

I looked at my watch. "Eleven-thirty. It's late."

"Not for me."

"It's late for any young woman to walk the streets without an escort."

"You want to come along with me?"

"I can't. I'm known in this neighborhood."

"We'll go to another neighborhood."

"I'm sorry, Vivian." I handed her the keys to my Ford Fairlane. "If you insist on going out, take my car."

She shook her head. "I prefer to walk."

"Please don't go out tonight."

She stared at me hard. "I won't go out if you invite me into your room. We can talk."

At the thought of bringing her into my room, my body filled with a hot passion. She was the woman I loved. "I'm sorry. I can't invite you to my room."

She shrugged and moved towards the next flight of stairs, was halfway down when I called to her. "Vivian, will you take the keys to my car?"

"No, thank you." Seconds later I heard her opening the front door…closing it.

I ran to a front window; saw her walking down the street with her head slightly bent. She was lonely, wanted company. I was lonely, too. I wanted company. I felt sorry for her and for myself.

Instead of returning to my room, I went to her room to examine the painting. I believed it somehow prompted Vivian to leave the rectory, seek companionship.

Hoping to find the painting covered with the two sheets, I was disappointed to see it was uncovered, propped on a bureau facing the bed. Moonlight filtered through Venetian blinds, illuminating the painting of Vivian in a strange and startling way. The light focused on her body in such a manner that everything else on the canvas was left in the dark.

The Vivian on the canvas was as real as the Vivian I spoke to moments ago on the stairs. Her arms were extended as if she wanted to embrace me.

Demon of Lust

Her smile was warm, seductive; her naked body, enchanting. She appeared to be alive!

Passion raced through my body. It had my blood boiling, my mind reeling. From past experience, I knew the woman in the painting was possessed by the demon Isacaron. Momentarily, I didn't care. Sexual passion destroys the mind...the body...the soul.

I told myself I was a priest and should resist the force pulling me towards the naked woman in the painting. I couldn't resist the force. But I had to! I had to get my eyes off the woman. Turning away, I focused on a table in the room. It contained lipstick, dusting powder, skin lotion, scissors, soap...a bottle of holy water. The Irish housekeeper used to sprinkle holy water on her plants to make them grow.

Grabbing the scissors, I threw them as hard as I could at the face of the woman. The throw was accurate. The point of the scissors was moving towards Vivian's face when suddenly, defying all laws of physics, the scissors veered up and over the painting. It struck the wall, chipped the plaster.

I grabbed the holy water. With all the force I could put behind it, I threw the bottle at Vivian's bosom. The bottle struck its mark, broke into a thousand pieces. Although the canvas didn't tear, a small red bruise appeared on the left breast of Vivian's bosom.

What drove me out of the room, down the stairs to my own room, was the look of surprise that appeared on the face of the woman in the painting. Not only did she appear surprised, her focus changed from me to her breast. She examined her breast; then looked down to examine the rest of her body. Her expression changed, as if she was wearing a new dress and someone had thrown mustard on it.

I stayed awake several hours that night, hoping to hear Vivian on the stairs. I wanted to know she was home, safe. I didn't hear her. Around three o'clock in the morning, I fell asleep; dreamed the picture of Vivian was in my room, balanced on the woodwork at the bottom of my bed.

Louis V. Rohr

The beautiful woman stepped out of the painting and got into bed with me. Running her hands over my body, she whispered, "Aren't you happy you're not holding out on me any longer?"

The face and body, so close to me, was Vivian's. Every characteristic she possessed was hers; except the voice. The voice was strange, hoarse, and foreign. It was the voice of someone who represented all cultures, all nations, all periods of time.

She ran her fingers lightly over my body.

"Vivian," I shouted. "You know I'm a priest. I can't…"

It was then she began to laugh, a low mirthless, irritating laugh. The laugh made me feel like a fool. If I were to kiss her, would she stop laughing? Could I muffle the laugh by placing my mouth on hers? I'd try…

She must have been able to read my mind, for the laughter increased in intensity, volume.

It stopped when an alarm clock went off in my room. I bolted up in the bed. The nightmare was over. My pajamas were soaked with perspiration.

CHAPTER 27

My morning schedule often troubled my conscience. Before reading my breviary and saying the six o'clock Mass, I felt the need of two cups of coffee. As a result, I was up at four-fifteen in the morning to get the coffee perking. Our former housekeeper, before leaving for Ireland, always had the coffee ready for me when I entered the kitchen. "The least I can do," she'd say.

I mentioned the early rising to Vivian, but I hardly expected her to lose sleep to serve me coffee.

The coffee pot hadn't quite perked when I heard her at the kitchen door, leading to the outside of the rectory. She let herself in. Standing transfixed inside the kitchen, with glazed eyes, she stared at the coffee pot and me. Her words were slightly slurred. "I wanted to get back in time to make your coffee," she said.

"You need not be concerned about coffee for me. I much prefer seeing you get your rest."

Her eyes met mine. "You worried about my rest?"

"Of course, I am."

She seemed puzzled. "Why worry about my rest, or anything else I do?"

How could I answer her question without telling her I love her. "Sit down, Vivian, have a cup of coffee with me."

She sat down at the table and observed me pouring the coffee, the cream, and the sugar. She observed me stir her coffee and mine. Her lips cracked into a smile. She was amused because I was doing for her what she was supposed to do for me. "Why do you give a damn what I do?" she asked.

I hesitated before answering. I figured the alcohol she consumed had loosened her tongue. "You and I have been friends a long time. You were kind to me after my mother died. You protected me when my father became intolerable. He's dead now. I'm alone. I've no one truly close…"

Vivian seemed to sober quickly. No longer were her words slurred. "You had a close friend…What was his name? Father O'Donnell, wasn't it?"

Vivian's question awakened vivid memories of the priest who befriended me when I was a boy of seventeen. He tried to help me destroy Togallini's paintings. How could I forget him? He helped me become a priest. "Shortly before my ordination, he had a breakdown, was taken to a mental institution on Staten Island. He lives in a deeply depressed state. He hardly recognizes friends who knew him for years."

Vivian appeared concerned. "I remember him as a big, strong man…well balanced. What ever happened to him?"

Tears came into my eyes. "I'm not sure. He was terribly depressed; thought the devil was winning the battle between good and evil. I believe he's being tormented now by Isacaron, who is punishing him for trying to help me destroy Togallini's paintings."

Like a black cloud blocking the sunlight, Vivian's expression changed drastically. It was no longer sympathetic.

Staring at me, she was about to protest my remark about the destruction of the paintings, when I spoke in a firm voice: "Vivian, whenever Father O'Donnell sees me, his demeanor changes so drastically, I become frightened. Normally, he's in a depressed stupor; but the moment he spots me, he becomes highly excited, shouts at the top of his lungs, 'The paintings! The paintings!' he cries. The nurses and doctors, who look after him, don't welcome my visits. They say I agitate him."

Vivian's words were sharp. "Well, don't you?"

"I'm not to blame. It's Isacaron, the demon. He's torturing that poor priest. He'll never forgive him."

"I won't forgive him, either. He had you doing some crazy things…"

Demon of Lust

Raising my voice, I said, "I'll not tolerate a single word of criticism leveled at Father O'Donnell."

"All right. I won't criticize him. I'm sure he's right about most things. But he was dead wrong about the paintings."

"He wasn't wrong about the paintings."

Vivian covered her ears with her hands. "Okay! Okay! I give up. Let's talk about something else."

While my temper was getting hot, my coffee was getting cold. I threw the cold coffee into the sink and poured myself another cup. "I feel responsible for Father O'Donnell's condition. He wouldn't have known the paintings existed if I hadn't asked him to accompany me to Togallini's studio to hear his confession."

"I thought we were going to drop the subject. Why not get back to the topic you were discussing before you got off on a subject that's taboo with me? You were saying we've been friends a long time." Vivian folded her arms, waited for a response from me.

"Yes, we have been friends a long time," I said, promising myself not to lose my temper again. "I want to continue the friendship, protect you as best I can. As far as I'm concerned, we're family. You're like a sister to me."

Her eyes popped open wide. "A sister?"

The idea seemed valid, I thought. I could love her like a sister, if I had one. I wanted to get used to the idea "Yes, Vivian, I love you like I'd love my own sister. And I worry about you. Tonight, for example, when I saw you leave the rectory by yourself, walk the streets, you can't conceive how much I worried about you."

"Why should you worry?"

"Why should I worry? Wouldn't a brother worry about a sister he loved if he thought she were in danger?"

"Take the danger out of living and you have the prescription for a dull life."

"Where'd you get that idea?"

"I don't remember. Probably in one of the better bars."

"The idea's not sound. A poor philosophy. Tell me, Vivian, where did you go tonight?"

"None of your business. And don't expect me to go to confession to you 'cause I won't."

"Have you made your Easter duty?"

"I told you, I'm not going to confession to you."

Vivian was successful in changing the subject by removing a pair of red shoes from her feet. The heels were four inches high. "These shoes are not the best for walking long distances. My feet are killing me."

I took a few seconds to admire her feet. They were perfectly formed. Then I recalled an event that occurred during the night. "Vivian," I said, hesitatingly, unable to think of a good way to approach the subject, "when you enter your room, be careful of the broken glass. You can cut your feet."

"Broken glass! Why would I have broken glass in my room?"

"I'll tell you about it sometime…"

"Tell me about it now."

I stood and patted her head. "Now is the time for me to go into the sacristy, say my office, prepare for Mass."

She frowned as I made my departure.

I spent an hour in the sacristy with my breviary and then said the six o'clock Mass, attended by twelve individuals. I knew them all. Six were members of the parish who faithfully attended daily Mass before going to work. The other six were vagrants whose only home was the church. The pastor and I agreed the church should never be closed to anyone wishing to enter, regardless of his motives. The policy prevailed despite the fact it often included those disposed to breaking open the poor box.

The presence of the vagrants gave me subject matter for a short sermon. Quoting John, I said to those who listened, "Don't allow your hearts to be troubled. Have faith in your heavenly father. In the Father's house there are many dwelling places, and He will prepare a place for you…"

Demon of Lust

I expanded on these ideas, thinking I'd like to find a place in the Bronx for the vagrants to live. They could live without troubled hearts, rather than live in fear, thinking they'd someday be found dead in a dark alley.

Returning to the rectory, I expected to find Vivian gone from the kitchen, asleep in her room. But there she was, serving the pastor breakfast.

He seemed to be enjoying her kindness, the attention she was giving him, her outgoing personality. I noticed him squinting at her. His eyes were bad but whether he could get glimpses of her beauty was questionable. I hoped so. Every man, regardless of his age and station in life, appreciates the beautiful.

We have a good housekeeper," he said to me.

Vivian smiled at the praise. "I'm not sure Father Tom agrees with you."

I didn't respond. No doubt about it, Vivian cleaned the dishes well, kept the house in order, and was the most beautiful housekeeper who ever cared for a rectory. But could she be called *good*? Theologians define *good* as an entity lacking evil. Human beings were made up of body and soul. Vivian's body was perfect, but what could be said about her soul? Was it good or evil? Was she more concerned about material things than spiritual? Was she unwittingly working with Isacaron to destroy me? Did she want Togallini's paintings distributed around the world, regardless of the harm they'd do to men's souls? Should I run from her like I'd run from a plague? Or should I stand by her, help her in every way?

Before I could answer the questions, Vivian spoke: "The Monsignor seems to think I'm a good housekeeper. I'm not so sure you agree."

"Vivian, you do a great job with the dishes, keeping the rectory in order, preparing delicious meals. What more can I say?"

"Thank you," she said, obviously pleased with my response.

The pastor excused himself, saying he had his office to read, a Mass to say.

When he was gone, Vivian asked, "You going to explain the broken glass in my room?"

"I'll explain the broken glass if you'll tell me where you're hiding Mario Togallini's paintings."

"Why do you want to know?"

"If ever you're kidnapped from here, I might use them as a bargaining chip. I might have other reasons."

"You don't have a reason good enough to satisfy me. I don't trust you when it comes to the paintings. I told you that. Besides, I think the broken glass in my room has something to do with the painting in my room. Why don't you admit you were in my room, tried to destroy my pet painting? I'm mad as hell about that. I demand an explanation. And I certainly expect you to help me pick up the broken glass."

"I'll help you pick up the broken glass."

As I entered Vivian's room, I believed I made a mistake agreeing to pick up the glass. One look at the painting convinced me of that, for the eyes of the woman were focused on the red bruise on her breast. Her angry expression gave me, and presumably Vivian, the notion I was responsible for the bruise.

Vivian lost no time pointing to the discoloration on the woman's breast. "See that?"

"See what?"

"The bruise!"

"I see it."

"Are you responsible?"

"What color is it?"

"You can see it as well as I can," she said irritably. "It's kinda red and blue and purplish."

I feigned innocence. "How could I do it? I don't have any kinda red, blue and purplish paint."

Her chin dropped. She was silent for a while. Did she have the same question in her mind that I had in mine? How could a blow from a clear glass container change the color of a painted cream-colored breast?

She dismissed the question with a flourish of her hand.

"Well, somebody damaged my painting, and you're the somebody I suspect."

"Let's pick up the glass. And try not to cut yourself."

Vivian and I began to pick up the glass, throwing each piece in a brown paper bag. Before the last piece was in the bag, I cut my finger. "Ouch!" I exclaimed, examining a wound resembling the crimson lips of a woman.

Vivian took my finger in her hands and examined it.

"What was the advice you gave me about not cutting my finger?" she asked with a smile.

She was close to me. My eyes met hers and my heart pounded madly against my chest. Without thinking, I viewed the face of the lady in the painting. She was waiting, smiling, and encouraging me to take Vivian in my arms, kiss her, drop her down on the bed.

Vivian whispered, "If you want me…"

"I want you to sweep the floor, vacuum it, before walking in this room in your bare feet. I don't want you to cut yourself." Turning away from her, I walked towards the door. I was down the stairs in a minute and on my knees in prayer.

CHAPTER 28

That afternoon I entered the confessional box and waited for a penitent. The box was dark and secretive, very much like a place where a sin might be committed. God sees through the dark, I thought.

Moments later, I heard the sound of footsteps, someone entering the confessional. I opened a sliding door in a panel separating the priest from the penitent. I saw the silhouette of a small boy. "Yes," I said, prompting him to start his confession.

The voice was a whisper. "Bless me, Father, for I have sinned. It's been three weeks since my last confession. I have...." The whisper trailed off.

"What did you do?"

The boy was hesitant. "I...I...looked at some dirty pictures. Ten times I looked."

"Anything else?"

"I'd some dirty thoughts."

"Did you entertain them?"

"No, Father. They entertained me."

I muffled a laugh. "For your penance, say ten Hail Mary's. Now say an Act of Contrition."

The boy knew about half the prayer, which he said. The second half was a mumble. "Thank you, Father," he added, rushing off.

The next penitent was a heavyset man whose nationality I couldn't identify. I could identify the sickening smell of perspiration. He started his confession by saying, "Bless me, Father, 'cause I frigged three girls eight times."

"Would that be a total of twenty-four illicit sexual acts?" I asked.

"I'm not too good with math."

"Is there anything else you wish to confess?"

"I know a woman whose husband is a wife beater. She likes me…flirts with me all the time. She needs protection."

"Have her call the police."

"She wants me to protect her. I'm wonderin'…"

"Forget her," I said quickly.

"Whadda ya mean forget her?" His voice was nasty, antagonistic.

"If you're interested in saving your immortal soul, you'll forget her. You certainly won't become involved with a married woman who flirts with you. Moreover, you'll have to promise to forego fornication and possible adultery. Otherwise, I can't give you absolution."

"I don't make promises I don't plan to keep."

"And I don't give absolution to anyone not sorry for his sins. Especially those who intend to commit the same sin…"

"I'll go to another church," he stated with a bluntness that startled me. "Catholics don't have a monopoly on churches in this country."

"You have that prerogative."

The man left the confessional, leaving me feeling bad and wondering if I should have handled him in another way.

There were other people who came into my confessional that day, more than the average number. They were predominately fornicators, adulterers, masturbators, homosexuals, lesbians, pedophiles, and bisexuals.

I was surprised to hear a college student from San Francisco, say he broke up with his girl friend and now satisfies his sexual desires with his boy friend.

"There's a middle ground between the two poles of heterosexuality and homosexuality," he informed me. "That is why the Church is falling behind the times. The Church must change."

"The laws of God don't change," I said. "We are unable to change fundamental laws even if we want to."

"You must change," he argued. "Otherwise you lose your people."

"Wouldn't it be more accurate to say the people lose the Church? And in the process, they run the risk of losing their souls."

Irritated, he asked, "Where do you get that crap?" Without waiting for an answer, he mumbled a curse and left the confessional.

Again, I felt bad, helpless, troubled. I was losing more people than I was winning. I'd failed to resolve a difference between a penitent and the Church. But some penitents were no longer penitents. They came to confession with a firm resolve to change any law that interfered with their mode of thinking. Isacaron and the other demons that infested the world influenced their mode. I was sure of it. Yet I couldn't convince them...

"Ah stole a car," my latest confessor told me.

Relieved that the teenager before me, a tall, thin black boy, was not going to relate a sin of a sexual nature, I thoughtlessly said, "I'm glad of that."

"Ya're glad Ah stole a car?" came the startled response.

"No! No! Stealing is a sin, but I'm glad you didn't commit a more serious sin. I emphasized the word *serious*.

"Dis was very serious," the young man insisted. "Dis wasn't no ordinary car. Dis was a new Rolls Royce. And Ah stole it out in front of de wreck-tory."

My voice was louder than I intended. "You stole a Rolls Royce in front of the rectory?"

"Yes, suh...I mean, Yes, Father."

"Where's the car now?"

"Gone."

"What do you mean, gone?"

"Ah lent it to mah friend, Ronnie Johnson. He lended me a hun'red dollars when Ah didn't have no money fer food. He said I could ferget payin' him de hun'red if Ah'd let him take his girl friend for a ride in de Rolls."

"And you let him have the car?"

"Ah did. Ronnie was mah bes' friend. Ah liked him a lot. And Ah liked his girl friend even better. Her name's Cathy Washington. Is she ever pretty. And is she ever fast."

Demon of Lust

My heart sank when I heard she was fast. So many young girls in the Bronx were fast. So many became pregnant. "I regret hearing she's fast."

"Why regret it? Cathy's broken de hun'red yard dash and de two-twenty yard dash records in her high school. She's gonna make de 'limpics."

"I misunderstood you. Now tell me what happened to the car."

"Cathy told me dis: Ronnie wuz drivin' up 'round de George Washington bridge. He wanted to show her de bridge. Her uncle told her de bridge wuz named after her grandfather. Along comes a black stretch limo carryin' four big gangstas. Dey forced Ronnie to a curb, dragged 'im outta de car, asked 'im a lotta questions. Dey wuz interested in learnin' where de Rolls wuz parked when it was stolen. Not too interested in de fact de Rolls wuz stolen."

"What did he say to them?"

"He said he didn't know. Dey knocked him down with a punch to de belly, and said that him and Cathy would die if he didn't tell 'em where de Rolls wuz parked when it was stolen. Ronnie said he didn't know 'cause he borrowed it from a friend. De friend never told 'im where de Rolls wuz parked when he stole it."

"And then what happened?"

"One of de men pulled a knife outta his pocket, put de blade against Ronnie's chest. He said, "You're gonna tell us your friend's name and address or you're gonna die a slow and painful death." The young confessor stopped. "Ah don't know, Father, if Ah can go on." He began to cry.

"Please go on. I'm terribly interested in this case. I want to help you; help your friend; help the girl."

The teenager wiped tears from his face with the back of his hand. He continued. "Ya can't help Ronnie now, Father. Not unless ya pray for 'im. He's dead. He laid down his life fer his friend. He laid down his life fer me! He wouldn't tell de gangstas my name, where t' find me. He wouldn't tell 'em even when a gangsta pushed a knife slowly, ever so slowly, into his heart. He let dat damn gangsta kill 'im before he'd betray me."

"Cathy Washington, what happened to her?"

"When Ronnie fell dead, his blood runnin' outta his heart and into de gutter, Cathy screamed loud and long. She surprised de man holdin' her. He loosened his grip. She broke away from 'im and dodged the other three men. She then began to run. Dey all chased her. But Cathy wuz too fast for 'em. Dey might just as well tried catchin' a subway train goin' full speed to Brooklyn."

"Cathy gave you all these details?"

"Yes. She's so scared she'd a hard time talkin' 'bout it. She won't go home. She's livin' with a married sister."

"A good idea."

The young man lowered his head and cried. When he gained control of his emotions, he lifted his head and asked, "Am Ah goin' t' hell fer stealin' dat Rolls Royce, gettin' Ronnie killed?"

"As long as you're sorry for stealing the car, God will forgive you. He forgives all sins, regardless of how horrifying they are. As far as Ronnie's death is concerned, you're not to blame. Believe me, I know I'm right."

"Ah feels better now, Father."

"The next time you're tempted to steal a car, or commit some other sin, remember this: Sins are contagious. They not only injure you, they often injure others; those you love. If you want a car, get a job and work for it. You'll appreciate it more."

"Ah'll never steal 'nother car, Father."

Feeling perplexed at the information the boy gave me, but anxious to relieve his mental burden, I said, "I'm pleased we've had this talk. If ever you'd like to talk again, call me. You can either call on me in the confessional or in the rectory."

"Thank you, Father."

"For your penance, say ten Our Fathers and Ten Hail Mary's. Now say the Act of Contrition."

After saying the Act of Contrition, he said, "Would ya do somethin' fer me, Father."

Demon of Lust

"What's that?"

"Say a prayer for mah friend Ronnie."

"I'll do that."

When I left the confessional, I knelt at the foot of the altar and asked God to welcome Ronnie into the Kingdom of Heaven. I told God I felt a responsibility for the boy. He'd be alive today if I hadn't been stationed in the Bronx and Vivian hadn't visited me in her Rolls Royce. Moreover, Vivian and her painting and the demon Isacaron were now living in the rectory. They wouldn't be living there if I hadn't been living there. And the Rolls Royce wouldn't have been stolen from the front of the rectory, if I hadn't been living there. Ronnie wouldn't have been killed if four gangsters weren't looking for the Rolls Royce.

Why would God allow an innocent boy to be killed as a result of incidents that occurred in my life, Vivian's life? Perhaps Ronnie was ready to enter the Kingdom of Heaven at the time he was killed. Later on, he might not be ready. In allowing him to die early, God did him a favor.

Is this the answer? I couldn't be sure. However, I'd never question the wisdom of God. He created Ronnie and me. His judgment is better than mine. He warned us to avoid sin.

My mind darted back to the sins told in confession that day. The majority were sins of the flesh, sins the demon of lust promoted. The more I thought about them, the more I thought they were sickening. Would I ever fall victim to sins of the flesh? I won't. But wasn't it Peter, the Rock upon which Christ built his Church, who said he'd never deny Christ? And he did! Wasn't his denial of Christ a warning for me? I had to be careful. After all, I'm no rock.

CHAPTER 29

That evening, after dinner, while I was helping Vivian with the dishes, I wondered if there was any way of telling her that a boy named Ronnie was killed as a result of taking his girl friend for a ride in the Rolls Royce.

Of course, I couldn't mention Ronnie's death to Vivian because I couldn't break the seal of confession.

Thinking about the *seal* led me to think about my first assignment after becoming a priest. I was sent to a large parish in Manhattan, where the pastor was a Bishop and the principal of the school was a dynamo in nun's clothes. At this particular parish, I learned that all members of religious orders are not necessarily at peace with one another.

The Bishop believed that every word spoken by the Pope was a word spoken by the Lord. The principal of the school didn't agree with him, and with her ability to drive a man up a wall with the intensity of her arguments, she said that qualified nuns should be able to become priests.

"By their very nature, they don't qualify," the Bishop retorted.

"And why not?" asked the nun, poised to rip apart any argument the Bishop would present.

"Take any ten nuns," he said. "Assume they become priests. Five will break the seal of confession simply because they can't keep a secret. The other five will attempt to keep the secret, but they'll burst."

I don't know if this dialogue was initiated by the Bishop to drive the nun up the wall, as she'd done to others; but I do know the nun wrote to the Cardinal in charge of the Diocese and asked him to transfer the

Demon of Lust

Bishop to a far away parish. The Cardinal responded by transferring me to my present post.

"Why me?" I asked myself when I was packing my bags. I felt like the civilian who was shot simply because he lived in a town run by a leader who was at war with a neighboring leader.

"A cookie for your thoughts," Vivian said, awakening me from my reminiscing.

"I was just thinking how I happened to be transferred to this parish...how the activities of some people have a bearing on the lives of others."

"You think my coming here has a bearing on anybody's life?"

"You can bet your last dollar on it? It certainly has a bearing on..." I was going to say it has a bearing on the life of the boy who stole your Rolls Royce, as well as Ronnie and his girl friend. I caught myself. "It has a bearing on Monsignor Blazer's life. He likes you...likes your cooking."

Vivian dried her hands on a towel, faced me. "How about your life? Does my coming here have a bearing on your life?"

"Of course, it does."

"Is that because you love me?"

Again, I felt a desire to hold her. "I told you before, I love you like a sister."

She pulled the dishcloth from my hands, pushed me towards the door. "That's not good enough for me. You'll drive me out of my mind. Get out of my kitchen, take a walk."

So I took a walk, aimlessly through the dark streets of the Bronx. My mind was a jumble of ideas. I tried to divert my thoughts away from Vivian by inspecting the graffiti on the walls of buildings, the foul words, the drawing of a large pair of women's breasts, the burnt-out buildings. People on welfare set some of the buildings afire. They were in hopes of getting better apartments, free of rats, if their accommodations were destroyed. I don't know how successful they were....

I walked into an area that could hardly be called a business district. Most of the businesses were out of business. They were either boarded up or contained broken windows or empty shelves. The few having merchandise were closed for the night. They sold used furniture, second-hand clothes, television sets, and groceries. One store had a dim light. As I approached it, I read a sign whose letters were worn thin from the weather: Sam's Funeral Home.

Looking through a dusty window, I saw fifteen or twenty African-Americans sitting with hands clasped together, listening to a thin black man wearing a Roman collar. He was praying for a young man in a casket. I'd never seen the deceased young man before, but I knew who he was: Ronnie Johnson, the unfortunate teenager who was killed by a gangster.

"Would you like to come inside?"

The voice startled me. I turned around to see a young black girl with bright brown eyes and a turned-up nose. She was just as pretty as a very young Lena Horne.

I said, "You startled me. I didn't hear you approach me."

"Sorry about that," she said. "I'm wearing sneakers. They don't make any noise."

"Aren't sneakers bad for the feet?" I asked. My question sounded foolish to me. I was afraid it sounded foolish to the girl.

She smiled warmly, revealing a perfect set of teeth. "I wear these sneakers whenever I feel like running. I try to keep in shape. I compete."

"Interesting," I said, thinking I didn't have to ask her in what sport she competed, for I knew she ran the dashes for her high school track team. And I knew her name was Cathy Washington.

She examined my collar. "I see you're a Catholic priest. Ronnie wasn't a Catholic, but I'm sure he'd welcome you to his funeral. He can use all the prayers he can get. Will you come into the funeral parlor with me?"

So I was right, I thought. The boy in the casket was Ronnie Johnson. "I've never met Ronnie."

"He was a good boy. Never did a dishonest thing in his life. Except once, maybe. He borrowed a stolen car from a friend, took me for a ride.

Some men who said they owned the car stopped us. They killed Ronnie because he wouldn't tell them who lent him the car."

"You're fortunate you weren't killed."

The girl nodded meditatively. "I know I am. I broke loose from the man holding me. I ran away."

I thought she was running a risk attending Ronnie Johnson's funeral. "Can you be assured the men aren't looking for you now? You witnessed a murder."

Before she had the opportunity to answer, a dark stretch limousine turned a corner, slowly approached us. Four men occupied the vehicle.

"Is there a rear exit in this funeral home?" I asked.

"Oh, yes," she said. "They bring the bodies in the rear." Her large brown eyes opened wider when she turned and spotted the approaching vehicle.

Taking her arm, I said, "Let's go."

We entered the funeral parlor, made our way past a mahogany casket containing Ronnie, through several rows of mourners, past the minister whose head was bent in prayer. Cathy kicked over a basket of flowers as we entered a room containing caskets on display. We raced through another room containing cabinets, tables, and medical supplies. A naked black man was on a slab. His lifeless eyes were fixed on a ceiling, badly in need of paint. A rubber tube ran from his arm to a sink.

We passed through a squeaky wooden door, ran out into a trash-filled alley, barely wide enough for a hearse to enter. I ran along side of Cathy, mindful that I could again taste the food I'd eaten for dinner. We ran about thirty yards down the alley when the explosion took place. The sound was deafening.

Stopping immediately, I turned around in time to see flame and smoke belching from the funeral parlor we'd left seconds before. Besides the smoke and flame, other things flew from the building: bricks, plaster, dust, and a jagged man's arm with a rubber tube attached. Buildings on both sides of the funeral home collapsed. Heat from the fire was so intense

I could feel it singe my face. There was no way I could save anyone from that inferno. I could only stare.

Cathy stared, too. She stared for a long time before she spoke. "All those good people are dead because of me."

"You're not to blame," I said quickly. "Unfortunately, you witnessed a murder. The man who killed Ronnie is to blame...the men with him are responsible."

She was too shocked to argue. She could only stare.

And while she stared, I asked myself if I'd been honest with her. Although the men who threw the bomb into the funeral home were directly responsible for the death of the people inside the home, I was indirectly responsible. I was an attraction for Vivian. She brought the Rolls Royce into the neighborhood. She brought her painting into the rectory. I should have exercised better control over her.

"What can I do?" the girl beside me asked.

"Nothing!" I said emphatically, thinking my response was a good one. "Do absolutely nothing to attract those killers to you. I'll get in touch with the police."

"You will?" she said. "You won't tell the police about me. I was in the car with Ronnie."

"I certainly won't. We'll not trust the police or anyone else with your life. Your safety is our primary concern."

"Thank you, Father."

Upon arriving at the rectory, I lost no time dialing 911 and informing the officer who answered the phone that I saw a dark stretch limousine, occupied by four men, approaching Sam's funeral Parlor moments before the explosion took place. "I'm quite sure the men are responsible for the murder of the people in the funeral parlor," I said. "They also killed Ronnie Johnson."

The officer taking the call responded: "Your name, address, and telephone number, please."

Demon of Lust

I hung up the phone, giving him no time to trace the call. I went to my room.

Reading my breviary for about an hour, I closed the book, realizing my concentration was poor. The events of the night continued to swirl in my mind. I felt exhausted. Taking off my clothes, donning pajamas, I fell on my knees and prayed for Ronnie Johnson and all the poor people who were in the funeral parlor when the bomb went off. I thanked God for saving Cathy Washington's life, as well as my own.

I recalled a question put to me by an atheist: "If we thank God for the good things that come our way, should we not blame Him for the evil things that come our way?" I pondered this question while trying to fall asleep. I was certain there was a sound, logical answer. But I was too tired to think of one.

Sleep came to me that night in an elevator. It carried me down at breath-taking speed through miles of smoldering coal. At what seemed an endless ride, the elevator stopped outside the entrance to a cave. The moment the elevator came to a halt, the doors slid open. I stepped out, and entered a cave decorated with diamonds. Twenty yards beyond the cave's entrance, I came upon a golden door, studded with rubies. Without knocking, I opened the door, found myself in an enormous bedroom.

Above the bed, Vivian's painting was on the wall. She smiled happily when she saw me. Stepping out of the painting, she slipped into the bed and beckoned me to join her.

"I can't. I'm...I'm a priest!"

"Priests have the same desires as other men," she said, extending her arms to me. "Join me, fulfill your desires."

A sense of passion surged through my body. I had to be crazy to say no to Vivian.

I moved towards her. No! I can't do it. I stopped short.

"You're not going to change your mind, are you?" she asked coyly.

"Vivian, you and I are friends. We must try to help each other. I'd do anything to help you save your soul. You must do everything to help me save mine."

"You must be joking."

"I'm not joking."

"If you're not joking, you're in trouble."

"Why should I be in trouble?"

Vivian spoke like a teacher informing a child: You don't seem to understand the laws of human nature. People want you to do what they want you to do. I want you to sleep with me. If you refuse, my love for you will turn to hate."

"You couldn't hate me. We've been friends a long time."

My remark brought a smile to her beautiful face. She laughed, the same sweet laugh I was accustomed to hearing. Then her laugh became loud, irritating, coarse. The laugh was so irrational, so unlike her, I thought she'd lost her mind.

As she laughed, her face became distorted, ugly, and wild. I wanted her to end the maddening laugh. "Vivian, will you please stop laughing?"

My request brought on additional laughter. It sounded as if it came from a hyena released from hell.

Suddenly, a thought struck me. I must be having a nightmare.

Awakening, I sat up in bed, aware that my pajamas were soaked with perspiration.

The laughter continued for five seconds or more after I was awake.

CHAPTER 30

After finishing the six o'clock Mass the following morning, I entered the kitchen and saw Vivian seated at the table with Monsignor Blazer. They were having a cup of coffee and reading the newspapers.

Lowering her paper, she said to the pastor, "There's an article here about a funeral home that was bombed last night. Fifteen people were killed and three dead bodies were torn to pieces. The funeral parlor is not far from here. What do you have to say about that?"

The pastor thought for a moment before replying. "I'll say the nine o'clock Mass for the people killed. May their souls rest in peace. We never know the day, or the hour, when God will call us."

Vivian folded the paper, put it on the table. "I can't understand why anyone would want to kill the mourners in a funeral home. Nor can I understand why anyone would have reason to bomb the dead. It's not the dead who'll harm you. It's the living who'll do you in."

The Monsignor nodded his head, smiled.

Vivian had an exemplary grace and confidence when discussing the bombing with the pastor. I wondered how much grace and confidence she'd have if I were to tell her the people bombed last night would be alive and well this morning if she hadn't parked her Rolls Royce in front of the rectory. Very often we fail to consider how our activities affect others, I thought. Should I, or should I not, tell her what took place?

I was leaning against the kitchen wall when the telephone rang. The ring was so loud; it startled me. I picked up the phone and said, "Father Tom Davis speaking."

"Did you read about the bombin' last night?"

The voice was familiar, yet I couldn't put a name to it. "With whom am I speaking?"

"Now don't tell me you've forgotten my name already. Must I have my boys throw a couple more bombs around the Bronx to stimulate your memory?"

"Mario Togallini!" I shouted into the phone.

I shouted so loud Vivian turned and faced me.

"So you do remember my name."

I remember it, but I wasn't sure if you were responsible for killing the people in the funeral home last night."

"I didn't say I was responsible, although I do have some guys workin' for me who play rough. I can't do a damn thing about them. Instead of rapin' girls when they go out at night, like normal guys would do, they get their kicks outta bombin' funeral homes, churches, rectories, schools."

"I may notify the police about you and your guys."

"I'll deny everything, except I went to confession to you. You went to the police, twisted the story I gave you in confession."

"You'd lie?"

"Of course, I'd lie. But I wouldn't have to lie about where I was last night. From ten till two in the mornin', I was playin' poker with the mayor of Jersey City."

"You provided yourself with an alibi."

"It's the mayor of Jersey City who provided me with an alibi, not that I need one. I've got friends in high places, on both sides of the law."

"I don't doubt it."

"Enough about me. Let's talk about you. The reason I'm callin' is because it strikes me strange Vivian's car was found in the Bronx. I'm wonderin' if her car was stolen while she was talkin' to you."

"If your imagination is undisciplined, you can imagine many strange things."

Demon of Lust

"It's possible the guys who bombed the funeral home have another bomb, one reserved for the rectory."

"They wouldn't…"

The voice was sinister. "They would if I give them the word. Just because you're a Holy Joe don't mean you're above the law. Vivian is a thief. A Holy Joe shouldn't help a thief get away with an honest man's prized possessions. I warned you before and I warn you again, if you attempt to help Vivian in any way, you and your rectory is gonna be blown apart."

"I can't believe you'd threaten a priest…"

"I mean business. If you hear from Vivian, you better find out where she's holed up. You let me know. Otherwise…." He banged the phone down onto its cradle.

The banging jarred my nerves, put my mind in disarray. I could hardly believe Mario Togallini, a millionaire many times over, would threaten me over paintings inspired by a demon. I was a priest, a disciple of God's, someone ordained to convert the pagan. But the pagan was trying to convert the priest. He wanted me to turn Vivian over to him. He'd torture her; kill her.

And now Vivian was staring at me with her mesmerizing eyes. She'd heard a part of the conversation, knew I was in danger. Monsignor Blazer was no longer in the room.

"Mario Togallini called you, didn't he?" she asked. Her voice was charged with emotion.

"He did."

"Did he threaten you?"

I nodded.

"You can be killed. You and the pastor. I better leave here."

"You have no place to go. You're safe here."

"You think so?"

"As long as Mario doesn't know you're here, you're safe. If you're off on your own, do your own shopping, you run the risk of being seen by one of Mario's thugs."

"You truly concerned about me?"

"Of course I am."

"You're a dear." She bolted towards me, kissed me.

I'd have protected myself against the kiss if I saw it coming. I didn't. The kiss struck like a live power line that snapped during a windstorm. It hit my mouth, gave me an unexpected charge. "Vivian, you must not kiss me."

"Why not?" she asked flippantly. "Can't a sister kiss a brother?"

"Not this brother."

"You love me and you won't admit it."

"I told you before, I love you like I'd love a sister."

"Next time you go to confession, tell the priest you told a lie."

"I'm not lying."

"Tell the priest you told two lies."

I'd no response to her remark. Maybe I was lying, I thought. My body was still in a state of shock from the kiss. It's one thing to love a woman from afar, another to be kissed by her.

Vivian spoke of confession. I recalled going to confession to Father O'Donnell when I was seventeen years of age. I told him a woman tempted me. He told me to avoid the woman. I told him I couldn't avoid the woman because I lived with her. Nine years after the confession, I found myself in the same predicament. I was living under the same roof with the same woman. If I asked any ten good theologians for a solution to my problem, the response would be unanimous: Get rid of the woman!

What an easy answer to a problem! About as easy as giving yourself a heart transplant. Nevertheless, I had to do it. The history of Christianity isn't a story of wearing your best clothes to Church on Sunday, tipping your hat to the ladies. It's a story of carrying a cross, wearing a crown of thorns, shedding blood, practicing self denial, tolerating miserable feelings. Happiness comes when life is over.

Demon of Lust

What could I do? If Vivian remains in the rectory, my soul is in jeopardy. If she leaves, her life is in jeopardy. But a soul is more important than a life. I'd have to let her go.

An article in the newspaper dealing with a Hollywood romance caught her attention. The article fascinated her. I was trying to think of some way to tell her she'd have to move, but I could think of no words to express the idea without hurting her. What a fool I was to say she'd be safer in the rectory than anywhere else.

Where could she go? She'd rented an apartment in Brooklyn to store the paintings she stole from Mario Togallini. Why couldn't she live in that apartment, take the painting in the rectory with her? I worried as much about the painting in the rectory as I worried about her. The painting in her bedroom was a place of refuge for the demon Isacaron. The demon had amazing spiritual powers. But did he have physical powers as well? I decided to give him a test.

Taking the stairs two at a time, I traveled to the fourth floor in record time. The woman in the painting had a look of anticipation on her lovely face. She appeared to be waiting for me.

I tried to concentrate on her face, not her body. Her body, poised and ready for fornication, would ignite the passions within my own body. I wasn't successful. The passions I tried so hard to control were stirring restlessly within me.

I spoke to the lady in the painting as if she were a live human being. "You and Vivian will soon leave here. A rectory is no place for either one of you."

Without my seeing any movement whatsoever, her head turned from left to right. The reaction startled me. She didn't want to go.

"You'll feel very much at home with the people in Brooklyn," I said with false enthusiasm. "The borough has a great number of rapists, wife-beaters, fornicators, adulterers, pedophiles and other deviates. There are more broken homes in Brooklyn than any other place in America." I believed my remarks were untrue, but I saw no reason why I had to be truthful to a painting possessed by a demon.

The woman in the painting smiled. A Mona Lisa smile. A smile studied by men for years. She knew I was making a statement without any basis in fact. She knew I was telling a lie. The lie pleased her.

Her eyes bore into mine like two laser beams. Then they shifted to the window. The lady in the painting wanted me to look out the window. Although I'd normally resist any suggestions she'd make, I found myself looking out the window. At that precise moment, a dark stretch limousine stopped in front of the rectory.

Two huge men emerged. One stood at the curb; the other man walked to the rear of the rectory. Both were carrying cell phones. The limousine pulled away.

I'd some difficulty understanding why the men were there. I didn't have any idea until I glanced at the smiling face of the woman in the painting. The men were there to observe anyone entering the front or rear of the rectory. Vivian was trapped. She couldn't leave the rectory.

CHAPTER 31

I lost no time notifying Vivian that Mario Togallini had posted two guards at the rectory. One was near the front door, the other at the rear door.

She sat in my office with her hands folded in her lap. She took the news better than I expected. Her voice was calm when she asked, "What am I supposed to do?"

"Stay out of sight," I said. "Mario doesn't know you're living in the rectory. He thinks you may visit me here. I also believe he wants me to feel his influence. He expects me to betray you if he applies enough pressure on me."

"But you won't?"

"Of course not."

Her brow furrowed. "How long will Mario have the rectory watched?"

"I have no idea."

"Do you think I could sneak past one of the guards, say around midnight?"

"You'll be running a big risk."

"I suppose so. But I'm not used to being confined. I like to get out at night, enjoy myself."

"There's no enjoyment in being kidnapped, beaten or killed."

"A woman's freedom is important. The bastards are taking away my freedom. Maybe you ought to call the police."

"I'll call the police if you want me to. But legally the paintings are Mario's. If he presses charges, you could go to jail for stealing them. You'll lose your freedom if you go to jail."

"Mario would be in trouble, too. He hasn't paid taxes on the money he's earned from the paintings. He's had copies made…"

"His being in trouble with the Internal Revenue Service won't help you."

She mulled over my words for ten seconds or more. "How come you think you're always right?"

"Vivian, you need not believe I'm always right. But believe I'm right about your painting. The devil's disciple, Isacaron, inspired it. The painting is evil. It should be destroyed."

"You're talking about my painting. It's more important to me than anything else in the world."

"I'm talking about a painting inspired by a demon. It can stain the soul of anyone who views it."

"My painting is beautiful."

"Sure it's beautiful. The devil offers many beautiful things to those willing to join forces with him. Your picture is a source of evil. It should be destroyed, as well as all the other paintings in your custody."

Vivian considered my statement for about three seconds before responding. "You're mad."

"I'm trying to save my soul, your soul, and all those who might be influenced by the paintings. I'd surely go mad if I knew you'd set yourself on a course leading to hell."

"I don't give a damn about hell," she shot back. "If there's a hell, you don't go there till you're dead. I'm very much alive. I want to live, enjoy myself."

Her words hurt me. How I wished she'd listen to me. How I wanted to protect her. The paintings will destroy her life. I'd have to do something about them. Soon.

"What are you going to do about the thugs watching the house?" she asked.

"I'm going to leave it up to you. If you want me to call the police, I'll call them."

"Do it," she said without hesitation.

So I called the police, waited ten minutes before getting an officer authorized to listen to my problem. I told him about the two men posted at the front and rear of the rectory.

He spoke with great authority. "Did anyone in the rectory ask the men to post themselves at the front and rear?"

"Of course not. I wouldn't be calling you if anyone here made such a request."

"Well, who made the request?"

"I can tell you whom I suspect."

He sounded a warning: "Don't give me a name unless you have proof."

"I have no proof."

"Then I can't help you."

"Can't you tell the men to move along?"

"The men may be pickets. Picketing is legal in the State of New York."

"Is it legal to picket a rectory?"

"A rectory, yes. An abortion center, no. Pickets must keep their distance when dealing with an abortion center."

"These pickets are thugs trying to harass me."

"Why would they want to harass you?"

I'd no answer for him. In desperation, I asked, "Is there anyone there who might help me? Your supervisor, maybe."

"Everybody here is going to give you the same answer I'm giving you. But, if you wish, talk to the Captain."

At last, I'm having some luck, I thought. "Let me talk to him."

"He's on vacation. Be back in a month. He's in Haiti helping the people there."

"Thank you very much."

With a sense of despair, I hung up the phone. The seminary didn't prepare me for dealing with the New York City police, the Bronx thugs, or Vivian. I hated to tell her I was unsuccessful getting the men to move on. I'd deal with them myself.

Going out the back door, and across a yard that was perhaps fifty feet deep, I opened a gate and met a powerfully built man in an alley.

He was seated on a box between two large garbage cans. His eyes, hair, beard, and clothes were all black. I wondered if his soul were black. He rose to his feet when he spotted me.

"I'm Father Tom Davis," I said in a friendly tone, offering him my hand. "I'm wondering why you're here."

He jammed his hands into his pockets and said, "I know who you are. You know why I'm here."

"You tell me."

He didn't hide his sarcasm. "You know as well as I do, we're looking for a woman who has stolen some valuable paintings."

"And you expect to find her in this alley?"

"We expect her to get in touch with you."

"My visitors generally ring the front doorbell."

"We have the front door covered."

"Since you believe a woman has committed a crime, why don't you notify the police?"

The man shook his head. "We don't deal with the police. The police are corrupt."

"Not all police are corrupt, only a few. Men like Mario Togallini corrupt them."

The huge man flinched. "I don't like to hear you criticize Mr. Togallini. I work for him, Father."

I'd taken a shot in the dark, struck a bull's eye. The man before me wasn't as hard-boiled as he pretended. "Unless I miss my guess, you're not proud to work for a man reputed to be the largest distributor of pornographic material in the country. The harm those filthy pictures do to children is a crime."

"I'll not listen to any sermons. I'm not Catholic anymore."

"But you were once?"

Demon of Lust

"I graduated from a Catholic elementary school, a Catholic high school."

"And the lessons you learned from the nuns is now so much garbage. Mario Togallini has better ideas. Is that your present way of thinking?"

"Not exactly, Father. But a man's got to make a living, decide things for himself. I had no money for college. No job."

I studied the big man more closely. I liked his sincerity…his features were finely cut. He was handsome, but unsure of himself. He'd be receptive to a good idea as well as an evil one. "It doesn't take a college education to distinguish between right and wrong."

"I know," he said meekly.

I decided to take another shot in the dark: "Are you the man who threw the bomb into the funeral home?"

A strange sound broke from his lips. "My God, how did you know?"

"You threw the bomb?"

"No! But I was in the limousine when it was thrown. I confess this to you so you won't tell the police or anyone else. Tony Barber threw the bomb. I'd no idea he was going to throw it. Not till he opened the window of the limo…threw the bomb into the funeral parlor. What a horrifying sight!" The big man shuddered, as if he could see body parts flying out of the funeral parlor.

I waited until the man wiped his brow with a handkerchief before speaking. "You don't belong with a gang of thugs. You're no killer. Any man who's spent twelve years with the nuns isn't a killer. Why don't you break away, leave New York, and find a job in some small town?"

"I'd like to. My conscience is killing me."

"You married?"

"No. I took care of my mother. She had many hospital bills. I couldn't afford marriage…couldn't afford to take a job that didn't pay well."

I thought of Vivian. She'd like this handsome guy. He'd make a good husband if he could break away from Togallini; let his conscience be his guide. "Will you promise me you'll quit the job you're now doing, leave

New York, and look for work in another city? You might not realize it, but you've a lot going for you. You don't belong in an alley, doing Togallini's dirty work."

"I need money to get away, Father. Give me another month on this job. I promise you, I'll take a bus out of town. Never again will I witness the murder of innocent people."

I offered him my hand.

He took it.

"Will you get in touch with me when you're settled in another town? I want to introduce you to someone. Someone you'll enjoy meeting."

He smiled, displaying teeth suitable for a television advertisement. "Do you know someone who'll give me a job out of town?"

"No, I'm sorry. I don't know anyone who can give you work. But when you leave town, let me know where you are. I know a girl I'd like you to meet."

"I've no trouble meeting girls."

"You'll never find another girl like this one."

"Why is that?"

"She's the most beautiful girl in the world."

He again showed me his perfect teeth. "If you recommend her, Father, she must be worthwhile."

The moment I left him, I began to worry. What had I done? A man was spending hours in an alley waiting for Vivian to show up. And I wanted to introduce her to him. Would he realize I was thinking of Vivian when I said she was the most beautiful girl in the world? Perhaps Mario told him the same thing. He might have seen her with Mario. He was no dummy. Wouldn't he know I was talking about Vivian when I opened my big mouth?

Too late now to rectify the mistake. I could only hope the man was honest with me, wanted to break away from Mario and his thug friends. He was a Catholic. But I knew from hearing confessions… sickening confessions, I might add…that Catholics were just as weak as other men. Their spirits were strong but their flesh was weak.

Demon of Lust

I decided to approach the man at the front of the rectory. If I could get some support from him, I'd offset the immediate threat Mario Togallini presented to Vivian.

"Good evening," I said to the man, trying to sound as pleasant as possible.

He was almost as big as the man at the rear of the rectory; however, he differed in many respects. He was ten years older, unkempt, and bore the smell of a neglected men's room. A scar disfigured a nose that had already been disfigured by too many blows. His left ear was a pink cauliflower. An ex-pug, I thought. He failed to respond to my "Good evening."

I'd try again. "I'm Father Tom Davis. I see you have the job of observing the rectory. Could I get you a cup of coffee or a bottle of beer?"

He stared at me without responding. He seemed puzzled by my approach. I suppose he expected me to come charging out of the rectory, swinging both fists.

"I want you to understand I hold no animosity against you or your friend at the rear of the rectory," I said, "so if there is anything I can do for you, like ordering a sandwich or a bottle of soda, please let me know."

Grooves appeared on the man's forehead. He was more puzzled than ever. Evidently, he'd never heard of a "turn the other cheek" approach to a problem. He continued to remain silent. He was accustomed to taking orders from Mario Togallini or someone else. He would do what he was paid to do, regardless of how evil it was. He wasn't accustomed to making a decision for himself. Man is a rational animal, I thought. This man is more animal than rational. I'll never receive any cooperation from him. Nevertheless, I was pleased with my efforts. I believed I had the cooperation of the man in the rear. He wouldn't hurt Vivian even if he spotted her.

Entering the rectory, I decided to refrain from telling Vivian I found a possible ally at the rear of the house. The man might be trustworthy; then again, he might not be. I'd not bet Vivian's life on it. Besides, Mario Togallini wouldn't expect the two men to work a twenty-four hour day.

He'd probably work them an eight or twelve-hour day. I could be coping with a stranger at the rear of the rectory.

Vivian greeted me in the kitchen with a smile of anticipation. "Where have you been?"

"Outside."

"Did you see the men?"

"Yes."

"Talk to them?"

"Yes."

"Did you talk them into leaving?"

"They won't be leaving for a while."

"Why not?"

"They're being paid to watch the front and the rear of this building. That's what they intend to do."

"And the police, you had no luck with them?"

"No."

"Then you must do something for me."

"I've already done what I can."

"You can do more."

"What more can I do?"

"You realize I can't sit alone in my room every night, twiddle my thumbs, stare at my painting. I'm accustomed to being entertained."

Vivian was being unreasonable, I thought. After all, it was she who stole the paintings, showed up at my doorstep. She brought the problem on herself. I felt my temper rise. "To be perfectly frank, Vivian, I've never stopped to consider if you sit alone at night, twiddle your thumbs, stare at your painting. Assuming I did, what more can I do for you?"

"You can make love with me."

CHAPTER 32

"Why not?" I heard her say. She tapped a foot while waiting for an answer.

I was speechless. My mind exploded with wild ideas. My blood boiled with a desire for the woman I loved. Is there a man alive who'd refuse to make love with the most beautiful girl in the world? Was the Church asking too much from its priests? Why must a man's passions burn if they can't be satisfied?

Vivian took my hand. It was like satin. "You can't expect me to live in the same house with the man I love without wanting to be close to him?"

I wanted to be close to her. But did I? My passions and intellect were at war. Would my passions win? Would I later go crazy because I'd broken my vows?

Subconsciously, I knew the demon of sex, Isacaron, was igniting my passions. He was also urging Vivian on, controlling her. He was beginning to control me. I'd soon yield. If only a guardian angel would appear, give me strength....

Monsignor Blazer appeared with a white slip of paper in his hand. "Father Tom," he said. "I've just spoken to a Mrs. Reilly. Her husband has been released from the hospital. He wants to die at home. Give him the last rites? Here's the address." He gave me the slip of paper.

Vivian gave the Monsignor a dirty look.

I took the paper from him. Without saying a word, I located the holy oils for the dying, was on my way to administer the last sacrament, known as Extreme Unction.

The apartment house in which Mr. Reilly lived was only five blocks from the rectory. The building was old, weather beaten, ready to collapse, and without an elevator. It was properly called a walk-up. Walking up five flights of stairs had me puffing.

The old woman who opened the door for me was short and heavy with an extremely pleasant face. She said, "Thank ye for comin', Father, and I hope the stairs didn't get ye."

"I don't know how you manage them."

Her answer sounded as if she'd used it many times: "We can manage the stairs better than we can manage a higher rent."

The interior of the apartment was much like the exterior, old and worn. It was furnished perhaps fifty years ago, with no regard for clashing colors. The furniture was still functional despite an exposed spring in a sofa and ripped fabric in a chair. I felt sure Mrs. Reilly gave little thought to the condition of her furniture at this stage of her life.

Her eyes moistened when she opened the bedroom door. Her husband, skeleton-like and bald, lay beneath worn but clean sheets. His eyes were blue and watery, fixed on the ceiling.

"Pat, this is Father Davis," Mrs. Reilly said. "He'll hear yer confession, give ye the last rites."

A faint "thank ye" came from the cracked lips of the man.

She left the room, closed the door behind her.

"I'll hear your confession now," I said to the man.

He whispered, "Bless me, Father. I've sinned. Two months, maybe four, since me last confession. Done nothin' bad lately…been too sick. I used to look at the ladies' arses with lust in me heart. I hope God'll forgive me."

"He'll forgive you. Are there any other sins you wish to confess?"

"That's all I remember."

"Can you say an Act of Contrition?"

The man started the prayer: "Oh, my God, I'm heartily sorry fer havin' offended ye…" His voice became inaudible and he fell asleep.

Demon of Lust

I gave him the last rites, a sacrament designed to give someone, at the end of his or her life, the strength, peace and courage to face death. The sacrament also renews trust and faith in God; becomes a fortress against the devil, who may offer discouragement and anguish to an individual as death approaches.

I closed the bedroom door behind me.

Mrs. Reilly met me with great anticipation. "Is he gonna be all right?"

"He's well prepared for death."

Nodding, she said, "I doubt if he's ever committed a grievous sin, except maybe buyin' a quart of gin when he was outta work."

"I'm sure he was a good man."

"Father, I'd offer ye a cup of tea if I had any tea. But the medicines were so expensive."

"A glass of water will be fine."

While she cleaned a cloudy looking glass and filled it with water from a worn faucet, I pulled my last ten dollars from a pocket and put it in the palm of my right hand.

"Here's the water, Father."

The water didn't taste quite right, yet I drank it all. "I'll say goodbye to you now, Mrs. Reilly. And call me whenever you need me." I expected her to extend her hand.

"Your blessing, Father." She folded her hands in prayer.

I made the sign of the cross over her head, asked God to give her the strength to carry on. I then extended my hand. When we shook hands, I gave her the ten dollars.

Her face registered surprise. She examined the ten dollars as if it were ten hundred. "I can't take it, Father."

"What Irish woman is without tea in the house? Buy some."

"Thank ye and God bless ye."

As I walked down the shabby stairs and out into the street, I felt good about giving the woman the money. I also thought about the man I'd visited. Evidently, he'd lived in poverty most of his life, had few worldly possessions, except a faithful wife. But on his deathbed he'd more to offer God than the wealthiest man in New York City. He'd lived a good life without worldly compensations. He'd go before God with few flaws on his soul.

In giving him the last rites, I'd given him the strength to die. He gave me more. He gave me the strength to live. I now felt better about myself. I'd not yield to temptation. Avoiding temptation required effort. It was so easy to fall, perform an evil act. The fact that I'd so many years ahead of me was frightening. If I could, I'd change places with the man who lived in the walk-up, the man about to die.

The elation I experienced in the Reilly apartment diminished when I approached the rectory. The thug was picketing the building. I said "Hello" to him. He stared at me as if I'd no right to greet him. I wanted to tell him he was wasting his time picketing the rectory. Only God knows how much time men waste doing useless tasks, especially those men in conflict with others.

At the rectory door, I fumbled for my key. Vivian opened the door. Fortunately, the big thug was looking the other way.

"You must not open the door of this rectory," I said, raising my finger to her. "You'll be spotted by one of Mario's men."

"I was anxious to see you," she said submissively.

"If that thug sees you, he'll grab you...break down the front door, if necessary."

"I don't care," she pouted.

"You don't care! Your life is at stake."

"I'd rather die than be in prison."

"You're not in a prison. You're in a rectory with people who care for you."

Her expression was child-like when she asked, "How much do you care for me?"

I said precisely what was in my mind. "I'd lay down my life for you?"

"But you won't make love with me."

Demon of Lust

A wave of passion swept over me. I tried to avoid revealing it with this remark: "I said I'd lay down my life for you. I'll not sacrifice my soul."

"You have a funny way of thinking."

"If you say so. All Disciples of Christ have a funny way of thinking. But I don't honestly believe the one who instructed the first disciples was a stand-up comic."

"You're impossible," she said, backing away from me, taking the stairs.

I was going to call after her, try to drum some sense into her beautiful head, but the telephone rang.

I took the call in my office, "St. Matthews rectory."

"You were lying to me."

I recognized the voice. It came as a surprise. "What makes you think I was lying to you, Mr. Togallini?"

"You know where Vivian is hidin'. You haven't notified me."

"I never agreed to notify you of anything. And I'm not saying now whether I know where she is living."

"I'm calling to give you a last chance. You gonna tell me where she is?"

"You'll get no information from me about Vivian."

"Is that your final answer?"

"It is."

"Look out the window?"

He had me puzzled. "What do you mean, look out the window?"

"Look out the front window, across the street."

I was in my office, where I'd picked up the phone. I put the phone down, went into Monsignor Blazer's office. I picked up a phone there and looked out the window. The big thug was nowhere in sight. Speaking into the phone, I said, "I'm glad to see you've removed the picket."

"Look across the street."

I looked across the street, saw a number of old brick homes, neatly maintained. I'd seen them many times before, never thought much about them. I knew several parishioners occupied the homes. "I'm looking across the street."

"You see the house in the middle?" Mario asked.

"I see it."

Suddenly, the house exploded. The noise shook the rectory... shook me. The sound was deafening. Smoke and fire belched from the house. Bricks flew in all directions. Several struck the rectory; others landed on the lawn. The window through which I observed the explosion was dotted with soot.

As I watched the flames demolish what was left of the house, I realized my will to resist Mario Togallini was being demolished. My will to resist Vivian was being demolished. My will to resist the demon was being demolished.

The voice of a man possessed by a demon came over the phone. His name was Mario Togallini. "Next time," he said, "it's gonna be the rectory."

CHAPTER 33

Fire engines clanked onto the street, followed by police cars, ambulances, emergency trucks, televisions vans, sightseers. A crowd gathered to witness flames shoot out of a massive crater. The houses on each side of the bombed home suffered from gaping holes. Bedroom furniture was exposed.

Putting the holy oils in my pocket, I rushed across the street; spoke to a fireman pulling a heavy hose. "Have you found any victims?"

"I don't believe there are any. The house was empty when the explosion took place. If you'll excuse me…" He pulled the hose closer to the fire. A hissing sound emerged from the crater when water hit the flames.

Several policemen shouted to the crowd. "Get back! Get back!"

The crowd moved back, away from the fire. There was one exception. A woman with snow-white hair remained standing in the center of the street. She appeared to be in shock. A policeman, standing close to her, made no effort to make her move. She needed help.

Approaching her, I said, "May I do something for you?"

Dazed, she looked at me with tears streamed down her face. "What can you do? My home is gone…blown to bits."

"I'm sorry." I felt more awkward than I've ever felt before. I also felt responsible for the tragedy that struck the woman. Her home, perhaps her one great possession, was destroyed. I was to blame.

"My home wasn't insured," she confessed.

Water from a fireman's hose sprayed us.

"We can't stay here." I put my arm around her waist, led her to the rectory. Opening the door, I guided her to my office, seating her in a large leather chair, worn but comfortable. I sat in my own swivel chair, faced her. "You can rest here as long as you like."

Casting her eyes to the floor, she said, "I'm not a member of your church."

"Many people aren't members of my church. As long as you're a member of the human race, I'll do what I can for you."

Her lips cracked into a brief smile. "Thanks."

"You'll need a place to stay. Do you have any relatives or close friends you can call?"

"I have a daughter."

"Is she married?"

"Not any more. Her husband caught her cheating."

"Could you stay with her?"

The woman shifted uneasily in her seat. "I don't know. She has boyfriends. A new one every night. She prefers them to me."

"Could I have her name and phone number?"

"Her name's Marlo. And here's her phone number." The woman took a small slip of paper from her purse, gave it to me. She stared at the paper as she spoke. "I don't like asking her for anything."

"Nonsense. I'm sure you did your best for Marlo."

"After my husband died, I used our savings to put her through college."

"So now she has the opportunity to repay you."

"I don't think she will."

Getting up from my chair, I said, "I'll give her a call. You stay here and rest."

Going into the Monsignor's office, I picked up the phone and dialed the number given to me by the woman.

The phone buzzed intermittently four times before I received a "Hello."

"Is this Marlo?"

Demon of Lust

"Yes."

"This is a Father Tom Davis. I'm stationed in a rectory across the street from your mother's home. I've some bad news for you."

"I've heard it. A neighbor called about the bombing. I also saw it on the boob tube."

I could hardly believe Marlo wasn't at the bombsite, searching for her mother. "Do you know the condition of your mother?"

"The neighbor who called didn't know if my mother was in the house when the bomb went off. Would you know if she's living or dead?"

"Your mother is living. She's as well as can be expected. But suffering from shock."

I waited to give the girl an opportunity to ask where her mother was at the present time. All I received from her was an awkward silence.

She finally said, "If you happen to see her, give her my regards."

My blood began to boil. "Your mother needs more than your regards. She's suffering from the mental distress associated with losing her home. She needs you to comfort her, love her. She needs a place to stay."

The girl's voice became whiney, disconcerting. "Too bad."

"What's too bad?"

"Too bad my mother and I don't get along. She doesn't like the way I live; doesn't like my boyfriends. I've a close friend with me now. What am I supposed to do, tell him to leave because some nut blew up my mother's house?"

"That's precisely what you ought to do," I said, pounding my desk.

The girl whined, "I don't have to take orders from you."

"The orders aren't from me," I said with a plea in my voice. "They're from your own conscience. We're talking about your mother; the woman who bore you, loved you, fed you, nursed you, educated you..."

"I don't have to take this shit," the girl said, slamming down the phone.

I was left weak with anger. What could I say to the mother in my office? Why wouldn't a daughter tear herself away from a boyfriend when her mother's life was in danger? Was the girl so involved with sex that all other activities were meaningless? Or was she possessed by a demon whose callousness had no bounds?

I didn't know. I only know the girl had no respect for her mother. No respect for anyone but herself. The tragedy here was not only the loss of a home, but also the loss of a daughter. What could I say to a mother with a broken heart?

Feeling her pain as I entered my office, I took the woman's hands in mine. "I discussed the bombing of your home with your daughter. She…"

"She doesn't want me with her, does she?"

"I didn't say she didn't."

The woman pulled her hands away from mine. "You didn't say she did, either. You can't, can you?"

"What I wanted to say is this: You're welcome to stay in this rectory. Our housekeeper is in Ireland. You can be a big help around here. We've more bedrooms than we need. There's an especially nice room on the second floor. The Bishop of the diocese uses it when he visits, which is rare. If you'll agree…"

"You'll take me in and my daughter won't?"

"We'll be happy to have you?" I said, wondering how happy the pastor would be.

The woman's face became contorted. She began to cry. I waited patiently for her to stop. But she didn't stop. The crying went on and on. I thought she'd become ill if she continued. I didn't know what to do. I ran into the kitchen, seeking Vivian.

She was on her knees, peering into the oven, examining something she was baking.

At my wit's ends, I said, "Vivian, there a woman in my office who won't stop crying. She's lost her home and daughter. Maybe you can talk to her."

Without reflection or comment, Vivian rose to her feet, went into my office and took the woman in her arms. She held her tight. What she had to say to her, I don't know. I spent the next fifteen minutes pacing the corridor.

Demon of Lust

What to do with a crying woman presented a problem. A problem I was unable to solve.

Vivian had the solution. She had her arm around the woman when she brought her out of my office. They appeared as if they were best friends. "I'm going to give her something to eat," Vivian said to me, heading for the kitchen.

"She may have the spare room on the second floor," I advised her.

The woman appeared safe with Vivian. She turned to me and said, "You have a wonderful wife."

A wonderful wife! "She's not my..." I stopped short when I saw Vivian smile. Well, let the woman think what she pleases...for today, anyway.

The doorbell rang.

Two men were at the door. They were in their mid-forties. One was built like a long distance runner. The other man, like a wrestler. The runner said, "I'm Detective Casey and this is my partner, Detective Warren. We're investigating the bombing. Mind if we come in?"

"Not at all." I ushered them into the Monsignor's office, sat them down. "I don't know how much help I'll be."

Without asking for permission, Detective Casey lit a large cigar and clouded the room with smoke. He sucked on it several times as if he were drawing in ideas. "You live across the street from the bombed home. We were wondering if you saw anything suspicious in the neighborhood?"

"There was a man walking up and down the pavement, in front of this rectory. I called the police station about him. I wanted him to move on. I received no results. I'd say the man is a suspicious character. You won't be able to question him. He's gone now.

"The man is just a picket. He doesn't like the position the Church is taking on the rights of women to choose. And he's not gone. Look out the window, you'll see him."

I looked out the window; saw the big thug picketing the rectory. He was carrying a sign I couldn't read. "He was gone during the bombing," I said, thinking I was making an important point.

"You can't expect a man to be on the job every minute of the day."

"I suppose not." I'd be unwise pursuing the subject any further. I couldn't talk too much about the man without talking about Vivian and her haven in the rectory.

For the next half hour, I used all my ingenuity ducking questions pertaining to the bombing of the home across the street and the funeral parlor. On no occasion did I lie. However, I did use many mental reservations to protect Vivian. If the police learned Vivian was hiding in the rectory, Mario Togallini would soon have the information.

"You don't seem overly cooperative," Detective Casey said, biting down on his cigar.

I shrugged. "What more can I tell you?"

Detective Warren entered the conversation for the first time. "If you don't know something, you don't know something."

His logic wouldn't find its way into the pages of a philosophical textbook, but I was happy to agree with it. "That's right."

The men bid me farewell and were gone.

I took a liking to the woman seated at the kitchen table, daintily chewing on a piece of chicken. I liked the way she brought a cup of tea to her lips. The woman knew how to eat. She was a lady, got along well with Vivian.

Why her daughter couldn't get along with her was a mystery to me. Or was it a mystery? The daughter belonged to a new generation, selfish and sex-saturated. It was a generation that failed to recognize basic traditions, saw no distinction between right and wrong. A generation that will someday self-destruct. I didn't know whether to feel sorry for the old lady or her daughter.

The woman touched her lips with a napkin and said, "I'm finished now. Thank you very much."

"We don't know your name," I said to her.

"It's Mary Smith. A common name but I'm not common."

"You certainly aren't," I quickly assured her.

Vivian added, "You're going to be a delight to have in this house."

Demon of Lust

"Thank you again. Now, if you don't mind, I'd like to rest."

Vivian took Mary Smith's arm, led her up the stairs to the spare room on the second floor.

I went to bed that night in a state of confusion. Mario Togallini had me confused with his threat to bomb the rectory. Mary Smith's daughter had me confused because I didn't know how to cope with a selfish daughter. Monsignor Blazer had me confused because he merely nodded when I told him I'd given shelter to an elderly woman. Vivian had me confused because she was perfectly willing to accept another woman in the house.

With these problems in mind, sleep that night was difficult. I tossed and turned for an hour or more before finding myself at the bottom of a smoking crater, talking to a lobster-red monster.

The monster said to me, "I want Mario Togallini to have all the paintings. He gets the paintings. You get Vivian. Do you agree?"

"How can I agree? Mario will use the paintings to promote sex in the world."

The monster reached for my throat with a huge claw. "Do you agree?"

"Yes, sir."

"Refer to me as Master."

"Yes, Master. I agree."

"You will enjoy making love with Vivian."

"No question about it, sir. I mean Master."

"You will conduct yourself in a sinful way?"

"Yes, Master."

"You will always do what I tell you to do?"

"Of course, Master."

" You're not strong enough to resist me, are you?"

"Of course not, Master."

The monster began to laugh. His laughter filled the crater, hurt my ears. The laughter was loud enough to drive me out of my mind. If I could only escape from the crater. But there's no escape from hell.

CHAPTER 34

My escape from the crater came when Vivian shook my arm, awakened me, and shouted excitedly, "She's gone! Gone!"

I was the one who was gone, I thought. I agreed to do what the devil demanded of me. I was a lost soul.

Vivian announced sadly, "Mrs. Smith is gone."

My faculties began to function. I sat up. "Did she die during the night?"

Vivian's voice revealed impatience. "She didn't die. She left the rectory last night or early this morning. I've searched the house from cellar to attic. She's not here. I've been to the bombed out area, walked the streets, called Missing Persons. I can't find her. She gone, but she had no place to go."

I was pleased to know Vivian was interested in finding the woman. "If you'll excuse me, I'll put on my clothes, see what I can do."

Vivian reluctantly departed from the room.

I fell on my knees, asked God why the woman left the rectory. No longer would she have the care and attention she deserved. God didn't answer. The only thought that came to mind: We can't foresee what others will do when presented with a problem. We're not programmed that way. It's the story of free will. Nevertheless, I felt more responsible than ever for the woman, the loss of her home.

As I dressed, I looked at my watch. Nine-fifteen! I'd slept through the time for my Mass. Monsignor Blazer probably said it. I'd do my best to locate Mrs. Smith. I called her daughter, the police, the Bureau of Missing

Demon of Lust

Persons. I walked the streets of the Bronx, and spoke to neighbors. All to no avail. Mary was gone. No one knew where.

I was feeling low when I returned to the rectory at three o'clock in the afternoon. I was also hungry, had nothing to eat all day. The one bright spot in my memory was Vivian. She'd been kind to Mrs. Smith, attempted to find her.

Vivian was drumming her fingers on the kitchen table when I entered the room. I intended to ask her what more could be done to locate Mrs. Smith. She had a different topic to discuss.

"They're back!" she said.

Ants had recently invaded our kitchen. I thought the ants had returned. "Who's back?"

The pepper and saltshakers jumped when she banged her fist on the table. "The men watching the rectory. Something has to be done about them."

"I don't know what we can do. The police aren't going to move them. Picketing is legal."

"Then you'll have to move them."

"How can I move them? Taken together, those two men are four times my size. I'd have to grow considerably before I could even think about moving them."

"If you can't move them, I'll will. They're not going to keep me locked up in prison the rest of my life. I must get out at night, enjoy myself. Life is short."

"Life will be shorter if either one of those men see you." I disliked arguing with Vivian. I wanted her to be receptive to all ideas regarding her safety.

During another such debate, Monsignor Blazer overheard us arguing. He rushed into the kitchen, looking excited. "Is there anything wrong?"

"Just a difference of opinion," I said.

Exasperated, Vivian remarked to the pastor, "Your assistant is a hard man to convince."

"He usually listens to me."

Vivian pointed a finger at her breast. "But not to me."

"Could I help?"

The pastor's question was an invitation to seek his counsel. We couldn't reveal our problem to him. "We'll work the problem out, Monsignor. The problem has nothing to do with Vivian's recipes, so you need not worry."

He seemed satisfied with my remark. He left the kitchen.

Vivian picked up the argument where she left off, saying she'd take her chances getting by the men without being seen. She thought she could do it if she studied their movements.

The reasons I gave her for not attempting it were as sound as any logician could offer, however, she closed her mind to every idea I offered.

The arguments lasted for days. Morning, noon, and night I heard the same story, "I've got to get out."

"Why is it so important for you to get out of this rectory? Is it necessary for you to talk to strangers, consume alcohol? What's so important about that?"

"You don't get it," she responded. With the stubbornness of a deaf mule, she repeated, "You just don't get it!"

What I didn't get wasn't explained to me. What I did get was the Pope's wisdom when he advised his priests to stay single.

Vivian used every device conceivable to get me to let her leave the house. Day after day I felt myself being worn down. The day she truly had my head spinning was the day she cried…and cried…and cried. Mrs. Smith's tears were nothing compared to hers.

I tried to console her by holding her in my arms, very much like a father would hold his daughter after her husband walked out on her. She drove me back onto a couch, gave me a hard kiss. I wouldn't want this information repeated, but I had to struggle to prevent myself from being raped.

Could I get her out of the rectory and back into the rectory by speaking to the man at the rear of the house? He seemed to be a decent type. As a matter of fact, I thought he'd make Vivian a good husband. But he was still working for Mario Togallini, a killer. I couldn't risk his life by speaking to him.

Demon of Lust

The only solution I reached was the one I initially had. Vivian had to content herself, remain in the rectory and avoid being seen. If she wanted alcohol, I'd give her a glass of altar wine. Mentioning altar wine to her was a mistake. A large carving knife was on the kitchen counter. Grabbing it, she pointed it at my throat. Her eyes were wild with anger; her voice, rough and crude: "The next time you mention altar wine to me, you're dead."

I didn't know if she were joking or not. I disliked thinking too unkindly of her, but I realized she wasn't the same Vivian I knew nine years ago.

I watched her put the knife back into a drawer. She took out a potato peeler, an instrument less threatening than the knife. "I'll be in the basement for the next hour," she said dramatically. "I'm going down there to peel potatoes and think."

Think about what? Was she going to think about apologizing for threatening me with a knife? Or was she going to think about how to get passed the thugs without being seen?

She departed for the basement and I departed for my bedroom. Reaching the third floor, I thought about her behavior. It had changed so drastically it was hard to explain. Never before had she acted so irrationally, so cruelly to one trying to help her. Never before had she put a knife to my throat. There must be a reason beyond her desire to get out at night.

The reason for her change in behavior could be on the fourth floor. Taking the steps two at a time, I entered Vivian's room and examined the woman in the painting. I steeled myself against any surge of passion I might experience when viewing the painting. The steel melted to butter when I saw her. She was so beautiful, so happy to see me, so enchanting; I was drawn close to her. I became engulfed in passion.

"I'm here to ask if you had anything to do with the change in Vivian's behavior?" I felt like a fool speaking to a painting, but I was desperate for an answer.

The answer came when the woman lifted her eyebrows, as if she couldn't understand why I'd ask her such a question. I didn't see her eyebrows move. I did see they were higher then they were before I asked the question.

"So you don't think my question fair?"

The head shifted from left to right. Again, I saw no movement, only the results of the movement.

"Can you suggest anything I can do to make Vivian contented, happy?"

The woman's arms were suddenly extended.

"Vivian wants to make love. Is that what you mean?"

The woman nodded.

I found myself magnetized by her. I wanted to be with her. But I forced myself to back out of the room. Enthralled as I was, I knew the woman in the painting represented an evil force. She was able to communicate with me even though she didn't speak. She let me know Vivian was restless, wanted to leave the rectory because I refused to make love with her.

Maybe I should! No, I couldn't. How can I teach others virtue if I'm not virtuous myself? Instead of listening to the woman in the painting, I should be thinking of ways to destroy her.

That night Vivian hardly spoke to me as we worked on the dishes. The moment the dishes were clean and put away, she handed me a broom. "The floor needs sweeping, so sweep."

She had a nerve asking me to sweep. Rather than argue with her, I swept the floor. While I swept, she retired to her room.

I decided to take a walk. A cool breeze struck my face as I stepped outside the rectory. The big man with the picket sign was pacing the pavement. He had a definite limp. Blisters, I thought.

He glared as me as if I were responsible for the miserable job he had to do.

"We have foot powder and band aides in the rectory, if you need them," I said to him.

He gave me a look of disgust. He'd accept nothing from me. I was responsible for his discomfort.

Men are forever blaming others for their problems, I thought.

Walking aimlessly through the streets of the Bronx, I was saddened to see the deteriorated condition of the homes in the area. Groups of men were huddled together on corners smoking pot. They turned their backs

Demon of Lust

on me when I approached them. Instead of wasting time on street corners, why couldn't they get together and repair the homes in their neighborhood? Why couldn't they make an effort to halt the blight surrounding them? People don't always do what they're supposed to do.

I walked past a dilapidated brick building with a red light in one window. A middle-aged Mulatto woman pressed her face against the glass. Her face was caked with powder and rouge. Her lips were fire red. She smiled, exposing a dull gold tooth in the center of her mouth. She beckoned me to come in. She was inviting a priest to enter a house of prostitution.

The buildings in the Bronx were deteriorating. So were the people. How to stop the deterioration?

I turned onto a poorly lit street; saw a tall thin black boy with an attractive black girl. They were about twenty yards ahead of me, walking much faster than I normally walk. My attention was drawn to the girl. There was something familiar about her. Although the boy was taking long quick strides, she was able to keep up with him. She could walk fast...run fast. Cathy Washington! She was the girl who witnessed the murder of Ronnie Johnson.

Wasn't she risking her life walking the streets of this desolate neighborhood? If that long black limousine turned onto this street, she'd be unable to get away. She couldn't outrun machine gun fire. The thugs would murder her...murder her friend.

For several seconds, I was tempted to warn her. I changed my mind. The girl was intelligent, aware of the dangers of walking the streets of the Bronx at night, conscious of the killers in the neighborhood. Who was I to tell her what to do, what not to do?

She and her friend soon disappeared from sight. I didn't know if they turned into one of the homes along the way or disappeared into the darkness.

I walked until I could walk no more. I wanted to be extremely tired when I went to bed; hoping for a good night's sleep without any wild dreams. I said "good night" to the big thug when I reached the rectory. He acknowledged my "good night" with a grunt.

Louis V. Rohr

Once again, I'd difficulty falling asleep. The sleep I finally experienced was worse than the struggle I had in getting to sleep. The woman in the painting was in bed with me.

"Why don't you do it, you prig?" she nagged. "You'll never rest until you do. If you fail to make love with Vivian, people will die. You'll be responsible. Your conscience will tear you apart. People have already died. How many must die before you're convinced?" The woman shook my arm.

I awakened with a start, bolted up in the bed. The woman was standing at the side of the bed. No! It wasn't the woman in the painting. It was Monsignor Blazer. He never looked more serious.

"Please get up, Father Tom. The police are here. They want to talk to you. Two people have been murdered."

CHAPTER 35

Glancing at my watch, I saw it was three o'clock in the morning. Dressing as quickly as I could, I followed Monsignor Blazer down the stairs and into his office, where I was met by the same two detectives I'd met before, Casey and Warren. Both men stood when I entered.

Detective Casey had a fresh cigar in his mouth. He spun it around with his tongue as he stuck out his hand to shake mine. "Nice to see you again, Father. But not under these circumstances."

Detective Warren failed to shake my hand or say anything.

"What circumstances?" I asked.

Monsignor Blazer answered for him. "Two men have gone to their eternal rest."

Detective Casey removed the cigar from his mouth. "The two pickets are dead. Come see for yourself."

With Monsignor Blazer trailing behind the detectives and me, we approached a man's body lying on the sidewalk. A dull moon cast an eerie light on the still figure. Blood seeped from his stomach. A picket sign was in the gutter.

The man was shorter, bulkier, and balder than the man who carried the sign during the day. A different shift, a different man, I thought, whispering a prayer for him.

"Get a load of this," I heard someone say.

Looking up, I saw Detective Warren nudging his partner with an elbow. The focus of his attention was on a woman, a very shapely and beautiful woman, walking towards us. Her walk was a bit unsteady as if she had one drink too many.

The detectives registered surprise when Vivian smiled at them and said, "Good evening, gentleman." She made her way into the rectory.

Detective Casey's question was blunt. "Who the hell is that beautiful woman?"

Monsignor Blazer answered matter-of-factly. "Our housekeeper and a very good cook."

Detective Casey munched on his cigar. "Where do you find beautiful housekeepers who can cook?"

"She's a friend of mine, filling in for our regular housekeeper," I said, almost apologetically. "Our regular housekeeper is in Ireland, taking care of a sick mother."

"Does she date?" Detective Warren asked.

Before I could answer, Detective Casey said to his partner, "Forget the housekeeper. We have work to do. How soon will the medical examiner be here?"

"Thirty minutes was his estimate, but you can't believe a word that guy says. I'll call him back, if it's all right with you." The detective reached into his coat pocket, pulled out a cell phone.

"Give him time to get here before calling. In the meantime, I'll have another look at the second body, the one behind the rectory. I might've failed to see some evidence the first time I looked. You stay here, wait for the medical examiner."

"I'll wait."

Detective Casey pointed the soggy end of his cigar at Monsignor Blazer and me. "If you wish to join me."

"I'll join you," I said. "I don't know about the Monsignor."

"I won't go," the Monsignor said to the detective. "Father Tom will represent me."

A thin flashlight in the hands of Detective Casey was helpful, as we made our way through the darkness to the rear of the rectory. The flashlight

Demon of Lust

illuminated the body of a man lying against a fence in the alley. He'd died in the same manner as the man at the front of the rectory. Blood seeped out of his stomach, into the dirt.

"May I borrow your flashlight?" I asked the detective.

He handed it to me.

I focused the light on the face of the dead man. It was like a statue, carved from granite...handsome, strong, familiar. It was the face of the man I'd met, the man I hoped to introduce to Vivian. My heart went out to him. He wanted to get away from Mario Togallini and his thugs, probably worked overtime to earn enough money to do so. Now he was dead. He waited too long.

Detective Casey knelt down and examined the dead man's right hand. It held a twig from a nearby tree. "Look here!" he exclaimed. "This man was trying to write something." He focused the light on the dirt, close to the man's hand.

Sure enough, the man had used the twig to write the following in the dirt: STABBED BY A WOMA...

"What's a woma?" the detective asked.

Without thinking, I said, "A woma is a woman with the n missing."

"You should be the detective," was the response. "This man is telling us he was killed by a woman. A woman he didn't know. Otherwise he'd have written her name. But now the question: Who is the woman?"

There was only one answer to the question. Vivian! She'd killed the two men for the simple reason she wanted to get out of the rectory, free herself from prison. She'd terminated two lives to satisfy a desire to have a night out.

Should I give this information to Detective Casey now, or should I give Vivian an opportunity to explain? Killers, such as Vivian... especially those possessed by a demon...always rationalize what they do. So why not reveal what I know to Detective Casey? He'd judge her objectively, put her in jail if she killed the two men.

But did she kill them? I can't be sure. In many respects, she's a wonderful person; kind, thoughtful, warm. On the other hand, she's a seductress, a hypnotist. She could stab a man while he was basking in her beauty. Stab him before he felt the knife going into his belly. She was quick....

While considering the pros and cons of Vivian's possible guilt, I barely heard the detective ask: "What do you have to say about this murder?"

"I don't know what to say."

"You're in a position to know who's responsible."

"Why me?"

"You know what's going on in this parish. You know why some crazy Catholic would kill a man picketing the front of a rectory, why he'd kill a man picketing the rear. Supply me with some ideas."

"I've already mentioned one idea to you. I believe the murdered men were connected to the bombings of the funeral parlor and the home across the street. Perhaps a woman who lost a loved one has decided to strike back."

"I'll look into the possibility."

"I wish you would."

"We can be sure of one thing," the detective said, lighting his cigar. "The owner of the bombed home was a woman. However, she'd nothing to do with the murders."

"She was too old to kill anyone."

"Not only was she too old, she was dead. She jumped off the George Washington Bridge yesterday afternoon."

If the detective had struck me in the face with his fist, he couldn't have hurt me more. I liked that lady. I wanted to find her, help her, and protect her. "I'm sorry."

When we returned to the front of the rectory, the medical examiner and his assistant were there, talking to Detective Warren. A policeman was also there, running a yellow tape around the crime scene. Detective Casey left me to relate his findings to the medical examiner, a thin Oriental with a goat's beard.

Feeling as if I were in the way, I excused myself and returned to the rectory.

Vivian was seated at the kitchen table, sipping a cup of coffee. Seeing me, she raised her cup and said, "Have some coffee?"

I'd a hundred questions to ask her before drinking coffee, however, I said, "I'll enjoy a cup."

She poured coffee into a cup, put a spoonful of sugar in it, and a little milk. "I hope this is the way you like it."

"It's fine. I took a sip and studied her face. She looked tired but just as lovely as ever. Actually, she looked angelic. Could an angel stab two men?

"Is the picket dead?" she asked.

"I'm afraid so."

"Do the detectives have any suspects?"

"Not to my knowledge."

"I didn't like the man who picketed in front of the rectory, but I regret he's dead. We live in a world in which one person doesn't think twice about killing another. Our world is animalistic, brutal, wild."

"Wild, indeed," I muttered. "Did you know a second man was killed, the man watching the rear of the rectory?"

The faintest flicker of surprise appeared on her lovely face.

"I didn't know."

Was she lying or wasn't she? I glanced at her dress. No blood spots. If she'd stabbed the men, would their blood spurt out, stain her dress? I'll examine her coat later.

I put my hand on hers. "Vivian, you know I'd do anything for you, don't you?"

She stared at my hand on hers, then into my eyes. "I think so."

"Then I want you to answer a few questions. I want some honest answers."

"About what?"

"About the two men who died. What can you tell me about them?"

"I've seen them from afar. And that's all. What other information could I possibly give you about them?"

"You went out tonight without my permission. I'd like to know if you had anything to do with their death…"

I never finished the sentence. Her eyes blazed, and with one stroke of her arm, she swept two cups of coffee, a pitcher of milk, and one container of sugar off the table. She shouted with indignation, "Are you accusing me of murdering those men?"

I failed to expect such an explosive response. "No! No! No! I'm merely questioning a strange coincidence. The night you decided to run the risk of leaving the rectory is the night the men were killed."

"I didn't kill them."

"If you say you didn't kill them, I believe you. I doubt if you'd lie to me."

I thought my statement would pacify her. It didn't. Her face was flushed when she said, "You have one hell of a nerve asking me if I killed those men. Why would I kill them?"

"Because you wanted to get out, do your thing, whatever that is."

"I wanted to get out, I won't deny that. The big thug at the front of the house had extended his walks to forty yards or more beyond the rectory. He walked slowly, going and returning. I think his feet were hurting him. I merely slipped out of the house, waited till he was lost in the darkness, and then I made my move. It was easy."

The explanation seemed logical enough. I wanted to believe her. Deep within the recesses of my mind, I knew I loved her. Yet I doubted her.

My doubts obviously showed on my face, for Vivian returned to her chair and spoke as if she were my boss. "I want to ask you this: How can you expect to sell the teachings of the Church to anyone? You couldn't sell the police the idea of moving those two damned pickets away from our home?"

I winced when she used the term damned for two men who'd just lost their lives. Stammering, I said, "The police follow certain rules and regulations. They have written policies…"

"Baloney!"

For an instant, I could understand why some men become wife beaters. Standing, I said, "I've heard enough from you. I must leave now, prepare for Mass."

"I wouldn't be surprised if you say the Mass for the two thugs who were killed."

"I intend to say the Mass for them. I'll also pray for Mary Smith."

"Think you'll find her if you pray for her?"

"I know where she is."

"You do?"

"I do. She jumped off the George Washington Bridge. Her body is in the City Morgue. Her soul is with God."

I was surprised to see tears run down Vivian's face. She tried to speak, couldn't. She wasn't so hard-boiled, after all.

CHAPTER 36

Shortly after lunch that day the telephone rang. I'd instructed Vivian not to answer the phone. I took the call. "St. Matthew's Rectory."

A familiar but sarcastic voice came over the wire, one I didn't wish to hear. It was the voice of Mario Togallini. "Haven't you learned the Ten Commandments yet?"

"I learned them years ago."

"There's an important Commandment that says, Thou Shalt Not Kill."

"All the Commandments are important."

"This Commandment is at the top of my list when two of my best men are killed. Why'd you have them killed?"

The accusation took me by surprise. "I didn't have them killed. Nor did I bomb an old woman's home and a funeral parlor filled with innocent people."

My remarks silenced Mario for several seconds. His tone was nasty. "Don't change the subject."

"I'm not changing the subject. A number of people have been killed, all in my neighborhood. The deaths can be traced to your desire to recover paintings your brother produced. All those paintings were inspired by a demon. Your brother didn't want you to have them, Mario. He wanted them destroyed. You'd rather kill people than forego the paintings."

"More people may die in your neighborhood if you fail to find Vivian for me. My property must be returned."

I felt as if I were talking to the devil. "Your so-called property is your ticket to hell. Forget the paintings, Mario. Forget Vivian. Forget the idea of punishing her. Above all, forget your desire to kill innocent people."

"You haven't seen anythin' yet," he said gleefully. "I've been told you teach in a Catholic school. How'd you enjoy seein' your school blown apart?"

My spine became an icicle. "You wouldn't…"

"I've already proved to you, I would."

"Then I'll go to the police."

"Your word against mine. I'll deny everything. I've the politicians and the police in my back pockets, guardin' my ass. You've no one."

"God is on my side."

"God ain't gonna help you. He wants you to suffer."

"He may not help me in the immediate future. Eventually, he'll help me."

"In the meantime, you can depend upon me if you give me some information."

"What information?"

" Who killed my two men?"

"Why ask me? I don't know. I can tell you this, I didn't kill them."

"I'm not surprised you didn't kill them. I doubt if you'd even have them killed. You're a Holy Joe. I've never met a Holy Joe who'd put a hole in anybody. But I think you know who…"

I slammed down the phone. I could no longer talk to the man. Even listening to him made me feel dirty.

Mario Togallini confirmed two thoughts I'd in mind. He didn't know who killed his men. And he didn't suspect Vivian. Not yet.

I suspected her, yet I couldn't be absolutely sure she was guilty. I couldn't be sure of anything.

I heard someone at the front door, trying to open it. I left the kitchen; saw Vivian struggling with the door.

"What are you doing?"

"I'm trying to open this damned door. It's stuck."

"Thank God it's stuck."

"What do you mean?"

"I mean you're risking your life if you go beyond the door. You should be aware of the danger."

Her tone was resolute. "I've told you before, no one is going to make a prisoner out of me. Besides, the goons are gone."

"I'm not so sure…"

"Look out the window."

I entered Monsignor Blazer's office, looked out the window. As far as I could see, no one was watching the rectory. The medical examiner, his assistant, the detectives, and the body of the picket were gone. I returned to the foyer. Vivian was again tugging at the door.

She stuck her tongue out at me. "Convinced?"

"I'm not convinced. I don't see anyone observing the rectory. That doesn't mean no one is out there. Mario could have this rectory under surveillance from a car or a building. You're risking your life if you go out today."

Vivian gave the door a hard yank. It opened. "I don't agree with you. I'm going out."

For twenty yards or more, I followed her down the street.

She walked with much deliberation, yet not too much in a hurry. No one came out of a car or a building. I felt a sense of relief. She wasn't going to be stopped. I couldn't understand why she ran the risk of being seen by one of Togallini's men.

Or was it understandable? Vivian wasn't being influenced by her common sense. Nor was I influencing her. She was being influenced by the demon dwelling in the painting propped up on a bureau facing her bed.

When I was a boy, I tried to destroy a Togallini painting. I'd try again. The power of a priest should surpass the power of a demon.

Taking a knife from the kitchen, I entered Vivian's room with a plan to cut the woman in the painting to shreds. I'd close my eyes, not look at her. I'd then turn the canvas around to face the wall; attack her with the knife.

Demon of Lust

Entering the room, I dropped the knife at the head of the bed. I closed my eyes, approached the painting, gripped both sides of the canvas, and turned it around to face the wall. The painting grew heavier as I moved it. I didn't have the strength to hold it for long. It dropped on the bureau with a thud. I had it turned around, surprised the demon with the speed in which I moved it. He surprised me by adding additional weight to the painting.

I examined the blank side of the canvas, wiped away a small spider web hanging from the top of the frame. Then suddenly the canvas was no longer blank. The woman was on the canvas, not a front view of her, but a rear view. She was standing, facing the wall and shivering. She apparently knew I'd strike her in the back with the knife.

Was this some demonic apparition I was viewing? I believed so! The demon was using an apparition to prevent me from striking the woman.

The apparition almost worked, for I found myself shaking at the strange sight. How could I strike a naked, living woman? I couldn't! Yes I could! Raising the knife above my head, I lunged towards the painting. When the point of the knife struck her back, she cried, "Ooooh!"

But instead of the knife ripping open the canvas, it struck what seemed to be hard rubber. The knife bounced back at me and brushed my face. A tiny cut appeared on the woman's back. Blood trickled down her back. Or was it crimson paint? Or perhaps some unknown liquid made in hell?

She was no longer shivering. She was sobbing. The more attention I gave to the sobbing sounds, the more I became convinced the sounds were better classified as muffled laughter. The woman was laughing at me! She defeated me in my youth. She defeated me again in my manhood.

Confused, I backed away from her, went to my room. I asked myself the same question I asked when I was a teenager. What can I do to destroy the painting? I had no answer.

Glancing at the alarm clock in my room, I realized I had to teach a Religion class in twenty minutes. I ran down the stairs and jumped into my Ford Fairlane, parked in the driveway near the rectory. The engine coughed a couple of times before starting. I gave the car the gas, made the trip in record time.

"Good afternoon, Padre," my high school students sang in unison when I entered the classroom.

"Good afternoon, Scholars," I responded. "What shall we discuss today?"

A thin black boy with a head of wire wool answered, "Sex!"

The students had a fit of laughter.

"Sex is a popular topic for discussion," I said, making an effort to have the last laugh. "If used within the confines of marriage, sex brings much joy. If used outside the confines of marriage, sex brings heartaches. You students are mature enough to know sex is a device God uses to people the world. Attempt to thwart God's plan by using sex as a plaything, and you're in trouble. Instead of following the will of God, you follow the will of the devil."

A bright looking teenager in the second row shook his head. "Nobody believes in the devil anymore, Padre."

"Nobody? I believe in the devil. And so should you. The devil is a former angel, driven out of heaven for rebelling against God. He's God competition on earth. His greatest wile is to convince you he doesn't exist."

A boy with the sallow complexion of an Oriental stated: "You've heard the joke, the devil made me do it…"

"I've heard it many times. It's no joke. It's a truism. The devil can influence your actions by placing sex and other attractions in your path. He can't force you into committing sin; do anything you don't want to do, but he can stir your passions, weaken your will, and have you believe there's nothing wrong in committing sin. You must be strong, resist his temptations."

As I spoke, I noticed a tall black boy in a corner seat in the rear row. As tall as he was, I hadn't paid particular attention to him before. He seemed interested in the lesson, but he didn't ask or answer any questions.

I found his name on a chart showing the layout of the seats in the classroom, the name of each student occupying a seat. I called on him: "Joshua

Demon of Lust

Roosevelt, please stand up, tell us if you believe in the existence of the devil? Give us your reasons for your belief or disbelief."

When he stood, I was surprised to see how tall he was. He was well over six feet, much taller than I'd estimated.

He seemed to be quite sure of himself when he spoke: "Ah believes in devils and demons, Father. Dey gotta be the ones in dis world who're promotin' trouble. Dey gotta be tellin' de gangstas in de Bronx, and other places, to knife dis woman, shoot dat man. Dey gotta be in Africa and Harlem where black men are killin' der black brothers. Dey gotta be in for'ign coun'ries where wars break out. Men slaughter der neighbors. Devils in dis country tell girls to kill dere own chil'run…smother 'em with a pillow…drown 'em." The boy sat down.

"Very good, Joshua. I hope you're ready to fight the evil forces when confronted with them."

"Yes, Father, Ah am."

While listening to Joshua Roosevelt speak, I realized there was something familiar in his voice. I'd heard it before, and it wasn't in the classroom. The moment he said, "Ah am," I knew where I'd heard it. It was in the confessional. He was the boy who stole the Rolls Royce, lent it to Ronnie Johnson…the boy who knew Cathy Washington.

A debate broke out in class between those who believed in the devil and those who didn't. Somehow I couldn't enter the debate, settle it. My mind was centered on Joshua Roosevelt. I wanted to talk to him about the death of his friend, Ronnie Johnson. I couldn't. The seal of confession had sealed my lips.

CHAPTER 37

Monsignor Blazer sat down for dinner that evening at six o'clock. There was no dinner to serve him. No Vivian. When I realized Vivian hadn't returned to the rectory, I began to worry. Had she been spotted by one of Togallini's men? Had she been kidnapped? Killed?

In an effort to hide my fears from Monsignor Blazer, I called a Chinese restaurant and ordered Chop Suey, enough for three. At six forty-five the doorbell rang. I answered the ring. The food arrived in a brown-paper bag, delivered by a young Italian wearing horn rimmed glasses. He handed me an invoice. I gave it back to him. "Bill the rectory, please. And add a twenty percent gratuity."

Without a "Thank you," he took the invoice from me and jammed it into a pocket.

I looked at him suspiciously. Was he one of Togallini's men? He could have paid off a Chinese driver, gained entrance into the rectory just to show me it could be done. Before I could question him, the Italian turned on his heel and departed.

When I entered the dining room, Monsignor Blazer had his breviary close to his nose, trying to read the small print. I served him the Chop Suey.

Without looking at the food, he asked, "Where's Vivian?"

"Her evening off."

"She deserves an evening off."

"She sure does."

"Father Tom, you know my eye sight is impaired. But there are rare moments when God gives me the ability to see well. Yesterday afternoon I observed Vivian in the kitchen, putting flowers in a vase. I was able to see her without the film, which normally clouds what I see. I saw her as you see her. She's remarkably beautiful."

"She is, Monsignor."

The Monsignor tasted the Chop Suey, nodded his approval. "You *are* aware of her beauty, Father Tom?"

I felt the blood rush to my face. "Yes, of course. I've known her a long time."

The prelate said: "A long time! If I'd known a woman as beautiful as Vivian when I was your age, she'd have influenced me. It's difficult to suppress human nature."

"Difficult to suppress? Yes, Monsignor. But with the help of God, it can be done."

His smile was pleasant. "With the help of God, all things are possible." He took a forkful of Chop Suey, chewed it and added, "You're a good priest."

"I try to be."

"Just one question, put my mind at rest. Since Vivian has joined us in this rectory, you haven't tried to kiss her, have you?"

Coming from the Monsignor, the question was a strange one. I answered quickly, "No, Monsignor, I haven't." I stopped to analyze my answer. Had I told the truth? I had! Vivian had tried to kiss me. I hadn't tried to kiss her.

"Just one more question…"

The onions in the Chop Suey seemed to sour in my mouth. Was the Monsignor going to trap me with the next question?

"Do you think the women in this parish will gossip when they see her?"

"I wouldn't be surprised if they do. But we can say Vivian is temporary. She'll be gone when our regular housekeeper returns."

"Another point," the prelate said with a funny smile. "We can say this is an affirmative action rectory. We don't deny a woman employment just because she's beautiful."

"That's right," I said with enthusiasm.

But was it right? My enthusiasm diminished when I realized I hadn't given my pastor the full story. I hadn't told him that Vivian was in the rectory because she was hiding from men trying to kidnap her, torture her, kill her. I hadn't told him about my love for her, the bombings, the stolen paintings, and the demon in the rectory. I didn't wish to deceive him, but I thought it best he didn't know all the ramifications connected with a highly complex Vivian.

Vivian's portion of the Chop Suey was cold when I put it in the refrigerator. I was in hopes she'd return before nine o'clock. My hopes weren't realized. I'd sit in my office and wait for her. I read my breviary until I could no longer concentrate on it. Was Vivian out for a good time? Had she been kidnapped? The two questions almost drove me out of my mind. I knew how a father feels when his daughter stays out all night. Or how a husband feels when his wife fails to return home. I couldn't doze off. I could do nothing but wait.

At two-fifteen in the morning, the telephone rang.

"St. Matthew's rectory."

"That you, Tom?"

I felt a tremendous sense of relief. "Yes, Vivian."

"I can't get in."

"What do you mean you can't get in?"

"I can't get in the rectory. The pickets are on the march again."

"You sure?"

"I'm sure. One is walking in front of the rectory; the other is sitting on a trashcan in the rear; waiting, watching. I saw them both."

I was tempted to give Vivian a piece of my mind for going out. I decided not to. "What do you want me to do?"

"Come and get me?"

"If I bring you back to the rectory, the men will spot you."

"They won't see me if we're careful. You can pick me up, drive back to the rectory. I'll lie down in the rear of the station wagon when you pull

Demon of Lust

into your parking spot in the driveway. You can get out of the car, walk back to the character at the front of the house, and open up a conversation with him. While you divert his attention, I'll get out of the Fairlane, run for the cellar door. He won't see me. Just be sure to leave the cellar door open. Savvy?"

"I savvy. I also understand you're risking your life. Why don't you stay where you are?"

"I can't. I'm out of money. I didn't bring enough cash with me. A taxicab driver charged me enough to put a down payment on a new bus."

"Well, if you're willing to risk it, I'll pick you up. Where are you?"

"In Brooklyn."

"Brooklyn! You realize I'm in the Bronx. It's quite a long drive…"

"It's not too bad at this hour. I'm in the Bay Ridge section of Brooklyn. Take the address down."

She gave me the address of her apartment and told me how to get there. After noting the information on a slip of paper, I ran down to the cellar, opened a side door, and was at the front door in one minute flat. Opening the door, I recalled I'd no money for gas.

My conscience nagged at me when I removed thirty dollars from a box reserved for the poor. I justified the theft by telling myself I was as poor as anyone I knew. Besides, I'd replace the money if the pastor remembered to give me my allowance.

Pulling out of the driveway, I came close to running down a bushy-haired Italian picket who cursed when he jumped out of the path of my car. He approached me with murder in his eyes. "Where ya tink ya're goin'?"

"An emergency," I said, hoping he'd enough education to know a priest often gets up in the middle of the night to take a sick call.

Whether he understood it or not, I was on my way, traveling through trash littered streets where old ladies and little children searched garbage cans for food. I saw drunks and dope addicts lying helplessly against buildings. Prostitutes were promoting their wares. Teenagers were peering into the windows of automobiles, contemplating which cars to steal.

Louis V. Rohr

I heard the sound of a gun fired several times. I slowed the Ford down, debated whether I should stop and investigate the shooting. I decided not to. No bullets had struck me. Nevertheless, they hurt me. Someone else was hurt. What was it Vivian said about me? I worried about the world. I couldn't help it.

My gas gauge read one-quarter full when I reached the West Side Highway. Travel on the Highway was quicker, more pleasant, and less distracting than travel in the Bronx. And I'd enough gas to make a return trip without filling the tank.

I used some of the poor-box money to pay the toll through the tunnel connecting Manhattan with Brooklyn. Several blocks beyond the tunnel's exit, I saw a look-alike family stripping a new Honda of its parts. A mother, father, teen-age son, and a twelve-year-old daughter, were busy removing parts from the Honda; loading them into a large Chrysler van.

The parents of this family were setting a bad example for their children. Should I speak to them about it? No, I shouldn't. I'd never get to Vivian's if I stopped to solve every problem I ran across. I continued on.

Locating Vivian's apartment was less complicated than I'd anticipated. And the building itself was far more elaborate than I'd imagined. It was an eight story, white brick structure that appeared recently built. It was as attractive as any on Park Avenue.

Vivian had given me the number of her apartment. I pressed a small brass button opposite her initials, was rewarded with her voice coming over the intercom. "You here already, Tom?"

"I'm here."

"I'll unlock the main door. Take the elevator to the eighth."

A buzzer sounded, unlocking the elevator door. I entered a cage lined with brass. Pressing button number eight, gave me the feeling of an astronaut shooting skywards.

When the elevator doors slid open, Vivian was waiting for me. She was wearing a red silk party dress I hadn't seen before. She gave me the impression she hadn't dressed for a trip to the Bronx.

Demon of Lust

"Let me show you the apartment," she said, linking her arm in mine. She escorted me into a living room furnished with black Oriental furniture and silk rugs. Shimmering silver drapes covered the windows. A huge ivory fan decorated one wall. The opposite wall contained the most striking object in the living room. It was a portrait of a golden haired woman, nude, poised and ready to seduce me or anyone else who viewed her. The few seconds I gazed at her caused my heart to beat madly against my chest.

I heard Vivian say, "It's one of Togallini's paintings. I have the others here, too."

No question about it. The painting was magnificent. But the woman in the painting fixed her eyes on me. My eyes met hers. My body heated up to such an extent I hardly knew what to do. I turned to Vivian, "Are you ready to leave now?"

"You haven't seen the other rooms in this apartment. Let me show them to you before we leave."

Anything to please her, I thought…anything to get away from this painting. "I'll take a quick look at your apartment."

The kitchen was something out of a Good Housekeeping Magazine. The floor was made of silvery marble. All the appliances, counters, cabinets, lights were sparkling new. A perfect kitchen, I thought.

"Let me show you the bedroom!" Vivian pulled me into a room containing a king-sized bed, with matching bureau, chest of drawers, chaise lounge, lamp tables, and….I saw nothing else. My attention was drawn to the most striking object in the room. It was another work of art by Togallini. A life-like painting of a nude brunette. The woman in the painting had the power to draw me to her, the power to fill my body with a desire to have sex. I couldn't take my eyes off her.

Suddenly, I felt Vivian's arms around me. She held me close to her. Again, I looked at the woman in the painting. She seemed to be telling me to go ahead, make love with Vivian.

Vivian whispered, "Could we make love? No one will know."

I wanted to make love. Everything encouraged me to do so: the bed, the woman I loved, and the portrait on the wall. I turned and faced Vivian. Never before had I felt so compelled to take her in my arms.

From somewhere within the recesses of my memory, I recalled words uttered on a mountain two thousand years ago: "All these things will I give you, if you kneel down and worship me."

The words were uttered by the devil to Christ. The devil had offered Christ all the pleasures and riches of the world if He'd fall down and worship him.

I glanced at the painting on the wall. The woman's chin had dropped. She'd read my mind, knew what I was thinking. She seemed to say, "What an inopportune time to have such thoughts. A time when Vivian was offering herself to you."

I took Vivian's arm, led her out of the bedroom. "Get your coat. We're going to drive back to the rectory."

CHAPTER 38

Vivian pouted all the way back to the rectory. I asked her several questions relating to the ownership of the apartment. She ignored the questions.

The only question she answered was one I should've asked before leaving the building: "Vivian, I saw two Togallini paintings. You have many more. Where are they?"

"I've already told you."

"No, you haven't."

"They're in a bedroom I use for storage."

"I didn't see a second bedroom."

"You didn't see it because you were so damned anxious to get out of the master bedroom. What's wrong with you, anyhow? If you're in love with me, why can't you make love with me? You make me feel as if I'm imposing on you. Aren't you a man?"

Now it was my turn to be silent. Her questioning my manhood hurt me more than I care to admit. Is a man less than a man if he refuses to be a rabbit? Why had I refused to make love with her? There was no explanation she'd accept. If I gave her reasons, she'd laugh at me, accuse me of preaching. What's wrong with preaching? Do we listen to God, or do we listen to the devil?

Arguments relating to the pros and cons of sex should be taught in schools. It was ridiculous to teach students how to circumvent the consequences of sex without giving them valid reasons for simply avoiding it. Not that it's so easy to avoid....

Dimming the lights of the Fairlane, I swung around a corner, headed for the rectory. Vivian slid low in her seat to avoid being seen by a man standing in the driveway. Putting on the high beams to blind him, I honked the horn and drove towards him.

Using an expletive, he leaped to the side of the driveway, avoided being hit.

Driving the car about twenty yards into the driveway, I turned off the engine and lights; hurried back to the man, hoping to divert his attention away from Vivian while she moved from the car to the rectory. Mocking annoyance, I said, "Don't you know enough to avoid standing in a driveway? I almost hit you."

"You're damned lucky you didn't. You hit me with your junk heap and I hit you with my…" His hand darted into an opening in his coat as if he were going for a gun. Evidently, he thought better of pointing a gun at me. He pulled an empty hand from beneath his coat, pointed a long narrow finger at me. "Be careful what you say to me."

I heard my car door close. Vivian had made her escape without being detected.

The man seemed to be studying me as if he couldn't decide whether to kill me or let me live. His eyes were devoid of humor. His lips were a thin line across the lower section of his face. I'd never met a killer before. This man, I thought, was a killer.

He was the direct opposite of the man killed at the rear of the rectory, the man who wanted to get away from his associates, and the man who revealed the name of the thug who threw the bomb. "Is your name Tony Barber?"

The thin lips tightened. "How'd you know my name?"

"I'm not in the habit of revealing all the information I have. For example, I may know who bombed the funeral home. That doesn't mean I'm going to the police with the information."

A profane word broke from the man's lips. Again, he leered at me. "Have you been informed that dead men tell no tales?"

"You threatening me?"

"I'm telling you I don't like this assignment. I'd like to end it any way I can. If I put an end to you, I put an end to this lousy job. Get it?"

"I'll have to notify Mario Togallini he has a disgruntled employee on the job. Perhaps he'll give you something more suitable to your talents, like blowing up an old folks hospital."

The man stared at me, long and hard. "You're asking for trouble."

"Not me. I'm just a simple priest, trying to keep peace and harmony in this parish. You don't contribute to the peace and harmony when you picket the rectory."

"I do what I'm paid to do."

"Were you paid to dispose of the men who preceded you?"

"You mean the two men who were killed?"

"I do."

"Of course not. We're looking for those killers. If you know who they are, it'll pay you to let us know their names."

"I can't give you their names. All I can give you is a warning: Watch your back."

The man issued a series of foul words. His vocabulary of expletives was so extensive; I could no longer remain in his presence. I made my way to the rectory door, took out my key. Before opening the door, I looked back at the man. From a distance, he looked normal enough. I wondered if he were possessed by a demon. A demon that prompted him to curse, to violate God's wonderful gift of speech...to kill.

Vivian was waiting for me when I arrived in the rectory. She was smiling. "Wasn't that easy?"

"Risky is a better term."

She shook her head. "Not risky at all. I no longer feel confined. With your help, I can come and go as I please."

"No, you can't. The man who stood in the driveway is a killer. He doesn't like the job he's doing. He'd like to put an end to the job by putting an end to you or me."

"We're too smart for him, Tommy Boy. He's not going to get his hands on me."

"There are people in this world who never learn, regardless of many sad experiences. I'm sorry to say, you're one of them. You leave this rectory again and you risk your life."

Again, Vivian shook her head. "There are people in the Bronx who worry unnecessarily. You're one of them. If you're not worrying about the world, you're worrying about me. I can take care of myself, so please stop worrying."

Thinking it was useless to attempt to change her mind, I said, "It's too late to argue. We better get to bed."

"Is my hero going to bed with me tonight?"

I was tired. That's why her offer sounded tempting. I thought about it for several moments, while she looked at me with great anticipation. I finally said, "No. I'm afraid not."

"And why not?"

"We've been over this before. You know why I can't. So go to bed, say your Hail Mary, and get some sleep."

Without further comment, she turned on her heel, and left me.

I watched her as she ascended the stairs. Although I was able to conceal it, my body cried out for her. I wanted to hold her in my arms, make love with her. Celibacy is a difficult state for some men. Unfortunately, I was among those who found it difficult.

As I undressed, a thought struck me. In view of the men watching the rectory, why hadn't I left Vivian in her apartment? She was without funds. But any money she had in the rectory, I could have delivered to her. Did I fail to leave her in Brooklyn because she wanted to be near me? Sometimes I've difficulty understanding what I do. Especially when I'm considering a problem relating to Vivian.

I'd no trouble getting off to sleep. My troubles began when I started to dream.

Demon of Lust

Isacaron was at the side of my bed, shaking me. "Wake up, Tommy. I am here to render you a great favor."

In the dream, I opened my eyes and saw an exceedingly handsome demon with wavy hair. His eyes were deeply set, piercing, and blood-shot. Muscles rippled all over his naked body. He was as colorful as a boiled lobster.

"I'll escort you to Vivian's bedroom." he whispered. "One flight up will bring you to heaven. She is waiting. She'll welcome you with open arms."

My response was automatic. "I can't go. I'm a priest."

"Priests are men with the same desires as other men," Isacaron said. His voice seemed to be from every nation, every town, and every hamlet in the world.

"Desires are cravings, Isacaron. Some are illegitimate. Such cravings must be controlled. Read St. Augustine. He didn't do what he desired to do. He did the opposite. What he did, he didn't desire to do."

The demon laughed, a deep irritating laugh. "You suggest I read Augustine. I knew that old reprobate from the day he was born till the day he died. When was he born? The year 354, I believe. I don't recall the day or month. My memory isn't as sharp as it once was. With each passing century, my memory grows dimmer. You will understand when you grow old."

"You knew him personally?"

"I knew him better than I know you. I was his guardian angel. When he was young, he accepted my counseling, allowed lust to take hold of him. He used to prowl the streets of Babylon at night, picking up the basest of women. I enjoyed watching him wallow in their filth. He accepted their aberrations, passed them on to his friends. As a fine logician, he could sway his friends, convince them that perverted acts were right for them."

"He deceived his friends?"

"You might call it deception. I call it truth. The devil's truth! He taught them to sin. Sin has its compensations. Would you not be compensated if you ascended one flight of stairs, fixed yourself to the woman you love?"

"I'd be breaking my vows, offending God."

"Vows are made to be broken. You can break them, go to confession, and you are forgiven. Forgiven for experiencing the overwhelming joys of fornication."

"You speak for the devil?"

"I speak for the pleasures of a short life."

"You are correct calling life short. My life will someday end. Then where will I be?"

"You will be with friends?"

"In heaven or hell?"

"Why ask meaningless questions? Look around you, millions of people are fornicating…the young and the old. The stars in Hollywood are fornicating. Fornication is a form of entertainment. Augustine fornicated…"

"But not always. He eventually recognized his sexual passions as evil. A peril to the salvation of his immortal soul."

" Uncontaminated nonsense."

"St. Augustine was sorry for his sins… apologized to God. He wrote: a mist hung between his eyes and the brightness of God's truth."

The demon screamed, "How dare you contradict me?" He cursed me, slapped my face till it felt as if I'd been branded with an iron.

Awakening, I sat up in bed, caught a glimpse of a lobster red body leaving the room.

CHAPTER 39

The following morning after Mass, the telephone rang.

"St. Matthew's Rectory."

"Is that ye, Father Tom."

"Yes."

"Ye told me to call when I need ye. I need ye now."

The voice was familiar. I couldn't put a name to it. "How can I help?"

"Me husband died last night, the poor dear. I don't know what to do, which way to turn. I called Flaherty's Funeral Home. They won't budge me husband's body till I give them thousands of dollars. I don't have any money to give them."

"Any life insurance?"

"I'd a twenty-five cent policy on me poor dear husband. It lapsed during the depression. They were hard times, Father."

"The funeral home won't help you in any way?"

"Not one bit. I think the Flaherty's must be from the north of Ireland. Could ye tell me, is that where they're from?"

"I don't know. Supposing I come over to see you."

"That would be wonderful, Father. You can bless Mike's body while I make ye some tea."

The woman's name popped into my head. "Yes, Mrs. Reilly. I'll be right over."

I made my way up the five flights of stairs, thinking Mrs. Reilly would have few friends visiting her. Who but the closest of friends, or a priest, would punish themselves climbing the stairs? How the Reilly's managed it, I'll never know.

Mrs. Reilly burst into tears when she saw me. I held her in my arms like a father would hold his child.

"I'm going to miss me husband," she sobbed.

"I know you will." But did I really know how an old, tired, worn, penniless woman would feel when she lost her mate? What a devastating experience. How would she survive?

"Will ye say a Hail Mary or two for Mike?"

"I'll say the rosary if you wish. The Sorrowful Mysteries."

" I'd like that very much," she said with great sincerity.

Mrs. Reilly and I knelt at the side of the bed, where we could observe Mike's face. He appeared to be sleeping peacefully. No longer was he concerned with getting a job, earning a living, or climbing those dreadful stairs. His concern now was meeting his Maker, presenting his report card to Him. I felt sure he had a good one.

"Shall we start now, Father?"

Blessing myself, I began the rosary: "The First Sorrowful Mystery, The Agony in the Garden. I believe in God, the Father Almighty, Creator of heaven and earth; and in Jesus Christ, His only Son, our Lord, Who was conceived by the Holy Ghost, born of the Virgin Mary, suffered under Pontius Pilate, was crucified, died, and was buried...."

I glanced at Mrs. Reilly. Her face seemed to glow.

She was a woman who knew how to pray. I said an Our Father and the first part of a Hail Mary. I waited for Mrs. Reilly to say the second half of the prayer.

She responded: "Holy Mary, Mother of God, pray for us, now and at the hour of our death. Amen."

Her response was short but powerful. As a priest, I had listened to many people pray, including cardinals, bishops, monsignors, fellow priests. Never before had I listened to anyone pray with the devotion manifested by Mrs. Reilly. She prayed as if the mother of God were in the same room with us. An aura of peace was reflected on her face. She had a good friend in heaven, I thought. And the good friend had made a trip to the bedroom to join us.

We finished the rosary and she proudly served me a cup of tea. I sat down on a chair in her kitchen, which was clean but worn. I sipped the tea. Steaming hot. "I'd like to make arrangements for Mike's funeral Mass," I said. "When do you wish to have him buried?"

"I don't know, Father. Mr. Flaherty was too busy to talk to me. He knows me financial situation, ye know. There was another funeral home offering cheaper prices. But it was bombed out of existence. I'm not accusin' Mr. Flaherty of the bombing, but people from the north of Ireland do throw bombs. I hate to do business with the critter. I've no choice. Besides, he won't talk to me."

"I'll talk to him. When would you like to have your husband buried?"

She gave me a date.

Later that day, I called Mr. Flaherty. He refused to talk to me when he learned I was interested in making arrangements to bury Mike Reilly. I spoke to an assistant, a Mr. John Diggins, and explained Mrs. Reilly was in need of financial help.

"For a burial, the plot, and everything else that necessarily goes with it, the best we can do is five thousand dollars. Can she pay that amount, sir?"

"She can't but I can."

"You will be responsible for her debt?"

I'd less than twenty-eight dollars in my pocket. I felt guilty saying, "Yes."

"All right, sir. We will pick up the body. You will be responsible for her debt. Now the address?"

I gave him the address and began to sweat. How could I raise five thousand dollars?

As I asked myself the question, Monsignor Blazer walked into my office. He squinted at me. "Are you perspiring on this pleasant day?"

"I am, Monsignor. I've committed myself to pay a five thousand dollar funeral bill and I don't have the money. Can you help?"

"You keep the records. How much do we have in the bank?"

"About twenty-two hundred. But we're due to receive an oil bill for the church and rectory, which will reduce our balance to zero."

"Take one thousand dollars from the bank and pay the oil bill on installments. We'll keep the thermo down for the winter."

"Thank you, Monsignor."

I took a list of the parishioners and scanned it for those who gave generously to the church. I checked off the names and telephone numbers. I also stared at the phone. I continued to stare, thinking my dialing fingers had grown immobile. If there's anything I hated to do, it was asking people for money...or to be more precise, *begging* people for money.

Many aspects of my life as a priest were unpleasant. I was out of bed every morning at an early hour, I worked for a "no pay" organization, my services were often rendered to unappreciative individuals, I couldn't marry, and a demon disturbed my sleep. Whom did I quote last night when the demon terrorized me? St. Augustine. What was the quote? The saint said he did what he didn't want to do.

So I picked up the phone and dialed every generous parishioner on my list. Some gave me excuses; others gave me a promise to deliver cash that evening to the rectory. I called the office of the Knights of Columbus and received five hundred. Another call to St. Vincent DePaul's gave me another five hundred. I'd collected a total of forty-five hundred dollars. I was still short five hundred.

While drumming my fingers on the desk, wondering whom I could call for the five hundred, Vivian entered the room.

"You haven't had any supper tonight. Aren't you hungry?"

"I hadn't thought about food. I'm trying to raise money for a funeral."

"Any luck?"

"A great deal of luck. But I'm still short five hundred."

"I can give you five hundred."

Demon of Lust

The offer came as a surprise. I shouted, "You can?"

"Yes. I'll stay home tonight and give you the money I'd normally take with me."

I was so elated; I said nothing about her plan to go out. I stood and kissed her on the forehead.

She smiled and said, "If I contribute another hundred, will you kiss me on the lips?"

As much as I wanted to, I didn't kiss her lips. I did relate my experience with the Reilly's, saying the wife was a true source of inspiration and a saint I wanted her to meet.

While I spoke, Vivian read the list of names of those who'd pledged money for the funeral. "Did you call Social Security? They'll make a contribution."

"I didn't think of it."

"They contribute upon the death of a member. It won't be much but it'll be enough to buy Mrs. Reilly a new black dress and give her some extra money."

"What a wonderful secretary you'd make."

"I'd make a better wife."

That night the doorbell rang many times. I was there to answer it and collect the money pledged on the phone. Two men doubled the amount they pledged, which meant I could buy flowers for the wake and put Mrs. Reilly's name on them. There are many good people in the world, I thought. I don't know why I worry so much about them.

Mike Reilly was laid out in the Flaherty Funeral Home, an old but well cared for establishment, whose owner, Timothy Flaherty, was one of the wealthiest men in the region. His wealth came from the high prices he charged for his services. The high prices bothered his conscience tremendously. So rather than face his patrons, especially the old confused and bereaved widows struggling along on Social Security, he employed a business manager, John Diggins, to extract as much money as possible from them.

This information was general knowledge in the parish. Of course, it was of no concern to Mike Reilly, laid out in a small chapel at the rear of the funeral home. He was laid out in a well-worn blue suit, perhaps twenty years out of style, a white shirt, a size too big for him, and a faded red tie, designed with jingle bells. He held rosary beads in his gnarled hands. How frequently had he said the rosary? I'd no way of knowing.

His wife stood before the casket, saying, "Thank ye. Thank ye" to those who came to see Mike for the last time. I was told they were friends who lived in the same tenement house, drank with Mike in a nearby tavern, and worked with him whenever work was available.

For over two hours, I stood at her side, wondering how she had the strength to stand for such a long period of time. I said the rosary and received a good response from the ten or twelve people who stayed for the prayers. Completing the rosary, I turned to Mrs. Reilly, who knelt at her husband's casket. She struggled to her feet.

"Sit down for a few minutes. I'll take you home."

Shaking her head, she said, "I don't want to go home. I want to stay here with Mike. He's all I got."

I knew there was a time when the Irish would sit up all night with a loved one in a funeral home; but those times were gone, especially in a Flaherty funeral home. I took her hand. "This chapel will close in a few minutes. We'll have to leave."

"Can't ye keep the place open?"

"I'm afraid not. I have no influence here."

"I don't mind sitting in the dark. No one will know I'm here. No one but God and Mike."

"Mrs. Reilly, do you have any sons or daughters?"

The question stung her. "I'd three sons, all killed in Vietnam. They'll be waiting for Mike in heaven when he arrives."

At precisely ten o'clock, John Diggins, an officious little man with sparse hair, a weak jaw, and a case of the jitters, appeared in the chapel. He told us we had to leave.

We could return the following morning at eight-thirty to witness the closing of the casket. The body would then be transported to the church for Mass before going to the cemetery.

I took Mrs. Reilly's arm, led her to the door. I felt someone tugging at my coat sleeve.

"Could I speak to you for a moment?" It was Mr. Diggins.

I told Mrs. Reilly to wait for me at the door. "I'll be with you in a minute." Entering Mr. Diggins' office, I asked, "What is it?"

"I want to thank you, sir, for raising it."

"Raising what?"

"The money. After picking up the body, I almost had a nervous breakdown worrying about the money. You work in a poor parish. I didn't think you could raise a dime there. If you hadn't raised the money, I'd have had to face Mr. Flaherty with nothing but a dead body on my hands."

I wanted to lash out at the man. Instead I said, "Raising the money wasn't so difficult, Mr. Diggins. It may surprise you to learn there are many generous people in the Bronx. You have my permission to pass this information on to Mr. Flaherty."

As I drove Mrs. Reilly home, I was thinking too much about Mr. Diggins and his fear of Mr. Flaherty. I failed to consider Mrs. Reilly. She'd find it impossible to climb the stairs to her apartment in her present condition.

"What do you do when you climb one flight of stairs in your apartment house, find yourself too tired to climb more stairs?"

She was slow to answer. "I don't like to tell ye."

"You can tell me. I've your best interest at heart."

"Ye do, I know."

"Well, tell me. I'll keep it a secret."

"What can I do? I sleep on the landing."

"Isn't that uncomfortable?"

"It is, Father, but I'm not the only one."

The whole idea was too disturbing to ask about the others. A solution came to mind. "How would you like to sleep tonight in the bishop's bed?"

"Sleep with the bishop?"

I had to smile. "No, his bed. We've a room in the rectory reserved for the bishop. It's rare when he visits."

"I'd feel uncomfortable sleeping in a rectory."

"You'll feel more uncomfortable sleeping on a second floor landing." I swung the car around, headed for the rectory.

As I drove, I decided to find suitable quarters for Mrs. Reilly. She was either going to live in the rectory or some other place that wouldn't drain her energy every time she had to leave or return to her apartment. She wasn't going to live in the tenement house. Not if I'd anything to say about it.

Mrs. Reilly was quite surprised to find a man picketing the rectory at a late hour. "What's the meaning of this, Father?"

"It's a long story, Mrs. Reilly."

"Is he objecting to the way in which ye're running the church?"

"He's just a paid employee, a thug who works for someone who wants us to conform to his ideas."

"I'd like to get me hands on the man who'd criticize the Church."

"You have your own worries. Don't worry about anything else."

The picket stopped at the driveway, glared at us as we drove past him.

"Git alone with ye," Mrs. Reilly shouted. "Git along with ye."

The picket released a string of expletives. To avoid hearing them, I drove the car into the driveway. Perhaps Mrs. Reilly would have been safer in the tenement than the rectory.

CHAPTER 40

Monsignor Blazer and Vivian were in the kitchen when I introduced Mrs. Reilly to them. "I've invited Mrs. Reilly to stay with us tonight," I said. "She attended her husband wake, is too tired to climb five flights of stairs in her tenement building to reach her apartment."

The pastor was sympathetic. "You look tired now," he said to her.

Vivian put an arm around her. "You can share my room if you can make it to the fourth floor."

The pastor was quick to respond. "She's welcome to sleep in the bishop's bed."

I was glad to hear him make the offer.

Vivian said to Mrs. Reilly. "I'll show you the room."

Mrs. Reilly turned to me. "Thank ye, Father." And to the Monsignor, "Thank ye."

When the two women had left the room, the pastor said, "The bishop's room is more comfortable than the one I have."

"You could enjoy that room, but you prefer to sacrifice yourself for the bishop."

He studied me as if I'd made a dubious philosophical point. "I'm afraid I don't make enough sacrifices for others. But I'm too tired to discuss my failings. I'll go to bed now and thank God I don't have to climb five flights of stairs to reach my room."

"Good night, Monsignor."

"Good night. And by the way, bringing that poor woman here is an act of charity. One I might not have considered if I'd attended the wake. You're a good priest, Father Tom." He left the room.

Vivian was all smiles when she returned to the kitchen. "Tell me something, Tommy Boy. Do you have a thing for old women?"

"What do you mean?"

"This is the second one you've brought home since I've been here. I'm beginning to think you find old women alluring. Must I wait fifty years before you find me alluring, make a play for me?"

"If you'd seen the stairs that woman climbs to reach her apartment, you'd have felt sorry for her too."

"I suppose so. I'm glad you brought her here. I love you all the more for it. I wouldn't be a bit surprised if you're out this week, looking for another place for her to live."

Vivian was uncanny. She read my mind. "How did you know?"

"I know because I know you."

Once again I'd difficulty going to sleep. And once again I'd greater difficulty while I slept. I dreamt the demon's voice came to me from somewhere in my bedroom. I couldn't see him, but I could hear him pacing the floor. Annoyed, he asked, "Why didn't you let that old hag fend for herself? She doesn't deserve to be here with us. She ignores me when I whisper into her ear."

"Mrs. Reilly is a good woman, Isacaron."

"Precisely why I hate her stinking guts."

"As far as you're concerned, good is evil and evil is good. Isn't that what you're saying?"

"You're beginning to show signs of wisdom."

"I showed signs of wisdom when I helped her tonight."

"You acted like an idiot. Help her again and she'll follow in the footsteps of Mary Smith."

"Mary Smith! Did you lead her to the George Washington Bridge, force her to jump?"

"Force her to jump? I had her so confused, she didn't know what she was doing."

"You drowned her. Do you intend to drown Mrs. Reilly?"

"Years ago, I told you we have many ways to kill the human fish. We need not use the same method twice."

Foolish trying to get an honest answer from a liar, yet I persisted. "Do you plan to kill Mrs. Reilly?"

"I won't kill her. I'll have someone else perform the task. In that way, the killer receives the devil's blessing."

He was making sense, I thought, in his own devious way. I wanted more information. "How would you find someone to kill Mrs. Reilly?"

"People are either with us or against us."

"Christ made the same statement."

"So He did. Nine percent of the world's population have listened to Him, the balance are with us. With ninety-one percent of the population, we have millions of killers available. All they need is a suggestion from one of Satan's disciples."

"You're a liar, Isacaron. The percentages you give are obviously fabricated."

The demon stopped pacing. For a moment, I thought he'd left the room. Then I heard his voice. He sounded like a defense lawyer. "Look around you. Every minute of the day, soldiers are killing men, women, children, and babies. The slaughter of innocent people is a never-ending fact of life. Killings aren't restricted to the battlefields. They're in the cities, homes, schools, shops, and recreational rooms. Women are killing their offspring, teenagers are killing parents, husbands are killing wives, and wives are killing husbands. Believe me when I tell you, evil is triumphing over good. A pity you can't see the multitude of killers marching to the devil's drumbeat. Marching to hell. Some day you'll march with them."

"I'll never join them. Never kill anyone. Never sin."

"You'll sin tonight. You have no choice. Unless you join Vivian tonight in her bedroom, Mrs. Reilly will die."

Was I actually talking to Isacaron? Or was I having a horrible nightmare? I tried to awaken, bring myself back to the real world. I was unable to do so. My voice sounded far away. "I'll not do your bidding, Isacaron. Nor will l believe your lies. Mrs. Reilly believes in me. I'll protect her."

"I'll have her killed."

"No, you won't. You can't hurt her. She has great faith."

"Legions of sinners have great faith. Faith in the devil. They enjoy eliminating those who have faith in God. One suggestion from me, they eliminate Mrs. Reilly."

"I don't believe a word you say. I do believe you belong in hell!" I shouted this so loud, I awakened myself. Sitting up in bed, I put my hands to my head. It was wet with perspiration. I listened for the demon's footsteps, heard nothing.

I watched the hands of my alarm clock go round and round. It was time to get out of bed, start a new day. I was scheduled to say the nine o'clock Mass for Mike Reilly's funeral. Monsignor Blazer said the six. I arrived in the dining room for breakfast; hoping food would give me a little strength.

Mrs. Reilly and Vivian were there when I sat down.

Mrs. Reilly greeted me with a "Good morning to ye, Father."

Vivian greeted me with this observation: "You didn't sleep well last night, did you?"

I put my hands to my face, could feel the puffiness under my eyes. "We all have our bad nights."

"You've more than your share."

She served me two eggs, four pieces of bacon, two pieces of toast, and three cups of coffee. I was able to eat one egg, one piece of bacon, no toast, and three cups of coffee.

The demon's threat was still on my mind. It retarded my appetite.

I'd no way of knowing how Mrs. Reilly had slept in the bishop's bed. She toyed with her food. Her appetite was no better than mine.

The Ford Fairlane carried Mrs. Reilly and me to Flaherty's Funeral Home. The chapel was empty when we entered. We knelt together at

Demon of Lust

Mike's casket, said five Hail Mary's and five Acts of Contrition. The moment we completed the prayers, John Diggins appeared. He had his hands on the lid of the casket, ready to close it.

"Just one moment," I said to him as firmly as I could.

He stopped as if shot.

"Give Mrs. Reilly a minute or two to say goodbye to her husband."

"Yes, sir," he said, looking at me as if I might strike him.

Mrs. Reilly viewed her husband with tears in her eyes. For several minutes she did nothing but fix her gaze intently on him. Then suddenly she bent and kissed him. "I'm gonna miss ye, Mike. And I'm gonna ask God to let me join ye soon."

John Digging stepped forward and closed the casket.

On the way to church, neither Mrs. Reilly nor I spoke. Whenever I glanced at her, I saw tears in her eyes. I doubt if she could speak or wanted to speak. What little comfort the world offered her was gone. She wanted to die and I wanted her to live, give her some of life's pleasures. How I'd do it, I didn't know.

At the opening of the funeral Mass, I read from the missal: "Give peace, Lord, to those who wait for you...listen to the prayers of your servants...guide us in the way of justice."

Glancing down at Mrs. Reilly, I saw she sat alone. Nevertheless, she was close to the one she loved the most, her husband. His casket was in the center aisle of the church, near the altar. The casket, I thought, was an inexpensive one. But what did it matter? A casket of gold was no ticket to heaven. It could be a hindrance.

Those attending Mass were few in number, maybe eight or ten friends from the tenement house. The number of friends he made on earth matters little. His friendship with God is priceless.

I read from the missal: "God, you have called your son from this life. Fulfill his faith and hope in you, lead him safely home to heaven, to be happy with you forever."

Mrs. Reilly seemed to be holding up well. At Communion time, she stood on wobbly legs, made her way to the front of the altar. Her face glowed as she received the sacred host. Her faith in God could not be denied.

After serving her Communion with five others, I read from the missal: "Father, all powerful God, we pray for our brother, whom you have called from this world. May the Eucharist cleanse him, forgive his sins, and raise him up to eternal joy in your presence."

At the end of the Mass, I entered the sacristy, removed my vestments, hurried through the church, and down the front steps. I wanted to help Mrs. Reilly into the Ford Fairlane, only one of two cars to accompany the hearse to the cemetery. I'd assure her she wasn't alone. But where was she?

I'd reached the sidewalk in front of the church when I felt someone's fingers tighten around my arm.

A familiar voice said, "Ah'd like to talk to ya, Father."

I turned and saw a tall lanky black boy. He was wearing a T-shirt and worn black sneakers. He was the boy who confessed stealing Vivian's Rolls Royce, the boy who sat in the rear of my Religion class.

He took me by surprise. "I can't talk now. I've a funeral...a burial"

"Ah gotta talk to ya now. Last night, somebudy tried to blow up our high school."

"What?"

"Somebudy drivin' a stretch limo. Ah seen 'im sneakin' into de parkin' lot wit' a keg o' dynamite under his arm. It had a long fuse. It wuz 'round midnight."

"Are you sure?"

"I seen 'im, Father. The moon was out last night. I was practicin' foul shots. I'm on de biskitball team, ya know. He didn't see me but I saw 'im. I saw 'im place de keg o' dynamite against de buildin', light de fuse..." The boy looked at me earnestly. "He wuz gonna blow up our school."

"What could you possibly do?"

"Ah could stop 'im, dat's what."

"But how?"

"As soon as Ah seen dat fuse sparklin' in de dark, I sprinted fer de man. He couldn't hear me comin' 'cause I wuz wearin' sneakers. I pulled out my knife…"

My heart seemed to drop to the pit of my stomach. "You didn't stab him?"

"Ah kicked 'im in de ass, Father. Knocked 'im down, cut de fuse, grabbed de keg o' dynamite, ran like hell. He didn't get a shot off."

"My but you were brave."

"He wuz gonna blow up our school, Father. And Ah'm tryin' to git an educa'shun."

"What did you do with the dynamite?"

"Hid it."

"I know you're in my Religion class, but I'm sorry to say I don't remember your name."

"It's Joshua. Joshua Roosevelt."

"Well, Joshua, supposing you stop by the rectory this afternoon, around three o'clock, and we'll make some decisions. The police should be notified."

The boy looked down at me quizzically. "Ah don't know about de police, Father. Some of 'em can't be trusted."

"Some can't and some can. We'll try to find one who can. We'll give him the information we have."

Suddenly I heard the roar of a car, a thud, a woman scream, and shouting. Turning away from Joshua, I saw people moving towards my Ford Fairlane. I also saw a long, black limousine; traveling at full speed, disappear around a corner.

I was unable to make any sense of the event until I reached the street. The door on the passenger's side of my Ford was open. I realized immediately Mrs. Reilly, who had grown tired waiting for me to open the door for her, had opened it. The limousine had struck her. She lay dead in the street with her hands folded in prayer. Despite an ugly gash on her head, a tiny smile appeared on her ashen face.

CHAPTER 41

Giving Mrs. Reilly the last rites, as she lay on the street, was a heartbreaking experience for me. Six policemen in uniform arrived on the scene with three detectives. Spotting Detective Casey, I told him that Mrs. Reilly was killed by a stretch limousine, driven by a hit and run driver. I suspected Mario Togallini employed the driver.

I also told John Diggins that Mrs. Reilly was to be laid out at the Flaherty's Funeral Home; given a new blue dress, new shoes, stockings, and the services of a good beautician.

With a meekness that was sickening, Mr. Diggins asked, "Who will pay the bill?"

I gave him a nasty look with my answer. "I'll pay the bill."

"Your credit is good with us," he said, feigning enthusiasm. "Anything else?"

"She will be buried next to her husband."

But first her husband had to be buried. A trip to the cemetery was necessary. Following the hearse, I pulled away from the church. A rusty old Honda, with worn paint and dented fenders, fell in line behind me. Three women and two men occupied the Honda. All had gray hair and somber faces.

When we arrived at the cemetery, they followed me on foot to the gravesite, listened attentively as I prayed for the repose of the soul of Mike Reilly. They bowed their heads when I said, "Remember man thou art but dust and into dust thou shalt return."

Demon of Lust

As I drove back to the rectory, my mind was in a state of disarray. I kept asking myself questions I couldn't answer: How did the demon Isacaron know Mrs. Reilly was going to die? Did he have her killed because I refused to lie down with Vivian? Was her death an answer to her prayers? Did God ever use a demon to bring about a desired result? I'd no answers. I couldn't even answer another troubling question: How was I going to raise money to bury Mrs. Reilly?

A name popped into my mind: Joshua Roosevelt! He was the one who grabbed my arm, told me that someone had tried to bomb the school. The information was so distracting; I ran off the road and almost turned the car over in an effort to get back onto the road.

I heard a dog yelp, saw it run across the road with its tail between its legs. Had I injured the dog? I wasn't sure. I couldn't be sure of anything.

Could I be sure that Mario would forego a second attempt to blow up the school? He'd blow up the school if the demon Isacaron put the notion into his head. Men were either inspired by God or the devil. I could be sure of one thing. God didn't inspire Mario Togallini.

Where did that leave me? Should I quit teaching at the school? Should I tell Mario where he could find his paintings? Should I deliver Vivian into his unholy hands? I didn't know.

What I need is a consultant, I thought. Funny, people consult me. I give them advice. But I can't advise myself. I was so puzzled I felt like jumping out of my skin. I thought of Father O'Donnell, my mentor and friend. But he was in a sanatorium, too ill to consider a problem. I thought of Monsignor Blazer. How I hated to tell him of my love for Vivian, the demon in the rectory, the threat of having the school and the rectory bombed. I'd no one to talk to. No one but Vivian.

She met me when I entered the rectory. "How did you make out with the funeral?"

"I managed to have Mike Reilly buried. I've another problem."

"I heard about his wife. I'd love to meet her killer in a dark alley."

"What would you do?"

"I can tell you what I wouldn't do. I wouldn't let him get away with murder."

Vivian's attitude depressed me. "You haven't told me what you'd do."

"I'd do something."

I studied her. She was not only a beautiful woman; she was strong…quick. I suspected her before of murdering two pickets. I suspected her again. The picket in the alley had left a clue. He wrote, a woma. He intended to write a woman. Who, but Vivian, would have sufficient reason to kill the two pickets?

"They're out there again," she suddenly stated in anger.

"Who's out where?" I asked absentmindedly.

"The pickets!" she snapped. "One is at the front of the rectory; the other, at the rear."

She read my mind, I thought. Had the demon Isacaron given her the power to look into my head, read my thoughts? A very obvious fact dawned on me: She was guilty of bringing Isacaron into the rectory, giving him a place to stay in her room. Had he given her some of the powers he possessed? I hated the thought, yet I had to recognize facts.

"I'm going out tonight. No one in the world is going to stop me," I heard her say.

"I wish you wouldn't."

"I won't go out tonight if you'll spend some time with me in my room. Say around midnight."

Her invitation opened the floodgates of my suppressed desires. I thought of meeting her at midnight. All would be quiet. No one would know what I was doing. No one but God.

"So what do you say?"

"I'm afraid not, Vivian."

"Are you turning me down?"

"I'm honoring the vows I've taken."

Her voice was harsh. "You're hopeless." She turned away from me, darted up the stairs.

Demon of Lust

I wondered if she'd sit before her painting; allow the demon Isacaron to churn up her passions. I knew her passions were strong She was willing to give in to them. I also knew my passions were strong. I had to hold them in check. Could we reconcile our differences?

I disliked the idea of her rushing off whenever we had a dispute. She allowed no time for a resolution. I thought she'd return to prepare lunch for me. We could talk some more. I patiently waited for her to come down the stairs.

She didn't come down the stairs. Monsignor Blazer had been invited out for lunch that day, so she didn't have to be concerned about him. I'd no invitation, so she had to be concerned about me. I soon realized I had to get my own lunch. I made my favorite sandwich: peanut butter and jelly. I also had a glass of milk.

After lunch, I read my breviary for an hour and spent another hour with the newspapers. The telephone rang.

"St. Matthew's rectory."

"Am I speaking to Father Tom?"

"You are."

"This is Joe McCabe from your parish and your local paper. I'm calling to ask for the details relating to the death of the woman killed outside your church this morning?"

"Mrs. Reilly?"

"She's the woman."

"What do you want to know?"

"Everything you know."

Giving the killing of Mrs. Reilly a little publicity would do no harm, I thought. So I gave McCabe the information he requested, saying I believed the ones responsible for the hit-and-run were also responsible for the picketing of the rectory, although I couldn't prove it.

"May I quote you, Father?"

"You may."

"Thanks a lot. And by the way, did Mrs. Reilly have any money?"

"She was as poor as a church mouse."

"Any insurance?"

"None."

"Who's going to pay for her funeral?"

"I am."

"You are? I've heard your parish is a poor one."

"It is."

"I'll bet you don't know how you're going to pay for the funeral, do you?"

"No, I don't."

"Tell you what, Father. I'll write the Reilly story in such a way that some people, I can't say how many, will contribute to her funeral. Any objections if I use your name and address?"

"None, whatsoever. I've committed myself to pay for her funeral."

"Thanks a lot, Father. And one more thing. Will you do me a favor?"

"I'll do it if I can."

"Say some prayers for me. I have a wife, two children, and a problem. The problem is my boss. She's a sexy woman who has her mind set on seducing me. She's quite attractive, and I must admit, I'm tempted. Yet I don't want to destroy my marriage."

"Of course, you don't."

"You're a priest, so you probably don't understand what I'm talking about; but believe me, Father, whenever I see that woman, my whole body craves for her. I'm tempted. And I don't know what I can do to resist her."

I was not alone, I thought. Isacaron is everywhere, doing the devil's work. "I'll say a prayer for you, a series of prayers, if necessary. But you must do your part. As best you can, stay away from that woman. She'll destroy your peace of mind, your family, your love for God, your soul."

A long pause followed my words. "Thank you, Father. I'm going to take your advice."

When the telephone call ended, I sat alone in the office with my hands clasped together. How easy it is to give advice. How difficult to follow it. I knew precisely how that man felt. He and I were free to act one way or the other. We could give in to our temptations or refuse to give in to them. We could follow our animal instincts or listen to the dictates of our conscience, which is nothing more than our intellects, passing judgment on moral issues.

I thought of Isacaron's master, the devil. His success dates back to the beginning of time...to the first man and woman on earth, Adam and Eve. He left them to fend for themselves after they had sinned...left them without a defense when God asked, "What is this you have done?"

I also pictured God presenting the same question to their son, Cain, after he had murdered his brother. "Cain, what is this you have done?"

Who can answer such a question from an all-loving God? There is simply no answer.

I spent more time in my office contemplating man's freedom, his responsibilities, and the consequence of his acts. How much time? I do not know.

Glancing at my watch, I saw the hour had reached four.

Four o'clock and Joshua Roosevelt had failed to ring the doorbell. I'd asked him to stop by at three. Three was a bad time, I realized. The students at the high school weren't released till then. He could have received permission to leave early if he'd told his teacher I'd asked him to be at the rectory at three. Even if he hadn't asked to leave early, he should be here by now.

Kids were irresponsible, I thought. Joshua was no exception. He convinced me he wanted an education. I'd have to tell him that responsibility is necessary for anyone pursuing an education.

The unexpected ring of the telephone jangled my nerves.

"St. Matthews rectory."

"Father Tom?"

"Yes."

"Dis is Joshua."

"You were supposed to be here at three o'clock today."

"Ah knows. But Ah'm not comin'. Ah don't trust de police. Ah don't trust nobudy but one pur'son…"

"You trust me, don't you?"

The response was slow in coming. "Well…"

"I'd like to know."

"Ah can't say."

"Either you do or you don't."

"Ah don't trust ya, Father."

I felt the blood rush to my face. I'd leave the priesthood if I couldn't win the trust of a boy in a Catholic school…a boy in my Religion class. "Why don't you trust me, Joshua?"

"If ya gotta know, Ah'll tell ya. Ya know de men in de limo killed my friend Ronnie, bombed de fun'ral home, and murdered a woman wit' der limo dis mornin'. Ya know all dat, yet ya never notified de police. And Ah knows yer not gonna notify de police. Dat's why Ah don't trust ya."

I couldn't have been more stunned if Joshua had slapped my face. "There are extenuating circumstances. Circumstances I'm not at liberty to reveal to you at this time. But I still want to talk to you."

"Ah shoulda let dat guy bomb de school."

"Don't make statements like that. Much blood, tears, labor, and money have gone into that school. I was proud to hear you risked your life to save it."

"Ah'm not proud o' myself."

I had an answer for Joshua I was unable to use. He dropped the phone into its cradle. The disconnect buzzing in my ear was annoying.

Frustrated, I placed my phone into its cradle, sat back in my chair. I'd a multiplicity of problems and no solutions. Of course, I knew the reasons for my problems. They were all explainable in terms of one word: Vivian.

She was a problem for me when I was a boy. Now that I'm a man, she's still a problem. I must face the fact she's a fornicator. A fornicator whom I love. Why do I love her? I don't know. I do know she's trouble. A possible murderess. And a woman who may drag me down into the lowest pits of hell. Why did God allow me to fall in love with someone who'd harm me? The answer may be found in any good theological book: Free will. But when a man falls in love with a woman, is he free? Isn't he trapped by his own emotions, his own passions?

Adam yielded to Eve in the Garden of Eden. His experience with a woman should be a lesson for me. A woman initiated the first sin. She brought the wrath of God down upon the world.

When we fail to conform to the laws of God, we receive subtle reminders of His displeasure: Tornadoes, floods, hurricanes, earthquakes, and other natural disasters. God lets us know He expects us to be guided by what is right and what is wrong.

Women today are demanding equal rights. What a laugh! It's the men who should be demanding equal rights.

So many people have been hurt and killed as a result of my efforts to protect Vivian from harm. The latest victim is Joshua. I must convince him I'm on his side, let him know I'm doing the right thing. I picked up the telephone, called the school.

The response was immediate. "This is Sister Agnes." Her voice was well modulated.

"Sister, Father Tom Davis calling. Would you be kind enough to check your files, give me the address of Joshua Roosevelt?"

"Just one minute."

In precisely one minute, she was back at the phone. "Father, I can't tell you where he lives."

From the tone of my voice, I let her know I was irritated. "Why not?"

"He's homeless."

I felt an urge to cry. "Thank you, Sister."

CHAPTER 42

When I went to bed that night, the day's events were on my mind, kept me awake for over an hour. Once asleep, I struggled to awaken. I'd a horrible nightmare. In my dream, I was seated in the rear row of my classroom, the seat normally occupied by Joshua Roosevelt. While waiting for the teacher to enter the class, I noticed my hands. They were black. I pulled up a leg of my pants and examined a bare ankle. It too was black. I was not only sitting in Joshua's seat, I was Joshua.

The classroom door opened. The teacher entered. He wore the Roman collar of a priest, looked precisely as I looked whenever I taught class.

I joined the other members of the class and sang, "Good morning, Padre."

He responded with a "Good morning, Scholars."

I asked myself the question: How can I be teacher and student at one and the same time?

The disagreeable voice of Isacaron whispered in my ear: "You're the teacher and the student. You walk in Joshua's worn sneakers."

I responded, "Ya can't do dat t' me."

"I've already done it?"

The sound of my own voice came from the teacher. "Joshua, will you please explain why your homework papers are stained with water?"

"Dat's rainwater, Father. Der's a hole in de cardbo'rd box Ah lives in. If Ah can't find mo' cardboard to fix it, Ah'll hav'ta move."

"You live in a cardboard box?"

"Dat's right."

Demon of Lust

"Your parents..."

"Never met 'em. Dey abandoned me."

"How did you survive?"

"Same as a stray cat."

"Dumbfounded, I repeated, "A stray cat?"

"Don't criticize cats. Cats don't never abandon der young."

"If you were my son, I wouldn't abandon you."

"Ah calls ya Father, but Ah don't see ya 'doptin' me."

"I wish I could."

Wishing ain't helping me, I thought. I was a black boy with no one to help me. A priest is supposed to help the poor. "Why can't ya help me, Father?"

Isacaron whispered in my ear. "There's a question you can't answer. Priests talk sacrifice. They don't experience it. They don't know what it means to be without shelter, food. Rather than spend time talking about poverty, why don't they experience it? They're all talk, no action. All talk, no action. All talk, no action." Throughout the night, these words were repeated over and over again.

I awakened at four in the morning with the demon's words ringing in my ears. Was he right about me? He could be. I hadn't done much for the poor. Maybe I could do something to help Joshua.

I skipped an early cup of coffee that morning, said Mass, and was removing my vestments when Detectives Casey and Warren entered the sacristy.

Casey approached me with a skeptical look on his thin face. "Did you hear about the murders?" he asked.

"What murders?"

"The two men picketing the rectory were killed."

I wondered if the detective had lost his memory. "Of course, I heard about the pickets being killed. We talked about them several days ago. Don't you remember?"

"I'm talking about the two men who were killed last night or early this morning. One of them was killed in the front of the rectory and the other, in the rear. Both stabbed to death."

I could hardly believe what I was told. "Two more men dead?"

Detective Warren put up four fingers. "A total of four."

"I was unaware of any killings last night or this morning."

Detective Casey gave me a stern look. "You certainly must know something." Not only were four men killed, an old lady...a Mrs. Reilly...was also killed by a hit-and-run driver."

"I knew her well. I was tending to her husband's funeral when someone driving a stretch limousine struck her down. I believe the driver works for Mario Togallini. I gave the police this information. I honestly believe the men picketing or observing the rectory work for him, too."

"We spoke to him. He's a highly influential man in Jersey City. He has an airtight alibi. We've no proof he's connected with the murders. That is, we have no proof unless you're able to supply us with some."

"I wish I could."

"So do I. Perhaps you can tell us why the pickets covered the rear of the rectory as well as the front."

"You'll have to ask them."

"They're dead."

"Yes, unfortunately, they're dead. However, there may be replacements. Grill them if they show up at the rectory."

"We'll see."

"Tell me something, Detective Casey. Do you believe in demons?"

"What kind of demons?"

"The kind you read about in the Bible, the fallen angels. The kind Christ believed in."

The detective studied my face as if he were searching for traces of insanity. "I'm afraid not."

For the second time, Detective Warren had something to say: "I believe in demons. I've believed in them ever since a local butcher was brought into the station. A clergyman said the butcher was possessed by a demon. The butcher killed twelve women, cut them up, stored them in the freezer

Demon of Lust

in his shop. If you'd seen the bloody body parts, you'd think the clergyman was right."

Detective Casey faced his partner. "The interpretation you give the story can't be verified."

"Maybe not," I said. "Some crimes that have occurred in the world are so heinous, they can only be attributed to men working under the influence of an evil spirit. Take the crimes committed by Hitler and Stalin."

Detective Casey was adamant. "You don't expect me to handcuff a demon, do you?"

"No, but..."

"No buts about it. Forget the demons. Take a look at something more practical, the crime scenes. You may see something we've overlooked."

Following the two detectives to the crime scene near the front of the rectory, I saw the body of Tony Barber, bent in a fetal position. He was the man who threw the bomb into the funeral home. Live by the sword, die by the sword, I thought.

Detective Casey nudged me on the arm. "Notice he's bleeding from his belly and back. He's been stabbed by a sword or a bayonet."

"Too bad," I said, feeling sick at the sight of the blood.

"See anything out of the ordinary?"

"Nothing but a man, killed outside the rectory."

"We'll take a look at the other body," the detective said.

I followed the two detectives to the rear of the rectory. Detective Casey introduced me to the medical examiner, a Mr. Harry Foo, and his assistant, a Miss Mary Jordan. They acknowledged me by nodding their heads. They were more interested in the body of a tall man, not more than thirty years of age, who died with his eyes and mouth open.

The medical examiner was an Oriental with bright eyes and a youthful face. His English was without an accent. "This man was stabbed with a long, sharp instrument. Possibly a bayonet."

Questions came to mind: Where did Vivian get a bayonet? Should I have the detectives question her? Or should I question her? I decided on the latter.

"Any ideas, Father?" Detective Casey looked at me with anticipation.

"Plenty of ideas. None worth exploring at this time…except, of course, the idea of a demon."

"Forget the demon."

"I wish I could."

His response was sarcastic, unexpected. "I wish you could, too."

"I must leave now," I said, with an abruptness that matched his. "I'll say goodbye to you and to Detective Warren."

When I entered the rectory, Vivian was in the pastor's office, looking out the window. No doubt about it, she was aware of the murders, attempting to see what was taking place at one of the crime scenes.

"Did you know two more pickets were killed this morning or last night?" I asked her.

"I suspected as much when I saw the police."

I noticed she hesitated, sounded guilty as hell. I also noticed she was wearing her better clothes. Clothes she wouldn't ordinarily wear around the rectory. "You were out again last night, weren't you?"

"So what if I was?"

"What time did you return to the rectory?"

"Between three-thirty and four."

"Did you see anything at that time?"

"As I matter of fact, I did. I saw a man lying on the ground near the rectory. I thought he was asleep. I hurried past him."

"You didn't recognize him as one of the pickets."

"No. I thought he was a homeless bum."

I winced at the term bum. I hated to hear anyone classify a man, one of God's creations, as a bum.

"Where did you go last night?"

"None of your business."

Demon of Lust

"You've left this rectory on three occasions since you've been here. On two occasions two men have died. Don't you consider that strange?"

"You accusing me of killing the men?"

"I'm not accusing you, I'm asking you."

"Asking me is either accusing me or insulting me."

"I'm not trying to do either, I'm trying to help you. The police are hot on this case. I'd not like to see them question you, find you guilty of anything."

"Wouldn't you protect me from the police? Lie to them if we found it necessary?"

"If we found it necessary? Vivian, I'll do anything I possibly can for you within reason. Don't ask me to lie, or cheat, or sacrifice my integrity for you."

She took a step closer to me. I could smell her perfume; feel her womanly appeal. "I'd do anything for you. Anything at all," she said.

"You would?" I'd a faint hope she'd say *yes*.

"Yes."

"Will you let me get rid of the painting in your room? We've had nothing but trouble since it arrived. As I've mentioned many times, that painting is the work of a demon. We'll get along much better if it's destroyed."

Vivian's face grew hard. "I'll give up my life before I'll give up my paintings."

"Then you won't do anything for me?"

"Anything but that."

Turning away from her, I ran up the stairs, saw a light in the Monsignor's room, entered.

He was seated in a large recliner, reading his breviary. "Good morning, Father Tom."

"Forgive me for breaking in on you, Monsignor, but I'd like to know if there's a bayonet or a sword in this rectory?"

"Why would you want to know?"

"I have my reasons, which I'd rather not discuss at this time."

The Monsignor appeared as if he were going to argue, then changed his mind. "Our housekeeper, the lady presently in Ireland, had a husband who died several years ago. He took care of the heavy chores around here. He was a Marine Corps veteran who retired from the service with a small pension and a bayonet. He used the bayonet as a machete to cut the weeds around the rectory. It's probably somewhere in the basement. Ask Vivian to find it for you."

"Thank you, Monsignor."

"You're welcome."

I went to my room, knelt down, and prayed for Vivian. As much as I tried to convince myself she was innocent, I found the task impossible. She'd killed four men! There was no way I could rationalize any legitimate excuse for her. Any woman who falls in love with a work inspired by a demon would have an evil end. She had the weapon, the opportunity, the motivation, and the strength to slay any man who attempted to stop her from doing what she wanted to do. Moreover, she had the demon Isacaron behind her, telling her what to do.

When I was a boy of seventeen, my mother died. Her death broke my heart. My heart was now broken a second time. I truly loved Vivian. I wanted her to be happy. But happiness isn't found in murdering another human being. Happiness isn't found in standing before a painting, allowing a demon from hell to heat the passions.

What can I do about her? Notify the police? Talk to her? I simply can't turn her over to the police. I'll try talking to her; get her to confess to the murders. She'll have to admit she killed the four men, express sorrow. Certainly, that's what God wants. It was He who gave us the Fifth Commandment: Thou Shalt Not Kill. No one has the right to take the life of a human being. Not even Vivian.

CHAPTER 43

For two days I performed my duties in a state of anxiety. The demon relentlessly tormented me at night. I was exhausted from lack of sleep; frustrated at the lack of success I had with Vivian. She not only refused to talk to me about the murders, she refused to talk to me about anything else.

I intended to ask her to leave the rectory after the police were through with their investigations, but I saw two black stretch limousines circling the block. Mario Togallini obviously planned to observe the rectory without losing any more men.

Despite this bad news, I received some good news from the newspaper. Joe McCabe wrote a fine article about the death of Mrs. Reilly and her husband Mike. McCabe wrote I'd committed myself to financing the funerals even though I'd no money in my pockets, and little money in the church treasury. All I had was faith in God and the good will of the people.

Almost immediately, checks flowed into the rectory. Within two days I'd enough money to pay for Mrs. Reilly's funeral. There are many good people in the world, I thought. People who offset the evil that other people do.

I was seated at my desk when the telephone rang. Automatically I picked it up and said, "St. Matthew's rectory."

A voice with a slight Irish brogue responded. "I'd like to speak to Father Davis."

"This is he."

"Father, this is Sean O'Malley, the owner of the building where Mike Reilly and his wife lived. I see in the newspaper you paid for their funerals. In my mind, that makes you heir to whatever they left behind."

"I'm sure they had no money."

"Not a nickel, but they left behind their furniture, dishes, pots and pans, an old television set, some other things. Nothing much of value, however, I'm willing to give you a fair price for it."

The caller gave me a great idea. An idea that seemed to lift the weight of the world from my shoulders.

"Why would you want the furniture, Mr. O'Malley?"

"Because I'm getting old, Father. I want to retire. I can't clean the building anymore. The damn stairs... Forgive me for my choice of words. The stairs are too much for me at this stage of my life. I'm going to offer the apartment to a couple, rent free, who'll keep the building clean, do other odd maintenance jobs. The only expenses they'll have are the utilities."

"Do you have a couple in mind?"

"Not yet, but I'll not have any trouble getting a couple if I spread the word around the building. I'll be able to get a poor couple, or maybe a small family, willing to accept my offer."

I said an aspiration before asking this question: "Would you consider giving the apartment to a young high school student who is desperately in need of a place to live?"

"Well, as I mentioned, I was thinking about a young couple. Two for the price of one."

"This boy will work hard. He's young, strong, tall, wouldn't mind the stairs. I'll vouch for his honesty, promise you he'll do a good job."

The man deliberated for thirty seconds or more. "All right, Father," he finally said. "I'll give him a shot at the job. Tell him he must do well with the building. He's not to have any women visiting him. No booze, drugs, loud music, noisy friends. I protect my tenants as best I can, and so should he. You never know what kids will do today."

"I understand your position perfectly, Mr. O'Malley, and I agree with it. I'll see the boy today in school; speak to him about the job. He'll call on you after school."

"I'll be waiting, Father."

I was so enthusiastic about getting Joshua a home, I arrived in my classroom early, long before any of the students arrived. As the students dribbled in, they were surprised to see me seated at my desk. Some said, "Good morning, Padre." Others remained silent. The classroom filled quickly with students. At the opening bell, all were present. All but one student…Joshua. It never occurred to me he'd take the day off.

Moreover, it never occurred to me that I had to conduct a class; that is, select a subject and talk about it. I spoke about the first subject that came into my mind.

"Scholars, I'd like to talk to you about angels. Like the boys and girls of today, as well as the men and women, angels have free will. They have the power to choose. Basically, they can choose to be servants of God or servants of the devil. Before time began, an angel named Lucifer enjoyed a high place in heaven. He had everything imaginable. Everything but the one thing he desired the most: God's power!"

A well-fed black girl in the second row shook her head when I met her stare.

"Lucifer spread his dissatisfaction among other angels, eventually led a war against God and those who supported Him. The angels who loved God, those willing to sacrifice themselves for Him, fought the war and defeated Lucifer and his followers. God cast the defeated angels into hell, where Lucifer became known as Satan. From the beginning of time, Satan roamed the world seeking the destruction of souls. His followers, the fallen angels, became known as demons. They hate God with the same intensity as Satan hates Him. Cunning and devious, they serve Satan by spreading their philosophy of evil throughout the world. Their primary goal is to snare your soul, have you join their ranks. Your primary goal in life is to save your soul. Your soul lives forever. The time you have on earth is limited."

I proceeded along these lines for another half hour or more. As I spoke, I kept thinking of Joshua. Where was he? Fifteen minutes before the class ended, I spoke to the students about him: "I've some important information for Joshua Roosevelt. Can anyone tell me where he lives?"

An emaciated Puerto Rican girl raised her hand.

"Do you know where he lives?"

"Yes, Padre."

"Marie, please tell me where?"

"I don't know where he keeps it, he lives in a cardboard box."

The students whooped and laughed at the response.

When the students were quiet, I glanced at my watch. Twenty minutes to three. "Is there anyone in this class who'll help me find Joshua?"

One hand went up, then two, then three. Eventually, twenty-four. Several students bounced up and down in their seats. They considered finding Joshua a game.

"Before I dismiss this class for the day, I'll give you some directions. We've got to use our heads for any job we do. Pointing to the first row of students, I said, "The first row of volunteers will go south; the second, west; the third, east; the fourth, north."

"Where's north?" one student asked.

"I'll show you. And check all empty lots and all buildings that have been burnt out. A prize for the first student who brings Joshua to me. I'll wait here at the school for Joshua and the winner of the prize."

The students rushed out of the classroom, making more noise than the rest of the school makes when released for the day. I'd a feeling someone would find Joshua.

In ten minutes time, as I waited outside the main entrance to the school, a girl had Joshua by the hand. She proudly brought him to me.

Joshua seemed puzzled when I greeted him at the door. "What's dis all 'bout?"

"Joshua, you and I are going to take a walk. We have something to talk about."

"Ah'm sorry Ah missed school t'day. Ah had a job. Ah hav'ta eat."

Demon of Lust

I tried to sound sympathetic. "You have to eat, work and sleep. You need a decent place to live. I've found an apartment for you, where you can live a normal life, be out of the rain, have a pleasant place to study."

"Ah can't 'fford no 'partment."

"You can afford this one. All you have to do is keep the building clean, take care of problems that arise, act as a superintendent. You'll have to pay for utilities. I believe you'll make enough in gratuities to pay for them."

"What're gratu'ties?"

"Tips. You'll have the opportunity to do jobs for tenants in the building. Chances are they'll show their appreciation by tipping you. If you don't get enough tips to pay for your food and utilities, see me. I'll make up the difference. You can repay me when you're a big success in the world."

"Ya think Ah can handle de job?"

"If I didn't think so, I wouldn't have recommended you. I want you to convince the owner of the building, a Mr. Sean O'Malley, you can handle the job. He doesn't want you to have any women visiting you. He doesn't want you to bring any booze, drugs, or noisy friends into the apartment. And he doesn't like loud music."

"It's his 'partment. He can lay down de rules."

"You don't object?"

"Oh, no. Ah'm grateful. Ah'd like to come in outta de rain, have a home. And one mo' thing..." Joshua failed to complete his thought.

"Yes?"

He wiped away tears from his eyes with the back of his hand. "Thank ya, Father."

He'd expressed his thanks at the precise moment we reached the front of the apartment. I took his hand, shook it "Good luck with your job interview. Remember, you're looking for a Mr. O'Malley. You'll probably find him in one of the first floor apartments. All you have to do is convince him you'll do a good job. Tell him you'll do everything he asks you to do. People like you and me must do as we're told. That's the way life is for us. Later on, when you're successful, you can be more independent."

As I walked back to the rectory, I prayed Joshua would make a good impression on Mr. O'Malley. I prayed because I didn't want to take God for granted. I knew God wanted Joshua to have a place to live. I was a mere instrument in His plan.

I became more convinced of that when Joshua called shortly before dinner. "Father, Ah got de job! Ah got de job!"

"Congratulations!"

"And Ah's got de 'partment! Father, it's beautiful! Beautiful! Got everything Ah needs, includin' a tel'phone. And de roof don't leak. Ah'm happier than Ah has ever been befo'. Thank ya again, Father."

"Don't thank me, Joshua. Thank God."

"Ah will. Ah will."

"I hope you'll be happy in your new home."

"It's a mansion, Father. A beautiful mansion."

"Take care of it and take care of your job."

"Ah will. Ah will."

As I sat down for dinner, I felt good about getting Joshua the job. He called the apartment a mansion. Compared to living in a cardboard box, the apartment…poor from the standards of many… was a mansion.

I was staring into space, thinking about Joshua, when a bowl of soup was placed before me.

I heard Vivian's voice: "What brings a smile to your lips?"

"Oh, nothing. I was just thinking about the events of the day."

"So nothing brings a smile to your lips?"

It was then I became fully aware of Vivian standing beside me. Monsignor Blazer was seated at the other end of the table.

He was smiling at me. "I've never observed you daydreaming before."

I felt the blood rush to my face. "Daydreaming! Was I? I thought I was thinking."

Vivian's question was blunt: "Thinking about what?"

"Oh, nothing."

She raised a finger. "There you go again with that nothing."

Demon of Lust

Monsignor opened a napkin, placed it on his lap. "Ordinarily, at this time of day, you appear as if you've the world's problems on your mind. Tonight, however, you're smiling. You can tell Vivian and me why you're smiling. Perhaps we'll smile, too."

As briefly as I could, I related my experiences with Mrs. Reilly and her death, Joe McCabe and his newspaper, Sean O'Malley and his vacant apartment, and Joshua Roosevelt and his homeless status. "All these people and their dealings with me led to my being able to remove a homeless boy from the streets. Of course, it was a plan designed in heaven. I take no credit…"

Vivian clapped her hands and exclaimed: "But you deserve a great deal of credit."

"You certainly do," Monsignor Blazer stated. "I'm proud of you."

"No reason to be proud of me."

"That boy may not be able to make enough money to pay for his food and utilities."

"In that event, I'll make up the difference."

"You're welcome to take as much as you like from the poor box," the Monsignor said. "I'll support you as best I can. You deserve much credit."

I deserved little or no credit for finding a home for Joshua; nevertheless I appreciated the Monsignor's words. Vivian's enthusiasm also gave me a boost. It was a pleasure having her in the rectory. A rectory can be a lonely place for a priest, who may or may not share the same interests as his fellow priests.

I was also happy to learn she was talking to me. She was now her usual self; warm, vivacious, beautiful, tempting. She was still my chief murder suspect, but I was so pleased with myself that night I went so far as to entertain the idea she might not be guilty.

I helped her with the dishes, felt as if I were walking on air. No question about it, I was in love with her. But what could I do about it? The answer was obvious: Nothing! Absolutely nothing! I was committed to be a priest and that's what I intended to be. Not only a priest but also a good one.

The vast majority of priests are good, I thought, but Satan and Isacaron are forever standing by to snare the ones who waver.

We finished the dishes and put them away. It was time to leave the kitchen, leave Vivian. "I have some work to do in my room," I said to her. "So I'll say goodnight."

"What kind of work?"

"School work for my class. Every time I read the newspapers, I find teen-age boys and girls in trouble. I'd like to design a program to keep them out of trouble. A deep understanding of the Ten Commandments should help. I'll focus on Thou shalt not steal; Thou shalt not kill; Thou shalt not commit adultery."

Vivian interrupted me with a question: "At least, one person must be married for a party to commit adultery, isn't that so?"

"Not necessarily so. Fornication is included in the Commandment. Fornication is a great offense against God. It should be confessed."

"Father, I've something to confess. I'll not ask you to open the church. Could we go to your room?"

"Not my room. We could go to my office or stay here in the kitchen."

"Monsignor Blazer may walk in on us."

"I doubt it, but..."

"Let's go to my room. I promise it won't take long."

Her request wasn't a wise one, yet I didn't want to discourage her from making a good confession. I wanted to hear her express her sorrow for murdering four men.

The moment I stepped into her room, I saw the naked form of the woman in the painting. And she saw me. She was alive, breathing lightly, and looking at me with great anticipation. My body grew hot with passion. An almost uncontrollable passion.

I felt Vivian's arms around me, heard her say, "I'm madly in love with you. I want you..."

"You don't want to go to confession?" I heard myself ask. It was the priest in me talking, not the frail human being.

Demon of Lust

"At this moment, I'd rather go to hell."

I glanced at the woman in the painting. Her eyes were fixed on Vivian. She seemed delighted to hear the remark. Delighted because somewhere in that canvas the Demon of Lust resided. The demon thought he was winning Vivian's soul...winning mine.

This information strengthened my will. I held Vivian at arm's length. "Never say you'd rather go to hell. Hell is not for you. And it's not for me. We'll talk more about it tomorrow morning when we're thinking clearly."

I left her looking sullen.

CHAPTER 44

I became aware of Isacaron hovering over me as I slept. He smelled like a decomposed body I once visited in a morgue. I heard his husky voice: "Happy to tell you, I've bad news for you."

"Bad news is part of my daily existence, Isacaron. I can take it."

"This news will cripple you."

I felt uneasy, but didn't want the demon to know he was a source of concern for me. "What information do you have?"

"Vivian will be kidnapped."

"What?" The news was so shocking; it almost awakened me.

"She'll leave the rectory tomorrow evening, not come back."

"You're not lying to me?" My question was a plea.

"No! No! I enjoy tempting Vivian; enjoy this assignment. When she departs from here, I'll have the task of escorting her to hell. Only the devil knows when I'll get back."

"Is there anything I can do?"

"You can travel up one flight of stairs, enter her bedroom, take her in your arms, make love with her. Your last opportunity."

The suggestion seemed to be a good one. The demon was offering me my last chance to make love with the woman who dominated my thinking. "Are you certain she'll be kidnapped tomorrow evening?"

"Trust me."

Could I trust the demon? He sounded sincere enough. He was once a good angel. Maybe there's enough good left in him to give me sound advice. He advised me to make love with Vivian before she leaves. I needed time to think.

"If you're going to make love with Vivian tonight, you'll have to get out of bed. So wake up. WAKE UP!"

I awoke, looked around the room. Empty. But I could smell something disgusting: the smell of a decomposed body.

Glancing at my watch, I saw I'd slept through my usual early morning coffee period. In ten minutes, I was scheduled to say Mass. Dressing quickly, I ran down the stairs, out the door, across a lawn soaked with a heavy rain, into the sacristy. Donning vestments, I entered the church and said Mass. I offered the Mass for Vivian, prayed she'd be free from danger.

Three vagrants came into church to get out of the rain. They approached the altar to receive communion. They had a reason to come to church. Vivian had a greater reason. She never came.

Later, at the rectory, she failed to acknowledge me when I entered the kitchen. Sitting down at the table, I waited for her to serve breakfast. Without uttering a word, she served me cereal and coffee. She then sat down in a chair next to mine, poured herself a cup of coffee. Taking a sip, she inadvertently put the coffee cup down on a bread knife, spilled some of the coffee onto the table.

Noting she was about to curse, I put a question to her: "Did you sleep well last night?"

"I'd a horrible night, dreamt I was kidnapped, taken to a warehouse in another state, and tortured. I suffered greatly. But I didn't tell Mario Togallini where the paintings are hidden."

I pictured the demon Isacaron going from my room to Vivian's room last night. "Do you place any credence in your dream?"

"Of course not. I'll admit, however, the dream I had last night frightened me."

"You still frightened?"

"I've no reason to be frightened. I studied dreams years ago. They take place when we're asleep and our powers to reason are suspended. They're produced by our imagination. They seem real because our intellectual faculties aren't working. We can't reason our way out of the situation we find ourselves in. Do you agree with that, Father Tom?"

"The philosophy is sound to a limited extent. If a spiritual force, good or evil, wishes to send you a message, he can do it by creating certain images in your imagination. He can also speak to you. A demon can do that. He can torment you while you sleep. I know that to be a fact…"

Vivian shook her head. "That's a lot of bunk."

"It may be bunk to you, not to me. You may be interested to know the demon Isacaron came to me last night, said you'll be kidnapped. Tonight!"

Vivian was puzzled. She stared at me for a long time. She waited, I thought, to hear me say I was only joking. She finally said, "You've been talking about a particular demon ever since you were a boy. You've even given him a name, Isacaron. He's a figment of your imagination, Father Tom. You've said he's troubled you for years. If that's true, he must be a nutty demon."

I met her gaze. "He's not nutty, Vivian. He's highly intelligent, an evil spirit from hell…alive before time began. He's out to snare your soul and mine."

"You actually do believe in demons and a devil, don't you?" she asked with exasperation.

"I wouldn't be a priest today if I didn't believe in them. Actually, if a devil didn't exist, the first parents wouldn't have disobeyed God. There'd be no need for priests and other religious leaders. We'd be in the Garden of Eden, enjoying the life God intended for us."

Frowning, Vivian said, "If God wants us to enjoy ourselves, why does He hold us responsible for sins committed by people who lived thousands of years ago? Call those people first parents, if you like, but their sins are not our sins. So why should we suffer? Why are so many individuals in pain from AIDS and cancer? Why the wars?"

"As I see it, Vivian, there are many tragic consequences for disobeying God. Our first parents disobeyed God. They were punished. All those who followed are punished. Is it fair to punish those of us who live in today's world? Absolutely! Not only must we suffer the sins of our parents, we make the same mistakes our first parents made: We yield to temptation, fail to obey God's Commandments."

"So what can we do about it?"

"You, in particular, can start by not tempting me."

"But I love you."

"If you truly love me, you'll keep me free from sin."

"No fun in doing that," she said wistfully.

She was a difficult girl to deal with, I thought. "There's something else you can do for me; that is, if you truly love me."

She looked at me suspiciously. "What's that?"

"Stay home tonight."

"I'll stay home if you'll stay with me."

"We'll stay together in my office. We can talk. Maybe have a few laughs."

"No necking?"

I could feel waves of passion rolling through me. Despite my theological knowledge, I still had difficulty controlling my passions. "None whatsoever," I said with an effort.

She put a finger to her cheek. "I'll have to think about it."

"What's to think about?"

"If I stay home tonight, you'll think I'm staying because the demon warned you I'll be kidnapped."

"On rare occasions, the demon tells the truth. He gave me the impression he likes his life here in the rectory. He doesn't want you dead yet."

"You can't be serious…"

"He was ambivalent. He doesn't want to see you dead because he'll have the job of delivering you to hell. He isn't sure if he'll be able to return here. On the other hand, he wants you dead because the devil wants you dead."

Vivian's beautiful coloring faded to chalk. "Why would you tell me something so…so gross?"

"Because it's the truth."

She stuck a well-formed finger two inches from my nose. "Even if it's true, you've no right to frighten the daylights out of me."

I had her on the ropes, planned to take full advantage of her. "Isn't it better to be frightened and learn the truth, than find yourself hand in hand with Isacaron, on your way to hell?"

She shouted the words: "I don't know anything about hell. I don't even know where it is, do you?"

"No, I don't. Isacaron does. He's anxious to show you the way."

"There you go again, frightening me."

I spoke as sincerely as I could. "Vivian, I'd give up my life for you, not harm you in any way. But your life is in danger. Since you arrived, the angel of death has followed you into the Bronx. The pickets, the woman who lived in the house across the street, the innocent people in the funeral parlor, the boy who drove your Rolls Royce… All have died since you moved into the rectory."

"I can't be responsible for them."

"Yes, you can. You've been associated with men who kill. I want you to go to confession before this day is over. You're a Catholic. That's what Catholics do when their lives are in danger."

Beads of perspiration formed on Vivian's brow. "You've got me thinking there's a chance I might die?"

"You may be at the end of the road."

She whispered the words: "Then I'll go to confession."

I felt a great sense of satisfaction. "You will?"

"I'll go to confession," she announced dramatically, "but not to you."

"Not to me?"

"You don't have the experience to deal with a sinner like me. Besides, what I have to confess is none of your business. I'm going to ask Monsignor Blazer to hear my confession. I'll look for him this very minute. He'll either be in his room or in the church."

Demon of Lust

Before I could comment, Vivian was out of the kitchen and up the stairs, calling. "Monsignor Blazer, Monsignor Blazer!" In less than a minute, she was down the stairs, saying, "He must be in the church."

I called to her, "I'll get him for you."

The front door slammed as I uttered the words. She was on her way to the church. I was on my way to a state of despair. If the men in either one of the stretch limousines spotted her, she'd be kidnapped...tortured...killed.

Blessing myself, I asked God to protect her, bring her back unharmed to the rectory. After saying the prayer, I felt better. Perhaps my worries had no foundation. She could have entered the church without being detected. I should learn to count my blessings. After all, I succeeded in getting her to confession.

Monsignor Blazer would do a good job. Like any other priest, he's not the master of God's forgiveness, but the servant, bound to keep secret any information he receives in the confessional. He's the Good Shepard, seeking the lost sheep; as well as the Good Samaritan, binding up injuries.

I poured myself a cup of cold coffee, put milk in it; drank it down without removing the cup from my lips. The taste was awful. I didn't care. I went into the Monsignor's office, looked out a window. I saw nothing of interest, except a bulldozer clearing debris from the lot across the street, the lot where the house had been bombed. I saw no pickets, no limousines, no Vivian.

Where was she? Was she praying at the altar, trying to atone for the sins of a questionable past? Was she still talking to Monsignor Blazer? I didn't know. I did know that pacing the floor wouldn't do a thing to help me. Nevertheless, I continued to pace the floor.

I was pacing the floor when Monsignor Blazer opened the front door. He'd hardly taken a step inside the rectory when I blocked his path. "Where's Vivian?" I asked him, a trace of hysteria crept into my voice.

"She was in the church an hour ago. I doubt if she's still there."

Without explaining my actions, I rushed past the Monsignor, ran to the church as fast as I could. The church was empty. A nerve-wracking silence permeated the interior. I examined the confessional boxes, hoping beyond hope I'd find Vivian in one of them. No Vivian. I examined every pew. No Vivian. I approached the altar, knelt down. No Vivian. Where was she? There was only one answer: She was gone!

I studied a life-sized crucifix hanging from the ceiling. A crucifix symbolizing the suffering of Christ. I'd seen it many times. Somehow its full significance hadn't struck me before. Christ suffered; we follow him. I'm now suffering. What can I do? Should I continue to suffer or should I do my best to find Vivian? I decided to do the latter. With God's help, I'll find her.

CHAPTER 45

Running up the rectory stairs and into Vivian's room, I stood before the woman in the painting. I spoke to her as if she were a living creature, which I considered her to be. "Isacaron, you came to me in a dream last night, told me a lie." A liar never likes to be called a liar, I thought. This fact might prompt him to speak to me.

The silence of the room was suddenly broken by a sweet voice emanating from the woman in the painting. "I didn't lie."

"You told me Vivian would be kidnapped this evening. She was kidnapped this morning."

"But I told you she would be kidnapped."

"You told me a half-truth, a form of articulation more deceptive than an outright lie."

"I'm truly sorry, Father Tom." Lines of deep regret and distress appeared on the woman's face.

"You can make it up to me," I said, thinking I'd settle for a half-truth or a clue to Vivian's whereabouts.

"In what way can I make it up to you?"

"By telling me where Vivian is being held."

"Oh, but I can't. I gave you the opportunity to save her when I suggested you take her into your arms."

"You gave me the opportunity to break my vows."

The woman appeared annoyed at my remark. "Nonsense!"

"Your method for luring souls to hell is obvious. You offer a brief period of pleasure for an eternity of pain. Anyone who listens to you is a fool. A fool with no sense of values."

"You're listening to me."

"Yes, and I'm a fool."

"At last, we agree. Tell me, Tom, what do you intend to do with Vivian's painting?"

"I'm not sure. I may trade it for her or destroy it. My options are twofold."

"You will never destroy it. Any attempt to destroy the painting is pure folly."

The demon could be speaking the truth. Many times I'd attempted to destroy a Togallini painting. On no occasion was I successful.

In the distance, I heard the ring of a telephone. I ran down a flight of stairs, into my bedroom. I picked up the phone. "St. Matthew's rectory."

"She won't talk."

"Who won't talk?" I asked thoughtlessly. Before receiving an answer, I knew the name of the caller, the name of the individual who wouldn't talk. Mario Togallini was the caller. Vivian wouldn't talk.

"You know who I mean?" Mario shouted into the phone.

Moments before I'd spoken to a demon. Now I was speaking to a man who followed the dictates of a demon. "I know you're talking about Vivian," I said earnestly. "Mario, I'm going to ask you not to hurt her."

"You've got a hellava nerve asking me for anythin'. You've been hidin' her for weeks. I warned you not to help her. You did, didn't you?"

"Vivian is my friend."

"Your friend, shit! She's your mistress. It's no wonder the Church is goin' to hell."

"I haven't touched her…"

"I'll believe you the day I buy the George Washington Bridge from some stinkin' vagrant."

"I don't care if you believe me or not. My main concern is Vivian. I don't want her hurt."

"She'll be hurt plenty if she doesn't tell me where she's hidin' my paintin's."

Should I tell him? The possibility of his killing her after receiving the paintings was great. He's killed others. "Mario, you and your friends are guilty of murder. I should notify the police and the FBI. Kidnapping is a federal offense."

"You call the police, or the FBI, and you call them to handcuff Vivian. She goes to jail. She's stolen a fortune from me. Some of my associates were also killed as a result of her theft. I'll involve you. You prepared to say you and some of your crazy parishioners didn't kill the four men legitimately picketin' the rectory? Can you convince the authorities Vivian didn't kill them? She's as strong as some guys I know."

He had a good argument. Vivian was strong, motivated.

Mario's voice suddenly became pleasant. "Tell me somethin', Father. Do you know where the paintin's are hidden?"

The question came so unexpectedly; I hardly knew how to answer it without telling a lie. "Well, maybe yes, and maybe no. I'm not saying. I'll have to decide."

"Vivian can die while you're makin' up your mind."

He had another good argument. I was dealing with a man influenced by a demon. "I don't want her hurt."

"Neither do I," Mario said as if he really meant it. "But I can't control the men who're holdin' her. They have some fiendish ways of pullin' information out of a person who won't talk."

"Are you saying they'll torture her?"

"They already have. And without success. When you get to know Vivian as well as I do, you'll learn she's not an easy girl to convince."

I felt sick at the thought of her being tortured. Yet I had to keep the conversation going. "I know she's hard to convince, Mario. I'm not so sure she won't die before revealing the information you're seeking."

"My thoughts, precisely. And that's why I'm callin' you. I want you to talk to her as a Holy Joe, convince her that her life is more important than a lot of paintin's she can't sell without bein' arrested."

"If you'll give me the telephone number where I can reach her…"

"I'm not that dumb. I give you the number, you find out its location, and where am I if you decide to call the police?"

"Well, how…"

"I'll have the men call you. Talk to Vivian, advise her to tell the men where the paintin's are."

"And then what?"

"Then everythin' will be fine."

"When you learn where the paintings are hidden, what assurance do I have she'll be released?"

"You don't have any assurances. You'll have to trust me."

"I'm not that dumb, Mario. Come up with a better plan."

"Why don't you come up with a better plan?"

"I will. Let me talk to Vivian."

"I'll have the men call you."

Before I could reply, Mario hung up the phone.

I sat down on a wooden chair in my room, waited for the phone to ring. Five, ten, twenty, forty minutes passed. The phone didn't ring. While waiting, I pictured the men making one last effort to pull the information out of Vivian before calling me. She refused to talk. They continued to torture her until she passed out. Finally, after a mind-boggling speculative hour, the telephone rang.

"St. Matthews rectory," I said automatically.

A gruff voice asked, "Is this the Holy Joe?"

"This is Father Tom."

"Somebudy wants to talk to ya."

Vivian's voice came on the phone. She sounded distraught, unhappy, in pain. "Father Tom. I should have listened to you. I'm somewhere in a warehouse. I don't know where. It's most unpleasant. I'm being forced to tell where I've hidden the paintings. I don't want to give them up. I'll die first…"

"Your life is worth more than the paintings."

"They belong to me."

"No, Vivian. They belong to the devil. Let Mario have them. He's one of the devil's disciples."

"I don't want him to have them."

"Have you seen him, spoken to him?"

"No. He has other people doing his dirty work. I'm with two men I've never seen before. They receive instructions by phone from Mario. Ooooh!"

Evidently someone ripped the phone from Vivian's hands. This was confirmed when I heard a gruff voice on the phone. "Knock the crap off. You're supposed to tell this slut to give us the info."

"Let me speak to her again."

Vivian came on the phone. "Father Tom, I…"

"You must tell the men I'll turn the paintings over to them when they turn you over to me."

"I don't want you to give up my paintings."

"I must."

"But I don't want you to."

"I'd rather give them up than see you lose your life. Have the men hurt you?"

"They put me in some kind of a machine. It pulls my arms out of their sockets. One of the men said, 'I'll look like a bloody Venus de Milo if I don't tell them where the paintings are hidden.'"

Tears formed in my eyes. I could truly feel her pain. I'd have gladly changed places with her; accepted the torture, the loss of my life. Why? Because I loved her. Why did I love her? A question not easily answered. I knew she was a fornicator, a potential murderess, a temptress, yet I couldn't control my feelings…my love for her. I'd help her without thought of recompense. I wanted her to be happy.

The gruff voice of one of the men came over the phone: "Ya've talked long enough."

"Vivian, tell me where you keep the key to your apartment."

She hesitated before answering, "I keep it behind a picture of St. Jude in my bedroom. I've been thinking about that picture today." She sobbed, "Did you know he was called the Saint of the Impossible?"

"I know. He was a martyr who suffered and died for his faith. I don't want you to suffer and die for the faith you have in paintings inspired by a demon."

"I don't like to suffer," she conceded.

"Tell the men we've agreed to release the paintings to them. But the release is contingent upon a plan agreed to by Mario Togallini and me. Have them pass this information on to Mario, and have him call me."

"I'll do that."

"And keep your chin up. It won't be long before you're released."

"Thank you, Fath…"

The familiar but annoying sound of a disconnect terminated the conversation.

Leaving the room, I took the stairs two at a time, reached Vivian's bedroom. The moment I entered the room, the woman in the painting fixed her eyes on me. Her eyes followed me as I crossed the room, stopped at the picture of St. Jude. Lifting the picture, I found a ring with two keys. One was for the front door of the building, one for the apartment. The keys were on a ring fastened to the wallpaper with chewing gum. The lady in the painting smiled when I tried to remove the gum from the wallpaper.

"Your friends are going back to Mario Togallini," I said to her.

A strange smile appeared on her beautiful face.

It occurred to me that Isacaron might not have any friends. He could be in more than one place at the same time. Or he, as a spiritual being, could travel with the speed of thought from one painting to another, as the need to corrupt demanded.

An idea came into my head that caused me to stop before the painting. With a super effort to control the passions surging within me, I gazed at the face of the woman. "I hope you realize your grand plan to bring Vivian and me together for illicit purposes has failed."

The beautiful head shook slightly.

She was showing her disagreement, I thought. "You brought Vivian into this rectory, thinking I'd yield to her beauty. Well, nothing happened. I'll admit I was often tempted, but I was able to control myself. I didn't touch her. Are you disappointed? And won't the devil curse you, punish you, when you report the failure?"

The expression on the lady's face reflected fear.

"I'd like to rescue Vivian...risk my life for her, bring her back to this rectory. She'll be so appreciative, who know what will happen between us?"

The woman in the painting appeared interested.

"You can help. Tell me where Togallini is holding her."

I was getting desperate at the lack of response. I'd good reason to be concerned. I was trying to deceive one of hell's most proficient liars. "If you help, Vivian and I may do what you've been trying to get us to do," I said, hoping God would understand my need to be dishonest.

The woman in the painting seemed to be reflecting on the idea presented to her. I waited ten minutes without receiving a response. Finally, I lay down on the bed and closed my eyes, hoping she'd speak to me. I waited and waited, still no response. Feeling exhausted from the events of the morning, I drifted off to sleep.

Isacaron came to me in a dream. I couldn't see him, but I could smell him...hear him.

"Look in the Jersey City telephone directory, you stupid bastard," he said to me. "You'll find Mario Togallini's name and home address. You'll likewise see the address of his warehouse."

CHAPTER 46

After being told I could find Mario Togallini's phone number and the address of his warehouse in the Jersey City telephone directory, I jumped into my Ford Fairlane and drove to the nearest library to obtain the information.

A scholarly looking woman with a no-nonsense approach to her job located the Jersey City directory for me. I found two listings for Togallini. One was for his home, the other for his warehouse.

Returning to the rectory, I went into my office and dialed Togallini's home number. A series of rings sounded before a woman with an Italian accent answered.

"Hallo."

"I'd like to speak to Mr. Mario Togallini. This is Father Tom Davis calling from the Bronx."

"He ain't here."

"Are you sure?"

"Father, he got a call a little while ago from somebudy about a meetin'. He told me he had to leave town for a couple a days."

"Is there any way I can reach him?"

"No, there ain't. I don't know where the meetin' is. After he got the call, he did a lotta cussin', so I figured it was the Mafia callin'. He always does a lotta cussin' whenever the Mafia calls. That's 'cause he's gotta drop everythin' and do what he's told to do. Father, just between you and I, he's not the big shot everybody thinks he is."

"I understand."

"Now that I've got you on the phone, would you tell me somethin'?"

"What would you like to know?"

"Is my husband talkin' to you about going back to church?"

"No."

"I thought maybe you was goin' to hear his confession. He hasn't gone to confession in fifty years. Maybe sixty."

"No, Mrs. Togallini. He hasn't asked me to hear his confession." I tried to think of some way to end the conversation. My primary concern was Vivian, how I could help her.

"Can a man like my husband get back into the church while he's sellin' pornography to the world?"

He can't work for the devil and God at the same time, I thought. But I said, "He and I can talk about it if he's interested, Mrs. Togallini. Will you have him call me the moment he returns home?"

"I'll have him call you, Father. I'd like to know..."

"I must run now, Mrs. Togallini. I've an important problem to work out. Nice talking to you." I hung up the phone.

I felt bad about hanging up on her. I've met other women like her. They could talk to a priest for hours because they'd no one else to talk to. Obviously, her husband gave her little attention. Her children were either gone from the home or of little comfort. She was a lonely woman with a great deal to say and no one to listen.

Her husband was her problem. And mine. So the Mafia has called him away from home. Where did that leave me? More importantly, where did it leave Vivian? Would she be required to suffer till he found time for her?

"Now, wait a minute," I said aloud to myself. Something I hadn't considered. Togallini would have a phone in his car. He could call me while traveling to his meeting. Even if he takes an airplane, he could call me. All I had to do was exercise patience, wait for him to phone.

I waited several hours. The call didn't come in. My imagination produced all sorts of wild possibilities, caused me to be sick with worry. Perhaps Togallini hadn't called because Vivian was dead. She couldn't take the torturing. She'd lost her arms, bled to death. I had to find out if she were still alive.

I needed help. But whom could I call? Not the police. Not anyone well established in the parish. I needed someone strong, athletic, who could climb a fence, if necessary. I glanced at my watch. Four o-clock. Joshua would be home from school. I'd find his telephone number under the name Mike Reilly. Finding it, I dialed the number.

The response was immediate: "Joshua Roosevelt, yore maintenance man."

"Joshua, this is Father Tom. Can you break away from your job long enough to make a return trip to Jersey City with me? I can pick you up in ten minutes."

"Yes, Father."

Joshua had the sweet, simple faith of an altar boy. He didn't ask me why I wanted to go to Jersey City, didn't offer me any excuses for not going. He simply said, "Yes, Father."

He was waiting for me in front of his tenement building when I pulled the Fairlane along side of the curb. He opened the door, sat down, stretched out his long legs, and didn't say a word.

I hoped he didn't feel I was taking advantage of him, simply because I'd found him a place to live and a job. Whatever was going through his head was something I couldn't figure out. Rather than keep him in the dark, I decided to give him an explanation.

"Joshua, this trip to Jersey City is for an old friend of mine, a woman who was kind to me when I was a boy. She made the mistake of taking some paintings from a pornographic dealer. Paintings she considers to be her own. And the dealer is out to get them back. He's kidnapped her, will kill her if she doesn't tell him where the paintings are hidden."

Joshua's head swiveled towards me. "Does he have anythin' t' do wit' de men dat pick'ted de rect'ry?"

"He assigned those men to the rectory, to watch and wait for the woman. Either he or they kidnapped her."

"Damn!" Joshua exclaimed.

"The woman, by the way, was the owner of the Rolls Royce parked in front of the rectory."

Joshua's eyes widened. "De Rolls dat wuz stolen?"

"Yes," I said, wondering if Joshua would admit to me, outside of confession, that he was the one who stole the Rolls Royce.

"Dere de men who killed my friend Ronnie."

"I know. And they won't hesitate killing my friend Vivian."

"Ya gotta stop guys like dat, Father. Ya gotta stop 'em."

Joshua's statement was a foolish one, I thought. How can I stop a gang of thugs without going to the police? I simply couldn't go to the police. I had to find some other way.

It was now seven o'clock in the evening. We reached Jersey City without difficulty. And after stopping at two service stations to make inquiries, we found the warehouse in an industrial area. The warehouse was a large, bleak, concrete structure, blackened with soot. Black, I thought, was appropriate for the building, which housed merchandise that blackened the souls of those who purchased it.

All the lights in the building were out, except one at the rear of the building. The window was at eye level. Too easy, I thought. Togallini, or his men, wouldn't hide a victim in a warehouse with a window anyone could look through.

But looking through the window wasn't easy. It was filthy dirty. When first we looked, Joshua and I could see only two vague images. Then Joshua pulled down the sleeve of his shirt and cleaned the window. He removed enough dirt to enable us to see two men playing cards. We also saw shelves stacked with boxes, a printing press, and the hands of someone grasping steel bars, built into a door.

"Ya see de hands?" Joshua asked."

"I see them. But I'm not sure they belong to Vivian."

"Dey belong t' her," Joshua said with some degree of authority. "She's in some kinda prison?"

"I think she's in some kind of payroll office. Evidently the door is locked."

"We could break it open," Joshua said, matter-of-factly.

"We could also get shot."

"Not if we had some weap'ns."

"Of course, we don't have any weapons. If we did, I wouldn't use them. I'd never deliberately injure anyone regardless of what he did."

"Ya believe in turnin' de other cheek."

"I do."

"Ya can git knocked out dat way."

"I suppose so. But we'd have a much more peaceful world if everyone believed in turning the other cheek."

"Dey don't believe dat in de Bronx and in Harlem."

"Maybe you can suggest it to them some day, Joshua. Suggest it when they're tired of fighting, tired of being injured and killed."

"Dey won't listen t' me."

Why was I rambling on with Joshua? I'd found Vivian and I didn't know what to do about her. I experienced some satisfaction knowing she was still alive. She was able to stand, grasp the bars in the door. Obviously the men were ordered to hold her until Mario Togallini returned from his meeting with the Mafia. There was nothing I could do now. I'll have to wait until I receive a call from him.

"We could open a window, sneak up on those guys," Joshua said.

"Too dangerous. I'll not risk your life for Vivian or anyone else."

"Ah'll be riskin' it for de gen'ral public, Father. Those guys tried t' blow up our school."

The school meant a great deal to Joshua, I thought. I was pleased to hear him offer to risk his life to protect it. "We'll have to leave now."

"Ya gonna call de police?"

"I can't call the police." I was tempted to tell Joshua that Vivian would spend the rest of her life in jail for murder if the police became involved. I thought better of it. "Let's go."

Demon of Lust

Reluctantly, Jonah left the warehouse with me. We were halfway through the Holland Tunnel when he spoke for the first time on the way back to the Bronx. "Those guys are gettin' away wit' murder."

"I know they are," I said despondently. "And to make matters worse, they'll receive a number of paintings that've been inspired by a demon from hell. Voluminous copies will be made, distributed around the world. If only I could destroy those paintings."

"If ya wanna destroy 'em, Ah'll help."

"Thanks, Jonah. You were a big help tonight. I might call on you again when I arrange to have my friend released. I'll have to deliver the paintings."

"Dat's somethin' ya don't wanna do, ain't it?"

"I'd much prefer to destroy the paintings. I've no choice."

After dropping Jonah off at the tenement house, I drove to the rectory and parked the car. Monsignor Blazer met me at the door.

He spoke with some concern. "I've been looking for Vivian. She's been gone all day. Do you have any idea where she is?"

"She's in Jersey City. She'll be back as soon as some arrangements can be made for her."

"Is she all right?"

"As far as I know, she is. I'll get her back here as soon as possible."

The Monsignor spoke as if he were revealing a deep secret. "I miss her."

My response was the same as his. "So do I."

It was well beyond two o'clock in the morning when I fell asleep. How long I slept before the demon Isacaron appeared to me in a nightmare, I don't know. I know his voice was harsher than usual.

"Listen for the bell!" he said excitedly. "Listen for the bell!"

"What bell?"

"The doorbell, you fool."

In my sleep, I puzzled over the order given me. Why should I listen for the doorbell?

The doorbell rang.

Seconds later, the voice of Isacaron: "The doorbell is ringing. The doorbell is ringing. Remember your promise."

"What promise?"

The doorbell continued to ring. A persistent ring as if someone had his finger on the button.

Awakening, I sat up in bed. The doorbell was ringing, loud enough to awaken Monsignor Blazer.

I swung out of bed, ran down the stairs in my bare feet. The bell was still ringing when I opened the door.

Vivian stood in the doorway with her finger on the bell, tears running down her cheeks. She looked hurt, disheveled, and dirty. Her clothes were stained with blood.

CHAPTER 47

I was so shocked to see Vivian standing in the doorway, with tears running down her cheeks and her clothes stained with blood, I couldn't speak. Nor could she. She stood like a lost child who'd somehow found her way home. And very much like a child, she rushed into my arms.

While still holding her, I closed the door and thanked God for returning her to me. Her heart was beating madly against mine. It was like the beat of a drum keeping pace with the rapid beat of a second drum.

She held me tight and I held her just as tight. I didn't kiss her. All I wanted to do was comfort her as a father would comfort a distraught child after experiencing a horrifying ordeal.

"Could we go upstairs," she said. "I don't want Monsignor Blazer to see me this way."

I accompanied her up the stairs and into her room. She closed the door. The lady in the painting smiled with anticipation when the door was closed. I sat down in a chair, observed her slip off the dress she was wearing. She examined the bloodstains, threw the dress into a hamper.

The bloodstains had my mind building up a series of questions. I could hardly wait to learn the reason for the blood. I wanted to learn every detail relating to the kidnapping. Trying to keep my voice at a normal level, I asked, "What happened?"

"Please don't ask me any questions," she said, putting on a bathrobe.

"Why not?"

"I don't want to talk about it." She massaged her left shoulder, then the right.

"Did you tell Togallini where you hid the paintings?"

"I'll die before I tell him anything," she said calmly. Then raising her voice to a hysterical pitch, she shouted: "I don't want to answer any questions?"

Her nerves were overwrought after the experience, I thought. She wanted to forget Togallini and the men who tortured her. So I'll not ask her any more questions. At least, not tonight. Besides, if she has another outburst, she might awaken the Monsignor. I'll speak to her in the morning, after she's had a good night's rest.

She sounded rational, in perfect control of her emotions, when she said, "I'd like to shower. Be back in short order."

A bathroom was next to her bedroom. I heard the shower running for five or six minutes. While waiting for her to return, I began to ask myself some questions: Why wouldn't she tell me what happened at the warehouse? Had she made a deal with Mario? That, I doubted. Had she managed to escape? That, too, was doubtful. Had she charmed the two men into letting her go? That was a definite possibility. What man would torture a woman as angelic as Vivian?

I should be satisfied in knowing she was free. Why should I be concerned about anything else? But I was. My mind burned with curiosity.

My questions and speculative answers ended when she came back into the room. She'd showered, brushed her hair, and applied a little powder, rouge, and lipstick to her face. She looked simply beautiful.

Before I could stop her, she sat on my lap. "How do I look now?"

I gave her an honest answer: "Beautiful."

"Beautiful enough to love?"

My body began to heat with passion. The heat became more intense when I looked at the woman in the painting. Her expression seemed to say, go ahead, make love with her. It will be a great experience. I was prone to do precisely that.

And that is precisely what Isacaron wanted me to do. I recalled him coming to me in a dream, suggesting I look in the Jersey City Telephone Directory to find the address of Togallini's warehouse. He'd given me the

Demon of Lust

information after I'd sought his help. I told him Vivian and I might do what he wanted us to do, if he'd tell me where she was taken after the kidnapping. That, of course, was pure deception on my part. To him, it was a promise he expected me to keep.

Could I keep the promise? No, I couldn't. I lifted Vivian off my lap, deposited her on the bed, moved out the door, and ran down the stairs.

Whether she and Monsignor Blazer could hear him, I do not know. But the loud voice of Isacaron followed me down the stairs, into my room. His voice ricocheted off the walls, into my head. "You promised me you would make love with Vivian! You promised me you would make love with Vivian," he repeated over and over again.

Yes, I made the promise. A promise I couldn't keep. My body wanted to keep the promise. My mind didn't. No man can follow the dictates of a demon and his God simultaneously.

The voice of the demon persisted: "You promised you would make love with Vivian. You promised you would make love with Vivian." The voice was so loud, so persistent, so maddening, I thought I'd lose my mind if it continued. Leaving my room, I ran down the stairs, out the front door, into the church. The moment I closed the door of the church behind me, the demon's voice was silenced.

Kneeling at the altar rail, I thanked God for the silence; thanked Him for giving me the strength to resist the temptation. How easy it is to yield to temptation, how difficult to resist.

I considered asking God to free me from Isacaron. Why should I have to cope with a demon every night? Isacaron was my cross. If I were to get rid of him, I'd be given another cross. Maybe another demon, more vicious than Isacaron. Perfect happiness in this life is a myth. I can't expect perfect happiness till I die.

But why does Isacaron spend time annoying me? He knows me, that's why. He revealed himself to me when I was a boy. He knows that I know him. He need not hide from me, as he hides from others. To that extent, I've an advantage over others. I know he's behind every sexual temptation driving men and women to fornicate, to commit adultery, to sodomy. Isn't that why he wants to destroy me? He doesn't want me to warn others, tell them to avoid illicit sex lest they lose their souls.

I knelt at the altar until it was time to say Mass. I offered the Mass for myself, asking God to give me the strength to cope with Vivian and Isacaron.

After Mass, I returned to the rectory. I found Vivian seated at the kitchen table, looking sleepy and drinking coffee. She greeted me with a weak smile, a cup of coffee and a bowl of cereal. I finished the coffee and cereal while she tinkered with something at the stove.

"So what do we do now?" she asked, sitting down next to me.

The question brought to mind my early morning experience with her. "What do you mean?"

"I mean Togallini knows I'm here in this rectory. Do you think he'll send his men after me again?"

"I can't answer your question, not till you give me some information. Did he let you go last night?"

She shifted uneasily in her chair. Hesitatingly, she said, "He didn't let me go."

I asked quickly, "Did you escape?"

Furrows appeared on her brow. She remained silent.

Awkwardly, I asked, "The blood on your clothes, will you explain it?"

She struck the table with a fist. "I told you last night, I don't want to be grilled."

"But why?"

"Because I don't. That's why."

"I didn't insist on your answering questions last night because I knew you were overwrought…"

"I'm overwrought now," she said with bitterness. "I'll be overwrought for the rest of this month; for the rest of my life."

I stared at a cereal flake on the table, wondered why she wouldn't answer my questions. The blood on her clothes bothered me beyond belief. It'd help me a great deal if she'd explain it. How best to approach her? Before I could think of a fresh approach, say, ask her an easy question, she was out of the kitchen and up the stairs. I was hurt. She didn't trust me. I pictured her standing before her painting, confiding in the demon. She trusted the demon, not me.

Going into my office, I sat down, opened my breviary to read...

The telephone rang.

"St. Matthew's rectory."

"Is this Father Tom Davis?"

"Yes."

"This is Detective Casey. I'm calling to ask if you're watching the news on television?"

"No."

"There's something that'll interest you on Channel Two. Take a look. I'll hold on, wait for your reaction."

There was an old, seventeen-inch television set in my office. I switched it on. The picture was slow to appear. It contained a few sparkles, but was clear enough to show the front of a huge building, soiled with soot. Policemen milled around the building. Radio and television vehicles were parked everywhere.

A cameraman brought his audience into the building, where pornographic pictures were on display. He passed cardboard cutouts of handsome men and beautiful women performing unnatural acts; passed life sized women in the nude, displaying whips, condoms, and other sexual devices of all shapes and sizes; passed printing presses and stacks of paper.

He finally reached the rear of the building, where policemen, technicians, and men dressed in civilian clothes, examined the blood-soaked bodies of two men. They'd fallen near an open door containing bars.

"The Togallini warehouse!" I gasped.

"What was that, Father?"

"I was talking to myself."

"I thought I heard you use the Togallini name."

"For many years I've known he owns the world's largest pornographic business. It wasn't difficult to conclude he owns a warehouse."

"Yes. And the men killed were the Ricco brothers. Have you ever heard of them?"

"No."

"They worked for Togallini. They're small time racketeers. The mystery is who killed them?"

I thought of Vivian on the fourth floor. She had blood on her clothes when she arrived in the rectory, early this morning. She had blood from the Ricco brothers?

"The reason I'm calling you, Father, is because I think the Ricco murders are connected in some way with the murders committed at the front and rear of your rectory."

"I wouldn't be surprised."

"Would you be surprised to learn the men were stabbed to death with a sword or a bayonet?"

If I'd been stabbed with a bayonet, the information couldn't have hurt more. I was dumbfounded, hardly knew what to say. I considered asking the detective to speak to Vivian about the murders. Would he believe she was under the influence of an evil spirit? He wouldn't. He'd say she was guilty of murder.

The voice of the detective interrupted my thoughts. "Are you still with me, Father?"

"I am. I wish I could help."

"You sure you can't? Certainly you must have some idea of the responsible party. We know a woman is responsible for the murders at the rectory. It's a ninety-nine to one bet it's a woman responsible for the murders in the warehouse. It's about time we learned who she is? We can stop the slaughters. The woman is a serial killer, Father I've never come across a woman who has such a wanton disregard for life. She doesn't kill one person at a time. She kills two!"

Demon of Lust

"You're right," I said to the detective. "Give me some time. I may come up with a name."

"A woman's name?"

"Yes."

I hung up the phone, watched the police on television put the dead men on gurneys, push them through an aisle, where placards of men, women and beasts were on display, performing unspeakable sexual acts.

The journey through life had ended for the Ricco brothers. What a pity they had to travel through an aisle of placards inspired by the devil. I said a prayer for them, hoping they'd asked God to forgive them before closing their eyes for the last time.

CHAPTER 48

Vivian served Monsignor Blazer and me lunch that day in the dining room. Her hand trembled as she placed a bowl of soup before the Monsignor.

He was quick to notice the shaking hand. "Have a disturbing sleep last night?" he asked her.

"None worse," she replied, without explaining her remark.

He tasted the soup, nodded his approval. "We all have bad nights, except Father Tom. He sleeps like a baby."

The pastor was wrong on that point, I thought. My nights were filled with terror. Isacaron simply wouldn't allow me to get a proper rest. "I haven't slept like a baby since I was a baby," I said, thinking he'd take my remark as a joke.

"You do all right," he replied.

How little we know of what others do and think. I observed Vivian putting a bowl of soup before me. She was still shaking. I longed to know what she was thinking. Was she reviewing the events of the past evening? Locked in the payroll office, how did she free herself? How did she kill the two men guarding her? Where did she get the bayonet? How did she find her way back to the rectory? Did she take keys from one of the dead men; drive his car back to the rectory? There were so many questions I wanted to ask her, I hardly knew where to start. But she wouldn't answer any of the questions, so why enumerate them in my mind?

She was seated close to me. I watched her trying to bring a spoonful of soup to her mouth. She was so nervous, she spilled half the soup in the spoon before it reached her lips. She'd reason to be nervous. She waged a one-woman war against a gang of racketeers, killed at least six of them. Members of the Mafia were known to retaliate.

Unquestionably, she'd have to leave the rectory as soon as possible. After lunch, I'd drive her and her damned painting to the Brooklyn apartment where...

"Oh, my God!" I heard her exclaim.

Looking up from my soup, I saw Mario Togallini and three of his thugs standing inside the doorway. They'd entered the dining room without making a sound. The three thugs had drawn guns.

Monsignor Blazer's chin dropped. "What is the meaning of this?" he asked, his voice quivering.

One of the men, whose face was disgustingly pimpled, pointed a gun at the Monsignor. "This is the meanin'."

The skin of the elderly priest turned deathly pale. He appeared as if he might have a heart attack. He made no further attempt to question the men.

Mario Togallini stood with his hands on his hips, glared at Vivian. His eyes were wet and wild. He must be out of his mind, I thought, to break into the rectory with three armed men. He made no pretense to hide his identity. Did he intend to kill us all?

"So this is where you've been hidin'?" Mario said. "Imagine that! We've been waitin' for you to approach the rectory, and you've been inside the rectory all the time. You fooled us, didn't you? You fooled me. And you know I don't like bein' fooled. And you've killed six of my men. Enough killin' to put you in jail for six lifetimes."

"I didn't kill anyone," Vivian sobbed.

"Don't lie to me," Mario snapped. "Your lies aren't cute any more. You're a liar, a murderer, and a thief. A thief who's stolen my paintin's. Paintin's I received from my dead brother. I want them back! You're gonna give them back to me or I'm gonna break your back."

Mario crossed the room and grabbed Vivian by the hair.

Clenching my fist, I stood up. I wanted to hit Mario with all my strength.

One of the thugs put a gun to my head. "Sit down."

I sat down.

As he tightened his grip on Vivian's hair, Mario Togallini looked insane. Rage distorted his face. He was possessed by a demon, I thought. He was being driven to do the unreasonable, the unexplainable, the harmful...the devil's work. Other men, similarly possessed, waged wars, murdered innocent people, raped and starved their victims.

Unmercifully, Mario twisted Vivian's hair. "You gonna tell me where the paintin's are hidden?"

Ignoring the gun and the thug who had it pointed at my head, I said, "Let her go, Mario. I'll tell you where the paintings are."

"Please don't tell him," Vivian sobbed.

Mario loosened his grip on her hair. "You know where they are?"

"I do."

Mario gave me a hard look. "I don't believe this slut would tell you where she hid them."

"She told me. And I'll tell you, if you release her."

"I don't trust you. You lied to me before, you'll lie again."

"I never lied to you. A few mental reservations, maybe, but no lie."

"You talk riddles. Riddles I don't have time to figure out. If you know where the paintin's are, you better tell me. Otherwise, you'll hear some guns go off."

I felt a chill go up my spine. I knew Mario Togallini was crazy enough to kill us all. I tried my best to keep my voice calm: "If you kill us, you'll never get the paintings. And you'll never be able to claim them. The police will know you had a motive for murder."

From the expression on Mario's face, my remark seemed to make sense to him. "All right," he said, "we'll take Vivian with us. You deliver the paintin's and we'll deliver her to you."

"Why take her with you?" I asked. "Why not leave her here? I give you my word, I'll deliver the paintings to your warehouse."

Mario gave me a harsh look. "You know where it is, don't you?"

"I found the address in the Jersey City phone book."

"I'll bet you did."

"Why haggle over the unimportant? I'll deliver the paintings to you tonight. But leave Vivian here."

"You'll deliver the paintin's to me tonight and we'll take Vivian with us. That's the deal. When we get the paintin's, you get Vivian. Not a fair exchange, but that's the way it's gonna be."

I looked at Vivian. Tears were running down her cheeks. She was dependent upon me. I could do nothing for her. At that moment, I knew I truly loved her, regardless of what she'd done. I'd have given my life for her. But sacrificing my life wouldn't help her. "Mario, I wish you'd reconsider..."

His negative answer came with a series of expletives.

Monsignor Blazer looked imploringly to heaven with each shocking word. He blessed himself several times.

Realizing that any reasonable appeal to Mario Togallini was hopeless, I finally said, "All right, Mario, I'll get the paintings for you, deliver them to your warehouse before ten tonight. Be patient if I'm a little late. I'll need a trailer or a large van to carry them. I'll also need someone to help me."

He studied me closely and warned, "Don't bring the police! If a policeman shows up with you, Vivian joins the faithfully departed. And you're dead. Priests today are rapidly becomin' extinct, so you better be careful."

"I won't bring the police. Nor will I endanger Vivian's life in any other way."

"Now you're talkin' business."

"Will you please release your grip on Vivian's hair? You're hurting her."

"I'll release her hair at your request," he said mockingly. "But if she runs, she'll get a bullet in her back."

"She won't run."

"My associates will escort her outta here." Mario nodded to the men. Grasping her arms, they led her out of the room.

Mario watched them depart. He then turned to Monsignor Blazer. "Sorry to break in on you this way, Father, but the woman you've been harborin' is a thief. I'm gonna hold her until the property she stole is returned to me."

"I suggest you let her go."

Annoyed, Mario said, "I'll let her go when I get back my property. And I won't sue you for harborin' a criminal if you don't call the police. All the police in the Bronx aren't in my back pocket. They can be expensive when I have to go over their heads. I pay through the nose."

"I don't understand…"

"There's a lotta things you don't understand, Daddy. You don't understand how a good lookin' woman like Vivian can be a thief. You don't understand how she could puncture the belly of an employee of mine. Nor do you understand why she'd run a sword through the bellies of five other innocent men. She's murdered six men! Family men! And you've been harborin' her," he shouted accusingly, pointing an index finger at the Monsignor. "Shame on you! Shame on you!" He then backed out of the room, was gone.

Rather than follow Mario Togallini to the main entrance of the rectory, and beg him to release Vivian, I sat immobilized in my chair in the dining room. I faced Monsignor Blazer, my pastor. Not so long ago, I'd a hundred questions to ask Vivian. Now that I faced the Monsignor, I could see from the expression on his face, he had a hundred questions to ask me.

"Is it true what that man said about Vivian?"

"Your question is difficult to answer, Monsignor."

"Why so difficult?"

"It dates back to my teen-age years. The answer is so complex, I hardly know where to begin." Beads of perspiration broke out on my brow.

"Suppose you begin by telling me if Vivian stole that man's property."

I wiped the perspiration from my brow. "In a way she did, in another way she didn't. The property belongs to him from one perspective; from another perspective, it belongs to the devil."

The Monsignor shook his head. "I don't know what you're talking about."

"Well, as I mentioned, the story behind the theft is a long and intricate one. It deals with Vivian when she worked as a model for an artist. The artist was possessed by a demon known as Isacaron. The demon inspired the artist to paint pictures of nude women. The paintings have the power to turn men's thoughts to sins of the flesh. I knew the artist well. He rented the attic apartment from my father. Before he died, he asked me to destroy his paintings. He didn't want them distributed around the world. He felt responsible for the damage they'd do to the souls of those who viewed them. He also feared the loss of his own soul."

"Did you destroy any of them?"

"I tried. God knows I tried. But I was coping with a demon. He is powerful. Much too powerful for me. The world isn't aware of a demon's power."

"Nor am I," the Monsignor remarked.

His words came as a surprise. "You don't believe me?"

"I didn't say I don't believe you. I'm saying I've been a priest for over fifty years. Never once have I had to cope with a demon. I don't focus on that which is evil. My mind centers on that which is good: God's love for us, His grace, His many gifts, and His promise to resurrect us after death. I focus on going to heaven."

"Getting to heaven isn't easy for some of us, Monsignor. God places obstacles in our way. He allows a devil and thousands of demons to roam the world, fight for our souls. They can destroy our chances of ever getting to heaven. You should understand the power of Satan much better than I."

"What you say conforms to the Church's teachings in many respects. However, I believe the notion of demons has become an obsession with you. I hate to listen to a young priest talk about paintings inspired by a demon."

I felt the blood in my body rush to my head. I stood at the dinner table, shouted, "You don't believe me!"

"Well, Father Tom..."

"Stay seated in your chair, Monsignor. I'll be back in a minute. I want you to see what I've seen." As quickly as I could, I left the dining room, ran up the stairs to the fourth floor, picked up the painting in Vivian's room. It alternately became heavy and light as I carried it down the stairs and into the dining room. I placed it on the table, leaning it against a brass chandelier for support. "Study this painting, Monsignor Blazer. It was done by an artist possessed by a demon."

"Surely, you don't expect me to believe..."

The Monsignor never finished his sentence. The woman in the painting mesmerized him. She was like a queen looking down critically on a subject who'd denied her beauty, her power, and her reputation. His face reddened and he tried, but was unable, to take his eyes off her. I thought his passions, dormant for decades, had been fired up beyond reason.

Almost imperceptibly, her lips moved. She whispered, "Now you believe..."

As if in a trance, he answered, "I do." Standing, he reached out with a finger, touched her stomach. It dimpled and reddened when he removed his finger. Then looking heavenward, he voiced a prayer of forgiveness, closed his eyes, and fell dead on the floor.

CHAPTER 49

Falling on my knees, I put my head on Monsignor Blazer's chest, listened for a heartbeat. I heard none. No doubt about it, he was dead. I obtained sacramental oils from a cabinet in his office and gave him the last rites. His eyes were open, fixed on the heaven above. What could he see now? Could he see the limitless rewards he labored so ardently to obtain? Closing his eyes, I asked God to welcome him into the Kingdom of Heaven.

Realizing I'd never heard the Monsignor speak of a living relative, I called the Bishop's office. The phone rang several times before I received a response.

"Bishop Mallery's office."

"This is Father Tom Davis. May I speak to the Bishop? It's important."

I recognized the well-modulated voice of the Bishop when he came on the line. "This is Bishop Mallory."

"Bishop, this is Father Tom Davis from St. Matthew's parish in the Bronx. I'm calling to report my pastor, Monsignor Blazer, died a little while ago."

A gasp came over the line. "Monsignor Blazer was a fine priest. I'm sure he's in heaven. Did he have a prolonged illness?"

"He died very quickly. We were in the dining room, having lunch...." I stopped talking immediately, realizing I couldn't tell the Bishop about the painting the Monsignor viewed. Nor could I tell him about Mario Togallini breaking into the rectory with thugs brandishing guns. Nor could I tell him our beautiful housekeeper was kidnapped. The Bishop would order me to notify the police. The police would hold the painting as evidence. I wouldn't be able to turn it over to Togallini.

"Are you still there?" the Bishop asked.

"Yes, I'm here."

"You have some work cut out for you today. Notify the local undertaker to pick up the body, embalm it. Select a casket, not an inexpensive one, but not too expensive. Prayers are more important. Check to see if the Monsignor has any living relatives. Write his obituary for the local paper and send me a copy. Be sure an organist is available for his funeral Mass. Call me if you have any problems and keep me posted...."

I'd heard the Bishop was a scholarly man, a deep thinker. There was no doubt about it when he recited all the things he wanted me to do for the Monsignor. As he talked, I found it impossible to concentrate on everything he said. How could I take care of a dead priest and a live Vivian? She'd soon be dead if I failed to live up to the agreement made with Mario Togallini.

Never before had I properly appreciated the telephone as a time saving device as I did that day. I called the Flaherty Funeral Home and promptly heard the voice of John Diggins.

"Flaherty Funeral Home."

"Mr. Diggins, this is Father Tom Davis. I've another funeral for you. Monsignor Blazer is dead. I want you to pick up his body immediately, prepare it for burial. He's in the dining room of St. Matthew's rectory...on the floor."

"Did you say he's on the floor?"

"On the floor. I'll leave the front door unlocked for you in the event I'm not here when you arrive."

"Now, wait a minute, sir," Mr. Diggins sputtered. "You'll need a death certificate..."

Using all the authority I could muster in my voice, I said, "Get it for me."

"Yes, sir," he responded obediently. "I will also need clothes..."

"You'll get them tomorrow morning. The Monsignor will be laid out in the church."

"We have a lovely chapel at a fair price…"

"He'll be laid out in the church," I said, hanging up on him.

I next called Joe McCabe, the newspaperman. I notified him of the death of Monsignor Blazer.

"I'm so sorry…"

"Could you write an obituary for him, publish it in your paper?"

"I'm one of his parishioners, but I know little about him."

"Neither do I. I do know he attended Holy Spirit High School in Atlantic City. The school is now located in Absecon, New Jersey. I also know he was graduated from Villanova. It's located in the suburbs of Philadelphia, Pennsylvania."

"I'll speak to someone there. I'll also call Holy Spirit High. Perhaps I can get enough information to write an article."

"Thanks very much. Monsignor Blazer will be laid out in the church in two days, buried the following day at Villanova. When you call the University about his obituary, make the funeral arrangements for him?"

"You want me to make the arrangements?"

"I'd do it myself, but I'm tied up in a life and death problem."

"Your problem sounds interesting. You know I'm always looking for a good story. Will I be able to print it?"

"I'm not sure."

"All right, Father. I'll do my best to get an obituary written and published, as well as a grave dug at Villanova University for the Monsignor."

"Thank you."

I next called Joshua Roosevelt to ask him to help me rent a van, pick up the paintings, and deliver them to Togallini. The phone buzzed ten times without a response. I examined my watch. It was well past three. He'd be out of school by now. Could he be practicing basketball, working in the tenement house, shopping? I didn't know. I had to find him, rent a van.

The van was most important. Examining the telephone directory, I found many auto rental establishments listed. Some were close to the rectory. I telephoned those that were close. I spent an hour talking to people who wanted to rent a small van. I finally found someone who had a van large enough to carry all the paintings that I described to him. His establishment was about three miles away. He gave me the impression he was doing me a favor, renting a van to me.

"I'll be there in a half hour," I said to him. "And I'll take the van."

His voice was gruff. "Get here as fast as you can, vans go fast. We have only one left. We require a deposit."

I was out of the rectory, into the Ford Fairlane, and halfway out the driveway when a thought had me slamming on the brakes. The car skidded to a stop. I'd no money.

Returning to the rectory, and into the dining room, I examined the body of my pastor. He was lying flat on his back. More important, he was lying on the wallet in his back pocket. I tried to get it without disturbing the body, which was now beginning to harden. In desperation, I rolled the body over on its side, removed the wallet.

The wallet contained seventy-three dollars, a credit card, a social security card, and a number of other cards that were useless to me. I regretted not asking the man renting the van how much of a deposit he required. Perhaps he'd accept a credit card, made out to someone other than me.

Thinking I'd park the Ford Fairlane at the rental establishment, I decided to try to locate Joshua Roosevelt to save time. Arriving at his tenement house, I examined his mailbox, expecting to find a button I could press to ring his apartment. I found a button. It was broken.

Pounding on the door to the owner's apartment, I received no answer. No help there, I thought. Maybe I'd find Joshua working on one of the floors. I climbed the stairs, searched each floor. No Joshua. After an exhausting climb, I reached the top floor of the building, rang Joshua's doorbell.

Demon of Lust

To my surprise, he answered the bell. His eyes widened in wonder. "Father," he said.

"Joshua, I hate to impose on you. I need your help again. Vivian, the woman who was kidnapped and held in the warehouse, escaped last night. She's been kidnapped again."

"Damn!" Joshua exclaimed. "Why didn't she hide after she 'scaped?"

"A good question. But the fact is, she came back to the rectory last night. This afternoon, while we were having lunch, Togallini and three of his thugs broke into the rectory. They took her again."

Joshua's face expressed pain. "Damn," he said softly.

"Togallini has demanded some paintings she took from him. He promised to release her if I deliver them to him before ten tonight."

"Can ya trust 'im?"

"Trusting him is like trusting a rattle snake, but I have no choice."

"Ah'll git mah jacket."

Joshua and I had no trouble finding the establishment for renting vans. The man in charge of the rentals was a rough looking individual who looked at me suspiciously, demanded a one hundred dollar deposit before releasing a van to us. I gave him Monsignor Blazer's credit card.

"You look kinda young to be a Monsignor," he said to me.

"Priests today are in short supply. Young priests are filling the positions of the older priests who are rapidly dying off."

"I guess that makes sense," he said, taking a set of keys from a board and putting them on a counter in front of me. He put the credit card through a machine and handed me a short form to sign.

I signed it Msgr. Blazer.

Joshua and I'd driven about two miles towards Brooklyn when he suddenly exclaimed, "Ah've fergot somethin'. We'll have t' drive back to mah 'partment?"

I figured he'd forgotten to go to the bathroom before leaving his apartment. "Couldn't we just stop at a service station?"

"Ah've gotta go back t' de 'partment," he insisted, staring at the road ahead.

Although I didn't like the idea, I turned the vehicle around and headed for his apartment. I found a parking space about thirty yards from the main entrance to the tenement. Joshua leaped out of the van before it was parked. He raced towards the building.

Ten minutes later, I heard him opening the rear door of the van, entering it, and shuffling around in the storage area. In less than a minute, he opened the passenger door and seated himself next to me. Not a single word of explanation escaped his lips.

"Take care of everything?" I asked.

"Yeah," was the response.

We were on our way again. It was now dark. Certain sections of Brooklyn were considered a war zone. I'd have to lock the van every time we left the vehicle unattended. I wasn't sure how many trips we'd have to make to Vivian's apartment to remove all the paintings. I'll worry about that later.

As we bounced over the broken roads, I wondered how Joshua would react to the paintings we'd soon be loading into the van. "Joshua," I said, "you don't know anything about the cargo we'll be handling tonight. Nor do you know anything about their history, which I'd rather not relate to you. If possible, just don't look at any of the art work." I said this with a certain solemnity, which I hoped Joshua would respect.

"Ah don't un'erstand."

"What I'm saying, what I'm asking you to do, is avoid looking at any of the paintings, if you possibly can."

"Why wud ya ask me t' do dat?"

In despair, I answered, "Because the paintings were produced by an artist inspired by a demon."

Glancing at Joshua, I saw that his eyes glistened in the dark.

"Wut's dat ya say?"

"I said the paintings we'll be hauling, delivering to Mario Togallini, were inspired by a demon. Demons work for the devil. If you look at the paintings, they can have an adverse affect on you."

"Wut kinda adverse 'fect?"

"They can turn your thoughts to sins of the flesh."

"Dey can?"

"Yes."

Joshua said nothing more about the paintings. I'd no idea what was going through his head. No idea if he'd be tempted to search for a girl after seeing the paintings. I grimly recalled the first time I viewed one of them. I sought Vivian, went to bed with her. The experienced changed my life...introduced me to a demon who encouraged me to sin. A demon that introduced me to a pleasant route to hell.

These thoughts filled my mind as I traveled the roads of Brooklyn. Before I became aware of it, I was on the street where Vivian had rented an apartment. I parked the van and looked up at the building. It appeared ominous.

CHAPTER 50

The speed at which the elevator traveled to Vivian's floor brought a smile to Joshua's face. "Ah could use an elevator like dat," he observed.

"You certainly could."

When I opened the door and switched on the lights to Vivian's apartment, Joshua had another remark to make: "Wut a won'erful 'partment! Nice as mine."

I glanced at him to see if he were joking. He wasn't. He loved his apartment, considered it beautiful despite its age and worn furnishings.

"And isn't it a pity this place is vacant," I said. "So many men, women and children are homeless, while this place remains unoccupied."

"Ain't Vivian ever gonna return?"

"I believe she will...after we rid this place of Togallini's paintings. I know where two of them are. I don't know where the others are. We'll have to find them."

Beyond the living room, there was a long hall with six-closed doors. Joshua pointed to them and said, "The paintin's gotta be behind one of de closed doors." With long strides, he crossed the living room, failing to notice one of the paintings on a living room wall. He began to open doors, turn on lights, and examine each room. It was the fourth door, and the fourth light he switched on, that brought forth a loud exclamation. "Here dey are!"

I hurried to the room; saw him transfixed by the contents of the room. He saw, as I saw, the room was empty, except for the paintings. There were five rows of them, seven in four rows, five in the one row. They rested against the rear wall. The outer painting in each row was exposed to view.

Demon of Lust

The women were nude, life-sized, and more beautiful than any Hollywood star I'd ever seen. They were not only life-sized; they were life-like. They looked out at us as if they were young women waiting for us to embrace them.

As I stared at each woman my body grew hot with passion. Each woman added heat. The lust within me was out of control.

"My! My!" Joshua exclaimed, feasting his eyes on them. He'd completely forgotten, or ignored, my warning: "Don't look at the paintings!"

"Joshua, try not to concentrate on the women in the paintings," I said. "They'll do things to your mind. Things you don't want done."

"How 'bout yore own mind?" he said.

I was surprised at his remark. It was one a student from a Catholic school wouldn't normally make to a priest and a teacher of religion. "They affect me too," I admitted. "I hope you understand why I asked you to avoid looking at them."

He dropped his eyes to the floor. "Ah understan' dat now, Father."

"Can you believe a demon from hell inspired these paintings?"

"Ah guess so," he said grudgingly. "But Ah can't understan' how a demon can produce anythin' so beau'ful."

"They know beautiful women can lure men away from God."

"Dat's why you'd like t' destroy 'em?"

"That's right. But we can't destroy them now. We must use them to free Vivian."

Joshua was silent for a while. His eyes were still focused on the floor. Again, I'd no idea what was going through his mind. If I were to guess, based on his expression, I'd say his mind was troubled. I wouldn't be surprised if he decided not to help me.

Not only was he troubled; the women in the paintings were troubled. Their deep concern was reflected on their faces. They heard me speak of destroying them. A mistake. I shouldn't have made such a remark in their presence. But how could paint on canvas *hear* what I said, react in such a manner? I couldn't answer the question. Only a supernatural force could supply an answer. From past experience, I knew the phenomenon was possible.

I counted the number of paintings in the room. "Thirty-three. There are two more," which I proceeded to obtain from the master bedroom and the living room. Returning with the paintings, I said, "Joshua, if we stack five paintings on top of one another, carry them to the elevator, we can load the elevator in seven trips. We'll take all the paintings to the ground floor before attempting to load the van. Do you like the plan?"

"Ah do."

There was hardly room enough for Joshua and me to get into the elevator when we finally had the paintings packed tightly into the cage. I pressed the down button. The elevator made a breath-taking drop.

A smile appeared on Joshua's face when the elevator reached top speed. The smile disappeared when a feminine voice emanated from one of the paintings: "Ooooh!"

"Did ya hear dat?" he questioned. Fear was reflected on his face.

"I heard it."

"It didn't scare ya?"

"I've been hearing sounds like that for a long while."

"But don't dey scare ya?"

"Not as long as I'm in the state of grace."

"But whut 'bout me?"

"You'll be all right. I promise. All you need is faith."

"Faith?" Joshua said as if the word were new to him.

"That's the word. As long as you're doing God's work, you need not worry about the devil or any of his demons."

As I spoke, Joshua shook his head. "But we ain't doin' God's work. We're deliverin' dirty pic'ures to a man who's gonna make copies of 'em, pass 'em 'round for everybody in de world t' see. Milluns of people will be sinnin' because of what we're doin' t'night."

Joshua was right. "But if I don't deliver the paintings, Vivian will die and I...."

"You'll whut?"

I couldn't tell Joshua I'd never be happy again if Vivian died. I had to do my best to help her. "Let's get the paintings into the van. Time is rapidly passing."

Joshua complied with my request. However, he worked sullenly, silently. He was disappointed in me for delivering paintings to Togallini that'd weaken the world's moral fabric. A fabric now torn and worn thin as a result of a multiplicity of sexual offenses.

Despite a cool October wind, Joshua and I were perspiring when we placed the last painting into the van. As I headed the vehicle towards New Jersey, I wanted to explain to him that Vivian's life was important to me. I hesitated in doing so. The cargo I was delivering was also important. Who could measure the life of one woman, beautiful though she may be, against the souls of millions of individuals who'd view a Togallini painting? Right or wrong, I had to free Vivian. I dreaded the thought of her being killed.

Evidently the women in the rear of the van became aware of my thought process. They knew I was willing to cooperate with Mario Togallini. They were happy, expressed their happiness in song. They sang a song containing words from all nations. It was melodic, spirited; sounding like something one might hear from a group of girls riding a school bus after an important football game.

"Ah didn't see ya turn de radio on," Joshua said, breaking his silence and looking at me with eyes opened wide with wonder.

I was tempted to circumvent the truth, give him some misleading story. I thought better of it. "You're not listening to the radio."

Ten seconds of silence passed before Joshua spoke: "Ya mean Ah'm not listenin' to de radio?"

"That's right," I said grimly.

"Den what'm Ah listenin' to?"

"You're listening to the women in the paintings. I've already told you, they're possessed by a demon. A demon called Isacaron. He has many powers…many voices…many tricks."

"Ya sayin' a demon is in dis van wit' us?"

"That's exactly what I'm saying."

"Ya can stop at de next corner, let me off."

"I'm not letting you off, Joshua. I need you. Besides, you're privileged to hear the voice of a demon."

"Ah've never been close to one befo'."

"You have. You just didn't know it. Demons are like hound dogs. They follows us, remains close to us, regardless of our status in life. You're privileged to hear the voice of one, or maybe more than one. You now know they exists. You can better defend yourself against the one assigned to you. If you thought he didn't exist, as many people think, you could easily fall under his spell. You could commit one sin after another, without realizing you're offending the God who made you."

"Ah don't wanna do dat."

"I'm sure you don't. Let the demon sing with his many voices, if he so desires. He's going to lose out in the long run. God will protect us. We're on the winning team."

The singing increased in volume, so much so it reached a pitch of madness. I understood why men like Hitler, Stalin, and McVey, possessed by demons, did maddening things. Other men did maddening things, too. In many parts of the world, acts of madness were common, a way of life. I glanced at Joshua. His skin had taken on a strange color. The singing was affecting him. The demon was having an influence on him, my co-partner. I didn't like to see it.

"Joshua," I've been dealing with this particular demon for nine years. In many respects, he's made my life miserable. In other respects, he's been a blessing. He's convinced me there is a hell, a devil, and legions of demons trained to carry out the devil's work. We have a choice: We either accept the devil or reject him. To accept him means we live with him in horror for an eternity. To reject him means we live with God in peace and harmony."

"Ah'm gonna reject 'im," Joshua said.

"That's great. Now do you think we should have our own Sing-A-Long? We can try to drown out the racket that's coming from the rear of this van?"

"Ya think we kin do it?"

"We can try. Any particular song you like?"

"Ah likes Old Man River."

I was pleased to hear Joshua suggested a song written years ago. Many contemporary songs, played on the radio, sounded worse than the static. I didn't know any of them. I did know Old Man River.

And so we sang Old Man River. I was surprised to learn Joshua had an exceptionally good voice. He pronounced each word with care and thought, making no mistakes. He had the natural talent of a good vocalist. At a more opportune time, I'd encourage him to take singing lessons. I'd even be willing to pay for them.

We sang all the way to Jersey City. There were periods when Isacaron drowned us out; other times, he didn't. When we stopped for traffic lights, we received the attention of people in other vehicles. They heard our booming voices as well as the multi-voiced Isacaron. They stared at Joshua and me as if we were mad. One driver gave us the finger.

We reached the warehouse long before ten o'clock. Pulling up to the front door, I stopped the van and said to Joshua. "Will you ring the bell? When someone answers, I'll say we have the paintings. They're ready to be removed from the van."

"Would ya mind if Ah removed 'em, put 'em up against de front door?"

"Why knock yourself out if it isn't necessary?"

"Ah'd like t' do it."

For the first time since I'd met Joshua, I realized he liked to do things his way. I was one of his teachers, but he wasn't always guided by my judgment. He wished to follow his own ideas. That was all right with me. He helped me considerably in the move. I was willing to accommodate him in any way I could. "All right, Joshua. Be my guest. I'll help you unload the paintings if you wish."

"Ah'll 'ppreciate yore help."

So I helped him unload the van. There were several times when I picked up a single painting, tried to carry it to the door of the warehouse. It became so heavy in the process that I had to drop it. Joshua had the same experience.

"Whut de hell…!" he exclaimed, dropping one of the paintings before reaching the door of the warehouse.

"The demon is playing tricks on you, Joshua. He has a sordid sense of humor. Don't let him rattle you too much."

Gingerly, he picked up the painting and placed it against the door.

Eventually, we had all the painting lined up against the door. The door was large enough for two trucks to enter, large enough for seven rows of paintings…five in each row. A full moon was shining, giving off enough light to illuminate the women in a way that was strangely romantic.

Joshua stood back, examined the women for a minute or more.

They examined him in a sexy sort of a way.

"Damn!" I heard him exclaim.

Despite the fact I told myself not to look at the women, I found myself looking. Passion surged through me, activated every nerve in my body. Had I made a mistake returning the paintings to Togallini? If Vivian's life were sacrificed for them, she'd conceivably receive a heavenly reward. Should I tell Joshua to load them back in the van, return them to the apartment in Brooklyn? I ought to notify the police, make a clean breast of everything. Telling the truth is normally the best way to untangle a difficult problem.

The beautiful women in the paintings read my mind, studied me with skepticism. They wanted to know what the outcome of my indecision would be. I felt sure they wanted to return to Togallini, help him carry out the devil's fiendish work. By returning the paintings to Togallini, I was also helping the devil. When men and women are driven to illicit sex, great harm may come to them...to their pre-born babies...to the world. Such a conclusion is a natural dictate of reason. Even poor Joshua, with little education, knew that much. I should've followed his instincts. Was I too late?

Yes, I was. The large garage door slid up, revealing three of the devil's advocates: Mario Togallini and two of his thugs. Another event of note took place: The paintings, stacked against the garage door, fell over when the door was opened. The women landed on their backs, smiled. They gave the impression they were ready to seduce all of us. The impression was so great that all of us were speechless. Even I was unable to utter a word.

CHAPTER 51

Mario Togallini was the first to recover from the emotional impact of seeing the women in the paintings on their backs. A malicious grin appeared on his swarthy face. "So you've kept your word, delivered the paintin's."

I met his gaze. "I've delivered the paintings. Now I expect you to deliver Vivian to me."

"You'll get her when I'm ready to hand her over," he said. "Why'd you lie to me, make a fool of me. You had my men waitin' for Vivian to show up at the rectory when she was already in the rectory?" He studied me like a general in the army would study a private who'd given him the raspberry.

"I didn't lie to you. I simply avoided telling you the truth. I didn't want you to harm Vivian. She took the paintings thinking they were hers. It's time for you to forgive her. We all make mistakes."

"I don't make mistakes," he said dogmatically.

It was best to avoid arguing with him. Nevertheless, I reacted to his remark in the same manner I'd react to a student whose ideas were heretical. "Your work is a mistake, Mario. You produce and reproduce pornographic material, spread it around the world, weaken the fabric of a universal moral order. You stain the souls of millions of individuals, promote sexual activity, the breakdown of families, disease, death."

He gave me a long look of disgust. "I don't wanna hear that crap." He then allowed a series of foul words to flow from his lips.

"You need not hear anything I have to say. Produce Vivian and we'll be on our way."

Demon of Lust

"First, deliver the paintings to the rear of this building. I want them stacked up against the wall, near my office. You're not walkin' away from here without doin' a little work."

"We'll help your men carry them."

Mario shook his head. "You and your black son will carry them."

"If that's the way you want it, Mario. Joshua and I will deliver the paintings anywhere that strikes your fancy."

"That's the way I want it."

Joshua and I stacked five paintings together, picked them up, and walked towards the rear of the building. On the way, I received several charges of electricity through my hands, up my arms, and into my body. As shocking as they were, I managed to hold onto the paintings without dropping them.

"De demon is playin' mo' tricks on me," Joshua said.

"On both of us. Soon we'll leave him in this warehouse. I won't regret saying goodbye to him."

"Ah regrets sayin' hello to 'im."

Joshua and I carried the paintings to the rear of the building. We stacked them neatly against the wall; then approached the office. The door was open. We peeked inside; saw Mario Togallini and his two thugs, reading girlie magazines. Vivian was nowhere in sight.

Togallini was quick to spot us, gave us a look of disgust.

A sense of despair swept over me. "I don't see Vivian," I said to him.

"You're not gonna see her either. Not till you finish your job. Get back to work."

Like obedient schoolboys, Joshua and I returned to work. We finally completed seven trips to the rear of the warehouse, had all the paintings lined up against the wall. In the semi-darkness, the women in the paintings stared out at us as if they were sorry to see us go. In one respect, I was sorry to leave them. I thought of the promise I'd made years ago to Mario Togallini's brother before he died. I promised him I'd destroy the paintings.

Now I was exchanging them for Vivian. I hadn't kept my promise. Why? I wanted Vivian to live. But where was she?

Once again, Joshua and I approached Mario Togallini's office. I put my head inside the door and said, "Mario, we finished the job. The paintings are lined up against the wall. Where's Vivian?"

"Where the hell do you think she is?"

"I don't know. You said she was here. I took your word for it."

"My word is a damn sight better than yours. And I'm no priest. Do you agree with that?"

"I agree with it, Mario. You're no priest."

His two thugs tittered.

Mario gave them a dirty look. "You guys wait outside." He pointed a thumb at the door.

The two men left the office. Joshua and I entered it.

I began to questions my own activities. Was Vivian dead? Had I made a mistake delivering the paintings without seeing her? "Where's Vivian?" I asked.

Before I tell you where she is, I'd like to know who killed my men?"

"I don't know, Mario."

"You think it was some of your parishioners?"

"I doubt it very much. No parishioner ever spoke to me about taking any action against the men picketing the rectory."

"I believe you. Catholics have gotten soft. They're not willin' to risk their necks any more for the Church. No crusaders. No martyrs. A gang of squealin' pussycats."

"You should have some insight into that area. Your wife tells me you were once a Catholic, but haven't gone to confession in fifty or sixty years."

"You been talkin' to my wife?"

"I've talked to her on the phone once. I was trying to get you."

"I hope you set her straight, told her I'm not interested in goin' to church."

Demon of Lust

"I gave her that impression."

Mario removed a handkerchief from his pocket, blew his nose, spoke reflectively. "You don't have to pay any attention to her. I keep her around because she makes good spaghetti. She takes care of my cats and the kids."

"She's your wife, Mario; for better or for worse. I'm inclined to believe she got the worse part of the deal. So don't criticize her."

Mario gave me an ugly look. "Now you're givin' me some of your pollutin' ideas, Father." The *Father* was said contemptuously.

I wondered why a man who gives so little respect to others expects to receive so much. "I'm not here to discuss your wife with you. I'm here to escort Vivian out of here. Now if you'll produce her."

Mario looked at me in a strange way. "Do you love the slut?"

"I assume you're asking me if I love Vivian. Sure, I do. Strange as it may sound, I also love you. Of course, I don't love what you do, but as a fellow human being, I love you. That is what God wants me to do, so that's what I do. Will you please produce Vivian?"

"You're not going to appreciate how she looks. Ordinarily, she'd take a bath, powder her nose, wear her best clothes for a young, good lookin' fellow like yourself who comes to call."

There was something in Mario Togallini's voice that made me feel uncomfortable. I could only hope, pray, that Vivian was all right. "Where is she?"

"You're standin' on her," he said with a grin.

Standing on her? I was standing on a throw rug, about four feet wide, six feet long. "I don't understand."

"She's under the rug."

Under the rug? Puzzled, I reached down and lifted the rug. Throwing it aside, I saw a bolted trap door. Thinking the worst, I knelt down and opened the door. Two large gray rats leaped out of the enclosure and into the room. They startled me.

Mario Togallini laughed at my reaction to the rodents. They scurried around the office, seeking an escape.

The hole from which the rats emerged was about four feet deep, four feet wide, and six feet long. At the bottom of the hole was Vivian, covered with mud and crouched in a fetal position with her hands covering her face. She didn't look pretty.

Not knowing if she were dead or alive, I dropped into the hole and felt her cheeks. They were warm. I took her arms and pulled her into a sitting position. There was little room to maneuver. I didn't know if I'd the strength to lift her out of the hole and onto the floor of Togallini's office.

"Could Ah help?" Joshua asked.

So concerned was I about Vivian, I'd forgotten Joshua existed. I was glad to look up, see his anxious face.

"You can help, Joshua, by getting down here, helping me lift Vivian out of this hole."

Joshua stepped down into the hole, swung an arm around Vivian's back. Together, we lifted her out of the hole, onto the floor.

Togallini smiled as he watched us. If ever there was a time when I wanted to throttle a man, it was at that time. But I had to devote my attention, my energy, to Vivian. I noticed she was breathing ever so slightly, but thank God she was alive. There was a sink in the office. Finding a washcloth, I soaked it with cold water, cleaned the mud from her face. She stirred ever so slightly. When her face was reasonably clean, I opened the doors to a number of cabinets and found a medicine chest containing smelling salts. Breaking open a capsule, I applied the smelling salts to her nose. Ever so slowly, she opened her eyes.

"Where am I?" she asked. She seemed unable to focus on me or anything else.

"You're here with me. You're with Father Tom. I'm here to take you back to the rectory."

In a daze, she asked, "Am I out of the hole, away from the rats?"

"You're out of the hole and away from the rats..." I hesitated, thinking I'd say you're away from all the rats but one. The rat Togallini was still with us. I didn't say it because I didn't want to antagonize the little rat.

Demon of Lust

"Did I hear you say you're Father Tom?"

"Yes, I'm Father Tom."

"He's the man I love."

I began to wonder if the ordeal of being in the hole with the rats had affected her mind. She no longer seemed to be her normal self. I had to help her. "Father Tom also loves you...in his own priestly way."

"His own priestly way! Is that what you said?"

"Yes."

"That's my problem. He's first and foremost a priest. I can't change him. No one can. Not even the devil."

"Would you want to change him?"

"I suppose not," she murmured. "He goes around doing good deeds for people. He helped two old women he hardly knew. I thought he had a crush on them. I was a bit jealous. Of course, he didn't have a crush on them any more than he has a crush on me. He's just bent on doing good for others. Where would civilization be if it weren't for men like Father Tom? And who am I to tell him to stop doing what he's doing?"

Mario Togallini was on his feet looking down at Vivian. "If that's not a lotta crap, I don't know what is." And then to me: "She's off her rocker, you know."

Again, I had an impulse to strike him on the nose. Instead I said, "If her mind has been affected from being in that hole with the rats, you're to blame."

"She's lucky she's not dead."

"We'll see how lucky she is; how lucky you are." I knelt down beside her and said, "Vivian, I want you to try to get on your feet. It's time for us to leave. Joshua and I will help you."

Which we did. With one of her arms slung over my shoulder and one over Joshua's, we had her on her feet. She was able to walk out of the office and into the warehouse. The two thugs were smiling as they watched us. Whatever they saw amusing in our plight was something I'll never be able to explain.

Mario Togallini stepped out of his office, observed us proceed towards the front of the building. "Hold it, right there," he shouted.

Stopping, we turned to face him.

"You don't think you're gonna walk outta here without payin' for your sins, do you?"

He had me puzzled. "What kind of payment?"

"Show him, boys."

One thug grabbed me by the hair, brought me to a wall containing handcuffs, fastened to a bar about three feet above my head. Raising my arms high, he put the handcuffs on my wrists.

I turned to see what was being done to Joshua and Vivian. Joshua was dragged by the neck to a similar wall, handcuffed, and left helpless. Vivian was thrown to the floor. She watched us with tears rolling down her face. She appeared dazed, weak, and unable to fully understand what was taking place.

I struggled to free myself from the handcuffs. They were tight, cutting into my wrist, holding me fast against the wall. "What is the meaning of this?" I said to Togallini.

"I've already told you. You've gotta pay for your sins." With that, he opened up my belt, pulled down my pants and underwear, leaving me naked from the waist down. Embarrassed, I pressed myself against the wall, attempting to cover myself as much as possible.

"Ya can't do dis t' me," I heard Joshua say.

Turning my head, I saw his pants had been pulled down, his buttock exposed.

"What do you intend to do?" I asked Togallini.

"We're gonna do to you what we did to Vivian. We're gonna beat your asses with a cane. That's a punishment I've introduced into the Mafia. The first infringement of rules requires a beatin' with a cane. The second infringement requires a bullet through the brain. You're lucky you're not gettin' a bullet."

"We're not members of your godless organization."

"That's true, but you butted into our business. So you've gotta pay. Let 'em have it, boys."

The two thugs struck Joshua and me at the same time. I heard his cry. I muffled mine. The pain was unbearable. Each strike was like a bolt of lightening hitting my body. My legs would no longer support me. The handcuffs held me up. The pain in my wrists was excruciating. Blood ran down my arms. Tears ran down my face.

"Oh! Oh! Oh!" Joshua cried with each strike.

"Seven strikes for each one of you," Togallini said. A lucky number. Next time, the seven becomes eleven, plus a bullet. Take a chance on foolin' around with me again, see what happens."

"Ah'll see ya in hell," Joshua shouted at him.

"One more peep outta you and we'll give you another seven lashes," Togallini bellowed threateningly.

Neither Joshua nor I had anything more to say. We were too weak, too beaten to argue with Togallini. One idea came to mind. The last time I said Mass, I felt the presence of God. When I was being beaten, I felt the presence of the devil.

I became aware of the handcuffs being unlocked, falling to the floor, striking my head. Somehow I remained conscious, knew what was taking place.

Togallini kicked my side; spoke with bitterness, "You've got a half hour to rest, say a penance for your sins. After that, I want you outta here, never to return. If I find you in this warehouse again, you'll qualify for eleven more lashes and a bullet through your stupid brain."

"Ah'm not sure Ah'll be able t' walk," Joshua said pleadingly.

"If you can't walk, I'll throw you in the hole with a couple of hungry rats."

"Ah'll be able t' walk," Jonah said, closing his eyes and falling aleep.

I allowed him to sleep for twenty minutes before calling him. "Joshua, it's time for us to go."

He stirred uneasily in his sleep, rolled over once, fell back to sleep.

Exercising all the willpower I possessed, I struggled to my feet, staggered over to him, grabbed his shoulders, and shook him. "Joshua, wake up! We must leave here."

His eyes popped open. He gave me a blank stare for three or four seconds before becoming alert. Without saying a word, he got up on one knee, struggled to his feet. Holding onto the wall for a few moments, he finally said, "Let's go."

Togallini watched us with great interest. He seemed to delight in our pain. "Take the slut with you," he said.

Vivian! Dear Vivian was no slut. I was so concerned with my own pain, I'd forgotten about her. How could I forget her?

She was lying on the floor, waiting for help.

Supporting each other, Joshua and I managed to reach her. We pulled her to her feet. With our arms around her, we walked through the warehouse towards the front door, staggering past many displays of naked women and various other inducements for committing sin. They had no affect on me at all. When one is in pain, or near death, sexual inducements are irrelevant. Prayer is more important.

I've read of death marches. I was on a death march that night, for Togallini lingered behind us like a cobra ready to strike. Whether he had a gun, I don't know. I do know he was a source of fear. Thinking of him, gave me incentive to keep walking, moving towards the door regardless of the pain. Somehow I managed to help Vivian on her march to freedom. Joshua helped, too. Despite his pain, he managed to help Vivian as much as I did. No complaints broke from his lips. He was perfect.

The van was a beautiful sight, parked close to the door. We'd reached our goal, no longer had to walk. Joshua and I helped Vivian into the passenger's side of the van. She moved into the middle. I tried to get into the van on the driver's side, learned I was unable to lift my right leg, thanks to the vicious kick Togallini had given me. "I'm afraid I can't drive," I said to Joshua.

He helped me into the passenger's side of the van, announced, "Ah'll drive."

I'd one comforting thought: If he can steal a Rolls Royce and drive it away, he can drive the van. I watched him get behind the wheel of the vehicle.

The sound of the starter was music to my ears. The engine coughed once, then hummed to life. Joshua put the vehicle into gear, we moved forward. At last, we were on our way…away from that hell.

CHAPTER 52

When I gave Joshua permission to drive the van, I expected him to head for the gate and get away from the warehouse as quickly as possible. He didn't do that. He drove the van onto a small strip of concrete alongside the warehouse, made a left turn onto another strip of concrete at the rear of the warehouse, and stopped the van at the rear and center of the building.

"Joshua, where are you going and why are you stopping?"

"Ah gotta return somethin'."

"What…"

Without giving me an answer, he opened the door, dragged himself out of the van. I then heard him open the rear door latch and enter the vehicle. He left the van and was gone for about three minutes. When he returned, he was in a big hurry; entering the cab rapidly for a boy who'd recently been beaten with a cane.

"Joshua, what are you doing?"

"We gotta get de hell outta here," he said, starting the engine, putting the van in gear, and jamming his foot on the gas pedal. The vehicle bolted forward, almost tilted over when he made a sharp left at the end of the building. Another strip of concrete encouraged him to hold the gas pedal down to the floor The van was moving at high speed when we shot through the gate, out onto the road.

We'd traveled about three hundred yards when a tremendous explosion shook the earth. In pain, and unable to put my head out the window, I looked at the side view mirror. I saw smoke and flame bellowing up from the warehouse. I saw something else! Visible in the smoke and flames, there were seven rows of naked women, five in each row, flailing their arms, screaming in pain.

The van followed a bend in the road. I lost sight of the women, the smoke, and the flames.

I turned to Joshua. His eyes were fixed on the road.

"What have you done?"

He was slow to answer. "Ah returned de bomb dat was meant t' blow up our school."

I could hardly believe him. I needed clarification. "You did what?"

"Ah blew up de supply house dat stores de stuff that teaches kids t' do de wrong thing."

"You may have killed Togallini and his two men."

Joshua spoke like an innocent child: "What's wrong wit' dat?"

I could have given him an answer. I didn't. I was thinking of my experiences with the Togallini paintings when I was a teenager; how often I tried to destroy them. I failed every time. Joshua had accomplished the feat in a few minutes. He'd also done it for me. He knew I considered the paintings inspired by the demon Isacaron, a source of evil for all mankind.

I was too tired, too hurt, to think about the possibility of Togallini and his two associates being killed in the blast. I wanted Joshua to follow the teaching of the Church, but there are times when an abused victim has to fight back. Joshua fought back. He didn't turn the other cheek after being beaten. He'd both cheeks of his bottom beaten because Togallini felt he should pay for his sins. Should Togallini pay for his own sins? Joshua figured he should.

Vivian was asleep beside me, her body pressed close to mine. I'd a great deal of satisfaction knowing Togallini was no longer a threat to her. She no longer had to hide from his thugs, fear for her life. I could only hope and pray she'd regain her health, find a decent fellow, marry and raise a gang of kids.

The trip to the rectory was a painful one. Blood seeped through my pants. I'd taken the worst beating I'd ever taken in my life. So had Vivian. I was more concerned about her than I was about myself. I prayed the beating, and her confinement in the hole, wouldn't affect her physically or mentally.

When we reached the Bronx, Joshua said, "Supposin' Ah drops ya off at de wreck'try. Ah'll bring back de van tomorrow mornin' and git yore car."

"That'll be fine, Joshua." I gave him enough money to pay what was owed on the van.

"Ya want me t' help ya git Vivian t' bed?"

"I can manage her."

I'd trouble managing myself. My legs buckled under me when I stepped out of the van. I grabbed the door to prevent myself from falling. The beating I'd received had taken its toll.

Vivian was either unconscious or asleep when I reached for her. I pulled her towards me and lifted her into my arms. Once again, the pain I experienced almost brought me to my knees.

"Ya sure Ah can't help ya?" Joshua asked.

"You've done enough for one evening. I'll manage."

How I managed to carry Vivian in my weakened condition was a mystery. I opened the door, carried her into the rectory, and brought her up one flight of stairs.

She stirred in my arms, opened her eyes. "You going to put me in my bed?"

"I'm going to put you in the Bishop's bed."

And that's what I did. When I had her tucked in, she opened her eyes again. "Kiss your little girl goodnight."

I kissed her on the forehead and said, "You're not so little any more. Say your Hail Mary and go to sleep. You've had a busy day."

She smiled and closed her eyes.

Returning to the first floor to obtain a couple of aspirin, I suddenly thought of Monsignor Blazer. Was his body still in the dining room? I rushed into the dining room to see. The body was gone. The Flaherty Funeral Home had done its job, after all. Tomorrow morning, I'll visit the funeral home, make arrangements...

Another thought struck me like a bolt of lightning. Vivian's painting! I'd forgotten all about it. I was supposed to deliver it to Togallini with the others. I hadn't done so. The painting was still here in the rectory. Like a fool, I showed it to Monsignor Blazer. He dropped dead. I put the painting against a wall. But what wall? I couldn't remember.

The painting should be easy to find. It was in or near the dining room. I searched the dining room, the kitchen, and all the other rooms on the first floor. The painting wasn't anywhere to be found.

Perhaps John Diggins, or someone else from the Flaherty Funeral Home, had moved it. Rightfully so. A painting inspired by a demon had no right to be in the same room with a deceased priest.

Where could it be? I searched the basement, Monsignor Blazer's bedroom, the Bishop's bedroom, and Vivian's bedroom on the fourth floor. The painting was gone. Perhaps it's just as well, I thought. I'd no longer have to cope with it. I regretted the painting hadn't gone up in flames with the others.

My bottom began to throb. Blood had crusted on my pants. The aspirin I'd taken did little to suppress my pain. I'd put medicated cream on my bottom, then go to bed. Tomorrow is another day.

Opening the door to my room, I switched on the light. A large portrait of a naked Vivian stood upright on the bureau in my room. It startled me.

The Vivian in the painting was also startled. She stared down at me as if I'd encroached on her privacy. She appeared more alive than the Vivian I'd left in the Bishop's bed.

I couldn't take my eyes off her. I wanted to ask her how she moved from the dining room to my bedroom. And why my bedroom? "You look unhappy," I said to her, not expecting a response.

She seemed to contemplate my words before speaking. "You're responsible for destroying my friends." Her words sounded as if they came from a far away source.

"I didn't know demons had friends."

"We are one," she said.

"One in harmony with the devil. Is that what you mean?"

"I am not at liberty to tell you."

"Are you at liberty to tell me how you traveled from the dining room to my bedroom?"

She shrugged. At least, I thought I saw her shrug.

"I'm going to move you out of my bedroom," I said to her. "I go to sleep at night hoping God will watch over me. I don't want a demon from hell watching over me."

She shrugged again and smiled.

She had reason to smile. When I attempted to lift her off the bureau I was unable to do so. The painting was so heavy I couldn't budge it. The effort caused sharp pains in my buttocks. Frustrated, I said, "Okay! Okay! You may share my bedroom tonight."

After undressing and donning pajamas, I prayed for a half hour, asking God to watch over Vivian, Monsignor Blazer and me. Turning off the light in my room, I was surprised to see the painting was still visible in the dark. The woman was smiling as she looked down at me.

As strange as it may seem, I slept well that night. Was the demon attempting to relay a message to me? Was he trying to tell me he'd leave me alone, allow me to get a proper rest, if I'd allow him to remain in my bedroom? Could that be it? I wasn't sure. I wasn't even sure if I should be referring to him as a he. I knew that God is God, and not a he or a she. I didn't know about the demon. He could be a he or a she, depending on the evil he wished to perpetrate.

After dressing, I peeked in on Vivian. She was sleeping soundly and silently. Do women of outstanding beauty ever snore? I didn't know. I reminded myself there were many things I didn't know.

I did know how to say Mass. It was now time to say the nine o'clock Mass. That's what I did. There were perhaps thirty people in church. I notified them of the death of Monsignor Blazer, that he'd be laid out in the church that afternoon, and buried at Villanova University the following day. Those wishing to travel to Villanova were encouraged to do so.

Unfortunately, I'd be unable to make the trip, as there was no replacement for me at St. Matthew's.

Once again, I peeked in on Vivian. She was still asleep. I'd let her sleep, hoping she'd soon recover from the traumatic experience of being in a hole with two rats.

I decided to skip breakfast, gather Monsignor Blazer's clothes together and deliver them to the Flaherty Funeral Home.

John Diggins put on a pair of rubber gloves before accepting the clothes from me. Obviously, he abhorred the idea of touching them. He paid more respect to an invoice he gave me. It enumerated services rendered and services to be rendered by the Flaherty Funeral Home. The list included a large number of items I'd never heard of before. The total amount of the bill numbed my brain, caused my rear end to ache more than ever.

Diggins promised to deliver the body of Monsignor Blazer to the church that afternoon at four. He'd pick up the body after the nine o'clock Mass the following day, deliver it to Villanova for burial.

"That's fine," I said.

"Now, about the bill…"

I held up an open palm before his face. "We'll discuss the bill another time."

"Yes, sir. Another time will be fine. I'll call on you in three days."

"I'll remember the date," I said, thinking I'd make a point of being out of the rectory on that date. How I'd pay the bill was a problem I didn't want to consider at the time.

I must admit John Diggings had Monsignor Blazer looking well when he delivered him to church that afternoon. The casket, resting on a bier, was located at the foot of the altar. A surprisingly large number of parishioners, priests, nuns, and school children crowded into the church to pay their respects to the deceased priest. Many of them shook my hand, asked how he died. With my developing excellence in equivocation, I avoided telling them I'd presented a painting of a naked woman to the Monsignor and he dropped dead when he saw it.

Louis V. Rohr

So busy was I that day, I'd forgotten to get myself something to eat. More important, I'd forgotten to feed Vivian. Leaving the church, I entered the rectory and searched the refrigerator for food. Finding a small tenderloin steak, I fried it in butter. I also toasted and buttered four pieces of bread, boiled a few stalks of asparagus, and poured a glass of milk into a tall glass. Putting the food and drink on a tray with the proper silverware, I delivered it to her room; or I should say, to the Bishop's room.

She was half-asleep when I entered. Her eyes widened when she saw the food.

"Are you hungry?" I asked.

"Famished."

"How do you feel?"

"Not too good. My head hurts and I can't walk yet. I tried to get out of bed, get myself something to eat. My legs buckled under me."

"You'll be all right in a few days."

"Hope so."

She began eating the food, smiling at me in the process.

"Anything else I can get you?"

"I could use a little medicated cream for my bottom, and a change of pajamas and sheets. I bled some last night."

My heart went out to her. She'd taken the punishment well. I was also relieved to know she was all right mentally. I'd worried about her mental condition the previous night.

I heard the doorbell ring.

Thinking it was someone in need of money, I took my time answering the door. Opening it, I was surprised to see a tall thin elderly priest whose gaunt face was vaguely familiar. I stared at him as if he were a total stranger.

He stared back at me in a puzzled sort of way. "I'm Bishop Mallory," he said. "You should remember me. I'm here to say Monsignor Blazer's Mass, spend the night with you."

Demon of Lust

"Spend the night..." I was unable to finish the sentence. Dumbfounded, I looked at him. He was here to spend the night in the Bishop's bed...his bed. Vivian was in that bed. The sheets were bloody....

CHAPTER 53

How could I tell the Bishop that a beautiful young woman was in his bed? That was the question in my mind when I reached for his bag, escorted him into the rectory.

"This old rectory hasn't changed in years," he said, fixing his eyes on the wilted curtains in the dining room. "I regret I didn't do more for Monsignor Blazer before he died."

"What more could you do?"

"Given him a few luxuries, a nicer place to live."

"He was happy here. On no occasion did he complain about this rectory."

The Bishop became reflective, stared off into space. "Nor have I ever heard him complain about his accommodations or anything else. He was an exceptionally fine man, willing to sacrifice himself for others. As a matter of fact, he'd go out of his way to sacrifice himself for others. I sometimes pray that I could be like him?"

"You do?"

The Bishop studied me closely; as if he didn't expect the response I gave him. Nor did I expect to put the question to him as bluntly as I did. If I were to guess what he was thinking, I'd say, he was thinking today's young priests can be pretty cocky, disrespectful of their elders.

The tension in the room was unbearably thick. Since I'd gone that far, I couldn't stop now. "Bishop," I said "our housekeeper was given a beating last night by some thugs…"

"Oh, the poor dear!" he exclaimed. "This neighborhood is going to the dogs."

Demon of Lust

"To the Mafia," I said. "But getting back to the housekeeper, I was unable to carry her to the fourth floor. I put her in your room."

"My room?"

"Yes."

"Well, God bless you, Father Tom. That was a wonderful idea. A little sacrifice will do us both good. Supposing I take your room on the third floor, and you take the housekeeper's room on the fourth floor. It is on the fourth floor, as I recall."

My spirits, which were heading for the moon, were now descending to the earth at record speed. My room contained the painting of a nude Vivian, activated by a demon…. "Bishop," I said in desperation, "would you be so kind as to take the Monsignor's room. He'd be happy to know you slept there."

"You think it appropriate?"

"Yes, I do. And I'll change the sheets."

Changing the sheets was much easier than thinking of some way of telling Vivian not to make any noise while the Bishop was sleeping in the room next to hers. While he was snacking away at the little bit of food left in the refrigerator, I was preparing the bedroom for him. I'd the room looking fairly presentable, when I spoke to Vivian about keeping quiet.

"Why should I keep quiet?" she asked, looking annoyed.

"Because he's my boss. He might not like your being under the same roof with me."

"Why wouldn't he like it?"

"I'm a young priest and you …you …you know what you are."

"Just what am I?"

"You're a beautiful woman who tempts the hell out of me."

"Is that bad?"

"I should say it is. And I don't wish to be reminded of it by the Bishop."

Vivian tried to sit up in bed. Wincing, she gave up the effort. She also gave my blood pressure a rise when she said, "I'd like to talk to the Bishop."

"Why talk to him?"

"I have my reasons."

"Give me one."

"He's a priest. Maybe I'd like him to hear my confession."

"Monsignor Blazer recently heard your confession." I thought she was looking for an excuse to talk to the Bishop.

"I was ashamed to tell him everything. When I was in that hole, I thought I was going to die. I regretted not telling him everything."

"Why didn't you? But if you say you didn't, I believe you. You can go to confession to me. I won't call the police," I added, trying to add a little levity to the subject.

"I told you before, I'm not going to confession to you. Send the Bishop in; I'll go to confession to him. He has more experience than you."

"Please, Vivian. No Bishop. I'll try to get someone else for you."

We left it at that. However, later that afternoon, I became concerned about her desire to go to confession. If she'd wanted the Bishop to hear her confession, I should have spoken to him about it. I'd take my chances on what he had to say about a beautiful housekeeper in the rectory. I talk of sacrifice, then think of myself. I wasn't proud of my decision.

Around five o'clock that afternoon, the Bishop telephoned a friend who invited him to dinner. A break for me. I didn't have to prepare a meal for him. Before he left, he called me into Monsignor Blazer's office and told me he had no replacement for the deceased pastor. I'd have to carry on alone. "A shortage of priests," he explained.

The life of a priest can be a difficult one, I thought. To carry on the work of a parish with two priests was difficult. With one priest, impossible. The thought of being burdened with work didn't bother me as much as the thought of being alone. I'd heard of priests taking to drink after being alone for a year or more. I wouldn't take to drink, but I dreaded the idea of having no one to talk to. No one but a housekeeper, whose topics were limited to domestic chores.

As I prepared supper, I thought of Vivian. I'd enjoy sharing a meal with her. There wouldn't be many more meals we could share. As soon as she was well, she'd have to leave the rectory. No doubt about that. I couldn't run the risk of having her close to me, even though I longed to be with her, watch over her…keep her out of trouble.

The telephone rang.

"St. Matthew's Rectory," I said, hoping I'd not have to respond to a sick call or an accident.

"Father, this is Detective Casey. I'm calling to ask if you read the newspapers today?"

"The papers, no. I haven't had time. Monsignor Blazer died…"

"Yes, I read his obituary. He was a very fine priest. I was sorry to hear of his death. I hope you get a replacement soon."

"There'll be no replacement…"

"Father, I'm calling to ask if you read about the explosion in Jersey City. Mario Togallini's warehouse was blown to bits. He was in the warehouse at the time. He and two other men."

My spirits dropped; the pain in my bottom intensified. "Was Mario killed? Were the other two men killed?"

"None was killed. All were burned. Mario lost a foot and the other two men suffered internal injuries. All are expected to recover."

"Thank God for that."

"I thought you blamed Mario Togallini for the bombings?"

"I did and I still do. I wouldn't want to see him hurt."

"Love your enemies. Is that the way it is?"

"That's the way it is."

"I believe you when you say, 'That's the way it is.' If I felt otherwise, I'd question you regarding the other murders; those involving the stabbings of Togallini's men."

"Rest assured, Detective Casey, I've never killed anyone. Never stabbed anyone or bombed anyone."

"I believe you, Father. Yet I can't help thinking you know more about the murders than you're telling me. You once mentioned demons involved in this case. I laughed at the idea. I'm no longer laughing. I questioned several individuals who witnessed the explosion from afar. They said they saw a large devil, or a demon-like creature, in the flames, surrounded by a number of screaming women. We searched the area carefully, found no devil…no demon…no women. What do you think of that?"

"I think a demon is present at the scene of every crime. However, he doesn't normally reveal himself. A demon is like a thief in the night. He does his dirty work and is gone without being seen."

"But why would this particular demon reveal himself?"

I thought of Isacaron who revealed himself to me. "He may be unique, different from other demons."

"I don't know, Father. I have difficulty believing in demons, yet I can't ignore the information given by witnesses. They convinced me they saw a demon, or a devil-like creature, in the flames. They also saw a series of screaming women. This case has me puzzled. I don't know how to precede, what to think. What do you think?"

"I think demons have been promoting murders and other evil acts ever since man first walked the face of the earth. The problem is this: few people are willing to accept the idea."

"If they were willing to accept the idea, what would they do?"

"They'd stay close to God to protect themselves."

"You think the murder rate in this country would drop if people stayed close to God?

"Absolutely. Not only the murder rate, but the rate of sexual activity, and other violations of God's laws."

"You could be right. But it's a hard sell."

"I know."

Detective Casey said "Goodbye."

I hung up the phone, contemplated the information given to me by the detective. I wondered if the bomb Joshua left behind was powerful

Demon of Lust

enough to blow up a large warehouse. Wasn't it more likely that Joshua's bomb had ignited other bombs stored in the warehouse for the Mafia? I disliked hearing that Mario Togallini and his two men were injured. However, I liked the idea that the contents of the warehouse were blown to bits.

Not wanting to spend any more time thinking about the problems Mario Togallini had brought upon himself, I completed the supper preparations, brought Vivian her meal on a tray. She rewarded me with a smile. I returned to the kitchen, fixed another tray for myself. Returning to the bedroom, I sat in a large comfortable chair, enjoyed the meal with Vivian. There wasn't a great deal of conversation between us. I took pleasure in being in the same room with her, thinking I'd never want to be anywhere else. From time to time, I stole glances at her. And she stole glances at me. I was at peace with the world. Never had I appreciated Vivian so much as I did that night.

The mind that God gives us can sometimes be an annoying entity. When I was at the peak of my enjoyment, I thought of Monsignor Blazer lying alone in church. I was missing my last opportunity to spend time with him.

"I must leave you now," I said to Vivian.

"Where do you have to go?"

"To church, to spend some time with Monsignor Blazer."

"But he's dead and I'm alive."

How well I knew she was alive. She made me feel alive. Yet I couldn't reveal my feelings to her. I said, "Monsignor Blazer's body is dead. His soul is alive. I'd like to be with him tonight as he moves from one stage of life to another."

"But wouldn't you prefer being with me?"

"Sure I would, but I'm going to spend the evening with him."

Vivian looked puzzled as I left the room.

I was puzzled, too. The idea of doing what I was supposed to do instead of what I wanted to do was difficult for me. However, I felt much better after spending several hours with the Monsignor. The church was quiet, a great place to reflect. I'll be happy if I can follow in the pastor's footsteps; do as good a job as he's done. The prayers brought me peace.

I went to bed that night without visiting Vivian. I wanted no one to disturb the peace I experienced.

What I wanted was not to be realized. After falling asleep, Isacaron came to me in a dream. He ridiculed me for not spending the night with Vivian.

"You still have time," he said. "It'll be fun having an affair with her while the Bishop is in the rectory. You can do it."

"Go to hell!" I shouted at him.

"You are destined for hell," he stated. "You might as well enjoy yourself while you have the opportunity."

"I'm not going to hell. I'm going where life is good, where I don't have to listen to you." For some inexplicable reason, I heard no more from the demon that night.

CHAPTER 54

For the first time since I'd been assigned to St. Matthew's, the church was filled with people. They were a diverse lot...some rich, some poor, some black, some white, some drunk, and some sober. All were there to attend the Mass said for the repose of the soul of Monsignor Blazer.

The Mass was celebrated by Bishop Mallery. I assisted him on the altar. He gave a moving talk regarding the final destiny of the soul. "Those who die in the state of grace will see God, live with Him forever. Whereas those who die in sin will be told by God to depart from Him forever, live in a place known as hell."

The reference to hell was a small part of the Bishop's talk. However, it had a greater impact upon me than the many kind words he said about Monsignor Blazer: how he helped the poor, the ignorant, and the indefensible. Hell was a concern of mine. Isacaron was a concern of mine. Vivian was a concern of mine. My love for her was a concern of mine. Put them all together and where did the mix propel me?

The Mass ended. Monsignor Blazer, locked in his casket, was wheeled out of the church and into a hearse. The hearse would bring his body to Villanova University, where it'd be buried. His soul would ride to heaven and be welcomed by God. No question about it. He was a good priest because he was a wise priest. He did what he was supposed to do.

I said goodbye to the Bishop, heard many automobiles start, watched the hearse, and a line of other vehicles, slowly pull away from the church. In a brief time, they were gone. That's the way life is, I thought. In a brief time, we're gone.

I watched the last vehicle in the line become a dot in the distance, thinking I was fortunate not having the Bishop discover the beautiful girl sleeping in the room next to his. But was I fortunate? Perhaps I'd be better off if he'd discovered her, reminded me that a priest has certain obligations. Obligations that preclude the care of a woman who professed a love for me.

Opening the door to the rectory, I became aware of a strange smell. A smell of death! I hadn't noticed it before. That's because my thoughts were filled with ideas relating to Vivian. So many people have died since she became a resident in the rectory. Was she responsible for their deaths? Was Isacaron responsible? Was Vivian unwittingly working with the demon? I wasn't sure. All were possibilities.

It was now ten o'clock in the morning. Vivian and I hadn't eaten anything. I prepared breakfast for two and carried the food to her room on a tray.

She looked serious. "How did the funeral Mass go?"

"Very well. Bishop Mallory gave a splendid talk."

"What about?"

"The destiny of the soul. You've heard the theme many times in many different ways."

"I have," she said, "although it never sank in until I was in that hole, close to death. Before that experience, I thought I'd live forever."

"You'll live forever but not in this life. You'll pass from this life to another. It'll be like getting married, for better or for worse."

I expected her to say, "You're preaching," however, she nodded agreement, and proceeded to eat her breakfast without arguing with me.

She spent a week in bed. And during that week I brought her food and many tales of the experiences I had with the people of the parish and the students in school. Although I was exceptionally busy visiting the sick and the poor, I found myself hurrying back to the rectory to spend time with her. The pleasure I had talking with her was unbelievable. I soon realized that such pleasure was not designed by God for priests. I'd have to say farewell to her as soon as she was able to leave the rectory.

That day arrived much quicker than I anticipated. One morning while I was preparing breakfast for two, she appeared at the kitchen door and said, "Could we have our breakfast this morning in the dining room?"

"I'm surprised to see you out of bed. Are you well enough?"

"As well as ever, except for a few bruises and blisters on my..." She patted her buttocks.

"If you feel well enough to be on you're feet, I'll gladly serve you breakfast in the dining room."

So we had breakfast in the dining room.

"You don't seem so happy this morning," she observed while we were having a second cup of coffee.

"I'm not happy at all. Now that you're well, I'll have to ask you to do something I don't want you to do, something you must do..." I struggled for words that wouldn't hurt her.

She supplied the words: "You're going to ask me to leave this rectory."

I wanted to tell her I loved her. I couldn't. All I could say was, "Yes. You must leave tomorrow."

"You really want me to leave?"

I wanted to say she could stay forever. Instead, I said, "I don't want you to leave, but you must. A priest can't have a beautiful woman living in a rectory with him. The temptation is too great. Especially with one of Togallini's paintings urging him to sin. That painting is like the serpent in the Garden of Eden. The serpent urged our first parents to sin. They followed his advice. The result was catastrophic."

"You still think my painting was inspired by a demon?"

"I know that to be a fact."

"I wish I could believe you."

"The demon is deceptive, Vivian. He's deceived people more astute than you. I know he's alive and active in this rectory. He's revealed himself to me, spoken to me."

She looked at me quizzically. "You sure you weren't dreaming when he spoke to you?"

"He usually comes to me in a dream, talks to me, tempts me. He makes the illicit sexual act sound so logical, so pleasurable, and so natural. He doesn't admit it produces unwanted babies, slaughtered by individuals under his influence. Nor does he admit the sexual act offends God. It's a device he uses to win souls for the devil. I wish you'd believe me."

Vivian sounded sincere. "With all my heart, I'd like to believe you. I've difficulty accepting what you say when you tell me the demon comes to you in a dream. We all have dreams, nightmares. You've been so wrapped up in religion; your dreams have turned to nightmares. You think you're hearing demons talking to you."

"That's not true." I said, feeling hurt. She wouldn't accept my word. Had the demon influenced her reasoning powers? Was she no longer sensitive to the truth after killing the men who were observing the rectory? If only I could read her mind.

"Is my painting still in my bedroom, or did it go up in smoke?" she asked suddenly.

How I wanted to tell her the painting had gone up in smoke. I couldn't lie. "The painting is in my bedroom."

She uttered a cry of relief. "In your bedroom? What's it doing there?"

I brought it down to the dining room to show to Monsignor Blazer and...." I could go no further. I didn't want to tell her the painting brought about his death. Nor did I want to admit the demon scored a victory over me. "None of your business," I whispered.

"Why would you want to show it to Monsignor Blazer?"

"None of your business."

"Okay, if that's the way you want to play. You don't mind probing me for information, but when I ask you a simple question, you become insulting. Just don't forget the painting belongs to me. When I leave this rectory, it goes with me."

Now she had the upper hand. "I'd like to destroy the painting," I said meekly.

"I know you would. But you're not going to do it. I'll see to that. It's Togallini's masterpiece. I intend to protect it with my life...with your friendship, if necessary."

What an obnoxious thing to say to me. But I was being obnoxious with her. Maybe that's the best course of action under the circumstances.

We finished the breakfast. I told her I'd be out for lunch and dinner. She could pack her things; prepare to leave the rectory the following day.

She was silent and sullen when she left the table. However, before leaving the room, she said, "I'll borrow your Ford Fairlane tomorrow morning, return it when I have the time."

When she has the time? Specifically, when would that be? I wanted to know, but decided not to ask her. I realized she was confused and hurt at the manner in which I asked her to leave. She was not only in love with me, she was aware I was the only true friend she had. She knew it and so did I.

On the other hand, she was my best friend. I thought more of her than any other person on earth. My life would be lonely without her. Yet I had to break away from her if I wanted to hold onto my priesthood. Life can be cruel to a priest, especially one who unwittingly falls in love with a woman. Falling in love with a woman is like falling off a building. There's no going back.

For hours, I walked the streets of the Bronx, considering the possibility of giving up my role as a priest, becoming Vivian's husband. The idea lifted my spirits. But not for long. I'd taken a vow to remain a priest forever. I'd break the vow if I married Vivian. God wouldn't like it. Isacaron would love it.

The fact that Isacaron would love it, score a victory over me, tipped the scales in favor of my remaining a priest. I simply had to get Vivian out of my mind. In my attempt to do so, I rationalized she was a killer, a fornicator, a woman who'd do anything to satisfy her passions. Why I loved her had no basis in logic. No basis in theology. No basis in anything that is good and holy.

Despite all my rationalizing, I learned that love couldn't be erased from the heart like a word written on a blackboard. Love clings to the heart, the soul, the mind, and the emotions. It won't let go, regardless of any attack made upon it.

To rid my thoughts of Vivian, I went to the movies. The picture started off with a boy meeting a girl. The story soon took a contemporary twist. The boy gave the girl a peck on the cheek. The girl ripped off the boy's clothes. He disrobed her. They fornicated! With my hands covering my Roman collar, I left the theatre. No question about it, the movie had me thinking about Vivian again.

Although the diner in which I ate my supper wasn't one with pleasing surroundings, I nevertheless spent considerable time there. I ate slowly, drank several cups of coffee, read three newspapers. I did all this because I was attempting to kill as much time as possible. I simply didn't want to go back to the rectory until Vivian was in bed, sound asleep.

I remained in the diner until the proprietor, a middle-aged man with a baldhead and a bulbous belly, stared at me as if he thought I was homeless. Embarrassed, I left the diner and took another walk. I walked until I was exhausted.

The rectory was quiet when I passed through the front door. It remained quiet as I made my way up the carpeted stairs. I reached my room without a call from Vivian. Evidently, she was asleep. My own body longed for the comfort of a bed. Undressing quickly, donning pajamas, and saying my prayers, I had no difficulty dropping off to sleep. I soon began to dream.

In my dream, I saw Monsignor Blazer at the foot of my bed. He wore a cassock and a pair of glasses with exceptionally heavy lens, which magnified his eyes to abnormal proportions.

"Father Tom!" he called. "Father Tom! Get out of bed. Vivian is waiting for you."

I'd a hazy notion his voice sounded as if it didn't belong to him. It was a harsh blend of many cultures.

"Why would she be waiting for me?"

"This is her last night in the rectory. The last opportunity you'll have to sleep with her."

"But I can't sleep with her, Monsignor. I'm a priest. I've taken a vow to remain chaste."

"Would you enjoy sleeping with her?"

"Sure, I would. But I'm not going to do it. When you get to heaven, talk to St. Augustine. He'll tell you we can't always do what we'd like to do."

"Don't be a damned fool."

"If I sleep with her, I'll be a damned fool. A fool damned to hell."

"You will not go to hell. God loves the sinner."

"God loves the sinner more when he stops sinning."

The Monsignor's eyes grew bigger, brighter. He shouted at me. "Are you disputing my word?"

"I'm not disputing the word of Monsignor Blazer, but the word of Isacaron. I'll dispute his word every night in the week."

The demon disappeared.

Awakening, I felt an urge to visit Vivian. However, I said a prayer and fell back to sleep. I'd no more dreams.

CHAPTER 55

The following day, a stained coffee cup and cereal bowl were in the sink at seven-thirty in the morning, which indicated to me that Vivian had an early rising. Looking out a side window of the rectory, I saw her loading her painting into the Ford Fairlane. A dozen dresses were draped over the back of the passenger's seat.

She was going to leave without saying goodbye. My first impulse was to rush out of the rectory, hold her in my arms. She looked sad, alone, bewildered.

I felt the same way. How I hated to see her go.

How I wanted to say goodbye to her, ask her to keep in touch with me. But that wouldn't be the proper thing to do. Her decision to make a clean break was the right one, even though it was a heartbreaking decision…for her and for me.

Watching her step into the Ford Fairlane, strap on the seat belt, and insert a key into the ignition was a torturous experience for me. Soon she'd be gone. Never again would I see her. Never again would I trust myself to see her.

As I pressed my face against the window to get a better look at her, yes, a last look at the woman I loved, I saw the Ford Fairlane turn into a huge ball of red flame and smoke. A loud explosion rocked the rectory, cracked the glass in the window, cut my forehead.

I was hardly aware of a small trickle of blood running down the side of my nose, as I watched a huge red ball of flame ascend into the sky. Within

Demon of Lust

that ball, I saw a demon-like woman screaming in pain. I asked myself, could that be Isacaron?

Isacaron was only a fleeting thought. I could think of no one but Vivian. She was gone from this world forever. Would I ever see her again? Maybe I would. I might see her in heaven if she and I make it. But making it was only a remote possibility, for me and for her. I should have been concentrating more on the love of God than the love of a woman. And Vivian had murdered some of Togallini's men. She showed no sorrow. She failed to confess the sins.

In a daze, I left the rectory to examine the wreckage. A large number of people had gathered around the burning automobile to witness an event that never before had taken place in the driveway of a home for priests.

The hood of the car was blown off and the roof of the car was gone. Vivian was still at the wheel, a burning skeleton of charcoal. If there had been any movement in her body, I'd have pulled her free of the car; regardless of the burns I'd have suffered. But she was still, lifeless, departed from this world. A beautiful work of God's art demolished by madmen.

How long I stood watching the flames, I cannot say. Nor can I say how many times I shook my head in response to the question, "What happened, Father?" I only know I was there until the Ford Fairlane was nothing more than a mass of hot steel, emanating smoke in the driveway.

"You ready to tell me about it, Father?"

I turned to see Detective Casey at my side. He had an arm around my waist, supporting me. I needed the support. I felt so weak; I thought I'd drop. "Sure, I'll tell you about it," I said with a voice hardly audible. "I'll tell you a sad story about a demon who travels around the world, seeking the destruction of souls. He's been working in the Bronx, working on me."

"I'm sure you had nothing to do with planting a bomb..."

"No, of course not. But a demon has many individuals under his influence, willing to plant a bomb, or commit a murder, or create conflict among nations, or have the word of God abolished from our schools..."

The detective interrupted me. "I've told you before that people aren't going to buy your demon and devil story."

"It's not my story. It started long before I was born…long before the world was created. It started the moment Lucifer and his followers were thrown out of heaven for violating God's laws. Lucifer and his followers roam the world, encouraging us to sin. They…"

"Can't you be more specific, give me a name?"

"The names are secondary. I've already given you one name. Mario Togallini is directly responsible for the bombings. The pornographic material he sells is indirectly responsible. Pornography corrupts the souls of men, makes them receptive to suggestions given to them by demons…"

"I'll never be able to sell that argument."

"Not if you don't try."

"I'll concentrate on Togallini."

"Togallini is a member of the Mafia. He uses thugs to force people to comply with his perverted ideas and the demands of the demons."

"You're certainly sold on demons."

"I have reason to be."

"You willing to testify against Togallini in court?"

"I certainly am."

"Father, when we go into court, will you promise me you'll keep quiet about the demon?"

"Do you think the judge and the jury will consider me irrational if I speak of a demon?"

Detective Casey ran his fingers through his hair, studied his shoes. "I'd rather not put it that way."

"How would you put it?"

"I don't know. I do know that if you bring religion into court, you anathematize our case. Such is the conventional wisdom."

"Which isn't wisdom at all."

"No, Father, it isn't. But that's the way it is."

Demon of Lust

"You're a crime fighter, Detective Casey. Are we winning the battle against crime or losing it?"

The detective was quick to admit, "We're losing the battle."

I shook my head. "The battle between good and evil is being lost. As a detective, are you proud of that fact?"

"No, I'm not."

"You ought to try another approach to crime. Realize there are spiritual forces in the world. Some good, some evil. They're battling for our souls. They influence our thinking, our activities more than we realize. All our laws should be based on this knowledge. In a perverted way, the knowledge is being followed. Satan is being encouraged to enter our lives, God is not."

"I wish it were up to me, Father."

Nodding my head, I said "goodbye" to the detective, entered the rectory. The house seemed extremely cold. Shuddering, I realized that all the warmth in the rectory had left when Vivian made her departure.

For some inexplicable reason, I took the stairs to Vivian's room. I once referred to it as the Bishop's room. The moment I entered, I saw a note on the bureau and a large diamond ring. The note read as follows:

Dear Father Tom,

This is my way of saying goodbye. Thank you for your kindness and the care you've given me. I realize my love for you can't compete with your love for God. You are a good priest. I won't bother you again, although I can't promise I won't think about you.

The ring I'm leaving behind is an expensive one. I want you to cash it in, buy yourself a nice new automobile. I won't be returning the Ford Fairlane. Any man who forgoes the pleasures of a wife deserves the next best thing. And that's a nice new automobile.

Love,
Vivian

Vivian's name blurred as tears welled up in my eyes. She was gone. I'd trouble believing it.

Putting the ring in my pocket, I decided to use it to pay for her funeral. A beautiful funeral with all the extras.

I called the Flaherty Funeral Home and spoke to John Diggins regarding Vivian's burial. "You'll have to talk to the police regarding the release of the body," I said.

"We're familiar with the procedure," Diggins said. "And, by the way, if you will hold on, Mr. Flaherty would like to thank you personally for all the business you've given us."

"Some other time," I said, hanging up.

Later that day, Joe McCabe, the newspaperman, rang the doorbell. He extended his hand the moment I opened the door.

Shaking his hand, I said, "Joe, it's nice to see you. What brings you here?"

"Father, I'm here to get the story about the woman killed in the bombing; your housekeeper. I've been to the police, spoken to a Detective Casey. He gave me what information he has about the bombing. He suggested I talk to you about the victim."

I liked the newspaperman, realized he'd helped me raise money for the burial of Mrs. Reilly. I wanted to help him all I could. "Come into my office. I'll try to answer your questions."

We spent several hours in my office. Without revealing my love for her, I gave the newspaperman as much information as I could about Vivian, her connection with the artist Togallini and his brother Mario, the pornographer, who evidently had the bomb planted in my car. I said nothing about the demon Isacaron revealing himself to me. However, I did say the pictures painted by the deceased brother of Mario Togallini were inspired by a demon and a source of evil.

"We're dealing with a controversial subject, Father. The majority of the public won't accept any reference to demons."

"Why not?"

"They don't believe in them."

"We have more demonic activity in the world today than ever before, and the public doesn't believe in demons. Witness the turmoil in our cities, the killings, the fornication, the adultery, the sodomy, the divorce, the broken families, the wars, the filth displayed on television."

"I'll write the article as you present it to me, Father, but many people will reject it."

"The best you can do is tell the truth."

"That's what a newspaper is supposed to do."

The article Joe wrote appeared in the newspapers the following day. I thought he did a remarkably good job presenting the facts. Other newspapermen thought differently, ridiculing the idea of paintings inspired by a demon. However, several newsmen agreed with Joe, singling out certain movies that appeared to be inspired by a demon. One writer reviewed a movie and said, "What more could a demon do to win the souls of viewers than that done by this movie?"

I'd little time to study the debate. Most of my free time was devoted to making arrangements for Vivian's funeral. Financing the funeral became a simple task, as Joe McCabe found a buyer who gave me full value for the diamond ring.

Despite the publicity Vivian's death generated, only two or three people showed up at the funeral home. I was alone with her most of the time. Her casket was closed. No picture of her appeared on the casket as none could be found.

She was moved from the funeral home to the church, where I said the Mass. I've only a dim memory of what I said to the few people who attended: She was a beautiful woman, kind, polite, considerate, one who held fast to her beliefs. I said nothing about her soul because I didn't know its status.

The status of her soul concerned me more than anything else. My concern was overwhelming when I saw her lowered into her grave. A grave I purchased next to the Reilly's. She'd be in good company with them.

Thinking of her soul caused me to say a daily Mass for her during the next two months. In many respects, she had a difficult life. I wanted God to be kind to her…kind to the only woman I ever loved. But God is a God of justice as well as mercy. If she'd killed the men who worked for Togallini, God would judge her accordingly. His mercy is replaced by justice after one dies.

This thought tormented me at night when I tried to sleep. No longer was I bothered by Isacaron, but the fact that Vivian could be in hell as a result of the murders she committed disturbed me more than the demon's worst attack.

I carried on the work of the parish as best I could, ever mindful that the woman who dominated my thinking might be in hell. As a priest, it was my job to steer those with whom I dealt in the other direction. I failed to do my job, the job for which I'd been ordained.

Several months after Vivian was buried, I heard confessions one Saturday afternoon in the church. I listened to a teenage girl confess she was having "protected" sex with her boyfriend. A dope addict confessed he'd robbed an old women to satisfy his craving for dope. Two unemployed laborers, one following the other, confessed they removed a safe from a liquor store because they needed money for food.

The same old stuff, I thought. I gave them some good advice, which they'd probably ignore.

The fifth confessor had something new to reveal to me: He said, "Bless me, Father, 'cause Ah killed four men."

I recognized Joshua's voice immediately. I couldn't help but exclaim, "You killed four men!"

"Ah did."

"But why?"

"Dey killed mah frien' Ronnie. An' dey blew up de funer'l home where mah frien' Ronnie wuz laid out."

I could hardly keep my emotions under control. "It's important for me, Joshua, to know…"

Demon of Lust

"In de dark, how'd ya know mah name?"

"I recognized your voice."

"Ah got de same voice as everybudy else."

"Never mind, Joshua. You came to me to confess your sins and you've done so. You've killed four men. Two in the front of the rectory and two in the back."

In the darkness of the confessional, I couldn't hear what he whispered to himself. However, I heard him stammer: "Ah...Ah killed one in de front of de wreck'try and one in de back. Dat's all. Ah stuck 'em in de gut with an old soldier's sword. Ah told 'em if dey wanna fight, well here Ah am."

"Four men were killed near the rectory. Who killed the other two?"

"A woman."

I felt sick to my stomach. "Could you tell me her name?"

Joshua's anger was revealed in the tone of his voice. "Ah don't have t' tell ya her name. She ain't no Catholic and she don't have t' go t' no confession. She killed 'em fer Ronnie. An' Ah...Ah'd like t' marry her some day."

My spirits rose. He was talking about Cathy Washington, the future Olympic runner. *Vivian didn't kill the two men* who observed the rectory. But she might have killed the two men in the warehouse, the night she escaped from them and returned with blood on her clothes.

"Joshua," I said, almost apologetically, "do you know how those two men in the warehouse were killed?"

"Ah killed 'em."

Suppressing my shock, I asked, "How could you have killed them? You returned to the Bronx with me."

"Ah borrowed a nice new Lincoln, wit'out de owner's permission. An' Ah got mah two swords and drove back to de warehouse in Jersey. Ah pried open a winder, snuck up on de men. Dey wuz torturin' yore housekeeper, stickin' pins in her bosom."

"She didn't tell me."

"She wuz cryin' a lot, pleadin' wit' de men. Ah let out a yell, ran fer 'em. Dey pulled out guns. Befo' dey could shoot me; I let 'em have the swords, right through their guts. I did it fo' you. I knew ya didn't wanna lose no housekeeper."

I pictured Joshua risking his life for Vivian and me. Should I praise him or chastise him for committing murder?

"Ah drove yore pretty housekeeper back to de wreck'try. She didn't want me to tell ya whut happened. Said she'd explain it in her own way."

"Thank you, Joshua."

"Thanks fer not givin' me no long penance."

"We're not through with this confession. You must be sorry for your sins…"

"Ah'm sorry."

"Realize you can't go around murdering people to solve your problems?"

"Ah knows dat. But Ah wuz tryin' t' git even wit' de men fer killin' Ronnie and de people in de fun'ral home. I also wanted to help ya."

"I know you were trying to help me. I appreciate your risking your life to assist me, but…"

"Ya can't let crim'nals bomb de school, kill good people," Joshua argued.

"I'm aware of that, Joshua, but the police have a function."

"Ah wuz wonderin' why ya didn't call 'em."

That was a legitimate question, I thought. Why didn't I call the police? I was trying to protect Vivian. I didn't want her to become involved with the police or the racketeers. Did I make a mistake? "Joshua, stop by the rectory sometime this week. You have asked a question that defies an answer at this time. I'll have to give it more consideration."

"Is de penance postponed?"

"Say the rosary every night before going to bed for the next week."

"Wow! Dat's some penance."

When Joshua left the confessional, I breathed a sigh of relief. Vivian hadn't murdered the men.

LaVergne, TN USA
06 August 2010
192274LV00003B/1/A